A Woman of Consequence

A Woman of Consequence

The Investigations of Miss Dido Kent

ANNA DEAN

MINOTAUR BOOKS

A Thomas Dunne Book

New York

This is a work of fiction. All of the characters, organizations, and events portrayed in this novel are either products of the author's imagination or are used fictitiously.

A THOMAS DUNNE BOOK FOR MINOTAUR BOOKS.
An imprint of St. Martin's Publishing Group.

www.thomasdunnebooks.com
www.minotaurbooks.com

ISBN 978-0-312-62684-6

Originally published in Great Britain by Allison & Busby Limited

First U.S. Edition: April 2012

10 9 8 7 6 5 4 3 2 1

Chapter One

Badleigh Vicarage, Wednesday, 8th October 1806

My dear Eliza,

I promised yesterday that just as soon as I had leisure for writing I should send you a full and satisfactory account of Penelope Lambe's accident at Madderstone Abbey; and so I shall begin upon it. Though I fear I may have to leave off at any moment, for there is a great deal of needlework to be done for the little boys at school and Margaret has already opened her workbox and begun to look at me with displeasure.

In yesterday's note I was kind enough to hint at some <u>very peculiar circumstances</u> surrounding Penelope's fall and I do not doubt that since receiving it you have enjoyed all the apprehensions and heightened imaginings which such hints can supply. And I trust my account will not disappoint you, for it was a <u>very</u> strange business indeed – one which I cannot, yet, understand at all.

The first thing you must know is that it all came about because of the ghost – I mean, of course, the Grey Nun of Madderstone.

And, by the by, it occurs to me...

'Well, Dido,' said Mrs Margaret Kent heavily, 'I daresay that when *I* was unmarried *I* had leisure for writing long letters.' She regarded her sister-in-law with the tragic aspect of a saint bound for the pagan arena in Rome. 'I declare it is more than a fortnight since I touched my writing desk.'

'Yes,' said the unrepentant Dido without ceasing to move her pen. 'It is quite one of the evils of matrimony, is it not?'

...it occurs to me, Eliza, that the Grey Nun is a remarkably important lady. The possession of a family ghost confers such dignity! I believe that every family which has any claim at all to grandeur should have a ghost. I consider it a kind of necessary which should be attended to as soon as the fortune is made and the country estate purchased.

Everyone's consequence is increased by the presence of a ghost.

For here are the two Crockford sisters, who are no more than some kind of third cousins to the Harman-Footes of Madderstone, but they must walk their visitor, Penelope, two miles across the fields to see the Grey Nun. Well, not perhaps quite her, for she cannot of course be relied upon to be always at home to morning callers – but at least the ruins in which she is reputed to appear.

I said to Penelope, when I was invited to accompany them, 'It is not enough, you know, that we should entertain you with parties and visits while you are here in Badleigh. We cannot send you back to your school in Bath without first chilling your blood and supplying you with nightmares to last a twelvemonth.'

And she, I discovered, was very grateful for the attention. For she had 'never set foot in a <u>real</u> abbey before' and she did 'most sincerely hope that it was <u>very</u> dreadful and just <u>exactly</u> like what one read about in books...'

Well, she is a sweet-tempered, good-natured girl and so very pretty that I always find great pleasure in looking at her – but I do not believe that she has more than common sense. However, since she is now lying abed with an injured head, I ought not to speak ill of her, and I confess that her eager naivety suits my taste a great deal better than Lucy Crockford's studied sensibility.

All the while that we were walking to Madderstone…

'It is a great pity,' said Margaret loudly, 'that Eliza is not here. *She* is a very fine needlewoman.'

'It is extremely kind of you to say so, Margaret. I shall be sure to pass on the compliment.'

'And so very obliging. Why, last spring, she sewed three shirts for little Frank in as many days.'

'Did she indeed? How remarkable!' Dido resolutely continued with her letter, but a glance across the green baize of the parlour table had shown colour mounting in Margaret's broad cheeks, her narrow mouth tightening. If there was not to be a state of warfare in the house, she must soon lay her pen aside. As she bent her head further over her page she rather fancied that she felt, prickling through her cap, not only the heat of autumn sunshine magnified by the window, but also a disapproving gaze.

And yet she could not help but try for a few lines more:

All the while that we were walking to Madderstone, Lucy was talking in her slowest, most languishing tones of the 'extraordinary atmosphere of melancholy which haunts the ruins.' An atmosphere to which she is herself 'most extraordinarily sensitive.' For 'no one – no one in the world

– feels these things more acutely' than she does. And there have been times when she has been 'almost overwhelmed by the <u>extraordinary</u> atmosphere of the ruins…'

So those two continued to talk of ghosts, with only an occasional digression in praise of Captain Laurence – who, I suppose, must be considered a secondary motive for our visit to Madderstone Abbey.

And, by the by, I cannot help but wonder that Lucy and Penelope should contrive to be both in love with the captain without any cooling of affection between themselves. Nor can I quite determine whether it argues most for the sweetness of their natures, the weakness of their understanding – or only the insignificance of their attachment to the gentleman.

The sunny silence of the room was broken by Margaret's searching noisily in the workbasket for a spool of thread. Dido began to write faster:

Harriet Crockford, I noticed, scowled darkly whenever her sister talked of the captain; I do not think she has a very high opinion of him. But I could not prevail upon her to discuss this interesting topic. And, while nuns and the navy were canvassed by the other two, Harriet and I were much less pleasantly engaged. It was roof leads and damp in the kitchen passage all the way with us.

Harriet informs me that there is a hole in the roof at Ashfield which is a yard and three-quarters long and twenty-seven inches broad. It would, I am further informed, 'break Dear Papa's heart' if he could see the hole in Ashfield's roof. And, if my memory were only a little better, I could relate to you the exact cost of the tiles and lead which will be required to repair it.

Poor Harriet: there are times when she goes beyond being sensible and is downright dull. And it is very disconcerting that a woman who is more than two years my junior can seem so very <u>old</u>. I find myself wishing that she would not wear such a dowdy bonnet, nor such a large and unbecoming cap beneath it; and I begin to despair of her ever having an original thought – I believe she only lives to reflect the ideas of dear dead Papa...

But now I am getting quite off the point. It is such a very great pleasure and relief to 'talk' to you, Eliza, that I cannot stop my pen from running away with me.

I must return to that woman of consequence: the Grey Nun. For it would seem that yesterday she was indeed at home to callers! Or so Lucy believes.

There was another, louder, sigh from the other side of the table.

'Well, well, I suppose you have nothing else to occupy your time,' said Margaret, 'but I confess that it makes me quite *envious* to see you writing away all day.' There followed some vigorous stabbing at a shirtsleeve. 'The truth is,' she continued, 'that when your cottage was given up and it was proposed that you should come to live with us, I told your brother: "Francis, my dear," I said, "I am sure I shall do all that I can for your poor sisters, but I do not know how I shall manage – with all the business I have to attend to – I do not know *how* I shall manage with having a *visitor* constantly in my house."'

It was too much. Reminded of her dependence, Dido bit her lip, set aside her pen – and reached for the workbasket.

Chapter Two

The room which Dido had been given possession of on the attic floor of her brother's vicarage had not much to recommend it. It was small and cold and airless; it had no hearth, and its ceiling sloped so steeply that anyone lying in the narrow bed might, with ease, place a hand on the plaster. There was but one small window and it could be reached only by kneeling upon the bed. However, the apartment had, in Dido's opinion, two material advantages: one was the very pleasant scent which crept into it from the apples stored in a neighbouring attic, and the other was the twisting narrowness of the stairs which led to it.

Margaret was not fond of climbing twisting, narrow stairs and only visited the attics when her constant dread of the housemaids stealing food became so great that she must make a search of their bedroom.

Tucked under the sloping roof, her icy feet wrapped in a counterpane, Dido felt herself beyond the reach of interference and was able to continue with her letter as well as her cold fingers would allow:

… Well, Eliza, I am sure that I have now sewn more linen than can possibly be required by two young gentlemen of twelve and ten, and I think that I may now go on with my story.

We had a fine sunny day for our walk to Madderstone yesterday – though with a sharp breeze blowing. And very glad I was to be able to go, for, besides the sewing, there is the bramble jelly to be made – and Rebecca began to pick the damsons yesterday. However, Margaret is as anxious as ever to show attention to Mrs Harman-Foote and, since she does not like to walk so far herself, I am her envoy.

We had a very pleasant walk through the fields and the park, but once we came into Madderstone's pleasure grounds there was an end to all pleasure in walking! For Mr Harman-Foote is very busy at his 'improving' again and there was nothing but dirt and puddles and confusion all along the path which leads from the park gate to the abbey ruins. There are new terraces laid out and half a dozen great oaks and Spanish chestnuts taken down to 'open up the vista' and I fancy that the stream is to be turned into a cascade or have its consequence increased in some such way, because the lower pool – the one we have always thought to be the abbey's fishpond – is drained. The old stone dam is breached below the overflow – and there was a great to-do, when we were there, over catching the carp in nets and putting them into pails.

And, by the by, I should be quite angry about the despoliation of such a fine old estate if I thought Mr Harman-Foote improved only for pride and show – but, knowing his character, I suspect it is rather to provide honest employment for his men after our bad harvest.

Well, it being still quite early in the day, we resolved upon paying our respects first to the Grey Nun and then walking on to the great house to call upon Mrs Harman-Foote. We made our way through the cloisters and came into the ruined nave. Penelope was delighted – for it seems

that Madderstone is 'so very much like a place in a book,'
and 'one can imagine very horrid things happening in it.'

Dido was compelled to stop, for she was shivering too
much to carry on. She unwound her feet from the
counterpane, went to the room's one small closet and took
out the shawl which her sailor brother John had brought
from the East Indies. Pulling it about her shoulders, she
knelt upon the bed and looked out of the window.

The moon – almost full – rode high and very beautiful
amid a flying wrack of cloud; its light silvered the
meadows and reflected palely on the little stream dividing
the glebe from the dark outline of woods.

'Look to nature when you are troubled, my dear.'
That is what Dido's governess, Miss Steerforth, had told
her many years ago. 'The beauty, the majesty, of God's
creation, will be sure to set your little worries at nought.'

Dido looked… But, tonight, all the serenity of nature
could not soothe her. The moon, lovely and indifferent,
had no power to make her forget that she was trapped
here for an indefinite period as Margaret's 'visitor', the dear
home which she had shared with her sister, Eliza, given up
in the cause of family economy. It was so very hard not to
feel injured, or to suspect that an injustice had been done.

But she must not allow such thoughts to intrude. The
failure of Charles's bank had involved all her brothers in heavy
losses. They had all been compelled to retrench: Edward's
hunters were sold and poor Francis, if Margaret prevailed,
might be reduced to taking in pupils again – a practice he
had given up with great pleasure when he was presented to
the rectory of Badleigh five years ago. In the light of these

sacrifices, it was only natural that her brothers should attempt to reduce the cost of their sisters' maintenance. They had not wished it. They had been very kind and regretted the necessity very much.

Indeed they had regretted it so much that, for a while, everything had hung in the balance and the rent of Badleigh Cottage might have been paid for another quarter, had not Margaret just chanced to remark that, of course she knew nothing about the matter – and she did not regard the cost at all, for she was sure she would divide her last farthing with her dear sisters, but she could not help but say – since the matter was now under discussion – that she had never been quite easy about Dido and Eliza living alone in that house. It had such an *odd* look, when their brothers had all homes they might be invited to share, which, she must observe, would be a much more *respectable* arrangement. Though, of course, she did not care at all about the *considerable* expense of maintaining a separate establishment.

The balance had tipped; the lease had been surrendered at Michaelmas. And now Margaret...

But this would not do at all! Blame and resentment would only make her unhappy – as Eliza reminded her every time she wrote.

The surest escape from misery was mental exertion – that was a maxim of which Miss Steerforth herself would have approved. And Dido had discovered that the very best kind of mental exertion was the solving of a puzzle or mystery.

She tucked her feet under the counterpane again, took up her letter and resolutely turned her mind once more to the strange, inexplicable events in the abbey ruins.

* * *

...We rested a while upon the fallen stones in the shelter of the nave, but the girls were quite determined to climb the narrow old night stair into the haunted gallery.

So up we all went and, as we climbed, the wind whipped about us horribly and we were forced to hold hard to our bonnets. However, we gained the gallery in safety and Lucy began explaining how the Grey Nun appears there to 'wail and wring her hands whenever there is trouble about to befall the people of Madderstone', and how, 'at this very moment' she herself could scarcely stand for 'the <u>extraordinary</u> *emotions' which the place aroused in her... And a great deal more of that kind.*

And Penelope's blue eyes grew wider and wider and she exclaimed that it was 'All quite dreadful! And so delightful!' And she wondered that anyone should ever have wanted to become a nun. For it must have been so very uncomfortable – and dull too, she did not wonder – for nuns never did anything but walk about with their hands folded in very nasty gowns, and tell their beads. And she did not know what it was that they told their beads – though she had always supposed that it must be their sins.

Meanwhile, Harriet and I stood beside the pillar at the top of the stairs and looked out through the great arch of the east window, across the ruined lawns, the workmen and the wheelbarrows, to the drained pool. After a time, Harriet observed that some gentlemen from the house were come down to see how the work went on; and then I was foolish enough to remark that Captain Laurence was among them. The girls caught at the name, and resolved immediately upon walking to meet him. I should perhaps have judged better, Eliza, and held my tongue, for, I suppose, the combination of narrow, crumbling stairs and eager passion _is_ a rather dangerous one.

However, Lucy got down the steps safely and I was next to follow her. When I reached the bottom I looked up and saw that Penelope was just moving towards the stairway. She bent to lift her skirt a little, for the wind was blowing it about her ankles. She went down the first two steps and then she stopped – holding on to the ivy that grows upon the wall with one hand, she turned back as if she would speak to Harriet.

And, in the instant that she did so – when she was turned back and looking full into the gallery – there came such a look of shock over her face. Her mouth opened – she put a hand to her lips – she stepped backward – and lost her footing.

She fell down onto the broken pavement of the nave below – and lay without moving.

There seemed, Eliza, to be a moment in which the world and everything in it stood quite still. Then movement came back suddenly; but not so smoothly as it ought. Everything, including myself, was moving in an awkward, jerking fashion. I was the first to reach Penelope and it seemed as if everything was to be left for me to do. Lucy was entirely occupied in screaming (which at least served the purpose of bringing Captain Laurence and one or two of the men running to our aid). And Harriet was still at the top of the steps, weak and shocked and struggling hard to hold on to her bonnet and cap which were almost blowing away in the wind. I think she was perhaps afraid of falling herself.

I raised Penelope up as best I could and began to rub her temples. But she was heavy and did not seem to breathe.

I called her name.

The eyes flickered and opened for a moment. The lips moved. 'I saw her,' she said. 'It was her…'

Chapter Three

Dido did not believe in ghosts. No, she quite definitely did not believe in them… But what had Penelope meant when she said, 'I saw her…'?

There was such an air of mystery about the whole affair as could not help but inspire the dullest of imaginations – and Dido's imagination was certainly not one of the dullest.

She had written so long her candle was burning low and the eerie light of the moon was throwing long shadows from the bedposts and the washstand across the bare floorboards. The wind was whining softly under the eaves and the clock upon the landing was striking the half-hour after midnight… At such a time, in such a place, it was only natural that the fancy should wander…

She could not prevent it, though she did not like to confess it in her letter – and she could not help but wonder what a certain Mr William Lomax might say if he knew about it.

'A *ghost*, Miss Kent?' She could imagine the look of wonder, the lifting of the eyebrows, the half-smile. 'You cannot truly believe that your friend saw a ghost upon the gallery?'

'No, no,' she said aloud, 'I do not say that there

certainly was a ghost – only that there was *something* – something which shocked her and made her fall.'

She smiled at herself and shook her head. Disputing with the absent Mr Lomax was become quite a habit with her. It was, perhaps, because there was so little rational conversation to be had in the vicarage; but she did not like it; it spoke of too great a dependence upon his opinions. And besides, he was too much inclined to win their disagreements, even when he was not present and she had all the trouble of devising his share of the conversation as well as her own – which did not seem quite fair.

But she would certainly not wish him – or anyone else – to think that she believed in such things as moaning, hand-wringing grey nuns. In point of fact, she had no patience at all with ghosts. They were so very *useless*.

There might for example be some purpose in this dead nun appearing, as she was reputed to do whenever disaster threatened the folk of Madderstone, if only she could be prevailed upon to disclose the nature of that disaster or advise how it might be averted. But, from all that Dido could gather, she had never performed such a service.

And, while they continued to be so very unobliging, she was determined not to put herself to the trouble of believing in ghosts.

It was an opinion which she might have expressed yesterday at Madderstone – if there had been an opportunity. For, no sooner had Captain Laurence carried the insensible Penelope into the hall of the great house, than Lucy had broken out with: 'She saw the Grey Nun on the gallery! And the fright made her fall. It is true. She *said* that she had seen the ghost.'

Dido had tried to intervene at this point with a suggestion that it was not certain that it was the nun she had seen. That she had not exactly named her...

But reasoned argument was quite out of the question just then, for all the while Lucy was talking, Mr Harman-Foote was booming out orders for a man to ride to the village for the surgeon, and his wife was giving very exact directions as to how Penelope must be carried up the stairs. And all the little Harman-Footes, who had, unluckily, been in the drawing room when news of the accident burst upon the household, were loitering about in the hall and adding their own noise to the uproar, despite their mama's pleas to the nursery-maid to remove them from the distressing scene. Two imperious little girls were clinging to the lady's gown and screaming to be noticed, while young Georgie – a stout-looking boy of eight or nine – was regarding Penelope levelly and demanding to know, 'Is she dead?' with very little sign of distress, but with a great deal of interest.

It was not until some hours later that Dido was at liberty to give her own account of the accident. By then the house was more at peace. Mr Paynter, the surgeon, had come and shaken his head and drawn in his breath, and finally declared that Penelope had a contusion to the head. However, he did not despair. Rest and careful nursing would probably set her to right – though they must not hope for a very rapid recovery.

The invalid was made comfortable in one of the abbey's best bedchambers and Harriet appointed herself her only nurse, sending away all the others. 'I know what I am about,' she said, flapping her hands at Dido. 'Too many cooks spoil the broth, you know.'

'But you cannot take all the trouble upon yourself,' Dido protested, still holding her place beside the bed, and gazing down at the pale face, sunk deep into the pillow, and the closed eyes which had not opened again since that strange moment in the cloisters. 'You must allow me to help.'

Harriet stepped back from the bed for a moment, and drew in a long, weary breath. Turning into the light which was coming through the half-closed curtains, she pushed up her large, ugly cap – and, without it shadowing her face, she looked positively young. Harriet was certainly the prettier of the two Crockford sisters – there could not be two opinions upon that point. She had a smooth white brow from which the hair grew in a delicate peak, small regular features, and an elegant figure; but her dress and air were those of an aging woman. Harriet Crockford had given up youth many years ago – or perhaps she had never embraced it.

'My trouble is of no consequence,' she said, now frowning seriously, 'and I cannot allow you to stay, for if you do, Lucy will demand it as a right that she stay too.'

'And why should she not? It is only fair that she should join with you in nursing.'

'Oh no, it will not do. She cannot look at Penelope without weeping. The greatest kindness you can do me is to take care of *her* and see her safely home. It would not do at all to have Lucy fixed here at Madderstone.'

Dido raised an eyebrow. 'You would not have her

living in the same house as Captain Laurence?' she asked curiously.

Harriet avoided her gaze. 'I think,' she said, 'that young girls should not fix themselves too soon. They should make hay while the sun shines.'

When Harriet could not express the thoughts of 'Dear Papa' it was her habit to fall back on maxims and received wisdom. It gave all her conversation a threadbare, made-over feeling – and rendered her real opinions difficult to comprehend.

'Lucy is three and twenty,' Dido observed. 'Time enough, I would have thought, to become *fixed.*'

'Oh Dido! Why must you always argue?' cried Harriet impatiently, her face reddening. 'When all's said and done, nursing must always belong to women like you and me – women who are too old for love.'

Fortunately Harriet turned away just then to gather up Penelope's clothes with efficient, angry little movements. She did not see her friend's blush and involuntary start. There was a short silence before Dido returned to the attack.

'But on this occasion I *must* argue. You cannot be the only one attending on Penelope,' she insisted. 'You need an assistant. And if I am indeed another aging crone who, by your account, is suited only to serve in the sickroom then I had better stay – my life is otherwise a dull blank!'

'Now,' said Harriet, folding her arms and frowning, 'you are being satirical – and you know that I particularly dislike your being satirical. Can you wonder at my not wanting such an argumentative companion?'

'But...'

Just then the patient began to stir and both women turned to look at her. Harriet went to her side immediately. 'Please, Dido, just do as I ask and take Lucy home. And... as for an assistant...' She paused and watched the face upon the pillow thoughtfully for a moment. 'If they can do without old Nanny at home, then tell them to send her. She is used to nursing... Yes, Nanny will do very well indeed.' She gave a weary smile. 'Now go please,' she urged. 'Our talking is making her restless.'

Dido left the sickroom and walked slowly down the elegant sweep of Madderstone Abbey's great staircase, pausing for a moment to gaze over the curve of the banister to the pattern of coloured marble on the hall floor below. She could not help but wonder why Harriet should be so very determined to keep Lucy away from the captain...

It was an odd little mystery and one which, she decided, she must get to the bottom of soon – but, meanwhile, there was something else troubling her: Harriet's theory that an unmarried woman of more than thirty should devote herself to being useful and give up all thoughts of love. It was – like most of Harriet's utterances – common cant. An unmarried woman over thirty was considered of no importance to anyone. She must make herself as useful as she might.

And, of course, Harriet knew nothing of Dido's true situation. No one but Eliza knew that, within the last half-year, she had been solicited – and solicited by a very agreeable, handsome man – to change her name.

The affair between herself and Mr Lomax was a cause of very real anxiety to Dido; she suffered all the anguish which strong affection, combined with profound doubts as to the wisdom of a marriage, can produce in a sensitive, intelligent mind. But, nevertheless, she found it rather provoking that she should have to suffer all the pain of indecision over his offer, while enjoying none of that consequence which a proposal of marriage usually bestows upon a woman!

Smiling at her own vanity, she continued down the stairs, but stopped again upon seeing below her in the hall the sleek black head of Harris Paynter, the young surgeon. There was something furtive in his movement: a looking-about to see whether or not he was observed. Dido could not help herself; she immediately stood very still – and observed him.

He was now standing irresolute, holding a folded paper in his hand. He appeared to be upon the point of delivering a note. In half a minute his mind was made up: he stepped to a small table where lay several letters – just brought from the post office. He slipped his note in among them, turned and hurried away towards the back of the house.

Dido waited until the sound of his steps died away and then slowly continued down into the hall. Propriety demanded that she walk directly to the drawing room door – curiosity argued for a detour towards the table… She stopped. The folded note could be clearly seen among the sealed letters. She took one step closer. There was a name written upon the note: *Mrs Harman-Foote*…

Now why, she wondered, was a humble surgeon writing messages to the lady of the house – and delivering them with such evident caution?

Chapter Four

Her friends were all gathered in the drawing room – an elegant, modern apartment with pink sofas, and a harp beside the pianoforte, a triple mirror above the chimney piece, some very pretty portraits, an abundance of small tables, and windows cut down to the ground – which ought to have opened upon lawns and trees, but which presently showed a view only of mud and toppled trunks.

The little girls, she found, had been tempted away to the nursery with toys and treats, but young Georgie still held his ground among the grown-ups, playing a rough, noisy game with a doll his sisters had left behind, and quite determined not to miss anything of interest which might be carrying on.

Lucy was seated upon one of the pink sofas, recovering from her distressing visit to the sickroom with the help of aromatic vinegar and the attentions of Captain Laurence – who was telling her a tale of a young seaman under his command who had once taken just such a fall as her friend and who 'was climbing up the mainmast within a se'night'.

The carriage was already ordered to take them back to Badleigh. As Dido entered the room Mr Harman-Foote stepped forward from his post beside the hearth to assure her of this. 'Best have you both home as soon as we can!' he declared. 'You must be feeling pretty well done-up. Damned bad business this!'

She thanked him, honouring his kindness even as she shrank from the loudness of his voice, which, she always fancied, was better suited to the Shropshire ironworks that had made his fortune than it was to the confines of a drawing room.

A large, red-faced man of forty or so, he was much addicted to the smoking of tobacco, and fragments of the 'blessed leaf' habitually festooned the straining buttons of his waistcoat. Mr Harman-Foote had the reputation among other men of being capable of great anger. There was even a – rather admiring – tale current in Badleigh and Madderstone of his having fought a duel and 'marked his man' when he was much younger. But his manner towards women was unfailingly courteous, and one could not help but like him.

However, he was now regarding Dido rather anxiously. 'What says the surgeon?' he asked. 'Must the young lady stay here long? Can she not be moved?'

She was rather surprised by the lack of hospitality which the question implied and, as she hesitated over an answer, Mrs Harman-Foote appeared at her side.

'Why, of course Miss Lambe must remain here, my dear,' she said firmly. 'We cannot think of moving her.' She took Dido's arm and led her off into one of the deep bay windows. 'An invalid must be disturbed as little as possible,' she declared firmly. 'There must always be complete calm in a sickroom, you see. Complete calm.

It is a principle of mine. Miss Crockford should ensure there is no noise and as little light as possible...'

She continued to talk for some time, settling Harriet's duties to her own satisfaction, the comfortable authority of her voice only a little impaired by its having to rise continually above the dreadful noise which her son was making.

The doll was now being made to climb the back of a chair in lively imitation of Penelope mounting the gallery steps. As it reached the top, it cried out (in Master Georgie's stentorian tones): 'Ah! There's a ghost!' There followed a scream so loud it interrupted the conversations of everyone in the room, and the unfortunate thing was dashed down violently onto the floor. There was an ominous cracking sound from its china head.

'Poor Georgie,' murmured his affectionate mother. 'He has been excessively upset by this terrible accident. He must be comforted and reassured.'

Dido could not quite think that it was comfort or reassurance which the child required just now. As she watched him begin once more upon the game and steeled herself for a repetition of the scream, she had some rather different ideas...

'It is of the first importance,' continued Mrs Harman-Foote, 'that he should be brought to believe that there was no ghost upon the gallery.'

'Yes...' said Dido doubtingly, 'but, in the meantime, do you not think...' She was prevented from continuing by a scream even louder than the first and an even more ominous crashing and cracking of china.

'Oh! Poor child!' grieved the mother and turned

confidingly to Dido. 'He is so easily upset. And by no means so strong as he looks – as I always tell his father when he argues for his going away to school.'

'Indeed!' said Dido, who, though not having a very high opinion in general of public education, was beginning to wonder whether, in certain circumstances, it might be of some utility.

'Now, Miss Kent,' continued Mrs Harman-Foote briskly. 'Is it true that Miss Lambe saw...*believed* that she saw the Grey Nun in the ruins?'

'Well,' said Dido cautiously, 'I would not put it down for a certainty. Though Lucy seems quite convinced of it.'

'I should very much value *your* opinion. Was it shock at seeing something frightening which made her fall?' A very earnest look accompanied the question. 'It is of great consequence. As you see, poor Georgie is so very distressed; he must not be frightened by this talk of ghosts.'

'Of course,' murmured Dido, glancing at the poor sensitive child who was now absentmindedly beating the doll's head against the leg of a chair. 'But I do not see how he is to be protected. Lucy is so very sure that the ghost appeared, and I daresay that by now half your household is talking about it.'

'And, if they are, they must be stopped,' Mrs Harman-Foote said firmly, and watched with a look of tender concern as her son began to wrench the limbs from the broken doll.

Anne Harman-Foote was a tall woman with features which were too well marked for beauty and she lacked that grace which makes height becoming. Her smile was not unpleasant; but there was such a forbidding air of knowing always that she was right, as made her seem older than her eight and twenty years – and her belief in her children's talents and virtues was unassailable. The consciousness of being Madderstone's heiress was very deeply ingrained: she was a woman who had not even surrendered her surname on marriage, but had merely added her husband's name to hers – as the substantial Foote fortune had been added to the even more substantial acres of the Harmans.

'Miss Kent,' she continued earnestly, 'you have not yet told me what your opinion is of this sad accident. I know I can rely upon *you* to speak good sense and not be carried away by fancies.'

'My opinion…' Dido hesitated, for she found that she must consider the events again before she could give an answer deserving of the compliment. Everything that had intervened: the bringing of Penelope to the house, the terrible suspense they had all been in while they awaited the surgeon's pronouncement, the writing of a hurried note to be sent express to Mrs Nolan, Penelope's guardian; all these things were already confusing and weakening her recollection of the terrible moments in the abbey ruins.

'I was not very close to Penelope when she fell,' she began carefully. 'I was at the bottom of the steps. But I saw her… She started to come down. She turned – when she was on the second step…' Dido remembered the hesitation, one little hand clutching at the wall. 'She seemed to be about to say something to Harriet and she was looking up at her – and into the gallery. And suddenly she looked so shocked…'

'As if she had seen something frightening on the gallery?'

'Yes,' admitted Dido with reluctance. 'That is how it appeared. Or, at least, if it was not a look of positive fright, it was one of very great surprise…' She struggled to remember, and to speak, exactly. 'As if she had seen something which ought not to be there. There was a kind of involuntary recoil. I am sure that step backward – which was the cause of her fall – was made quite unconsciously.'

'Of course,' said Mrs Harman-Foote with a dismissive wave of the hand, 'there was no ghost. But what was it that Miss Lambe saw?'

'It is a great puzzle,' acknowledged Dido. 'But I daresay we shall only be in suspense for a day or two. For then Penelope will be sufficiently recovered to tell us all about it.'

'But I have spoken to Mr Paynter on the subject,' said Mrs Harman-Foote anxiously, 'and it his opinion that, after such an injury, it may be several weeks before the patient is well enough to recall the exact circumstances of her accident. Indeed, he tells me that he has known cases where these memories are lost for ever and that even after a perfect recovery, the time of the accident remains a kind of blank in the brain.'

'Oh dear!' cried Dido. 'How very inconvenient!'

Mrs Harman-Foote laid a hand upon her arm and gazed tenderly across the room to Georgie who had now abandoned the doll and was standing between Lucy and

Laurence, teasing them with questions. 'It is a great deal more than inconvenient,' she said, 'for here is my poor Georgie – and his sisters too – wanting so very much to know the whole story. And children must *always* be told the truth. It is a principle of mine. I must have a rational account to give them. I cannot allow their heads to be filled with stories of ghosts.'

'Yes, yes, of course,' said Dido anxiously. She might care little about young Georgie's delicate sensibilities, but she cared a great deal about unsolved conundrums. 'There must be something we can do to come at the truth,' she said eagerly. 'It cannot be so very obscure. Perhaps if I were to return to the ruins and look into the gallery again...'

'Yes. That is precisely what is needed. So you will enquire into the matter and find out the truth?'

'Well, I shall try, but...'

'It is extremely kind of you Miss Kent. I am very grateful indeed.'

'But I cannot promise...'

The protest went unheard. The carriage was announced and everyone was on the move.

And, as she watched Lucy cross the hall still flushed with heightened imagination, Dido could not help but think that a cool sensible explanation of events might benefit her as much as Georgie. In fact, the sooner the spectre of the Grey Nun was laid to rest, the better it would be for all concerned.

Chapter Five

It was not until the third day after the accident – and rather late in the afternoon – that Dido was able to revisit the abbey ruins. The demands of sewing, damsons and jelly-making did not permit an earlier escape. But her determination to solve the mystery was, by that time, increased rather than diminished.

For, although Penelope was recovering more rapidly than they had dared to hope, and her periods of consciousness becoming longer, it seemed that Mr Paynter had been right to doubt her memory of the accident. Questions on the subject elicited no more than a gentle shake of the head. She remembered nothing after their leaving the nave to climb the stairs.

And meanwhile, Lucy Crockford had altogether too much to say upon the subject for Dido's liking.

'Oh my dear friend,' she murmured when she visited the vicarage two days after the accident. 'I blame myself! I blame myself entirely! *I* who *knew* what terrible forces haunted the ruins! I should *never* have taken my poor friend there. Indeed I should not.' She put a hand to her brow and arranged herself upon the hard sofa of Margaret's parlour with all the grace that her stout little form would allow.

'I am sure you have nothing to reproach yourself for,' said Dido briskly. 'Penelope lost her footing...'

'Oh Dido!' exclaimed Lucy so slowly that there seemed to be an eternity of pity in the words. 'You do not understand.' And she sat for a moment sorrowfully shaking her head, too much overcome to continue.

She had a plump, freckled face which was, in truth, ill-suited to sensibility: the eyes were too small and sharp, and there were ill-natured little lines between her brows betraying the peevishness which broke out all too easily when her languishing sentiments passed unheeded. She wore her brown hair pushed back in a careless tumble of curls. Lucy professed to be indifferent to her appearance; but Harriet had once confided to Dido that the careless curls were sustained only by the constant use of papers – and the freckles received generous, but unavailing, applications of Gowland's Lotion.

'It is all so very awful,' she continued in a slow, thrilled voice, 'for, you know, there must be some kind of trouble coming to the family of Harman-Foote. The ghost would not otherwise have appeared. She only comes as a warning.'

'I do not think,' said Dido firmly, 'that we need concern ourselves with imagined woes. We have trouble enough with poor Penelope lying sick...'

'Oh! But it cannot have been Pen's fall the ghost came to warn of. Because...' she paused a moment to add weight to the announcement of her great insight, '*Penelope is not a part of the Madderstone family.*'

'No, of course she is not, but...'

'No, Dido,' Lucy shook her head. 'I am afraid it is

indisputable. There is some other disaster yet to come.'

'Good heavens!' exclaimed Dido, tried beyond endurance. 'We do not even know that Penelope saw a ghost!'

Lucy sat up sharply, her small mouth contracted, her brow furrowed. 'I declare,' she cried in a quick, peevish voice, 'you are quite determined to find out that there is no ghost in the ruins, are you not?'

'I am determined to come at the truth.'

'But the truth is that there *is* a ghost. Everyone in the place has seen her now.'

'Have they?' cried Dido in amazement. Then, immediately suspecting the information, she asked, 'And who, precisely is "everyone"?'

'Oh, all the housemaids – well, I believe that two of them have. And Jones, who is Mrs Harman-Foote's maid.'

'They have seen the Grey Nun?'

'Oh yes! Did you not know? – Well, they have not quite seen the nun herself. But they have seen a light – late at night, on the gallery – *moving about*. Which is as good as seeing the nun.'

'Is it?'

'So you see it is proved.'

'I cannot at all agree that it is proved.'

'You are determined to ignore the evidence.'

'No, I am determined to consider *all* the evidence – not only that which supports my prejudice.'

'And what, pray, is all this other evidence?'

'Well... I do not yet quite know.'

Lucy smiled with insufferable satisfaction and resumed

her languid accents. 'Oh! My dear friend!' she said pityingly, 'I fear you listen too much to your head and too little to your heart. If you would only allow yourself to *feel* a little more. You would instinctively know, as I do, that there is something dark and terrible in the ruins...'

Dido promised herself that, come what may, she would *prove* there was no ghost.

As she passed through the little side gate which led from the park into the gardens of Madderstone Abbey, Dido paused a moment to catch her breath and gaze across the muddy lawns and felled trees to the house. A pleasant, rather rambling building standing on slightly rising ground, it had been built and added to and embellished ever since the first Harman had bought the land at the time of the Dissolution. Every generation had made 'improvements' according to its own taste, so that now the old Tudor core was flanked by many-windowed wings from Queen Anne's time, a grand ballroom built by the late Mr Harman and a conservatory and orangery of the present owner's creation.

At a short distance from the house stood the broken outline of the once great religious foundation; its mass of tumbled, ivy-covered walls appeared rough and irregular in the fading light, the great broken arch of the east window loomed against flying, red-tinted clouds. *A likely home for a ghost*, thought Dido as she set off through the mud towards the ruins.

And there had been a ghost at the abbey for as long as anyone in Madderstone or Badleigh could remember. Everyone could tell a story of the Grey Nun – though, as is generally the case with apparitions, she had usually been seen by a relative – or a friend – or the relative of a friend – rather than by the speaker himself. And Dido could not admire the originality of her story, for it was one which had probably been told of every ruined abbey since Henry VIII turned the nation to the Protestant faith.

In the 'old days' a rich young girl had fallen in love with a poor knight and had been parted from him by her cruel father – a baron (for barons are, by common consent, much more addicted to mistreating their daughters than any other class of men). The girl had refused the grand suitor her father would have forced upon her, become a nun and pined to death within the abbey walls. Her spirit had haunted the place ever since. Though why she should haunt the abbey, Dido did not know. She could not help but think that it would have been much more to the purpose to go off to the wicked baron's castle and haunt *him*…

But by now she was approaching the ruins and, as she looked about at the red sky, the lengthening shadows, and the rising moon gleaming palely through an ivy-clad arch, she found that she was not quite above a superstitious shudder. Perhaps she should have deferred her visit to a more propitious time…

No, there was no rational reason why twilight should be feared more in a ruined abbey than in the parlour at home. She walked on resolutely, but a minute later there was a lurching of the heart. A dark figure was just visible among the great fallen stones of the nave, pacing towards the night stair – mounting towards the gallery above, and vanishing into the shadows.

She stopped and, before she could quite reason herself out of the notion that she had seen a ghost, another, smaller figure appeared, rounding a corner of the ruins and dawdling towards the house. Fortunately there was no mistaking this for a spectre. It was, very certainly, young Georgie, walking slowly: dragging and scuffing his good boots mercilessly. The injuring of shoe leather was a crime Dido never could regard with equanimity and, for a moment, she forgot all about ghosts.

'Pick your feet up, Georgie!' she cried indignantly. 'You are spoiling your boots!'

'Well, what if I am?' He stopped in front of her, thrust out his plump chin and stared up defiantly, then put out one foot and scraped it slowly and deliberately against a stone that edged the path. A pale, ugly scuff mark appeared on the dirty, but costly, brown leather.

Dido withdrew her eyes from the distressing sight – and found herself looking more closely at the fat little face which was watching eagerly for her disapproval. There was a fresh red bruise upon his cheek.

'Your face is hurt, Georgie,' she said – glad of the distraction. 'How did you do that?'

He quickly put his hand up to cover it. 'It's nothing,' he said. 'I just fell – on the path back there.'

'You had better have some witch hazel put upon it immediately.'

He shrugged and began to walk away, saying something quietly which sounded remarkably like, 'It's none of your damned business.'

'Georgie!' she called after him angrily. 'I do not think your mama would like to hear you using that word.'

'But she can't hear me, can she?' he said and he was off – still scraping his boots with all his might.

She watched him swagger away along the path, greatly angered by his self-consequence. He looked so disgustingly easy and prosperous in his fashionably cut blue jacket and his pale pantaloons…

'Ah!' she cried aloud.

Her anger suddenly forgotten, she turned from contemplation of the retreating little gentleman and looked instead at the path along which he had come – a path which the traffic of 'improvements' had left almost an inch deep in mud… And she thought again about those pale, *clean* pantaloons…

No one could have fallen upon that path without staining his clothes. It was an impossibility…

So how had he come by such a bruise? And why had he lied about it?

She almost ran after him, but stopped herself and stood irresolute on the muddy path in the gathering dusk and encroaching shadows of the ruins. Her curiosity – that powerful motive of her character – was now pulling her in two directions: urging her to pursue the boy with a question or two, but also demanding that she discover who was in the gallery.

For someone *was* in the gallery; she had seen no one descend during her conversation with Georgie. And, since the boy had seemed to come from the shadows surrounding the nave, the person up there might well be the cause of the bruise. And besides, she would dearly love to know who else was taking an interest in the haunted ruins…

She hurried into the deeper, slightly damp gloom between the high walls and picked her way across the broken pavement of the nave, where fallen pillars and great blocks of fallen masonry lay about, choked with weeds and ivy and deep drifts of dead leaves. A bird clattered up from a twisted ash tree which grew in the sanctuary, making her start foolishly. But she continued up the night stair, clinging with one hand to the ivy on the wall, and came into the deeper dusk of the gallery, which smelt of moss and damp stone – and which seemed, at first, to be entirely deserted.

She stared along it, her eyes gradually accustoming themselves to the poor light. Parts of the roof had long since fallen away and the walls were dank and fringed with moss; tiny ferns grew in the gaps between stones. Beneath the holes in the roof, the floor was worn into hollows by rain which had fallen in upon it for centuries: in one particularly deep hollow water glinted darkly. On one side the arched front of the gallery gave a dizzying view down into the great nave of the old abbey church and the magnificent Gothic outline of the east window. And through the remains of the window's stone tracery could be seen the muddy pool and the blazing red of the beeches and yellow of the chestnuts in the park.

There was a movement beside one of the pillars that supported the roof of the gallery. A dark shape stepped out – and resolved itself into the figure of Captain Laurence. His back was towards her and he did not see her immediately. He stood instead gazing out through the great window towards the drained pool and the park. He raised a hand, rubbed his chin thoughtfully then turned back into the gallery with a look of great calculation on his face – and saw Dido watching him.

'Miss Kent!' he stepped forward and bowed with a very uncomfortable look. 'What are you doing here in the gloom?' he cried. And then, changing his expression to one of tender concern: 'Are you too hoping to discover what it was that frightened poor Miss Lambe?'

She acknowledged that that was indeed her errand and he eyed her keenly. 'And have you found out anything?' he asked.

'I have as yet had no opportunity to look about me,' she said returning his keen gaze with interest. 'I met young Georgie on the path just now. Has he too been searching for the ghost?'

No, he hastened to assure her, he had seen nothing of the boy. There was a momentary hint of alarm as he spoke, but whether that arose from the consciousness of lying, or the fear of having been overlooked, Dido could not quite determine.

She knew no positive harm of the captain, but she did not like him. He was a big, loosely made man of one or two and thirty, handsome in what she considered to be a rather coarse style, with a great deal of colour in his face, heavy brows and a lot of thick black hair. In Dido's opinion, he was altogether more *masculine* than a man had any cause to be. Wherever he went there was likely to be jealousy among the other men – and folly among the ladies.

He was now looking about him and exclaiming that it was 'a mighty strange business. I cannot account for it. Now, if we were on board ship, it would be a different matter. Some men get overwrought when they have been a long time at sea, Miss Kent, and imagine that they see all manner of things. Why, I remember one occasion...'

'But we are not at sea, Captain Laurence,' interrupted Dido who was in no mood for naval talk. She began to walk along the uneven stones of the gallery. 'What did Penelope see?' she mused. 'What did she mean when she said "I saw her".'

'There cannot have been anyone here in the gallery,' said the captain as he followed her, 'for you see there is no door here,' he waved a hand at the blank walls. 'And here,' he continued as they reached the end, 'is only this broken wall and a drop of twelve feet or more down into the nave. Even a sailor could not have climbed up – though on board ship, you know...'

'Yes, quite so,' said Dido quickly as she turned away and continued to pace the old flagstones. She was impatient of his habit of bringing everything around to a discussion of the navy, but she could not help but admit he was right. There was no way in which anyone could have got into the gallery. There could have been no one standing behind Harriet when Penelope turned back.

'The only way into this gallery is up those steps,' said the captain.

'And Harriet and I were standing at the top of the steps all the time our party remained here,' she said firmly. 'No one could have come past but we would have seen them.'

She had now come back to the head of the stairs and she found that she was rather cold. She pulled her pelisse closer about her and descended the first two steps – to the place from which Penelope had fallen. She turned and saw that her companion was now lounging against the nearest pillar, watching her thoughtfully.

'From here one can see clear along the gallery,' she remarked.

'And nothing else?' he asked.

'No… Except through the great window I can see a little of the grounds… But very little; from here I can see only trees – and the drained pool.'

'The pool?' Captain Laurence straightened up abruptly. 'Are you sure?'

'Yes,' she said, puzzled by his sudden interest. 'Perhaps you would like to look for yourself.' She returned to the gallery and he hurried to take her place on the steps.

As he passed, his long overcoat stirred something very small which was lying on the stones. She stooped down – but found only a little brown and green feather which seemed to have blown in from somewhere. However, as she was standing up again, she caught sight of something much more sinister.

A foot or so away lay the pool which, on first entering the gallery, she had taken for a puddle of rainwater. But, now that she was so close, it was possible to see that it was too dark for water. She took off her glove and touched the gleaming surface with the tip of a finger; it was thick and sticky. She examined her finger – and saw blood…

'Good God!' cried the captain. She turned to him thinking that he had seen the red stain. But he was still on the step, and he was staring, not at her, but at something behind her. A frown was gathering his black brows into one thick, bristling line above his nose.

She stood up and looked about to see what had alarmed him. The gallery was empty and, for a moment, she feared he had glimpsed some fleeting apparition… But then, through the east window, she saw the cause of his surprise.

Down beside the drained pool there was a scene of consternation.

Two workmen were shouting and pointing down at the dried mud, while a stout young man in gaiters – whom Dido recognised as Henry Coulson, the landscape gardener responsible for the present deplorable state of Madderstone's grounds – was standing with his hat in his hand and rubbing at his thatch of fair hair.

Laurence came to stand beside her. 'There is something amiss,' he said with keen interest. 'They have found something.'

Dido had already turned towards the steps, but the captain took her hand. 'Miss Kent, I think you had better wait here,' he said earnestly. 'I will go to see what it is and return to tell you.' He bowed and was gone, running down the steps, through the fallen stones and out into the cloister.

Dido, who had a rather better opinion of her own nerves than Captain Laurence, felt equal to any surprise which the pool might supply and began, almost immediately, to make her way towards the men.

The captain was perhaps fifty yards ahead of her. Mr Coulson had now left the side of the pool and was hurrying past the fallen trees and through the lengthening shadows towards him. They met upon the lawn and an eager conference ensued with the smaller man waving his arms about a great deal while Laurence listened attentively.

As Dido came close enough to distinguish words, Mr Coulson seemed to be cursing and saying something like, 'I don't understand.' He laid his hand upon the captain's arm, 'Damn it, Laurence,' he said urgently, 'we need to talk about this.'

But Laurence shook him off. 'Not now,' he said. 'I must go up to the house and tell them the news. You go back and set the men to…getting it out of there.'

He turned to Dido with an upheld hand. 'Miss Kent,' he cried, 'I would not advise you to go any closer. The men have found something…rather unpleasant at the bottom of the pool.'

'Indeed?' she said with keen interest. 'What precise nature does the unpleasantness take?'

'I am afraid it is a skeleton.' He paused, but Dido showed no sign of fainting away. 'A *human* skeleton,' he added.

Chapter Six

...Well, Eliza, as you may imagine, there is not another topic on anyone's lips but the skeleton in the pool. As Rebecca solemnly assures me, 'the whole place is alive with this dead body, miss.'

And it is, of course, the mortal remains of the Grey Nun. Lucy is quite sure that it <u>must be</u>.

That the bones of a woman who died four hundred years ago should have been preserved so long and should, furthermore, be accompanied, as these were, by a quantity of sovereigns, many of which bear the likeness of our present king, does not seem to astonish her at all. It is undoubtedly the Grey Nun.

However, the coroner, Mr Wishart, when he held his court at the Red Lion this morning, failed entirely to identify her correctly. You know how it is on such occasions. These fellows in authority are all too inclined to be blinded by commonplace evidence and probability and so are quite insensible to all the thrilling possibilities of what <u>must be</u>.

Lucy is sorely disappointed.

The other great cause of his failing to recognise the nun, was a ring which was upon her finger. It seems that just such a ring belonged to a Miss Elinor Fenn – a governess who disappeared from Madderstone Abbey some fifteen years ago.

So the coroner has declared that the remains are those of this Miss Fenn. A verdict with which Lucy is most displeased. And I very much pity poor Silas for having to report it to her.

For she would have Silas attend the inquest so that she might have the earliest intelligence, though I believe he has as little liking for frequenting public houses as any young man of one and twenty can have. And the viewing of bones would be a great deal less to his taste than his sister's. However, the customs governing such occasions protect only the sensibilities of women, not sensitive younger brothers, and since Lucy had no other gentleman to attend on her behalf poor Silas must go. And he is so accustomed to doing just as both his sisters command, that I doubt he raised half a word in protest.

But he looked quite unwell when he returned...

I happened to be at Ashfield when he came in. I would not have you believe that *I* was at all anxious to hear Mr Wishart's verdict; for, of course, being of such a remarkably incurious disposition, it was a matter of complete indifference to me...

But it did just so happen that I was with Lucy when Silas returned – and I have never seen him look so ill. He is but just recovered from his last great attack of asthma and should not, in my opinion, have risked his health in a public assembly. He was exceedingly white and shaken.

You may imagine him, Eliza, sitting on the old sofa by the window in the breakfast parlour, with Lucy upon one side and me upon the other, stammering out his account.

'Miss Fenn?' repeated Lucy again and again. 'Miss Elinor Fenn? But who is she?' For she seemed to feel that, if the coroner could not oblige her with a romantic nun, then he *might at least furnish a name with which she is familiar.*

And then, in the next moment, she was tugging at the poor boy's arm and demanding to know how the woman had died. And I quite lost patience with her, for she should know that such treatment, besides making him nervous and risking another attack of the asthma, will always make his stammer worse. When it came to pronouncing the cause of the woman's death, he could only stare from one to the other of us with a trembling lip.

'Does Mr Wishart believe that she fell into the pool by accident?' I suggested by way of helping him out.

He shook his head. 'N…no,' he managed at last. 'It was not thought possible. The sides of the pool slope so gently, you know. So, n…no, not an accident.'

'Murder!' Lucy reached for her lavender water and I was in fear of the hysterics. But, luckily, the delay caused by his stammering prevented it. She could not very well give way to hysterics while she must wait and coax him into an answer.

At last he managed to explain that the verdict was not murder but, 's…s…su… In short, it seems that Miss Fenn took her own life.'

'Self-murder!'

There was a silence while Lucy considered this – and I began to hope that she might after all forgive poor Mr Wishart his shortcomings, since his opinion at least furnished her with a great deal to feed her imagination.

While she was lost in thought, I questioned Silas about the reasons for this verdict; and it seems that Mr Harris Paynter could prove that the young woman was much troubled with melancholy in the months before her death. Of course, this Mr Paynter is not more than one or two and twenty and so the death occurred before he was surgeon here. But his uncle, Mr Arthur Paynter, was Badleigh's medical man before him: and, by Silas's account, he (that is, the uncle) kept a journal of his patients. It was this journal which was presented as evidence in the court today.

'Well,' said Lucy at last, 'one thing is quite certain. It was this dreadful discovery which the Grey Nun came to warn us of.'

And I was on the point of arguing against her… But I found that I must pause and think a little more carefully about the matter. For, though I certainly do not believe that there was a ghostly warning, yet…

Yet I must confess to being puzzled, Eliza. It does seem so very strange, does it not, that two such unusual events – first Penelope's fall, and now this discovery in the pool – should occur within the course of only a few days? And within a few hundred yards of one another. It seems so very improbable that they should be random occurrences coming together only by chance. But I cannot come at any explanation which might join the two together.

Nor can I escape the feeling that there was something wrong – no, not wrong exactly, perhaps I should rather say strange – about the discovery of the bones. I keep remembering that moment when the captain and I first saw the commotion down beside the lake and I feel as if there was something decidedly odd…

A knocking on the house door stilled Dido's pen. She waited, fervently hoping that the visitor would not be admitted to disturb her precious hour of solitude. Margaret was gone to pay calls in the village and she had been quite determined to finish this letter while she was alone.

But, after a minute or two, there were the usual sounds of approach, the parlour door was opened and the round red face of Rebecca, the vicarage's upper maid, appeared.

'It's Mrs Harman-Foote, miss. I told her the mistress was gone out, but she says she most particularly wishes to speak with *you*.'

'Then you had better show her in, Rebecca,' said Dido with a sigh. And she put the letter away in her writing desk, wishing very much that she had some success to report concerning her enquiries after the ghost.

But, meanwhile, the maid was hesitating in the doorway and looking quickly about the room as if to be quite sure Margaret was absent before venturing upon an opinion. 'She's looking but poorly to my mind, miss,' she said in a half-whisper before ushering in the lady – who was looking very 'poorly' indeed. Dido had never seen her so pale – nor so agitated.

She took a seat beside the hearth and clasped her hands together tightly in her lap. Rebecca hurried forward solicitously to mend the fire, hoping, no doubt to hear something of interest, but Dido waved her away with a frown. As soon as they were alone, the visitor raised her eyes.

'You have heard the news, Miss Kent? I mean, the news of the inquest.'

Dido replied that she had.

'It is all so very unpleasant,' began Mrs Harman-Foote, then seemed unable to go on. She pressed her lips together, swallowed and fixed her eyes upon a spot just behind Dido's head, as if she was suddenly very interested in an old silhouette of Mr Kent which hung there. She had, altogether, the appearance of a woman who was endeavouring to hold back tears.

Dido waited rather awkwardly for, though they had been acquainted for a little more than five years, there had never existed between them the kind of intimacy which could authorise her to notice her friend's distress. 'It is all very shocking,' she said at last.

'Yes.' Mrs Harman-Foote struggled for her usual assurance. 'But there can be no doubt – I mean as to her identity. I knew the ring for Miss Fenn's immediately. It was always upon her finger. It is certainly her, Miss Kent, but…' Again it was necessary for her to study the silhouette and, as she did so, Dido's mind turned to some hasty calculations which she had not thought to make before.

The woman had died fifteen years ago. Fifteen years ago Anne Harman was a girl of (a pause while Dido counted, arithmetic did not come easily to her,) thirteen or fourteen years old. And, since she was the sole heiress of Madderstone, it was probable that she had been the only young person in the family at that time. *Elinor Fenn had been her governess.* And the struggling face, the gleaming eyes, proved the pupil had been very much attached to her teacher.

'I am very sorry,' Dido said quietly. 'The lady who died in the pool was a good friend of yours, I think?'

'She was the woman who brought me up. For many years – since I was six years old – Miss Fenn had supplied the place of the mother I never knew.' The words were

pronounced with quiet, feeling dignity – but a slight
flicker of the eye as she spoke sent a single tear running
down her cheek. She drew out a handkerchief and wiped
it away briskly.

'This discovery,' said Dido gently, 'and the publicity of
the inquest must be very painful indeed for you.'

'It is, of course, distasteful,' she said, and tucked away
her handkerchief as if resolved upon not needing it again.
'But not because I have ever doubted…' She stopped,
drew in a long breath and straightened her back. 'I have
known for many years, almost from the time of her going,
that my dear friend was dead. There could be no other
explanation. She went out one evening, you see, and
never returned. She was searched for, but never found.'

'So,' said Dido cautiously, with curiosity and propriety
making their usual battle inside her, 'this late discovery
has not surprised… That is, I hope, it has not pained you
so much as…'

'It has, of course, shocked me. It has raised unhappy
memories. But it has not recalled me to grief,' came
the firm, quiet answer. 'That would not be right. It is a
principle of mine *never* to waste time upon empty regrets.
I have mourned my friend already and I have long ago
committed her soul to the loving care of that greater power
which I *know* has received her.' As Mrs Harman-Foote
spoke these comfortable phrases of Christian reassurance,
her usual confidence seemed to be gaining ground. There
was something positively defiant in her emphasis and in
the setting of her jaw. 'But,' she continued resolutely, 'I
know that the verdict of the inquest is wrong. I *know*
that Miss Fenn did not take her own life. Every principle

which she possessed – every principle which she taught to me – would have cried out against such a wicked, irreligious act.'

'I am sure it is very much to your friend's credit that you should remember her so kindly,' said Dido. And she sat for some time in very thoughtful contemplation of the woman before her. There is always a kind of fascination in seeing a familiar acquaintance act in an unfamiliar way; and tears in the eyes of Madderstone's assured mistress were an odd sight indeed. But Dido's interest in the present case went deeper. Doubts as to the coroner's verdict must raise the possibility of a mystery…

Meanwhile Mrs Harman-Foote was struggling for composure. 'I have spoken,' she said at last, in the same quiet, feeling voice, 'I have spoken to Mr Portinscale…' She broke off. Dido wondered why Madderstone's clergyman had been consulted. 'He is quite unpersuadable…' She stopped. It was necessary to take the handkerchief out again and wipe away a fresh tear. 'My dear Miss Fenn is to be buried in a suicide's grave on the north of the churchyard. In *unhallowed ground.*'

She stopped, her face working with emotion, the handkerchief pressed firmly to her lips. And Dido watched in silent sympathy; for a little while she was beyond words herself. Poor lady! To see a beloved friend laid outside the benediction of the church; to be denied all the natural solace of religion in her loss. The idea must frighten even Dido into silence, still for a while even the workings of *her* mind…

They sat together for a while saying nothing. The little fire smoked sullenly; there was a loitering footstep in the passage and Rebecca's face peered once around the door, full of questions, but upon receiving nothing but a frown, it was withdrawn.

At last, with a great effort: 'You are wondering I am sure, Miss Kent, at my calling here – at my speaking so openly. I hope you do not feel that I intrude too much upon our friendship.'

'No,' stammered Dido hastily – and a little untruthfully. 'No, not at all.'

'But I must do something you see.'

'Oh, yes, quite.'

'And I have no one else to whom I may speak without reserve on this subject. My husband does not wish me to concern myself over the matter, you see. He believes that my making any enquiries will only add to my distress.'

'Yes, I quite understand,' murmured Dido, though she was beginning to wonder where all this might be leading.

'And so I have decided that I must ask for your help, Miss Kent. For, you see, I have always had the highest regard for your good sense and understanding – I have always felt that you are someone whose judgement may be relied upon.'

'Thank you,' said Dido, surprised and flattered by a good opinion which she had never had much cause to suspect. 'I am sure I should be very glad to be of any assistance.'

Mrs Harman-Foote looked pleased and put up her handkerchief. 'You see,' she said, 'I am quite sure that, if only a few enquiries were made into the matter, it would be possible to establish that dear Miss Fenn is innocent of this terrible crime which is charged against her.'

'I suppose it might be possible to find out a little more,' said Dido thoughtfully, rather intrigued by the problem. 'Her friends might be questioned. The history of her last days examined more closely…'

'Excellent,' cried Mrs Harman-Foote. 'Then it is agreed – you will make the enquiries my husband will not permit me to make. You will find out about Miss Fenn's death – so that we may *prove* to Mr Portinscale that she did *not* take her own life and her body must be laid in consecrated ground.'

'Oh! But…'

'I am very grateful to you for undertaking the matter Miss Kent.' Mrs Harman-Foote stood up to take her leave. 'I know the matter could not be in more capable hands.'

'It is very kind of you to say so, but…'

'I should be particularly glad to have the whole matter settled before the All Hallows ball at the end of the month. I must have the poor, dear lady removed from that dreadful grave by then.'

Dido hesitated, disconcerted to find herself imposed upon again – and yet not entirely unwilling to undertake the commission. For it was shocking to think of a woman cast needlessly into a suicide's grave. And, besides, her own curiosity was piqued. Had there been another cause of death? Or had the young pupil been entirely deceived as to the character of her governess?

However, her ever-active curiosity was at war not only with propriety, but also with memories of previous enquiries of her own: enquiries which had brought upon her responsibilities she had neither expected nor welcomed.

'Mrs Harman-Foote,' she said, 'please forgive the question: but have you thought about the consequences of any enquiry into the events surrounding your friend's death?'

'The consequences?'

'We have to consider Mr Wishart's opinion,' Dido explained. 'I mean his opinion that the death could not have been an accident. I understand that the nature of the pool – the way in which the edges of it slope so gradually – makes it most unlikely that Miss Fenn could have fallen into it unintentionally.'

'Of course there was no accident. Miss Fenn was neither clumsy nor imprudent.'

'And if she did not fall…and if she did not take her own life…then someone else…' She stopped.

Mrs Harman-Foote was regarding her impassively.

'You believe that Miss Fenn was murdered?' cried Dido in amazement.

'I rather think that she must have been,' was the calm reply. 'Mr Wishart says that an accident was not possible. And, since I *know* that it was impossible for a woman of her character and principles to harm herself, I have no choice but to believe that someone else was responsible for her death.'

Chapter Seven

...Well, Eliza, be warned by this simple little tale: great ladies of Mrs Harman-Foote's stamp are no less dictatorial for having tears in their eyes! Grief does not make such a woman any less determined upon getting her own way.

I am fairly caught!

Though I confess that I am not entirely sorry to be caught. The question of Miss Fenn's death intrigues me. Mrs Harman-Foote seems so <u>very sure</u> that her principles would have prevented her from ending her own life. And I should be very glad indeed to help exonerate her if I can – an unconsecrated grave is a terrible thing.

I am to dine at Madderstone on Monday – rather to the surprise of Margaret. At first she was inclined to be offended by an invitation which does not include herself or Francis, but now she has very wisely decided to be delighted, and says again and again how perfectly charming it is that Mrs Harman-Foote should show attention to <u>her</u> family.

So the invitation does not, at least, disturb the peace of the household. Whether it will produce anything of interest remains to be proved. I am to be shown the governess's room and also her ring. And I should very much like to look for myself at the place in which the remains were found...

Dido was forced to break off. There had been, all through the last few lines, a voice of protest attempting to make itself heard: a voice which was none the less insistent for being entirely imaginary.

'My dear Miss Kent!' it was saying. 'Is it wise to interest yourself in such a very…unpleasant business?'

She closed her eyes. 'Perhaps it is not exactly *wise*, Mr Lomax,' she replied in a whisper, 'but it is certainly humane. Poor Mrs Harman-Foote is so very distressed.'

'And, tell me honestly, is her distress the real motive here? Do you not seek rather to satisfy your own curiosity?'

Dido coloured. His knowing tone – even in imagination – made her uncomfortable. 'Curiosity may play a part,' she consented reluctantly. 'It certainly qualifies me for the task. But I cannot allow it to lessen the force of the poor lady's distress.'

She was rather pleased with this argument. Mr Lomax was forced to attack on different ground.

'And are you sure that investigation is the best way to comfort your friend?'

She faltered. 'I hardly know…'

'Consider the consequences. Once questions begin to be asked, all manner of secrets may be revealed – things which are much better left in obscurity.'

'It is true…' she began thoughtfully. But just then the wind caught in the eaves outside her window, producing a loud, desolate howl. She opened her eyes upon the cold attic room: the bare floorboards, the clothes hung upon pegs on the wall – the sleeve of a morning gown stirring slightly in a draught of air from the window. An apron cast aside upon the foot of the bed, and a large basket of interminable sewing beside it, reminded her of the pleasant diversions which awaited her on the morrow.

'No, Mr Lomax,' she said as she reached for her pen, 'I see no reason why I should suffer the inconvenience of your opinions when I have not even the pleasure of your society.'

She turned her attention back to her letter with great determination.

The difficulty lies, Eliza, in proving for certain that a woman did not commit such an act. For it would be necessary to look into her mind, would it not?

It is not, of course, difficult to believe Miss Fenn might have been affected by melancholy — and even despair. The extreme loneliness of the governess's life: the humiliation of an intelligent, feeling woman reduced to a situation of dependence upon people of inferior understanding is universally acknowledged.

Dido paused a moment and frowned a little uncomfortably at her own words before continuing.

But a great deal must depend upon her character. Exactly what kind of woman was Elinor Fenn?

Anne Harman-Foote's affection for her governess — and her extreme youth at the time of the death — mean that her testimony upon this subject cannot be entirely relied upon.

Indeed, I confess that at first I had the gravest doubts as to the accuracy of her memories. We have often remarked upon

*the strange contradictions in her character, have we not? That
a woman who sets herself up for clear-sightedness should be so
deceived in the nature of her own children – so weak and blind
to the faults in their behaviour – has always been a matter of
amazement to me. And I could not help but wonder whether
she might have been similarly taken in by Miss Fenn.*

*So I have been asking a few questions among people who
remember the governess – at least, I have hardly needed to
ask, but only to listen, for, just at the moment, the good folk
of Badleigh and Madderstone need no prompting to talk
upon this interesting subject.*

*And the general opinion seems to be that she was neither
pretty, nor beautiful, but very handsome. Handsome, I
always feel, says a great deal. A woman may be pretty and
silly, beautiful and bad. But handsome is a different matter.
'Handsome' generally approves the character as much as the
features.*

*And Elinor Fenn was, undoubtedly, 'handsome'. In the
haberdasher's and in the milliner's and also in the post office,
there is but one opinion: Miss Fenn was a very handsome
woman.*

*Another point of interest is that there is hardly a woman
who knew her who had not planned a match for her. Rebecca
is of the opinion that her employer, old Mr Harman himself,
should have married her. And this remarkable school of
thought has other adherents in the village, though mostly
among the poorer sort. Mrs Philips, the abbey's housekeeper,
seems to have been content to settle Miss Fenn in Mr
Portinscale's modest, but comfortable, parsonage house – and
most gossiping ladies were in agreement with her. Though
there were some who recognised the utility of an experienced*

governess in a family with two daughters and would have had the late Mr Crockford make the proposal – if only he had not been so inconveniently devoted to the memory of his dead wife.

It is by no means usual for a neighbourhood to marry off its governesses to every prosperous bachelor and widower within reach. So I cannot help but conclude from all this that Miss Fenn was a very superior woman – or, at least, a very superior governess.

For the rest I can only discover that she was quiet, religious and came from 'somewhere in Shropshire'. Nothing more definite is ever hazarded than 'somewhere in Shropshire'. She was, by all accounts, an orphan with no living family.

This picture of her character – the high regard in which she was held by her neighbours and, above all, her religious principles – certainly argues most strongly against self-murder. It would, I think, have required something quite remarkable to overcome such a mind and drive it to despair.

I do not know that anything more may be gathered. But tomorrow I shall see what I may discover at Madderstone.

And in the meantime, Eliza, I have been considering again the facts which came out at the inquest. I should certainly like to know more about the journal which Mr Paynter's uncle wrote. But, above all, I am deeply interested in those coins which were found with the bones. It seems to me very unlikely that a woman setting out from her home intent upon self-destruction should take the trouble of furnishing herself with money...

The parish church of St James at Madderstone had been built in Norman times, and was older even than the great Cistercian abbey which had once been its close neighbour. It was a rather humble little building of low rounded arches, crouching amid its yews and gravestones, embellished only by a short, half-timbered tower. On this particular morning, when Dido stopped there on her way to her dinner engagement, the yews were dripping from a recent shower. A shaft of sunlight was just breaking through the clouds and sparkling on the drops which hung under the arch of the lychgate.

She scarcely knew why she had come. But, passing by the gate, her mind full of recent events, she had felt compelled to turn aside and visit the grave of the unfortunate Miss Fenn.

She followed the path which led among the mounded graves of the poor and the stone-boxed tombs of the gentry, but turned aside from the porch, skirted the blunt west end of the church and came into the sunless northern corner of the graveyard, where the air struck cold against her face and the path was green and greasy with lichen.

The grave she was seeking was not difficult to find. A little path of downtrodden grass led to it. It would seem that half the inhabitants of Madderstone village had come, like her, to gaze upon the suicide's resting place.

It lay under the overhanging boughs of an ancient yew, just beyond the low wall of mossy stones which marked the boundary of the church's mercy: a raw wound of reddish earth among the yellow grass and dead docks of the waste ground. And it was too small; it would seem there had been no coffin to decently house the bones. They had been tumbled into the ground here with no care, no dignity.

Dido looked back towards the church with the graves of all its dead gathered close; even the most humble, grass-covered mound safe within the benediction of the little stone cross which topped the tower. Then she gazed down at the unforgiving wall dividing this one soul from grace. The sight was terrible, even to her. How much worse must it be to Anne Harman-Foote, who had loved this woman like a mother?

Insensibly her fists clenched in the shelter of her cloak. 'I *will* find the truth,' she whispered, half to herself and half as a promise to the wretched bones. 'I will do everything within my power...'

She stopped at the sound of the lychgate opening. Footsteps sounded along the path and the figure of a man appeared, walking briskly past the end of the church. There were a few pale-pink late roses in his hand and Dido expected him to stop by one of the tombs, but instead he hurried towards her, making directly for the grave of the outcast.

As he drew closer she saw that it was Harris Paynter, the surgeon.

He was a young man whose firm figure, black hair and dark, heavily lidded eyes had their share of admiration among the ladies of Madderstone and Badleigh; but set against these advantages were his reputation as 'a precise, plodding fellow', his being 'nothing but a surgeon-apothecary' – and a rather sallow complexion.

Though Dido could not help but notice that, just at the moment, his complexion appeared rather better than usual. There was a slight but becoming flush of colour on his cheeks, a hint of emotion that made him seem rather less dull. There was a happy easy confidence in his stride – and even in the sitting of his hat on the very back of his head. The fine eyes were animated.

'I am sorry!' he stopped abruptly as he caught sight of her. 'Good day, Miss Kent.' He bowed and, as she returned his greeting, there was an odd little movement of his hand – as if he half-attempted to hide the roses from her view, but then thought better of it. Instead, after a moment's hesitation, he leant across the wall and placed them upon the turned earth and they both stood for a moment gazing down at the delicate flowers lying softly on the ugly brown clay. A drop of water fell from the overhanging branches of the yew and settled in the curve of a petal.

He cleared his throat. 'I was walking up to the great house, to visit Miss Lambe,' he said in his clipped, precise voice. 'And thought I would just stop – to look at the grave.' He paused, his eyes still fixed upon the little patch of turned earth. 'This is a very sad business, is it not?' he said.

Dido tried to study his face, but it was impossible to make out the expression of his eyes. 'Were you at all acquainted with the lady?' As she spoke she was busy calculating that he would have been a child of only six or seven at the time of the death – strange, then, that he should seem so very concerned: that he, of all the people who had visited this grave, should be the only one to bring flowers…

'No,' he said quickly. 'No I did not know her at all.'

'Oh…' Dido's eyes wandered back to the roses. He looked at them with embarrassment and seemed to feel that some explanation was required.

'I gave evidence at the inquest,' he said abruptly. 'I feel…'

He hesitated; he was a man inclined by nature and by the demands of his profession to choose his words with care, '...connected. It is – in part at least – on account of my testimony that she is...excluded from the churchyard.'

'And you are grieved at the result of your testimony?'

He sighed and put up his hand to lean against a low bough of the yew tree. 'Yes, I did not foresee this.'

'It could have made no difference if you had,' said Dido gently. 'You were under oath and so had no choice but to tell exactly what you knew.'

He raised his eyes to hers with a very grateful smile. 'That is true,' he said.

It was too fair an opportunity to miss. 'If it were possible, you would be glad to see the verdict changed?' she ventured.

'I doubt that it is possible.'

'Perhaps Mr Wishart cannot be persuaded,' she said. 'I know very little of coroner's courts. It may be that, once it is written down, a verdict is beyond the reach of reason. But this...' she glanced down at the grave. 'This is the decision of a clergyman. And it may be that, if we could supply sufficient reasons, Mr Portinscale might amend *his* verdict.'

She had certainly gained Mr Paynter's attention. He eyed her keenly. 'I should,' he said, 'be very glad to be of service to Mrs Harman-Foote.' He spoke simply but with great feeling – as if he was particularly anxious to please the lady – and Dido could not but be reminded of that note he had left upon the hall table...

'Then perhaps,' she suggested, still eyeing him suspiciously, 'you might be so kind as to walk up to the abbey with me – so that we may consult together.'

He looked surprised but, when she turned away, he fell into step beside her and listened very attentively as she told him of her promise to find the cause of Miss Fenn's death.

'It is an admirable enterprise,' he said solemnly. 'But I do not see how I can assist you.'

'Well,' she began carefully, 'a great deal must depend upon this journal which your uncle kept.'

'Yes.'

She stole another look at his brooding face, but still could make out nothing of his expression. They rounded the end of the church and emerged, blinking a little, into the autumn sunshine.

'Miss Fenn's consultations with your uncle,' she ventured, 'when did they begin?'

'Two years, three months and one week before she died,' he answered promptly.

'And were they frequent?'

'Tolerably frequent. He seems – and I have only his journal to inform me – but he seems to have visited her once every week.' He checked himself, held up a finger, and proceeded with exactness. '*Usually* a week passed between his visits. Once it was just six days. On...' he thought a moment, 'on *two* occasions, it was eight days.'

'Your memory is very precise.'

He looked at her in some surprise. 'I was required to state these facts in a court of law,' he said. 'Naturally I would wish them to be correct.'

'Yes, of course. And her complaint was always one of melancholy?'

'Usually it was melancholy: on one occasion he has written "depression of the spirits". Though *that* may be no more than a variation of expression. Even to a medical man there is little to distinguish the two conditions.'

'And had Miss Fenn asked your uncle to visit her during the last few days before she died?'

'No. No, she had not,' he said gravely. 'It had been…' He paused under the lychgate as he again sought the exact memory, '…twenty-six days since he last attended her.' He pushed open the gate and began to take his leave of her.

'But I thought you were walking up to the great house, Mr Paynter.'

'I am,' he said hurriedly, 'but I find there is something I have forgotten to bring with me. Unfortunately I must return home to fetch it – I shall not be able to accompany you.' He bowed, but then hesitated and stood, hat in hand, staring down at his feet.

'You seem troubled, Mr Paynter.'

'I am thinking of Miss Fenn. It is a sobering thought,' he said, 'but perhaps if my uncle had attended the lady during those last days… In short, it may have been the lack of his usual cordials and restoratives which drove her to the terrible act.'

'Yes,' said Dido thoughtfully. 'It may have been.' She paused – thought a moment. 'However,' she added, 'it may be that her not calling upon your uncle's services in those last weeks argues instead for her feeling better and being in no need of his cordials.'

'Yes,' he said doubtingly. 'Perhaps it may.'

'In point of fact,' she said, 'your uncle's journal does not prove that Miss Fenn was suffering from melancholy when she died; but only that she had suffered such a complaint *twenty-six days earlier*.'

Chapter Eight

Dido walked on slowly to Madderstone Abbey, her mind full of Mr Paynter's tribute of roses – and those six and twenty days during which Miss Fenn had, quite contrary to her habit, sought no help from her physician.

In order to establish whether or not this was a case of self-murder, it would be necessary to discover how the lady had appeared during those six and twenty days. Was she happier than usual – or sadder? Was it possible that, after fifteen years, anyone would be able to remember such a detail?

She passed through the park gate and came into the spoilt gardens. The sun was sinking low, casting long shadows from the fallen trees and turning the many puddles a deep, bloody red. The path from the gate ran above the bank of the old pool – and was particularly difficult to negotiate for a woman determined upon keeping her petticoat clean. But at the end of it there were four stone steps which led down to the pool, and it had been Dido's intention to descend these steps to look at the place from which Miss Fenn's body had been taken.

However, when she was only halfway along the path – and balancing precariously on a stone beside a deep patch of mud – she heard footsteps and the booming voice of

Mr Harman-Foote down by the pool. 'Well it must be put to rights at once, d'you understand?' he was saying in a tone of grave displeasure.

She paused, swaying dangerously on her stone. Another, quieter voice was murmuring an apology. She looked down the bank and saw Mr Coulson, the landscape gardener, scratching anxiously at his head as he spoke.

'Well, well,' cried Mr Harman-Foote, a little mollified, 'I daresay you meant no harm; but you've caused a great deal of trouble. You should not have…'

Unfortunately he never finished his speech, for just as he reached this most interesting point, Dido overbalanced and gave a little cry as she trod deep into the mud. Mr Harman-Foote stopped speaking immediately; both gentlemen turned in the direction of the sound and bowed when they saw her. She was obliged to call a greeting and hurry on – doomed never to hear what it was that Mr Coulson should not have done.

Which was very provoking, for she was almost sure he was about to be upbraided for draining the pool. At least, that is what she thought at first. But, by the time she reached the ruined cloister, she had begun to revise her opinion. For, she reasoned, the draining of the pool could not have taken the owner of the grounds by surprise. He must have seen that it was to happen when plans for the improvements were first drawn up; and if he had not wanted it done, he would certainly have vetoed it immediately…

She was shaken from this engrossing reverie by the sight of other dinner guests. Ahead of her on the gravel sweep, Silas Crockford was handing Lucy out of his chaise. And just rounding the corner of the cloister was

Mr Portinscale, walking up from his vicarage.

'Ah Miss Kent!' he began immediately upon seeing her, and bowed with great formality. 'This is indeed a heaven-sent opportunity! I had been very much hoping that I might, in the course of the day, avail myself of the pleasure of a few minutes private conversation with you.'

'Indeed?' she smiled up at him politely. He was a tall, very solemn man who had, no doubt, been rather handsome in his youth; but his youth was almost twenty years distant now and in those years he had grown thin and dry. And when he removed his hat, it was clear that his hair – though still tolerably black – was so thin atop as no amount of brushing about was quite able to disguise.

'Yes, I fear,' he clasped his hands in the small of his back and rocked himself forward on his toes – very much as if he were about to preach a sermon, 'I fear that you have been *suborned*.'

'Suborned? Oh dear! I hope that I have not, for it sounds very disagreeable.'

'It is, my dear,' he continued seriously as they walked on. 'Very disagreeable indeed. It appears that your good nature has allowed you to be imposed upon. You have been led into error, Miss Kent, and, as a clergyman, I feel it incumbent upon me to set you right.'

'Oh!'

'I am aware,' he said, sinking his voice almost to a whisper to prevent it being heard by the Crockfords – or by Mrs Harman-Foote who was now come out onto the steps to meet them. 'I am aware of the service which your friend,' a glance here towards the steps, 'has asked you to perform – I mean, of course, with regard to her dead governess. But you do wrong to interfere. Suicide is a grievous sin.'

'It is indeed, Mr Portinscale,' said Dido, matching his solemnity, 'and no one should be accused of it falsely.'

He shook his head and a little colour tinged his thin cheeks. 'These matters should be left in the hands of God, my dear.'

'But they are not in the hands of God,' Dido pointed out gravely, 'they are in the hands of the coroner.'

'Who would not be suffered to remain in authority if God did not will it,' he answered quickly. Then he seemed to recollect himself and spoke more calmly. 'We must trust in the Lord,' he insisted. 'We must not meddle with what He has ordained.'

'No! That is nonsense!' The words burst from Dido involuntarily as the weakness of his position struck her. The colour in his cheeks deepened with displeasure. She forced herself to speak less violently. 'This philosophy, sir, would argue against all good works and make inertia the greatest of all virtues. I cannot believe but that we are sometimes required to exert ourselves in the cause of charity.' She drew a long breath. 'I do not doubt Mr Wishart's good intentions. But his verdict *may* be mistaken. An injustice may have been done. I cannot believe it wrong to try to discover the truth.'

He was about to reply, but he was prevented by the approach of their hostess.

They all walked on into the house together and it was not until some time later that Dido was calm enough to wonder just why Mr Portinscale should interest himself so much in the business. Why should he care so very much that the coroner's verdict remain unchallenged?

* * *

... Well, Eliza, there were nine of us at dinner, for besides the Crockfords and Mr Portinscale there was Henry Coulson, the landscape gardener, and of course Captain Laurence, who is staying once more with his cousins at Madderstone. (By the by, I do not know whether Captain Laurence has a home of his own when he is not aboard ship, but, if he has, I fancy it is not so comfortable as Madderstone Abbey.)

Well, as you may imagine, Mrs Harman-Foote's duties as hostess did not allow for any conversation between us while we remained in the dining room, beyond an assurance, almost shouted along the table, of her intention of taking me to see Miss Fenn's bedchamber as soon as she should be at leisure.

Indeed it was hardly possible for female voices to be heard at all. For Mr H-F himself pays his compliments, talks about poachers and tells his jokes so loud that, if you do but listen carefully, you may hear the glass drops on the chandelier tinkling in answer to his speeches.

And then there was Mr Coulson braying down his nose and shouting 'Quite so!' and 'Very good, sir!' whenever the master of the house might be deemed to have said anything clever. Mr Coulson, by the by, is an addition to our society since your going to London, so I had better introduce him. He is a very young man – a relation, I believe, of both the Harmans and the Crockfords and the ward of old Mr Harman at whose expense he has been educated. He is not long finished at Oxford and intends to make his mark upon the world. He fancies himself very clever in the landscape gardening line and, once he has demonstrated his skill at Madderstone, he means 'to make a mint of money at it in no time at all'.

It would seem that at one time or another Mr Coulson

has considered devoting his talents to every profession from the navy to the church, and does not doubt that he could have, 'made a pretty fine show' at anything he set his mind to. But – as he gave the whole table to understand – it is in medicine that his genius might have had full rein. And he would have done a great deal more good than that 'dunderheaded sawbones Paynter', who is 'as dull-witted as any medical fellow he ever met'.

I rather wondered why he should wish to speak so slightingly of poor Mr Paynter – a gentleman he can hardly know – but I had no opportunity to enquire. For meanwhile Mr Portinscale was busy denouncing the iniquities of the entire world, with all the force of the pulpit; and Harriet and Lucy were making a great to-do because poor Silas was attempting to eat a ragout which they were sure was too rich for his constitution. And all the time our old friend James Laurence was talking to me incessantly about the navy.

I cannot like Captain Laurence. He is too much inclined to pressgang the conversation and carry it away aboard ship. And once he has got it there, what can his listener do? One has nothing at all to say and can only exclaim upon the captain's bravery and hardihood – which becomes excessively dull after the first five minutes. But Lucy, I fancy, would have been exceedingly happy to do the exclaiming and was rather aggrieved that it fell to my lot rather than hers.

Well, so much for dinner. But I wish particularly to tell you about what happened afterwards. And the first thing is that Anne Harman-Foote and I had the drawing room to ourselves for a little while before tea. Harriet returned to Penelope straight after dinner and Lucy, I think, went with her. The men, I believe, were occupied in the billiard room, for I could hear the clatter of

*cue and balls all the time that we were talking. Anyway, Anne
(you see how our intimacy is increased! I have been authorised
to use the name) and I were left alone in the drawing room and
I took the opportunity of finding out as much as I might about
Miss Fenn.*

*My first business was to discover all that I could about her
family and connections – but there I more or less drew a blank.
Miss Fenn, it seems, was a woman of 'very respectable' family,
but poor; she was a neighbour of old Mrs Foote in Shropshire
and she came to Madderstone upon her recommendation.
Mrs Foote, by the by, seems to have been a great recommender
of maids, governesses and companions; she was generally
regarded as being very 'sensible and straightforward' in these
matters and it was quite the accepted practice to apply to her
when any such appointment was to be made.*

*I asked next about Miss Fenn's life at Madderstone. What
were her pursuits? Her friends? And – that all-important
question for every governess – how much did she 'mix in the
family'.*

*Well, if she had any friends in the neighbourhood, her
pupil knew nothing of them; and her pursuits seem to have
been only attending church and visiting the poor. And as to
mixing in the family – Anne was puzzled by the question.*

'Why, she was with us as much as she chose to be!'

'And when there was company?' I pressed. 'Dinners? Balls?'

*'She generally dined with us,' said Anne, 'but she did not
attend balls – except, of course, the All Hallows ball. That
she always attended.'*

*And I thought that point rather telling, Eliza. That she
should be present for Madderstone's famous All Hallows
dance when the greater tenants and the half-gentry of the*

place are invited but absent herself from the later, grander balls of the winter, speaks to me of a woman with a delicate sense of her own place. A woman with scruples, determined not to impose too far upon her employer's goodwill.

And, finally, I asked about the day of her disappearance.

It was, it seems, the sixth of June 1791 — a Monday, and a very warm day. There was a large party staying in the house: all the Laurence cousins were there and Mr Harman-Foote — plain Mr Foote as he was then — had arrived that morning with his mother. It had been too hot to take much exercise during the day but the evening was a little cooler and Miss Fenn left the abbey quite soon after dinner, saying that she had an appointment to keep.

I asked, of course, what this appointment was, and I wondered for a moment if Anne might know more of it than she was telling. But when I pressed her she only said she supposed it to be a charitable errand — that was the usual cause of Miss Fenn visiting the village.

And did her manner seem at all unusual? I asked. Was there anything to mark this day as different from any other?

Oh no, Anne assured me, nothing at all. Absolutely nothing at all. It had been a day just exactly like any other and she had expected Miss Fenn to return before tea — it had been agreed that they should all drink tea in the summer house.

Well, I rather fear that if there <u>was</u> anything unusual about the day it may now be irretrievable. Anne is either unable or unwilling to recall it.

So I turned my attention to the coins and the ring which were recovered from the lake. There is perhaps five or six pounds in money: the gold still remarkably fresh-looking — the silver coins very much tarnished and one or two of them positively misshapen with decay. As for the ring – it is rather a plain thing. Which, I am told, is entirely in keeping with the lady's taste. It seems she had quite a horror of finery. There is nothing to this ring but a narrow gold band and a simple setting holding a curl of fine hair. The curl is dark, almost black; but, upon reflection, I am not at all sure that that is its natural hue. I think it may have been darkened by lying so long in the water.

'Do you know,' I said, 'whose hair is in the ring?'

But she said she did not and, when I pressed to know whether she had ever asked about it, she smiled. 'I did once,' she said, 'and was rebuked for impertinence – I never asked again.'

I looked more closely and saw that, within the gold band, there is engraved a single word: 'Beloved'.

Dido laid down her pen and blew upon her chilled fingers to warm them. The rain was beating hard at her attic window, the wind moaning under the roof like a lost soul and the landing clock had long since struck midnight. She was determined to finish her letter before sleeping, but was unsure how to go on.

The ring had raised so many speculations in her mind, she was ashamed to reveal half of them to her sister. Had there been a secret lover? Had he played a part in the woman's death?

Of course Miss Fenn's character and reputation argued against it. And it was entirely possible that the ring was a remembrance of a father or mother, a brother or a sister; but if that were so, why had she not acknowledged it?

The fact was that, in this case, investigation seemed to breed suspicion. And the visit to Miss Fenn's bedchamber had aroused even more questions in Dido's mind…

Chapter Nine

There had been no time to visit Miss Fenn's chamber before tea, and when tea was over the card tables were placed immediately. So it was not until Mr Portinscale, Silas and Lucy had all gone home that Dido was able to go to the room with her hostess.

All was quiet within the house as they set off from the drawing room, candle in hand; but outside, the wind was rising, driving handfuls of rain hard against the windows with a sound like thrown gravel. Mr Harman-Foote had been for some time shut up in the library talking with Captain Laurence, but as the two women crossed to the stairs he came out of the library door, pipe in hand, looking rather displeased and breathing port wine and tobacco smoke. Dido could not quite escape the idea that he had been listening and waiting for their leaving the drawing room.

'Well, my dear,' he bellowed across the echoing hall, 'what are you troubling poor Miss Kent with now?'

His wife coloured a little but named their errand calmly enough.

'It is very late,' he said, drawing out his watch. 'Very late indeed. Do you not think I had better order the carriage and have it take our guest home. I am sure she is very tired.'

'We shall not be ten minutes,' said his wife.

He looked as if he might protest again, but Dido declared that she was not at all fatigued and he knew his manners well enough not to hold out against her. 'Well, well, have it your own way! Have it your own way! Ought to know better than to try to change a lady's mind! But I shall ring for Thomas immediately and have the carriage at the door in ten minutes.' There was another look at his watch. 'There's a storm coming on. You had better not delay any longer than that, Miss Kent.'

'He thinks,' said Mrs Harman-Foote as they climbed the stairs, 'that I would be less distressed if I left matters alone. He thinks I should forget all about my poor friend. He means well, I don't doubt, but he does not understand my feelings. So I shall tell him as little of our investigations as I can.'

At the top of the stairs they turned along a broad, carpeted passageway, into the east wing – where the best rooms were – and Mrs Harman-Foote threw open the door of a chamber close to the one which had been given over to Penelope. It was a fine, large room – a room such as a woman of consequence might be given on a visit – a room such as Dido had *never* been offered in any country house. There were mahogany wardrobes, a large mirror, tall sash windows, very pretty wallpaper and bed-hangings embroidered with fabulous Chinese birds.

The room had the musty smell of a place seldom entered; but there was also a faint scent from old lavender laid in the bed and closets… And there was something else too, very faint, another sweet scent which was familiar, but so very out of place that it was a moment or two before Dido could identify it – as tobacco smoke...

'It is a pretty room, is it not?' said Anne as she set her candle down upon the toilette table.

'Oh yes! Your father must have held Miss Fenn in high regard, to have placed her in such a room.'

'He held her in the highest regard possible. She was quite part of our family.'

They were both conscious of the ordered carriage and began to look about them as quickly as they might. Dido could not help but feel the strangeness of entering the domain of a woman so long dead, and the few plain possessions – the wooden-backed hairbrush on the toilette table, the simple writing desk upon a window seat and the black bible and prayer book lying on a table beside the bed – all had the air of things but just laid aside, whose owner might return at any moment.

She walked about touching things here and there, keenly aware of the character which seemed still to inhabit the room – austere in the midst of luxury. Above the bed there was a text worked in faded cottons. *Thou God seest me...*

'They are gone!' cried Anne suddenly.

Dido turned to see her standing beside the open writing desk, staring in disbelief.

'They are all gone!' she repeated.

'I beg your pardon?' Dido went to stand beside her and looked into the opened desk which held only two uncut pens and some blank sheets of paper turning brown at the edges. 'What are gone?'

'The letters. There were letters here, letters which she had received. They were here in the writing desk.' She sat down upon the bed among the Chinese birds, staring at the desk in disbelief.

'Are you quite sure they were in the desk? They were not somewhere else? In a drawer, perhaps?'

'No! I know they were in the desk. They have always been there.'

'Have they?' Dido felt her interest quicken. She looked more closely at her friend's face, pale with confusion and shock. 'Anne, who were these letters from? What was written in them?'

Mrs Harman-Foote raised her eyes in a look of amazement. 'I had not *read* them,' she replied.

At first, Dido – judging from her own unmanageable curiosity – was scarcely able to believe this. Letters left for fifteen years unread! How remarkable!

But then, allowing for a difference in character – and the profound influence of the governess upon her pupil – it began to seem less strange. Looking about the room, which seemed still to bear the imprint of its mistress, she could, after all, comprehend that the respect in which Miss Fenn's memory was held, might make Anne reluctant to come in here and violate all the rules of honour by reading what was not addressed to her.

'When did you last see the letters?' she asked.

'Today. Just before dinner. After dressing, I came in here for a moment or two. And I looked into the desk, so I know the letters were there. I was wondering, you see, whether it might be right to look at them now. Whether the higher good might not be served. I meant to ask your opinion whether reading the letters might help us discover the truth about her death.'

'I see. So it would seem someone has taken them from the desk since then.'

'And someone must return them,' said Anne, regaining her usual assurance. 'I cannot permit such a theft! But, Dido, I do not quite understand. Why would someone take them?'

'I think we must assume that it was in order to prevent them being read.' Dido smiled. 'Anyone who knows *me* could guess that I would hesitate less over looking into them than you...' She was forced to stop a while to consider all the implications of the letters' disappearance. 'Of course,' she said very slowly, 'anyone who was at the dinner table would have heard that you intended to bring me here. Any one of those present *could* have come to this room after dinner and removed the letters... And there is another point...' She stopped.

'Yes, what is it?'

'Nothing... No, it is nothing of consequence.' She had decided it would be better not to mention that little hint of tobacco smoke which she had discerned upon entering the room.

Chapter Ten

The strange disappearance of the letters haunted Dido's dreams and occupied the many waking moments of the night. But she came to the breakfast table next morning with no clearer notion of what was carrying on – only a certainty that the nature of her mystery was changed entirely. For it would seem she faced not only the death of a woman fifteen years ago, but also a more immediate puzzle – the motives of someone who was acting *now*.

Who had cared enough about those letters to risk drawing attention to themselves by removing them? Was there something written in them which would cast light upon the circumstances of Miss Fenn's death? Might they point to the guilt of someone still living at Madderstone?

There was a great deal more to investigate than she had previously supposed. Somehow she *must* circumvent Margaret's demands upon her time and get herself to the abbey again as soon as she might. She had, as yet, not even looked at the place in which Miss Fenn's remains had been discovered. And there were a great many questions which might be put to the abbey servants…

'I declare, Dido, you are very quiet and sullen this morning. Does dining at the great house not agree with you?' Margaret leant across the sunny table with the teapot in her hand. She looked irritably from her sister-in-law to the back of the newspaper which was engrossing her husband, in the expectation that one or other of her companions should supply her with a little conversation – and seemed to decide that Dido was the more promising subject of the two. 'Well,' she said, as she poured the tea, 'you have not told me one word about who was in the party yesterday, or what you had to eat.'

Dido sighed and was on the point of giving as good an account of the evening as she could, when her brother saved her the exertion by making a sudden announcement from behind his newspaper.

'I have had a letter from my friend Lomax,' he said. 'He is coming here again on Friday.'

Dido laid down her knife and stared across the bread and butter and the tea-things of the breakfast table, to the window sill where a tray of windfall plums had been laid to ripen in the sun; she noticed the deepening marks of bruises upon one, the small wasp holes in another… But, though she would not look at her, she knew that Margaret's lips were thinning as she set down the teapot and swept a few invisible crumbs from the tablecloth.

'And how long,' said Margaret in her most gentle tones, 'how long do you think Mr Lomax will remain with us, my love?'

Alerted by the extreme softness of her voice, Francis lowered his paper an inch or two; a bushy grey eyebrow and a very wary eye appeared. 'About a week, perhaps?' he hazarded, his voice rising into a question.

Margaret closed her eyes and sighed.

Francis retreated behind his newspaper. 'He is on his way to somewhere else – perhaps he will only stay five days – or four. I daresay it will not be so very long.'

Margaret looked once more as if she were bound for the pagan arena, but, as wives all over the country discover every day, it is peculiarly difficult to argue with the back of a newspaper. And Dido was soon wishing that she could employ such a protection herself.

For the expectation of a visitor threw Margaret into a frenzy of activity. She was determined that curtains must be washed and beds aired – though the motive seemed to be rather less the comfort of her guest than the discomfort of her husband. And through it all she had a great deal to say about the inconvenience and expense of visitors and also her surprise that Francis should take such extraordinary pleasure in the company of a man who was, after all, not much more than the steward of his daughter's husband.

It was a very great relief to escape at last for another walk to Madderstone.

By then it was so late that Margaret very much doubted there would be time to reach the abbey and return before dark, and she thought that if Dido was wanting air and exercise she had much better walk out into the kitchen garden and watch over Robert digging the potatoes, for the fellow was so lazy he had left half of them in the ground last time.

But Dido held out. She would walk fast, and not stay long, and the necessary business of 'finding out how Penelope goes on' provided a very convenient excuse for the visit.

By the time she left the vicarage, the sunshine of the early morning was all over, the clouds were gathering and there was a threat of rain in the breeze. But still she was determined to go. Madderstone and its mysteries intrigued her more and more, and besides, the two miles between Badleigh and the abbey provided a little peace, a break between one society and another in which she might indulge her own thoughts.

And she found that today, as she walked, even thoughts of ghosts and governesses must give a little ground to thoughts of Mr William Lomax...

His proposed visit must discompose, though it did not surprise, her. Unlike Margaret, she found it very easy to understand why her bookish brother should value the friendship of another clever, well-informed man. She had not forgotten to anticipate, when her living at the vicarage was first proposed, that the move must throw her more into Mr Lomax's way.

But did she wish to meet him again, or not? It was a difficult point which two whole miles of brisk walking could not quite decide.

It was now nearly four months since Mr Lomax had made her an offer of marriage – and been refused. There had been, at that time, such a serious difference of opinion between them as had convinced her they could not be happy together – despite her considerable affection for him. He had objected to that part of her which was particularly dear to her – her curiosity. They had argued; but still he had made his offer. He had even been so foolhardy as to pin his hopes for their future happiness upon a change in her character. She might, he had suggested, be so influenced by the advice of a husband as to adopt his opinions rather than arguing against them.

It was, she thought, a strong proof of his regard that such a sensible man should wilfully blind himself to the evidence around him: evidence which must cry out against finding happiness in marriage through so momentous a change. Was there a couple in the world who had ever succeeded in it? And even if it were possible, she doubted she would find it desirable. Her own opinions were very precious to her: she did not wish to give them up.

All in all, she had felt it incumbent upon her to save them both from his dangerous optimism. She had spoken her 'No' as firmly as she knew how. And if the matter had only rested there, there would be sufficient embarrassment in this recontre. But there was more.

She had given her answer and walked away – and he had followed her. He had, in point of fact, *run* after her and called upon her to stop.

This last memory brought a little flutter of pleasure. At nineteen she would have been affected by this evidence of passion; at six and thirty she was quite delighted to find that she had such power over a man.

She remembered him, there in the lime walk at Richmond, bareheaded in the sunlight that twinkled through the leaves, earnestly pleading his cause. For she had, of course, done as he requested and stopped – just before reaching the end of the avenue.

'Miss Kent,' he said breathlessly, 'forgive me… I know that I am not acting the part of a gentleman… to force myself upon you in this way when your answer is already given. Please, do not think I would be such a brute as to distress you by asking you to reconsider your decision now… But I cannot help… I must just beg one favour.'

'I am sure…' she began, but her voice was unsteady and she paused. Exertion was absolutely necessary. If this was to be their last interview, she would not wish him to remember her stammering. 'I am sure I would do anything in my power to prove my friendship.'

'Then may I be allowed to ask you again… Not now, but in the future…' He too was forced to break off. 'As you know – as I have explained,' he began again more calmly, 'the burden of debt which my son has laid upon me makes an immediate marriage impossible. In two, three years at the most, I shall be free. Do I have your permission to ask then – if, of course, you are still unmarried – to ask you again to be my wife?'

Dido remembered staring down at the trodden earth of the lime walk; she remembered very clearly how the interlacing roots of the trees had stood out like veins on the back of an aging hand. Her mind had been in turmoil, flattered, confused…and yet, suspecting him. 'I do not think such an arrangement would be wise,' she said quietly. 'I would not wish you to feel bound to make an offer which – three years hence – you may no longer wish to make.'

He shook his head very seriously. 'My dear Miss Kent, I *am* bound to you. It cannot be helped, though it is very kind of you to attempt to grant a liberty I do not even desire.'

She bent her head lower so that he could not see her

smile. 'I cannot suppose,' she insisted, 'that time will change my reply.'

'But we cannot any of us predict the future,' he argued eagerly. 'Three years…two, even one year may encompass any amount of change. I beg you: allow me to hope.'

The indecision had been dreadful: her heart had been all for giving way and consenting immediately, while her head… Her head had been calmly noting the inconstancy of his argument. The passage of time was to produce no change in him – *his* feelings were not to alter, and yet it was to be supposed that *hers* might undergo a very material change. He was no doubt thinking that she would soon regret her answer – and decide that she must give up her opinions, cease to argue with him, and become all that he required in a wife… In fact, his request was intolerable presumption…

But he was regarding her with such tenderness, and he had never looked so well as he did now, his usual dignity all put aside, his brow furrowed, his eyes so anxious.

Her heart had won the day. She had granted the favour. When the gaming debts of his dissolute son were at last paid – when he had a home to offer a wife – Mr Lomax was authorised to apply to her again.

Of course, she remained determined against accepting. She instinctively shrank from that image which her lively imagination readily supplied – of esteem and affection all sunk into marital discord and resentment…

However, there was another image of the future which had lately begun to haunt her: an image of a lonely old maid shivering perpetually in Margaret's attic – and that was sufficient to touch even Dido's cheerful mind with despair.

Chapter Eleven

…Well, Eliza, I have very wisely determined to give myself no more pain by worrying over this visit of Mr Lomax. The resolution is, I think, a great proof of my strength of character. Though the keeping of it may prove my weakness…

But I shall write no more upon the subject — except to remind you of your promised secrecy — which you must be particularly careful to preserve if you should happen to see our cousin, Flora, while you are in town looking after Charles. I would not for the world have any of my acquaintance know of Mr Lomax's offer, for I do not think there is one among them — excepting, of course, your dear self — who could resist advising me upon the subject. And that would be insufferable.

I certainly have more than enough carrying on here to distract me. And I hope, instead of pining, to prove myself worthy of my resolution by being useful to poor Mrs Harman-Foote. For the more I look about me, Eliza, the more certain I become that a <u>very great injustice</u> has been done: that Miss Fenn is innocent of the dreadful calumny which is charged against her and has been cast out into that terrible grave for no reason.

I must tell you about the drained pool.

I went to look at it yesterday, you see, and it provided a

great deal more interest than one could reasonably expect
from a muddy depression in the ground.

It was a bleak enough sight! Indeed there seemed to be
a kind of gloom hanging over _everything_ yesterday. Though
it pains me to admit it, Margaret was right in supposing it
would be rather dark before I reached the abbey. The sun
was low in the sky. It was cold and still and damp, with the
smoke from the house chimneys hanging low and sullen, and
the grounds deserted, except for two men up on the lawns
lopping branches from the fallen trees.

There was a sad, winter smell about the place: smoke
and freshly cut wood, mud and bruised grass. When I first
descended the steps in the bank and looked down into the
pool it seemed unpromising. But there is this to be said for the
business of mystery-solving: it can enhance the dullest scene
with the thrill of discovery. For here was only an expanse of
gently sloping mud, with a sort of large puddle collecting at
its centre and its edges dry and cracking, except for the great
wet hole – a yard or two from the bank and all trodden
round with boot prints – which showed where the remains
had been dug out.

And yet, there were two great points of interest. Can you
discern them from my description? I charge you not to read
on until you have tried to find them out...

Well, did you notice, first of all, that I said there was
water collecting in the centre of the pool?

As yet it is no more than an inch or two deep, but it
alerted me and, when I looked to the end of the lake, I saw
that the dam is repaired. The pool is being refilled! Soon the
place in which Miss Fenn lay will be lost once more beneath
the water – and all its secrets sunk with it!

Do you not think that this has a very suspicious appearance? Why has the plan to redirect the stream been changed? Does it not seem as though <u>someone</u> is anxious to have the place, and any information it can offer up, concealed? Who, I wonder, has decided it should be done? Was Mr Harman-Foote giving orders to effect it when I passed him and Mr Coulson on my way to dinner yesterday?

All this, Eliza, is puzzling enough, but… I wonder whether you have yet noticed the other strange detail in my description: the fact that the place where the bones were discovered is no more than a yard or two from the bank?

Now, I am sure that this is of the very greatest significance.

For, as Mr Wishart observed, the sides of the pool slope very gradually indeed. And, though I am inclined to agree with him that this renders an accidental falling-in unlikely, I cannot agree that, in this case, a suicide is more probable.

I shall tell you what I did. I took up a stick from the bank: as long and straight a one as I could find. And, putting one end of it against the place where mud ends and grass begins – the place which marks the margin of the old pool and the level of its water – I held it out towards the hole. By this means I was able roughly to calculate the depth of water in which Miss Fenn lay.

It was, I am sure, no more than three feet!

And so you see, even allowing for her sinking six inches or so into the mud of the lake-bottom, she <u>cannot</u> have been beyond her depth in that place. The water would not have reached to her shoulders – unless she was <u>remarkably</u> small of stature. And I have certainly never heard her described so.

I confess that this observation threw me into a very melancholy train of thought.

I stood upon that muddy bank in the gathering gloom, with no company but the ringing of axes echoing back from the house-front, and I imagined coming there in a state of utter despair and loneliness. I imagined walking down into the green, weedy water with the intention of extinguishing life, of ending for ever worry and pain. I declare that I could almost feel the chill of the water rising against my shrinking flesh, the soft silt sucking at my feet as I surrendered up misery, loneliness and humiliation...

You are perhaps wondering, Eliza, why I should distress myself — and you — with such terrible thoughts. But there is a purpose. You see, it is all but impossible to imagine <u>lying down</u> to die in the water. I am sure, that if one had made up one's mind to self-destruction, and had the determination to carry out the intention, the only way to accomplish it would be to walk on until the water became so deep it was impossible to save oneself. In short, I believe that, while the continuation of life remained possible, the body would insensibly struggle for it, even though the heart and brain were determined upon destruction.

A woman bent upon suicide would have no choice but to walk out into the deep water at the very centre of the lake — and that is where her remains would be found.

Well, this conclusion was as grim as the thoughts which had brought me to it, and you may imagine how I began to shiver in the gathering dusk. For it would seem that I am being forced to agree with Anne Harman-Foote's opinion and declare, with her, that it is impossible for Elinor Fenn to have taken her own life. And little by little, I am being brought to contemplate the alternative: murder...

Chapter Twelve

Dido woke from an odd dream of despair, loneliness and cold, encroaching water, to find that she had fallen asleep remarkably awkwardly. Her writing desk was still upon the bed and the covers were slipping away from her, leaving her feet exposed and thoroughly chilled.

It was still rather early. The light falling through the little window was thin and grey, and there was no movement from the house below, only the slow heavy sound of Rebecca descending the attic stairs to begin her duties.

She pulled up the covers and attempted to rub some warmth into her frozen feet, but the gloom and wretchedness of the night seemed still to hang about her. Nor was there much comfort to be found in anticipation of a day carrying out Margaret's orders as the vicarage was prepared for its visitor.

In fact, there was but one way to dispel desponding thoughts: she drew the little writing desk back onto her knees, turned herself about to gain as much light as she might from the window, and resumed her letter:

...I mean to be rather selfish this morning, Eliza. I shall keep to my room until Margaret has gone out upon her early morning errands and then I shall attempt an escape

to Madderstone. It is not a course of which I think you will approve, but I am quite determined to pass as much of the morning at the abbey as I am able – for once Mr Lomax is here it may become rather more difficult to pursue the matter of Miss Fenn's death.

And, while I wait for Margaret to leave the house, I shall attempt to divert your thoughts – and my own – by giving an account of an amusing and very surprising little encounter which followed my discoveries at the pool yesterday.

I was just turning away when I saw that I was not alone. Silas Crockford was walking along the opposite bank, with a very distracted look upon his face and a pencil and a tablet in his hand.

Poor Silas… It is odd, is it not, how often the epithet accompanies his name? But I cannot help it, it is nearly always 'poor Silas' with me. Perhaps it is his sickly air; or his sisters' constant chiding; or his great brown eyes and little pointed chin which always put me in mind of a child. I do not know why it should be, but there is something which never fails to arouse a pitying fondness whenever I see him. And yesterday he appeared more than usually pathetic, for, can you guess what he was about, Eliza?

He was attempting to write a poem.

It is true: little Silas Crockford has turned poet! He told me all about the poem he is writing: it is the tragic story of the Grey Nun's doomed love and is to be composed 'in the style of an old-fashioned m…minstrel'. Of course, he begged that I would not mention the matter to Lucy or Harriet. For he was sure there would be 'a g…great carry-on' about it if they knew.

I agreed immediately upon secrecy, but I doubt my complicity will result in a work of towering literary merit, for the poor boy did not seem to be going on very well. He showed me his page and was very eager to know whether I could suggest a rhyme for 'drooped' or 'b...bonnet'. 'W... what do you think, Miss Kent? I should be very g...glad to know your opinion.'

Altogether this did not seem to be a proper way of going about the business of poetry to me. At least, I do not think that Mr Pope ever asked advice, nor can I suppose that dear Mr Crabbe is forever troubling his friends for rhymes. Though, of course, I may be wrong. I know very little about poetic genius... Except that I believe I know what has turned young Silas into a poet.

He is in love, Eliza!

I began to suspect it as soon as he mentioned poetry, for the two generally go together, do they not? But I became sure of it soon after, when he asked in a <u>very anxious</u> voice if I could assure him that Miss Lambe was quite out of danger.

I said that I believed she was, but his anxiety did not seem to be entirely done away. He shuffled his feet about like an embarrassed schoolboy, evidently wishing to ask more, though it was some minutes before he could manage to stammer out, with flaming cheeks, 'I s...suppose that she is a great deal in c...company with C...C...Captain Laurence?'

Poor Silas! Oh dear, I have said it again. But the pain in his eyes cut me to the heart. 'Oh no,' I said quickly, 'I am sure she is not in company with the captain at all. She is still too unwell to leave her bedchamber. So, of course, he cannot visit her.'

'I am very g...glad of it,' he stammered. 'That is, I am glad she does not see the c...captain, I am not g...glad she is unwell...'

He stopped and we both stood quietly for a moment or two, looking down at the muddy waste, and the dark pool of water in which were reflected flying storm clouds and the last light of the day.

I was thinking he had little chance of succeeding with Penelope if he were indeed opposed to such a man as the captain – and I believe his thoughts had taken a similar turn. For he soon shook his head regretfully and said – very fast, in the way he does when he wishes to express his thoughts before the stammer can intervene – 'I had hoped, that while Pen... Miss Lambe was with us at Ashfield, we – that is, she and I – would be able to improve our f...friendship. I hoped that before she returned to Bath I should be able to d...d...dec...to tell her how I feel. But then there was this c...confounded accident, Miss Kent, and now she is sh... shut away from me... And C...C...C... And Laurence is there on the spot with her all the time...' His poor face burnt as red as the sunset reflected in the water.

I expressed my concern at this unfortunate situation – and he became confiding.

'Henry,' he said eagerly, ' – that is, Mr Coulson, you know – he says that I should declare my passion, that I should write such an ardent letter, Miss Lambe could not resist. That I should tell her I will d...die if she is not k...kind to me. Henry says that that sort of thing never fails with women.'

I ventured to suggest that Mr Coulson's information might be a little inaccurate.

'So you think I had better not?' he said

Oh dear, Eliza, he looked so wretched! I could not help myself: I turned matchmaker on the spot!

'But,' I said firmly, 'it may be possible for you to convey

your sentiments – to raise yourself in Miss Lambe's esteem – without an outright declaration.'

He looked doubtful. 'The devil of it is, Miss Kent, if I don't d…declare myself, then I cannot write to her at all. For that would be most improper – c…corresponding, you know, when there is no engagement. Harriet w…w…w…'

'Harriet would be very angry indeed. Yes, I quite see your point.'

We both considered a while. It was becoming more gloomy than ever. The sound of the workmen's axes had ceased, and, overhead, rooks were calling harshly as they flocked to roost in the park. I was wondering how such a dear, gentle boy as Silas might gain the advantage of a worldly fellow like Captain Laurence with his coarse good looks and his interminable stories of high-seas gallantry, and I confess that, for a while, I was utterly perplexed.

But then I considered the character of the lady… And I saw a possibility.

I suggested to Silas that his poem might make a great appeal to Penelope's romantic disposition…and that the character of a poet might make an even greater appeal.

He looked more than a little frightened, but he is not lacking in understanding and he caught my meaning well enough. And so, before we left the side of the pool, we had agreed upon our plan. When he has written some part of his great ballad – I was careful not to condition for the completion of the whole, which I rather fear may never be accomplished – when some part of it is completed, he is to show the work to me; and I am to convey it to Penelope.

Do you not think it a rather good plan, Eliza? I am extremely proud of it.

I grant that there would seem to be some danger in the probable badness of the verse; but I am trusting that Penelope's taste in such matters is not too nice.

It will not be easy, for Harriet has always opposed any attachment of her brother's – love no doubt being considered as dangerous to his constitution as ragouts and port wine. But I confess that I am very glad to have another scheme on hand to divert me a little from gloomy thoughts. And I would dearly love to rout Captain Laurence. Somehow, I just cannot like the man. Nor can I escape the feeling that I have detected in him some kind of duplicity or deception. And yet I cannot quite remember what it is that has made me suspect him.

For some reason my mind keeps returning to that moment upon the gallery when we saw the men discovering the bones. It seems ridiculous to suggest it, Eliza, but I feel as if in that moment he revealed something about himself: something very suspicious.

Chapter Thirteen

Dido emerged cautiously from the vicarage sweep and looked about her.

It was a dull, raw morning; shreds of mist lay about the gravestones in the churchyard, and all the spiders' webs on the vicarage railings were thickly beaded with moisture. There had been rain in the night and the ruts of the village street were full of puddles. Beyond the black and white front of the inn, the usual little knots of women were gathered upon the steps of the baker's and the milliner's shops; but, though Dido looked very carefully, she could not distinguish Margaret among them.

Very much relieved, she set off along the street at a brisk pace, her thoughts all fixed upon a stile beyond the village forge which led, through a little copse, to the Madderstone footpath. Once over this stile she would be beyond Margaret's sight – and free to spend the morning as she pleased.

She passed the Red Lion in safety, and the baker's, with its warm yeasty scent. She was passing under the chestnut trees on the village green and was just daring to hope… when a voice called out her name.

She gave a guilty start. However, it was not Margaret, but Lucy Crockford who was hurrying over the yellow carpet of fallen leaves.

'My dear friend!' she cried, 'I am so very glad to have met with you! For I must speak to you on a matter of the utmost importance…and…delicacy.' Her face coloured coyly – until it matched almost exactly the pink satin lining of her bonnet.

'Indeed?' said Dido looking anxiously about her. 'But I am afraid I am in rather a hurry just now.'

'Then I shall walk with you.' Lucy linked arms and leant close to talk as they walked on. 'You are on your way to Madderstone to visit the poor invalid I suppose?'

'Yes.'

'Oh! It makes me quite *wretched* to think of dear, dear Penelope lying sick,' said Lucy in her slowest most languishing voice. 'No one feels these things as I do! I declare, I had rather be sick myself than see someone I care about suffer! You will laugh at me for it, I am sure, but it is quite true.'

Dido showed no inclination either to laugh or to reply, but only to walk on as fast as Lucy's dragging arm would allow.

'I wish,' continued Lucy, 'that I might come with you to Madderstone and sit a while with poor Penelope! But I dare not attempt it!'

'I see no need for caution. I do not believe there is any infection in a broken head.'

'Oh, but it is so dangerous to my nerves. I feel things so *very* deeply. Captain Laurence…' there was a conscious glance as she spoke the name, 'says that it is extremely uncommon for a woman to be so exceedingly sensitive, so very *alive* to the feelings of everyone around her. He thinks it something quite remarkable. But I am sure that, if I am remarkable, I had much rather *not* be. As I tell the captain, it is a dreadful trial to me. Harriet of course is different. She is much better suited to a sickroom.'

'I do not doubt she is.'

Lucy pressed Dido's arm and sunk her voice almost to a whisper. 'In point of fact, it is Harriet I wish to talk to you about.'

'Oh?'

The pressure of Lucy's fingers increased. 'Dido,' she whispered urgently, 'you *must* speak to Harriet on my behalf!'

'Must I? On what subject must I speak?'

Lucy cast her eyes down modestly. 'Captain Laurence,' she whispered.

'Oh!'

'You must tell her,' Lucy said eagerly, 'that she should not attempt to separate...' She stopped speaking, looked conscious, tossed her head. 'She seems determined to part us. And I declare it will break my heart...' She stopped again, and gave Dido's arm another squeeze. 'I am sure you understand.'

But Dido was quite determined not to understand so easily. 'Has the captain made you an offer?' she asked.

'Well...'

'Has he?' Dido was so eager to know – for Silas's sake – whether Captain Laurence was, indeed, an engaged man that she momentarily forgot the risk of capture to herself. She drew Lucy to a halt outside the open front of the village forge – where the light of the blacksmith's fire shone out into the dull morning, and the smells of hot iron and coal mixed with the damp air. 'Is there an understanding between you and the captain?' she asked firmly.

Lucy bent her head. 'Nothing has quite been said,' she admitted. 'There has been no outright proposal. For you know it would not be proper to announce an engagement whilst my poor friend is lying sick. I could not *bear* to do anything so indelicate myself, and the dear captain is so very considerate…'

'Is he?' said Dido suddenly, half to herself. The description did not quite chime with her own opinion of the man – and yet, for some reason, it had raised again the troubling memory of that moment when she and Laurence had stood together on the gallery… Why?

But meanwhile Lucy, who had not heard the question, was running on eagerly with her own narrative.

'Of course he cannot speak until Pen is quite out of danger. But…' She stopped with such a look of happy consciousness as cried aloud to be prompted.

Dido put aside her doubts about the captain's character. 'But?' she prompted obligingly.

There was a little lifting of the eyes. A sigh of great sensibility. 'But… I believe I do not say too much if I confess that there is an *attachment* between us.'

'I see.' Dido was rather surprised by this news; she had been almost certain that – if Captain Laurence settled on either of the two friends – it would be the lovely Penelope. She looked doubtingly at Lucy's unremarkable little face: the ruddy light of the blacksmith's fire deepened the rather excessive colour on her freckled cheeks and laid a faint red gleam across the lank curls clustering under the pink bonnet. Could a man such as Laurence be charmed by the person or the mind of Lucy Crockford?

Of course, there was money to be considered. But the Ashfield estate, she knew, was entailed upon the male line. It was not a subject ever entered upon by Lucy or Harriet, but it was generally known in the village that there was somewhere a distant relation who could 'turn them out of the house if anything should happen to their brother'. It was also universally supposed that Lucy and Harriet's marriage portions were small – a thousand – two was the most that even generous gossip allotted to them.

Two thousand pounds was certainly no great inducement to an ambitious man. And Dido would take an oath that Laurence was ambitious. It was possible that Lucy was deceived – either by her own wishes, or by the gentleman himself…

Meanwhile Lucy was chattering on. 'Two days ago, on the evening we all dined at the abbey, Captain Laurence and I were in the conservatory *alone* all the time between dinner and tea. And he was *very* attentive.'

She smirked and raised her brows in a way which invited her companion to beg for confidences – but Dido was in no mood to oblige her. 'And you are certain,' she said briskly, 'that Harriet would oppose an engagement?'

'Oh yes.'

'But why? Why should Harriet wish to prevent your happiness?'

Lucy primmed up her lips. 'It is not in my nature to be suspicious,' she said, 'nor to speak ill of a sister.'

Dido stared a moment, then understanding dawned. 'You suspect her of…admiring the captain herself?'

Lucy tossed her head. 'Why do you suppose she has

insisted upon staying at Madderstone with Penelope?' she cried in a sharp, quick accent.

'Why, she is nursing her!'

'But why cannot she leave the house? The business of nursing could be safely left in the hands of Nanny and the Madderstone housekeeper. But there is no shifting her from the place! She is *determined* to remain where he is.'

'I cannot believe...' began Dido, but just at that moment, Margaret's unmistakable green and yellow bonnet emerged from the butcher's shop. Forgetting everything but her own need for liberty, Dido began to hurry towards the stile, pulling Lucy with her.

'Please, please say that you will speak to Harriet for me.'

'I do not know,' Dido said distractedly... The stile was just a few paces away now. They had reached it. She was climbing the step; but her companion was dragging upon her arm, preventing her from crossing over. 'Very well! Yes, I shall speak to her.' She broke away: climbed the stile.

'Oh thank you! Thank you!' Lucy clapped her hands together like a child. 'You will be sure to do it without delay, will you not?'

'Very well,' said Dido resignedly. 'I shall speak to her this morning.'

The trees of the copse at last cut Dido off from the sight of the village street. She stopped among the dripping branches, drew a long, grateful breath of damp leaf-mould and considered this new responsibility which had been laid upon her.

She found she was rather angry at what had just passed. She had more than enough to occupy her at present and she certainly had no wish to be deeply involved in Lucy Crockford's affairs. She was determined to fulfil her promise of 'speaking to Harriet' as briefly as possible.

She gave no credit at all to Lucy's notion of Harriet being in love with Captain Laurence – she had seen no symptoms of it... Although there was no denying that Harriet had seemed determined to fix herself at the abbey, and she did appear to be opposed to a match between her sister and the captain. Dido had observed as much herself.

Now, why should she oppose such a match? Was it possible that she knew something about Captain James Laurence which made her fear for her sister's happiness?

That was a very interesting thought indeed!

As she began to hurry along the path away from the village, Dido gladly abandoned all thoughts of love affairs for the rather more interesting subject of the Captain's character. Why did she distrust him so very much herself?

And why, when Lucy spoke of Captain Laurence as considerate, had she suddenly remembered again that moment when she had been with him upon the gallery? – the moment of the bones' discovery. Why should that moment have come into her mind?

She stopped walking and pressed her hand to her head in a great effort of memory. The trees dripped disconsolately around her. A pigeon broke cover suddenly and whirred up into the sky.

She tried to recall every detail of that moment on

the ruined gallery. The dying light, the damp, gloomy stillness of the abbey, the captain's fingers laid gently on her own hand, his very considerate words: 'Miss Kent, I think you had better wait here. I shall go to see what it is and return to tell you…'

'Oh!' The answer came upon her so suddenly and forcefully she could not help crying out. How stupid she had been! Of course, it was not his consideration which must be suspected, but its *cause*.

On noticing that something was discovered in the water, Captain Laurence had immediately advised Dido to remain where she was, while he went on alone to investigate. But why? How had he known – how could he have known – that the discovery was unsuitable for a lady's eyes?

'He knew!' she cried wonderingly to the dripping trees. 'James Laurence knew that there was a body to be discovered in the pool.'

Chapter Fourteen

How, thought Dido as she walked briskly towards Madderstone, could the captain have known about the body before it was discovered?

She ran eagerly through everything she knew about the man. He had certainly been at Madderstone on the day Miss Fenn disappeared. Anne had spoken of 'all the Laurence cousins' being in the house. But he cannot have been more than... (A little bit of rapid calculation and counting of fingers.) No, he cannot have been more than sixteen or seventeen years old at the time. One did not like to suspect anything of a boy of just sixteen or seventeen... And yet, he was a big man; even at sixteen he would have been strong enough...

It would certainly be very interesting to know whether James Laurence had been on familiar terms with the governess: whether he might have had any cause to harm her.

She stopped as she came at last within sight of the abbey, wondering how best to pursue this subject. The mistress of the house had already told all that she could – or would – tell, and the master did not wish the matter to be discussed. But there were certainly those among the servants who remembered Miss Fenn. And, in Dido's experience, the testimony of an intelligent servant was always worth attending to.

She turned aside from the main sweep, passed the hothouses and the wall of the kitchen garden, and came into the poultry yard. Here she paused and looked about for anyone she might talk to.

It was a well-kept yard, enclosed by a wall so ancient it might be a relic of the abbey's domain, and furnished with a dozen or so low wooden poultry houses. The hens strutted and fussed in the dusty earth and strings of black and yellow chicks hurried, cheeping, behind them. In one corner there was a rough bench and sitting on that bench, plucking a chicken, was…Harris Paynter.

She stared; but there was no mistake. It most certainly was the young surgeon sitting there with a sack spread about him to protect his clothes, his hands full of brown feathers which he was diligently stuffing into a bag, the limp body of the bird hanging across his knees. His hat was tilted onto the very back of his head and stray pieces of white down were clinging to his black hair.

How very odd!

'To be quite candid with you,' she said, glancing at the half-naked hen as she approached, 'I rather think that this patient is beyond hope of recovery.'

'Oh no!' cried Mr Paynter who was constitutionally deaf to humour. 'I am only collecting a few feathers, Miss Kent.'

He said it as if it were the most natural thing in the world for a gentleman to do, but Dido could not help but ask why he should find himself so urgently in need of feathers that he must gather them for himself.

'They are required for a little…enquiry which I am carrying out at present.'

'Oh?'

'Yes a…*medical* enquiry.' He laid aside the bird and the sack and dusted a few stray feathers from his person.

'Indeed?' said Dido, 'I did not know that feathers were a cure for any illness.'

'Oh no,' he said very seriously and raised his finger as his habit was when he wished to make a precise point. 'In point of fact, I suspect they are a *cause* rather than a *cure*.' He picked up his bag.

'What? Poisoned by feathers? This is a new thing.'

'On the contrary, Miss Kent,' he said with a bow, and not even the hint of a smile. 'The case I have in mind is an old one. Some fifteen years old.' And with that he hurried off. She almost called him back; but he seemed very anxious to be gone and, besides, she did not know exactly what she could say – what she would ask – if she did succeed in delaying him…

'Well! He's a strange one, isn't he?' said a voice close beside her. She turned to see Mrs Philips, the housekeeper, picking up the half-plucked chicken from the bench and frowning in puzzlement beneath her well-starched cap.

'Oh, yes, it does seem rather…unusual behaviour, does it not?'

The housekeeper shook her head. 'Came here saying could he have some feathers. Said it was for his "enquiries". "Well," said I, "you're welcome to all the feathers you care to take out of this bird" – and off he goes to pluck it! Ah, but he's always been a strange one, Miss Kent; has been ever since his uncle took him in when he was just five years old.'

'Indeed? Has he?'

'And, in my opinion, he takes the strangeness from old Arthur Paynter. For he was a great one for "natural philosophy" and "experiments" and young Harris admired him very much.'

'And now the nephew has taken to "experiments"?'

Mrs Philips nodded. 'Last month,' she said, 'it was eggs gone bad he wanted for his enquiries. Comes here solemn as a judge – "Have you got any eggs gone bad, Mrs Philips?" "Well," said I, "I might, but I don't see why you'd want them." And he says it's a "medical enquiry" for finding out why they make folk sick.' She folded her arms and stood with the bird dangling over her crisp white apron. 'Don't know what the sense is in that for I'm sure we all know a bad egg will give us a powerful bellyache. Seems to me a surgeon'd do better reckoning out how to cure folk, not how to make them sick.'

'Oh, yes, yes indeed.'

'Ah well, as I often say, there's no accounting… And so, Miss Kent, what brings you here? Was there anything you wanted?'

'Oh no…no. I just came to look about me and see how your chickens go on… I see the new clutches are all hatched. And you seem to have done remarkably well! I do believe you have hardly lost one!'

'Well!' Mrs Philips cheeks glowed with pride. 'It's very kind of you to say so, miss. And, though I don't like to boast, these new pullets are coming on very nicely…'

Mrs Philips was an old acquaintance of Dido's and she fell comfortably now into a conversation which, beginning upon the merits of her pullets, moved very naturally to the depredations of foxes, and thence to the even worse depredations of poachers on the estate, to the deplorable state of all the estate's walls, to their long-awaited repair, to repairs and improvements in general, and so, at last, to the draining of the lake – and the relics which it had revealed.

'And that,' remarked Dido, watching her companion closely, 'is an extraordinary business, is it not?'

'Dear, dear, yes, a very odd business indeed,' said Mrs Philips. 'There's no accounting, is there? Poor Miss Fenn lying up there in the water all this time and no one knowing anything about it! That fair makes me shudder.'

Dido nodded kindly. 'It must have been a very great shock to everyone who knew the poor lady. And you, Mrs Philips, who had known her ever since she came to this house, must feel it very deeply indeed.'

'Dear, dear, yes,' she sighed, very well pleased to have her share of sympathy.

They stood together for a while without speaking, watching the hens pecking up corn. A large cockerel with a fine green and gold tail flew up onto the broken wall and crowed importantly.

'I understand,' said Dido as indifferently as she could, 'that poor Miss Fenn had been low in her spirits for some time before she died.'

'Yes…' said the housekeeper, a little doubtingly. 'There's no denying she *had been* a little low… But… Well, there's no accounting, is there?'

'No accounting for what, Mrs Philips?'

'Well, that did seem to me she'd got a bit brighter in

the last few weeks. More at ease with herself.'

'Indeed!'

They watched the poultry a little while longer. A very fat hen shuffled herself luxuriously in a dirt bath and a frantic line of chicks peeped and scuttled out of her way. Dido was considering risking a very particular question – and decided at last that it must be hazarded.

'Was Miss Fenn at all acquainted with James Laurence?' she said, her eyes still fixed upon the hens.

The housekeeper looked surprised. 'Why, yes, of course. All the Laurence boys knew her, for they used to come often on visits – their mother being Mr Harman's sister, you know.' She stopped, smiled fondly. 'The truth is – and I wouldn't mention this to anyone else – but young Mr James was rather struck with Miss Fenn that last summer. We all used to laugh about it a bit. Nothing improper of course – just following her about and leaving flowers by her place at dinner.'

Dido ceased to study the hens. 'He was in love with her?' she cried.

'Oh no! I would not call it love. Not in a boy of sixteen for a woman of nine and twenty.'

'Well, you and I may call it what we wish, Mrs Philips,' said Dido meditatively, 'but to a boy of sixteen I think it might seem very much like love.'

'Perhaps you're right, miss. But it wasn't to be wondered at, you know. She was such a very handsome woman and she had such a way with her. And if young Mr James *was* in love with her…' She bent over the dead chicken in her hands and began to tweak a feather or two from its neck, 'he was not the only one.'

'Oh?'

Mrs Philips continued with her plucking.

'Who was this other admirer?' Dido prompted.

'Well – quite between ourselves…'

'Of course.'

'Mr Portinscale.'

'Indeed? You believe Mr Portinscale was…paying attentions to Miss Fenn?'

'Oh yes, there can be no doubt about it! All that last summer she was here, he'd call regular at four o'clock – just when he knew she was at liberty. And they'd walk out across the lawns and down to the pool nearly every fine day. "Mark my words," I used to say, "we'll see her settled in the parsonage before Christmas." But then… Well, there's no accounting, is there, miss?'

'No accounting for what, Mrs Philips?'

'Why! The way it all went off.'

'Mr Portinscale never made an offer?'

'Ah well!' cried Mrs Philips. 'I wouldn't know anything about that.' But she folded her arms and began to look about at her chickens with the air of a woman who knows a great deal.

Dido waited a moment or two – long enough to raise the fear in Mrs Philips' mind that she had lost the opportunity of displaying her superior intelligence. And then… 'I suppose,' she mused, 'Mr Portinscale was deterred by Miss Fenn's being only a governess…'

'Oh no!' cried the housekeeper immediately. 'He was not deterred at all!'

'Oh? You believe he made an offer?'

'Well…' lowering her voice as if she feared the hens

might overhear. 'I've never mentioned this to anyone before – on account of her disappearing so soon afterwards – but I believe he did.'

Dido said nothing, only raised her brows a little.

'It is all in the sitting of a gentleman's hat, is it not, Miss Kent?'

'The sitting of his hat?'

'Oh yes, a gentleman wears his hat in a very particular way when he is in love. On the very back of his head – with a sort of a tilt to it.'

'Perhaps you are right. I confess I have never observed it myself.'

'Well, I have, miss. And when I saw Mr Portinscale walking to the door that afternoon, I looked at his hat and I said to myself, "It is coming to a crisis. He'll speak today for sure."'

'And do you know what the outcome was?'

Mrs Philips looked suspiciously once more at the spying hens and whispered, 'I'm sure he spoke that afternoon – the afternoon before she went away. Oh yes, he spoke – and was refused. I know, for I was watching and I saw him leave the house.'

'And his hat?'

'Pulled right down over his eyes. And a look like thunder on his face. She'd certainly refused him.' She frowned thoughtfully. 'And refused him in a way he did not like at all!'

Chapter Fifteen

As Dido approached the front of the great house, Anne Harman-Foote was just setting off through the shrubbery with her basket to instruct the poor and the sick of Madderstone village into a state of plenty and well-being.

Mrs Harman-Foote was most particularly glad of the meeting, for she wished to hear everything that Dido had discovered about Miss Fenn's death; but, since the poverty of the villagers was rather urgent this morning, she could not very well afford the time to turn back. So it was somehow decided that Dido must accompany her a little way and, before they had gone many yards, it had also been decided that she must carry the basket.

They started down a damp gravel path between some fine rhododendron bushes which old Mr Harman had planted and which had mercifully escaped the attentions of Mr Coulson. 'I am taking broth and baby linen to the family at Woodman's Hollow,' Anne explained with a sigh of long-suffering, 'though I doubt they deserve it, for I am quite *sure* the boys have been allowed to go poaching again. And it is a principle of mine to give only to the deserving; but Mr Harman-Foote is so very lenient…' She paused to remind Dido to be careful with the basket.

'It is quite shocking,' she said, hurrying on, 'the way the poor allow their children to act without restraint, do you not think? If I could only spare the time, I should establish a school in which proper behaviour might be instilled.'

Trailing in her wake with the heavy basket, avoiding as best she could the broad leaves of the shrubs which dripped water at the slightest touch, Dido was taken with a notion of the village children all exhibiting the restraint and proper behaviour of young Georgie. To distract herself from the horrible idea she began upon a succinct account of her discoveries.

'It seems to me,' she said, 'that there are three arguments against your friend's having taken her own life…' And she explained rather breathlessly the significance of the coins, the position of the remains in the water and the housekeeper's belief that Miss Fenn had recovered from her melancholy before her death.

'That is excellent,' said Anne when she had finished. She paused a moment, beckoning Dido to hurry and then turned into a broader walk. 'I shall tell Mr Portinscale all about it as soon as I have an opportunity. And I shall tell him that the grave *must* be moved.'

'I doubt he will agree to it yet. He seemed very determined upon denying her the church's blessing when last I spoke to him.' Dido took a few quick steps along the gravel in order to look into her companion's eyes. 'Do you know of any particular reason why he should be her enemy?'

'No.' Anne paused as they reached a little side gate which led from the park into the village lane. There was just a flash of doubt upon the assured face – enough to raise the suspicion that she had known of the clergyman's rejection. 'No,' she said, pushing open the iron gate. 'I know of no particular reason. But he is a very stubborn man and I think you had better continue with your enquiries in case we should need more evidence to persuade him.'

Since Dido had every intention of continuing with her enquiries, but did not like being ordered to do so, she was rather at a loss for a reply. And, as she searched for words which might combine independence with acquiescence, Anne turned busily to another topic.

'Now, I must talk to you about Mr William Lomax,' she said.

'Mr Lomax?' cried Dido, struggling through the narrow gateway with the basket.

'Yes. He is to pay a visit to your brother, I understand,' she said, but stopped, distracted from the subject for a moment by the sight of her village.

And Dido must wait, full of half-formed apprehensions, as Anne looked busily to right and left. There were thatched cottages and a newer little row of brick almshouses – all looking trim with smoke from their chimneys hanging low in the damp air. There was a green with a well and stocks, geese and sleeping curs. A woman who was beating a rag rug against her garden wall stopped and curtsied. All seemed to be as it should – but for two small boys who had climbed onto the stocks and were balancing there with waving arms for as long as they might.

Anne hurried forward with a reprimand immediately.

The boys both started, fell and struggled to their feet, attempting to rub their bruised shins, pull off their caps and apologise at the same time.

'Now,' said Anne turning briskly back to Dido, 'of what were we talking? Oh yes! Mr Lomax. He is a very gentlemanlike man, and I have been wanting to get him a wife for some time.' Dido's apprehensions began to take on a very unpleasant form. 'It is almost six years since his wife died,' continued Anne as they skirted the green 'and that is long enough for a man to repine, is it not?'

'Is he repining?' asked Dido – from the corner of her eye, she could see the two boys putting out their tongues at Anne's back.

'Well, I suppose he must be repining. For I am sure he was devoted to her.'

'Oh.' Dido was uncomfortable, but she had never heard anything of Mrs Lomax and could not help asking, 'what kind of a woman was she?'

'A charming woman! Very quiet and proper…' Anne paused and cast a rather anxious, assessing look at her friend. 'And always *very* smartly dressed.'

Dido set the basket down and endeavoured to catch her breath. But Anne's look made her suddenly aware not only of her hot red face, but also the mud on the hem of her petticoat and one or two white feathers which were clinging to her dark pelisse.

'Exactly what age are you, Dido?'

'Oh! I am old enough to wish not to answer the question!'

'Lucy Crockford supposes you to be forty.'

'Then Lucy Crockford is wrong!' she cried

immediately. 'I only turned six and thirty in August.'

'Yes,' said Anne with satisfaction, 'that is just about as I thought. It is not so *very* old. I think, after all, I may make a match of it – if I put my mind to it. Though I would, as a friend, counsel you to take a little more care of your appearance when he comes – and perhaps try to be a little less…odd and argumentative.' She turned and hurried on along the lane.

'I thank you for you advice! But I do not think…'

'Whatever is the matter? Do you dislike Mr Lomax?'

'He is a very pleasant gentleman, but…'

'Well then, it is decided.' She turned back again – this time with real concern in her eyes. 'I have been very worried about you of late and I am sure marriage will be the best way of securing your future happiness.' She was too well-bred to allude to the sinking of Charles's bank, the consequent loss of income to the Kent family – and Dido's residence in her sister-in-law's household. But there could be no doubting that it was all very much in her mind. 'It is a very eligible match, and I mean to do my utmost to promote it. I shall insist that he attends our All Hallows ball, and make him dance with you. And, while he is here, I shall talk to him particularly about your sense and economy.'

Dido sighed inwardly. Why, after a woman turned thirty, must 'economy' become her greatest recommendation? It had such a very *unappealing* sound. Not that she wished to appeal to Mr Lomax, she reminded herself hastily. But, nonetheless, it was mortifying to be accorded such dull praise.

They had come a little out of the village now to a

place where the lane crossed a brook in a shallow, noisy ford and, to one side, a single plank gave passage for pedestrians. Beyond the stream, a path wound down through coppiced hazel trees to Woodman's Hollow where a thin streak of smoke could be seen rising from ragged grey thatch. Anne took the basket into her own hands and stepped onto the bridge, but did not immediately hurry away to distribute advice, broth, linen and disapproval to the unfortunate family in the cottage. It would seem she had something further to say.

'The fact is, Dido, we must act quickly over Mr Lomax, or I fear we shall lose him to another woman.'

'Another woman? Do you believe he is paying attentions to another woman?' The question came out a great deal more sharply than it should have done.

'No. But I rather fear that other women may begin to pay attentions to Mr Lomax. For he may soon become much more eligible than he has been.'

'I am not quite sure I understand you.'

'Well, you may know that he is encumbered with a very dissolute son who seems bent upon spending all his father's money.'

'Yes,' said Dido. 'I have met Mr Tom Lomax.' It was not an experience which she wished to repeat. And, since she had once succeeded in thwarting the young man in a particularly unpleasant, but profitable, scheme, she did not doubt that the feeling was mutual.

'The existence of the son,' continued Anne briskly, 'has, I know, deterred many women who would otherwise have found the father very agreeable indeed.'

'Ah,' said Dido. The notion of other women finding

Mr Lomax agreeable was surprisingly disagreeable. 'But,' with a great effort at indifference, 'what is the change? Am I to suppose that Mr Tom Lomax has undergone a revolution in character?'

'No, but he has undergone a revolution in fortune. It seems his father may soon be rid of him. I had it in a letter from town this morning that Tom Lomax looks set to become engaged – to a woman with *twenty thousand pounds*.'

'Oh!'

'Dido, are you unwell?'

'No, no I am perfectly well. Just a little tired from all the walking I have done this morning.' But all the heat had drained suddenly from her face and her legs were weak. She sat down hurriedly on the end of the bridge.

'Well then,' said Anne, 'I shall leave you to rest and be about my business, for I have a great deal to do. But, remember, we must act quickly before news of Mr Tom's match gets abroad and other women begin to make a play for his father. And, Dido, please,' she added with one last critical look as she crossed the stream, 'give a little thought to your appearance. An unmarried woman *must* pay attention to her appearance if she would make a match. It is a principle of mine...' Her voice trailed away through the hazel thicket and Dido was left alone with the chatter of the water and her own thoughts.

It was alarming how very significant this news of Tom's prospects appeared. Why should it matter? It was true that once she had looked forward to just such a prosperous marriage for the son as the surest route to happiness for the father – and for herself. But that had been before their disagreement at Richmond. For many months now she had considered her own curiosity, Mr Lomax's unbending disapproval, and the fear of horrible marital discord as much greater barriers to their union than the debts of his son.

So why, she demanded of herself as she watched the yellow leaves drift and twist upon the water, why should the prospect of Mr Lomax unshackled and free to marry take the breath from her body and the strength from her legs? Could it be that her resolve to refuse him was faltering?

It must not. That was her immediate thought – for there could be only one cause of the change and that was the wretched alteration in her own circumstances.

In the summer, as a free woman, with a home of her own, she had refused him. And was she now, wretched and dependent, to accept him? No. If she did, she would know that her motives were base. And, in addition to all the misery of conjugal disharmony, she would suffer the pain of despising herself as weak and mercenary.

Chapter Sixteen

'Harriet,' said Dido reluctantly. 'I have promised Lucy that I will speak to you on her behalf.'

The scene, she thought, had better be got over quickly and this was as fair an opportunity as any she was likely to have. The abbey was very quiet just now. The gentlemen were all gone out shooting, the little girls were in the nursery, young Georgie was at his Latin lesson with Mr Portinscale, and Mrs Harman-Foote had not yet returned from Woodman's Hollow. So Dido had come to sit awhile with Harriet and her patient.

Outside, the morning had turned dark and rain was pattering on the windows; but within the bedchamber everything was pleasant and comfortable. There was a good log fire in the grate and lavender had been burnt upon it to cleanse the air. A jug of pale pink roses stood upon a dark oak chest, and Harriet was sitting upon the window seat beside it, her head, in its all-engulfing cap, bent over her tambour frame. In the wide bed Penelope was sleeping peacefully – a half-smile on her lips – as if the book, just slipping from her fingers, had amused her and was now supplying very pleasant dreams.

'Your sister,' said Dido looking earnestly across at Harriet, 'wishes me to…plead Captain Laurence's cause.'

Harriet gave a start. Her hand went to her mouth. 'He has made an offer to Lucy!'

'No, not quite. But she seems determined that he will. And I am commissioned to tell you that it will break her heart if you oppose their union.'

'Oh dear!' Harriet sighed heavily, but showed no particular sign of jealousy. She put a hand to her brow. 'I had hoped,' she said, 'that if Lucy was out of the house… Out of sight out of mind, you know. I hoped… Well, I hoped the hare would run another way, as the saying goes.' Her eyes strayed to the bed and its sleeping occupant.

'Yes,' confessed Dido, 'I too thought he would choose Penelope.'

'And she thinks it still,' said Harriet drily. 'And there she lies her silly head just full of the navy! Do but look at what she has been reading.'

Dido stepped to the bed and looked at the book in Penelope's hand. 'The *Navy List*?' she cried. 'I would not have thought that provided much entertainment for an invalid!'

'But she is an invalid in love, Dido. All morning she has done nothing but read about the ships Captain Laurence has served in.'

'I see.' As Dido bent over the sleeping girl she saw something written upon the book's cover. She gently disengaged the book from the drooping hand, and read, in strong, looped letters: *To Miss Lambe, wishing her a pleasant study and a very rapid recovery. James Laurence.*

'She asked most particularly for it,' said Harriet. 'And you may be sure the captain was eager enough to supply it.'

'Was he indeed! So it would seem that Penelope has good reason to think him *attached* to her.'

'Oh yes! Though I do not doubt he has encouraged Lucy too.'

'This then,' said Dido thoughtfully, 'is why there has never been any symptom of jealousy between the two girls. They have *both* felt secure of the gentleman!'

'I fear the captain means to have his cake and eat it too.'

'You do not have a very high opinion of Captain Laurence?'

'Papa would not have liked him. This attachment of Lucy's will not do at all, you know,' said Harriet firmly. 'Here at Madderstone we hear only what the Captain wishes us to know about himself. He is always singing his own praises. But when we were in Bath last month we saw him in his true colours.'

'Why? What did he do?' cried Dido eagerly.

'Oh, it was not so much what he did, as who he consorted with,' said Harriet. 'I saw him again and again in the company of such dissolute men! It would seem he has recently become acquainted with Lord Congreve, who was divorced after his wife ran away on account of his abominable behaviour; and Sir James Dearing, who eloped with an heiress two years ago, broke her heart and gambled away her fortune – and other men of the same stamp. Men such as…'

'Such as Papa would not have approved?'

'Well, no, he would not.'

'And you fear the captain might be inclined to follow the example of his acquaintances?'

Harriet primmed her lips and bent her head over her work. 'Birds of a feather fly together,' she said.

Dido studied her friend's averted face for a minute or two. What exactly did she suspect the captain of? When Harriet began to talk entirely in proverbs it was not easy to distinguish her meaning. Even 'Dear Papa' was to be preferred to an endless parade of proverbs.

'She is very beautiful,' Dido mused turning away to look down upon the lovely, faultless oval of Penelope's face where long dark lashes curled on soft white cheeks.

'And very poor,' added Harriet, her eyes still fixed upon her work. 'Penelope has nothing at all beyond a small allowance.'

'Do you suppose then,' said Dido carefully, 'that the captain is *mercenary* in his pursuit of Lucy?'

Harriet laid aside her work. 'I love my sister dearly,' she said quietly, 'but I am not blind. I cannot help but see that she has not one half of Penelope's beauty. If such a man as the captain truly means to give up Penelope for Lucy, I *must* suspect him of being mercenary. Money, as they say, gilds a woman's features – and Lucy has twelve thousand pounds.'

'Twelve thousand pounds!' The words burst from Dido before she could check her surprise. She stopped. Apologised.

'Oh, there is no need to be sorry!' said Harriet. 'I can see you are full of curiosity, Dido. You are no doubt wondering how the Ashfield estate can supply such a claim – and I tell you honestly, I do not know how it can. But it must! For that is the provision which Dear Papa made in his will for Lucy's marriage portion – and mine.

We are entitled to twelve thousand pounds apiece, you see. And if Lucy marries a man who insists upon her rights, then Ashfield must be ruined to pay him as much of that twelve thousand pounds as it can. The roof would remain unrepaired, money would have to be borrowed; the mill at Great Farleigh sold, every inch of alienable land mortgaged. And I would be left...' She began to wring her hands. 'Oh, poor Papa would be so distressed to know we were got into such a muddle.'

'But why...' Again Dido bit back her curiosity.

'Why did Dear Papa arrange things so ill?' Harriet smiled fondly. 'Because he was a *very remarkable* man, Dido.' There was a sad shake of the head. 'I do not believe there are many men who love their wives and daughters as he did. He wished us to have an equal share, you see...' She stopped, sighed again. 'His intention was that, as soon as Silas came of age, they should join together in cutting off the entail. Then the estate could have been broken up and the value of it divided among his three children.'

'But the entail was never cut off?'

'No.' Harriet shook her head sadly. 'Dear Papa died before Silas was one and twenty. They were never able to undertake the legal process necessary for ending it. For that process, you know, requires the consent of the present owner and the legal heir. So now the estate must remain entire.' She turned back to the window. 'The only *safe* possibility of marriage for Lucy or me would be to find a man who is rich enough or...' there was a moment's hesitation, 'or *good* enough to be indifferent to money. It is of course of no consequence to me, but Lucy...'

The shadows of water streaming down the window shimmered like a veil of tears on Harriet's pale cheeks. Perplexity lined her brow, and yet there was a half-smile on her lips – no doubt a tribute of affection to Dear Papa – a man Dido remembered only indistinctly from one or two meetings in her earliest days at Badleigh: a big man with a large, slightly purple nose, a blue coat, silver buttons, very strong opinions and a doting fondness for his daughters. His beloved wife had died giving birth to Silas; and after that his children had been all the world to him.

'I do not suppose,' Dido ventured gently at last, 'that your sister could be persuaded into seeing things as you do – I mean, might she be brought to suspect the captain's motives?'

Harriet raised her head with a sigh. 'Oh I can never make Lucy understand money matters,' she cried bitterly. 'Her sensibilities are too delicate! And now she is in love. Love conquers all, you know, and there are none so blind as those that will not see.'

'She cannot conceive that the captain might be mercenary?' Asked Dido in an attempt to cut through maxims to meaning.

'No. He has told her of course that he cares nothing for her fortune – and she believes him. But once they are married, I make no doubt he will sing a different tune. And then of course it will be entirely in his hands. A woman owns nothing after she is married: her fortune will be his. He will be entitled to wring every last penny he can get out of Ashfield.'

'Oh, Harriet!' cried Dido feelingly, 'marriage is so very

final, do you not think? I do believe a woman needs all her wits about her for the business – and she had better not choose a husband while she is distracted by love.'

But Harriet's mind turned more upon particulars than general principles. 'Soon,' she said sadly, 'Penelope will be recovered enough to return to Bath. Silas, Lucy and I are all to accompany her. But I fear that Captain Laurence is planning to go too. I think he plans to meet us there – and make his offer to Lucy during our visit.'

'It would, I suppose, be his first opportunity to speak without appearing inconsiderate of your friend's illness.'

'Dido, you *must* come with us and help me prevent it.'

'Upon my word, Harriet, now you are telling me what I *must* do. It would seem that I am never to have a moment's peace between you and Lucy and Mrs Harman-Foote!'

'But you will come, will you not? It will be an opportunity to put all your satirical cleverness to good use.' Harriet gave a weary smile. 'You can do some good for once instead of only laughing at us all.'

'What a very kind invitation! I shall consider it.'

Harriet was about to press the point but was prevented from doing so by the appearance of a housemaid come to say that Mr Paynter was out in the passageway and would like a short conference with Miss Crockford before coming in to see his patient. Immediately Harriet was on her feet, setting her cap straight, smoothing her gown and preparing to give an account of her nursing. But, at the door, she hesitated a moment to say, 'Remember, I am relying upon you.'

The door closed behind her and Dido was left alone in the still chamber with only the sleeping girl, the gentle lapping of flames and the tap-tap of rain at the window for company.

Her thoughts were far from comfortable. She was deeply concerned for Harriet – and for Lucy too. And then, when she turned her head and looked upon the peacefully sleeping Penelope, she felt an even graver disquiet.

For here was an unscrupulous man who had deliberately made two young women in love with him. Two young women who were – to put the matter kindly – not remarkable for their sense. Why had he done it? And what would be the end of it all for them?

For the plain woman with a fortune it might end in a loveless marriage which would bring ruin on her brother and sister. But what was to be expected for the beautiful and penniless girl…? What were his motives in pursuing her? A girl with no father or brothers to protect her, guarded only by the mistress of a common school.

The fate he had planned for her might be infinitely worse.

Expelled from the sickroom by the surgeon's arrival, Dido walked slowly out onto the landing which overlooked the hall and leant thoughtfully upon the gilded stair rail. Below her was spread Mr Harman-Foote's dazzling new floor of coloured marble. High above her head rain pattered on the cupola, but otherwise the house seemed unusually quiet – there was only the murmur of voices in the room behind her, and the faint beating of a toy drum drifting down from the nursery.

Harriet's communications had, she found, depressed her spirits and disturbed her in more ways than one. For now her mind was making invidious comparisons…

It was, of course, regrettable that Edward Crockford had failed to safeguard the futures of his daughters – but at least he had *tried*. Her own father had made no attempt to circumvent those severe laws of inheritance which impoverished daughters to the benefit of sons. The bulk of his small fortune had been spent on the education of his sons, and the remainder inherited by them…

She stopped herself. She was too near to being angry with her father – a man who had never been anything but kindly and tolerant towards her. Naturally he had never doubted that the boys would provide for their sisters – as they had. Eliza and Dido might be poor, but they would never be destitute, never lack for a home – though that home might not always be to their taste…

She must not succumb to self-pity. A diversion was absolutely necessary and she began immediately to look about for a suitable means of continuing her enquiries.

Beyond the high sash windows, rain continued to sweep across the lawns, cutting off the possibility of a visit to the ruins or the pool. Her eyes strayed on along the carpeted length of the passage – and came to rest at last upon the door of Miss Fenn's room… Thus fixing her wandering thoughts upon the disappearance of the letters.

This would be an excellent opportunity for taking a look about the bedchamber alone. Would it be allowable to venture in there unaccompanied…? Yes, she thought that it might. She crept quietly to the door. She would, of course, explain her actions later to Anne. She was sure that she would not disapprove.

And yet, as she opened the door, she could not quite escape a feeling that she was doing something wrong: intruding. It was maybe the lingering presence of the apartment's mistress which caused such a feeling of awkwardness.

The room seemed larger by day, and the stronger light falling through the tall, unshuttered windows also brought forward the intricate pattern of the wallpaper, the beauty of the needlework in the bed-hangings, the rich wood of the furnishings.

It was a very fine room indeed. And, as she hesitated just inside the door, Dido wondered again at its having been allotted to a governess. The most comfortable attic – or the very humblest family room – would have been a more usual choice. An idea insinuated itself into her mind: an idea she would have been ashamed to speak aloud…

It would have been the widowed Mr Harman himself who decreed where the young woman was placed; was it possible that he had chosen this room because Miss Fenn was more than a governess? Dido blushed at framing the thought – but framed it none the less: was it possible that she had been the old gentleman's mistress?

She looked about and Miss Fenn's few, simple possessions, thrown into sharp contrast by the room's luxury, rebuked her for the thought. The plain hairbrush and writing desk, the text above the bed, certainly had not the appearance of belonging to an immoral woman. The black bible looked particularly humble and virtuous on the fine polished mahogany of the bedside table – and cried aloud against the horrible idea.

She crossed the room, picked up the bible and found that it bore every indication of constant use. She turned a page or two and saw the marks of a pencil everywhere – underlinings and neat little commentaries crammed into the margins. It would seem that Miss Fenn was one of those exceedingly pious women who make notes upon the sermons they hear every Sunday.

There is something about the writing of those who are dead – it seems to promise a connection with the past. Dido moved eagerly towards the light of the window to read more closely. And, once there, she was taken with the idea of trying to discover whether there was any page which had been studied more than the others. A favoured passage might reveal much about the lady's character.

She closed the book, placed its spine in one hand and, carefully giving way to the inclination of the pages, waited to see at what place it would, most naturally, fall open.

The attempt was more successful than she had dared to hope.

The leaves hardly fluttered before opening at one place so very decisively that there could be little doubt of the book having been held in that position for some time. She turned into the full light of the window.

The bible had opened at the third chapter of Saint Paul's letter to the Colossians and there were two verses underlined: *Wives, submit yourselves unto your own husbands, as it is fit in the Lord. Husbands, love your wives, and be not bitter against them.*

And in the margin was written: *Mr Portinscale spoke*

very movingly in his sermon today upon the second part of this commandment – the duty of tenderness which a husband owes to his wife.

Did he indeed? thought Dido. It was not a subject upon which she could imagine Madderstone's clergyman being eloquent…

But, before she could pursue her thoughts any further, there came the sound of quick footsteps outside in the gallery. She started – as guilty as if she were about to be detected in a crime – and hurriedly closed the book. And, as she did so, something – something which had been shaken loose by her handling – fell from inside the back cover onto the floor.

She snatched it up and had just time to see that it was a letter directed to _Miss Elinor Fenn_, before a hand turned the lock of the door. And there was but half a minute to decide between satisfying honour and satisfying curiosity: between taking the letter and replacing it.

The temptation was too great; it was decided in the instant. The door opened. Mrs Harman-Foote walked into the room. Dido was laying the bible back in its place beside the bed – and the letter was hidden away in her pocket.

Chapter Seventeen

Dido was not in the habit of thinking of herself as a bad woman. While acknowledging her many faults, she had always believed the balance to be, overall, in favour of virtue. But she found that now, facing her friend with Miss Fenn's letter concealed in her pocket and reminding her of its presence with a little rustling every time she moved, she could not be quite so comfortable with herself as usual. It had been theft – a kind of theft. She ought to tell Anne about it. She ought not to read it…

'Why, Dido, I believe you *are* unwell. You still look very pale.'

'Oh, I am quite well, thank you.'

'Well, I am glad of it,' cried Mrs Harman-Foote immediately. She sat down on the window seat and clasped her hands anxiously in her lap. 'I must talk with you. I have had a dreadful shock!'

'A shock?' Dido sat down beside her and watched emotion working in every feature of her face. 'Whatever has happened?'

'The ring! It is gone!'

'I beg your pardon?'

'My dear Miss Fenn's ring. It is gone from my jewel case.'

'But it cannot... Are you sure?'

'Oh yes. I have searched the whole room. It is gone. It was certainly there yesterday. But just now I went up to my bedchamber to change my wet clothes – and I found that the ring is gone.' She drew a long breath. 'I am this minute going to my housekeeper. I shall insist that the house is searched.'

Dido smiled. For all the pretence of talking the matter over, it was clear that Anne had already determined upon her exact course of action. 'Yes,' she said thoughtfully. 'You are quite right, of course. It is very important that we find it – and even more important that we find *who* has taken it. For why should anyone steal it? It is of gold, and so must have some value,' she mused, 'but not so very much.'

'There were a dozen beside it in the jewel case which were of much greater value – and they were left untouched.' Anne stood up, very eager to begin the search, for commanding activity was a great deal more to her taste than contemplation.

But Dido was still puzzling over the matter. 'Who would have had the opportunity to take the ring?' she asked.

'No one except the housemaids. There is my own maid, Jones, but she is above suspicion. She has been with me for more than ten years.'

'And you can think of no one else? What of...visitors to the house.'

'Visitors!' cried Anne. 'I could never suspect my visitors of such a thing!' And then, having paid this necessary tribute to good breeding, she considered the

matter carefully. 'It cannot have been a visitor,' she said
at last. 'A visitor could certainly not wander away to the
bedchambers without my being aware of it. No one but a
servant could have gone to my room.'

Except, thought Dido, *your husband…*

This disappearance of the ring was intriguing, but
there was nothing to be gained from staying to watch
it searched for. It was, Dido knew, a matter with which
Anne Harman-Foote could be safely entrusted. And
the letter in her pocket was continually demanding her
attention. So she left the house just as soon as the rain
held off – and when the search was at its height, with
Anne confidently issuing commands from the hall, like a
general directing a battle.

She hurried through the gardens and into the park,
busily calculating whether she must walk the full two miles
to Badleigh before looking at the letter – or whether the
path afforded some secluded place in which to satisfy her
curiosity. She still could not quite explain to herself why
she had decided so quickly to conceal her discovery in the
bedroom, nor why she had continued to say nothing of
it all the time she remained in the house. Perhaps it was
because she was half-afraid of the contents: afraid that
they would reveal something which Anne Harman-Foote
would not wish to know… Something which might make
her call a halt to the enquiries…

But the removal of all the other letters pointed to the
significance of Miss Fenn's correspondence… And this one
letter, which had by good fortune escaped the attention
of the intruder, seemed by its privileged position in the

bible to be more important even than the others...

In short, the only thing she was sure of was that she could not bear to remain any longer in ignorance of its contents. And when she had left the open parkland and the church, and had followed the path into a small wood, she decided that its great oaks and hazel thickets provided secrecy enough, and a fallen log a sufficient resting place. She sat down and there, amidst the drifts of curled, bronze leaves, with the busy sound of a small stream filling the stillness, she drew the letter from her pocket.

It was rather thick – there seemed to be two sheets of paper. The direction was written in a strong, slanting hand...a man's writing perhaps? And there was no mark of a post office on it. It had certainly been delivered by hand – which argued for its having come from no great distance. She turned it over: the broken seal was of red wax, and did not bear the imprint of any device.

She opened it and found that it was not, in fact, a single letter of two sheets, but rather one letter enclosed within another. Her interest quickened.

She smoothed the outer sheet and read, in the same firm hand as the direction:

4ᵗʰ June 1791

Dear Madam,

I am returning under this cover your recent letter. And I beg you to send no more.

I cannot conceive that you truly intend to inflict pain upon one whom you profess to love, nor to end that security, happiness and contentment which he presently enjoys.

Therefore I must remind you once again that such might be the end of your continued protestations of affection. I beg you will leave them off.

You <u>must</u> forget what is past.

There was no signature.

She quickly picked up the inner letter, but was instantly disappointed. It bore no direction – nothing to show to whom it had been sent. She unfolded it and found, written in the same small, neat hand which she had seen in the bible:

3ʳᵈ June 1791

Beloved,

I must tell you how dear you are to me.

I see you, again and again, with your friends about you and I feel so lonely, my dear. You scarcely notice me and I must watch you in silence. Once I was everything to you – now I am nothing. And yet, dearest, I care more deeply for you than anyone else ever can. Believe me, no other woman will ever, can ever, love you as I love you – as I will always love you.

The pain of being apart is terrible. I can no longer endure this separation. We must be together. I see now that I was mistaken in ever thinking that I could give you up. I was wrong to ever agree to it.

Your ever loving
Elinor Fenn.

Dido stared, read the letter again to be sure she had not mistaken its contents, then let it drop into her lap.

The little noises of the forest flowed about her:

the song of the stream, the rapid, broken stutter of a woodpecker, the furtive rustling of a mouse or a blackbird in the dead leaves. But in her head she heard only the echo of those passionate words in the letter. Words which showed Miss Elinor Fenn to have been a very different creature from the quiet, religious woman her neighbours had taken her for.

Chapter Eighteen

... You are, I know, Eliza, too generous to glory in your better judgement; but I must confess that you may have been right to advise against the enquiries I have lately been making. For I am now got to such a point I do not know where to turn.

The finding of these letters has taken me into very dangerous territory indeed. I know not what I ought to do next. And indecision is, I believe, of all states of mind, the most painful.

I find now that I am in possession of information about Miss Fenn which her friend would find almost as distressing as an incontrovertible proof of self-murder. For it would seem that the lady did, indeed, have a lover and, since secrecy was imperative to him, one cannot escape the conclusion that it was a guilty, clandestine attachment.

I am all amazement. I cannot make out how such a business could have carried on at Madderstone without any of her neighbours suspecting it. How were meetings contrived? How were friends deceived? For it is certain – from the way in which the neighbourhood talks about Miss Fenn – no shadow was ever cast upon her reputation.

Eliza, I certainly do not feel equal to revealing this attachment to Mrs Harman-Foote, and there would seem to be no reason for destroying her esteem of her governess.

Except that this lover would have had a powerful motive for murder.

The passionate nature which her letter betrays must have put him in a perpetual fear of disclosure. Here was she – just a few days before she met her death – declaring that she 'could no longer endure' their separation, insisting that they 'must be together'. Did she intend some desperate action which would expose him? Did he act to prevent that exposure?

I cannot help but suspect that it was this lover with whom she had an appointment on the day of her disappearance. Nor can I forget that purse full of money and the last weeks of life, during which, by the housekeeper's account, Miss Fenn had seemed recovered from her lowness of spirits.

These arguments against suicide, combined with the motive – and opportunity – for murder, make me fear that a terrible injustice has been done: that not only is a woman cast out needlessly from the church's mercy, but also that a murderer is walking freely among us…

And I do fear that he may be walking among us.

The fifteen years which have passed since the lady's death might have produced the hope that the guilty man was already gone beyond the reach of human law to face a much surer and more terrible judgement. But the removal of the other letters – those in the writing desk – robs me of that comfort. Someone is acting now to obscure the truth. The disappearance of Miss Fenn's ring must put that beyond doubt. Someone wishes to remove every remembrance of this woman: every clue to her secrets. And I cannot escape the conviction that that person was among the company collected at the dinner table when Anne promised to take me to Miss Fenn's room.

Under these circumstances, can I, in all conscience, stand by and do nothing? Every principle of humanity and morality cries out against it...

And yet it will be impossible – or, at least, exceedingly difficult – to proceed with my enquiries without revealing the things I have learnt to Anne Harman-Foote. And that I cannot face, for I would be forced not only to reveal the improper behaviour of her friend, I would also have to cast the shadow of suspicion upon her own husband.

For you see, Eliza, I am sure that Mr Harman-Foote is the guilty man... No, no, I am not sure at all. But the evidences against him are very strong.

That hint of tobacco smoke suggests that it was he who took the letters from the desk – that is the first, and most powerful, argument against him. He would also have had the opportunity of taking away the ring. (Which ring, by the by, Anne informs me was not found in her search.) Mr Harman-Foote, you will remember, has been from the very beginning quite determined that his wife should make no enquiries into her friend's death. And he seems to have ordered the refilling of the pool – as if he wishes the matter to be forgotten as quickly as possible... And then there are the details which, while not exactly proving his guilt, certainly make it plausible. We know that he was staying at Madderstone when Miss Fenn met her death; and their both originating in Shropshire makes possible a connection between them before her coming into this country.

Eliza, what am I to do? My mind is in turmoil. For when I am not doubting the husband I find that my suspicions fall upon the father, who, for some reason, installed a governess in luxury. Though Mr Harman's being dead does, I confess, rather excuse him from being the thief of the letters and the ring. I certainly do not wish to start the possibility of there being <u>another</u> ghost haunting Madderstone…

But then there are strong evidences against the cousin, Captain Laurence, too. I am certain he knew of the existence of the body <u>before it was discovered</u>. We know that he was also staying in the house at the time of Miss Fenn's disappearance. And, by the housekeeper's account, he was quite in the habit of following the governess. Well, supposing he followed her upon that fateful evening, and saw something – perhaps her meeting with a lover – something which turned his boyish love to jealousy and anger…

Of course, there is the possibility that Mr Portinscale is the guilty man! Now there is a better thought, Eliza! It would certainly be a great deal more agreeable to suspect a man unconnected with the family. Might he have been so enraged by Miss Fenn's rejecting his offer that he persuaded her to walk to the pool with him one more time and there exacted a terrible revenge?

Well, I grant that it does seem rather extreme. Revenge for such an affront usually amounts to no more than a little coldness and formality in future meetings, and, at the very worst, a hasty marriage to someone else. Murder is not a common sequel to a rejected proposal. But perhaps there was something which made her refusal particularly objectionable… Mrs Philips spoke of him being very discomposed when he left the house – 'A face like thunder.' That is what she said.

Oh dear! Forgive my rambling, Eliza. I am writing down my thoughts as they arise and I doubt you will be able to make any sense of them.

I do not know what I should do next and I have come to such a pass that I am almost glad that Margaret makes it impossible for me to carry my enquiries any further just now. The expectation of our visitor has thrown her into a paroxysm of housekeeping and, what with washing glasses, overseeing the polishing of silver, and rehanging curtains, I am quite unable to leave the house.

And, within a few hours, Mr Lomax will be here…

In a corner of the orchard at Badleigh Vicarage there was a moss hut. Made by a previous incumbent with a taste for rustic simplicity, it had stood for the most part unregarded by the present family – except when the little boys were home from school and had a mind to turn it into a ship or a robbers' stronghold – until Dido discovered it.

So sheltered as to be habitable on a fine day even in October and so conveniently overrun by spiders as to deter any visit from Margaret, it formed an excellent hiding place. If she provided herself with a basket of plain sewing, Dido had found she could often sit there a whole hour undisturbed.

And she retreated to it on the morning after Mr Lomax's arrival – meaning to sew and to think. Her plan had been to think about Miss Elinor Fenn, but, as she drew a cravat of Francis's from her basket and held her needle to the light to thread it, it was rather more immediate matters which concerned her…

The meeting yesterday with Mr Lomax – the first meeting since that extraordinary interview in the lime walk – had been keenly anticipated, looked forward to with such dread and such pleasure as could not but lead to a kind of disappointment. It had passed, as such meetings frequently do, quite unremarkably. He had been pleased to see her – he had said it, and he had certainly looked it; but he was too well-bred to give any hint of what had passed between them. For which she was, of course, grateful…but…

She frowned at the cravat as she began to sew its hem. She could not explain why she should feel so very restless this morning.

She had, as yet, had little opportunity for private conversation with the visitor. The talk at dinner yesterday had been only a general telling over of news. But that news had necessarily included the recent events at Madderstone. And later, when Margaret and Francis were busy at backgammon, Mr Lomax had taken the opportunity of coming to Dido and saying very quietly – with just that lifting of his brows as appeared in their imagined conversations – 'And what is *your* opinion of the ghost in the ruins, Miss Kent?'

'Oh,' she replied in some confusion, 'I do not have an opinion, for I do not believe in ghosts.'

'No, I would not have expected it of you.' He steepled his fingers together, rested his chin upon them and regarded her with mock gravity. 'But I would have thought your very disbelief would give you a strong interest in the business. For if there is no ghost, then there is a *mystery*, is there not?'

'Is there?' she said, smiling as innocently as she knew how. 'I assure you I had not thought about it.'

'Indeed?' he said disbelievingly.

Dido had turned away her face and rather wondered at herself. Why should she attempt to hide her curiosity from him now? What did it matter if he thought ill of her? Could it be that, although she was determined not to marry him, she wanted him still to wish for it?

That, she told herself severely, was very selfish indeed.

Meanwhile he was considering – and the result of his consideration was: 'Well, well, I suppose someone had got into the gallery. A servant perhaps. A figure appearing suddenly in the shadows might well frighten the poor young lady.'

'Oh no!' cried Dido immediately. 'That is not possible. There is no door, you see, and no other stairway – and there is only a ten-foot drop at the end, guarded by a wall this high.' She leant forward eagerly and held up her hand to indicate the size of the wall.

He began to laugh.

She froze for a moment with her hand still extended. She dropped her hand. 'I assure you,' she said demurely, 'there was no one in the gallery that morning besides ourselves. But I do not see why you should be amused by it.'

'I am not,' he said. 'I am only amused to find that a woman who has not even thought about the matter should be able to give such very exact information.'

As she sat at her sewing in the orchard remembering this conversation, Dido could not quite determine whether she should regret, or rejoice in it. She upbraided herself for having betrayed herself. And yet there had been a kind of pleasure in the discussion – he had not seemed so *very* disgusted by her interest in the ghost...

A heavy footstep and, 'Ah Miss Kent! I hope I do not intrude too grossly upon your domestic labours!' roused her abruptly from her thoughts. Much to her surprise, Mr Portinscale was picking his way delicately through the long grass of the orchard.

'Not at all, sir,' she replied putting the cravat back into its basket and closing the lid. 'I am very happy to suspend domestic duties for the pleasures of society.' (For some reason, she found Mr Portinscale's ponderous manner rather infectious.)

He stepped into the moss hut and looked rather warily at a particularly fine spider which was resting in a web of its own making only inches above her head.

'I was in hopes of a private conference with you,' he said.

She obligingly lifted her basket from the bench to make room for him. But, remembering their last 'private conference', she could not help asking, 'Have I been so unfortunate as to incur your displeasure again, Mr Portinscale?'

He looked uncomfortable, attempted a laugh, took a handkerchief from his pocket and made a great to-do about dusting a few fragments of moss and dead leaves from the seat before settling himself and smiling in a way which, to Dido's mind, could only be described as *conciliatory*.

'Ah! No, no, not at all. Not at all!' he assured her. 'On the contrary.' He attempted another laugh which sounded more like a snort. 'On the contrary. I was, in fact, rather hoping to consult with you, Miss Kent.'

Dido raised her brows in surprise.

'That is, I am come upon business to visit your brother. But, finding I must wait for him… I hoped that I might – as I said – *consult*.'

'Yes?'

'About dear Mrs Harman-Foote.'

'Oh?'

'I do hope,' he said, folding his narrow features into an expression of mournful concern, 'I do sincerely hope that she is not so very distraught as she was – I mean, of course, in relation to the dreadful demise of her governess.'

Dido stole a glance at his face: it was red, shiny and exceedingly anxious. Was he relenting? Might he consent to a removal of the grave? 'I do not think,' she said carefully, 'that it is the loss of her friend which hurts the lady so badly as the nature of Mr Wishart's verdict – and its consequences. The death she has been long resigned to; but the disposal of the corpse is a fresh – and unexpected – blow.'

She looked steadily at him. He was sitting uncomfortably on the very edge of the bench, his ankles crossed, his thin, delicate hands clasped upon his knees. His eyes were resolutely turned from her, fixed in a study of the buttons on his gaiters.

'Mrs Harman-Foote,' she continued, 'is very certain that Miss Fenn's principles and character would have prevented her taking her own life.' Still he would not look at her. She longed to know the emotions which kept him silent. Was there still tenderness in his memory of the dead woman? Or lingering resentment for her refusal of him? Was there perhaps even guilt?

'And everything I have heard,' Dido concluded, 'would

seem to support Mrs Harman-Foote's view that self-murder was…unlikely. Miss Fenn was, by all accounts, a very *religious* woman.'

The colour deepened on the clergyman's face and he looked up at last, scowling stubbornly. 'I am very well aware of how the young woman appeared to her neighbours,' he said with considerable force. 'But appearances can deceive, Miss Kent. The Lord God looks not upon appearances but upon the secrets of our hearts.'

'Yes, I am sure He does,' said Dido – but she was more concerned to know whether, in this case, the Reverend Mr Portinscale had looked upon the secrets of the heart. Was he suggesting that he knew something to Miss Fenn's disadvantage?

Meanwhile the clergyman appeared to be considering. At last he raised his eyes to hers with a look of determination. 'Miss Kent, I have been at a loss to know what I should do – what it is *right* for me to do – in the face of your extraordinary determination to continue upon your enquiries, in spite of the very strong advice you have been given to desist. I am afraid that you leave me with no alternative but to be a great deal more *explicit* upon this subject than one would wish to be with a gently reared lady.'

'Oh!' A gently reared lady ought, of course, to disclaim immediately – to prevent him from continuing. Dido did not; she waited instead – with considerable eagerness – for him to be explicit…

He sighed, deeply and with great disapproval. 'The woman you are interesting yourself about,' he said stiffly, 'was not at all what she appeared to be – she was not what she *ought* to be. Her religious principles were a pretence. She was, I fear, capable of anything – even of destroying the life which the Good Lord had seen fit to bestow upon her.'

'Oh?' Dido waited for more, but he appeared to have finished speaking. 'Oh, but I cannot believe it!' she cried provokingly, watching his face for a response. 'The world could not be so deceived! There is no proof of her wickedness.'

'There is indeed proof! There is the proof of her own words!' he stopped, aware that she had driven him too far and looking about for a way in which to retract.

'That is a very serious accusation,' said Dido quietly.

'But it is a well-founded one.'

She raised her brows – she would not be so discourteous as to say she doubted him, but there was disbelief in every line of her face.

'I cannot give you my proof, Miss Kent, without disclosing matters…of a personal nature.'

'I would not wish to make you uncomfortable, Mr Portinscale. But you may rely entirely upon my discretion – and I confess myself to be very surprised by your poor opinion of a woman who is spoken of so very highly by the whole neighbourhood.'

He sighed again. 'There was a time,' he said, 'when I was more disposed to admire her than anyone else.' He stared down at the thin hands clasped upon his knee. 'I asked her to be my wife,' he said quietly. 'And it was then I discovered…'

'Yes?'

'It was then that she confessed to…another attachment.'

'Miss Fenn was engaged to another man?'

'No,' he replied stiffly, 'she was not. She spoke of an attachment and, when I asked...' He stopped, cleared his throat, seemed to force himself to go on. 'When I asked if I should...soon suffer the pain of witnessing her marriage to another man, she told me – with decision – that, no, that would never happen. I should never witness her marriage.'

'Oh dear...'

'In short, Miss Kent, it was an improper attachment – one of which she should have been ashamed, against which she should have struggled – but which she preferred over an honourable offer...' He stopped. His face was now very red and his clasped hands were tapping up and down upon his knees.

Dido watched him with concern – a little ashamed of herself for forcing the confidence. She was wondering how best to soothe him when Rebecca made her appearance with the news that Francis was returned and awaiting his visitor in the library.

The gentleman jumped up immediately, very glad to hurry away – though he very much regretted the necessity, and was greatly obliged to her for the honour she had done him in bestowing her time upon him...

And she was left alone, watching his narrow black back retreating through the fruit trees and wondering very much about his response. The information he had given was not new to her – though she was rather surprised to find that the lady had spoken so...*explicitly*.

But the great revelation of the interview was Mr Portinscale's palpable emotion.

There had been such an air, not only of the resentment which she had expected, but also of very great suffering. He had been so badly hurt by the rejection that there could be no doubt of his having deeply loved Elinor Fenn. And furthermore, he had believed that she returned his affection. He must have done, for he had been sorely disappointed by her refusal. And disappointment had found expression in cruel resentment.

The pale autumn sun warmed the sheltered corner of the orchard, raising a sweet scent from overripe fruit lying in the long grass. But, all of a sudden, there seemed to be something of melancholy in the mellow warmth – and in the singing of a blackbird on the roof of the moss hut.

Dido was deeply affected to discover that Mr Portinscale's insistence upon the poor woman's eternal punishment – her casting out from God's grace – arose not, as she had thought, from narrow, unbending piety, but from thwarted, human love. She pitied him from her heart – she even wondered whether there had perhaps been a more general souring of his character. Perhaps it had been this injury which had turned the handsome young clergyman capable of preaching eloquently upon such a text as 'husbands love your wives' into the dry, narrow moralist that he was today...

And yet she could not excuse him. It was wrong: it was monstrous and hypocritical to use religion in inexorable punishment of a personal slight.

Chapter Nineteen

Deep in thought, Dido sewed carelessly, putting untidy stitches into the cravat which her fastidious brother would be sure to remark upon later.

The interview with Mr Portinscale troubled her greatly.

She recollected that her original task – the justification for beginning enquiries – was the removal of Miss Fenn's grave. And that removal lay within the parson's gift. If she was correct in supposing his resentment and disappointment were the main causes of his consigning the corpse to unhallowed ground, then overcoming that resentment was a matter of first importance.

But how was it to be accomplished? How was he to be worked upon? A man tormented by an old unrequited love was a formidable opponent. He would not easily be won over.

At the opening of their interview there had seemed to be some hope. He had certainly been fearful of offending Mrs Harman-Foote. She could not help but wonder why he was so very anxious for the lady's good opinion.

Her hands stilled upon her work and she looked through the arching curtain of yellow damson leaves to the bow window of the library, dimly perceiving two figures within. What was Mr Portinscale's business with her brother? she wondered. Was it perhaps connected with this anxiety over Mrs Harman-Foote?

Now that she considered the matter, she acknowledged that it was rather strange to see Mr Portinscale here at Badleigh Vicarage. For, although they were close neighbours, the two clergymen were, most certainly, not friends: Mr Portinscale being of rather an evangelical turn of mind which did not suit Francis Kent at all.

Suddenly restless, Dido jumped to her feet, picked up her workbasket and started towards the house.

She would not, of course, be so dishonourable as to try to overhear the gentlemen's conversation... But she might, perhaps, gain a sight of the visitor as he left and be able to judge something of his mood...

As she passed the library window she caught a glimpse of Francis sitting beside his desk – and Mr Portinscale pacing about on the carpet. And then, as she came into the hall from the garden door – and just paused for a moment in the shadow of the stairs – she saw that the library door was standing ajar.

She became suddenly very dissatisfied with the lacing of her boot; she put her basket on the hall table and stooped down to put the lace to rights... And, as she was doing so, Mr Portinscale's voice rang out very clearly from the library.

'In God's name, Kent! You have been in my situation; you know how difficult it is. Will you not put in a good word for me?'

'It would have no effect,' came in her brother's calmer voice. 'He is the master of Madderstone and will have all his own way. You had much better confess the truth.'

'Please! I beg you!' cried Mr Portinscale. Then he seemed to recollect himself and began to speak more quietly.

Dido lifted her face, struggling to catch the words. And, rather unluckily, it was just at this moment that Mr Lomax, rounded the corner of the stairs – and saw her.

Her little round face was tilted and sunlight from the stairs' window showed cheeks glowing with fresh air, a curl escaping from her cap onto the softness of her neck and wide green eyes which had all the eagerness – though not perhaps the innocence – of a child's.

'Miss Kent! Whatever are you about?' The blunt words were just saved from discourtesy by the unmistakable affection in his voice.

She looked up, blushed and began to stammer out an account of coming in from the garden…and noticing that her bootlace was unfastened and being obliged to stop just here…and put down her workbasket…and…

He raised his brows. His eyes strayed to the library door.

'I was not…' she began, but before she could say any more, the door of the parlour opened and Margaret sallied forth, dressed in her outdoor clothes and just pulling her gloves onto her hands.

'Oh there you are Dido!' she cried and stopped as she noticed her guest upon the stairs. She acknowledged him with a brief nod, before turning her attention back to her sister-in-law. 'I have been looking for you this last half-hour and I assure you I can very ill spare the time. For I absolutely *must* pay my visits this morning; I am quite ashamed of how I am neglecting my neighbours. But now I find the apple pies are still to be made, and I would be very much obliged to you, if *you* would just spare a moment or two to speak to Rebecca about them and see that they are done. It will not take above ten minutes I am sure and then you may enjoy your walking about and letter-writing as much as you please.'

And so Dido was obliged to quit the hall, without being able either to hear the end of the conversation in the library or to assure Mr Lomax that she had not been listening to it. And, as she started down the chilly stone passage to the kitchen, she did not know which circumstance to regret more.

What was the situation which Francis had shared with Mr Portinscale? And why did Mr Portinscale wish Francis to intercede with Mr Harman-Foote? And did this matter relate at all to Mr Portinscale's anxiety over offending that gentleman's wife? These were questions which must occur and yet to even ask them was to feel ashamed. She was mortified to have been discovered by Mr Lomax in so base an act as listening at a door… Well, she told herself comfortingly, she had not actually been *at* the door. She had been on quite the opposite side of the hall; her ear had not been pressed to the lock…

But still, she could not be comfortable about it. She ought not to have done it. This was curiosity at its most inexcusable. And he had known what she was about. The skin upon her neck prickled with discomfort at the thought.

She pushed open the kitchen door and stepped into warmth and the smell of damson jam. At the wide, scrubbed table, Rebecca was just securing the lids upon the last of the pots.

Dido delivered her message and then, obligingly, sat down at the table to peel apples while the maid carried away the jam to the pantry and began upon making pastry.

It was a rather peaceful place in which to think, well away from Margaret's intrusions – and the observation of Mr Lomax. The air was sweet with the scent of fruit and sugar and the bundles of drying rosemary and mint which hung above the table. An outer door was standing open upon the kitchen garden and pale October sunlight was streaming across the scrubbed flagstones, bringing with it a smell of warm damp earth and scraps of song from a particularly impertinent blackbird who now and then bobbed up to peer curiously into the room.

Slowly Dido began to regain her composure and, as she watched the long green curls fall away from her knife, she told herself that she must never, never again let her curiosity lead her into impropriety…

'That's odd Mr Portinscale coming to see the master, ain't it, miss?' remarked Rebecca as she spooned flour into her bowl.

Dido's knife stilled. She looked up to see Rebecca with her round red face tilted questioningly, waiting for encouragement to go on. She resumed her peeling. 'Yes,' she said offhandedly, 'I suppose it is. He does not often come.'

'He ain't a great one for visiting at all.'

'Is he not?'

'No, I reckon he thinks most folks are a bit too sinful for him to want to go visiting them.' Rebecca paused a moment in her spooning and gave a quick half-smile.

'He is certainly a very severe moralist,' Dido acknowledged. And she smiled back – though she knew she was breaking one of her grandmother's strictest rules and 'being familiar with servants'.

'Ah yes, miss,' said Rebecca significantly, 'he's certainly got a great deal to say about *other folk's* sins.'

And that, reflected Dido, was the great danger of breaking strict rules: it so often achieved precisely what one wanted... She could not resist. It was clear that Rebecca was full of some gossip which she was quite longing to share. Despite the resolution she had taken only minutes before, she leant a little closer across the table. 'Do you suspect that he is…a little less harsh upon himself?' she asked.

'Well, it ain't my place to say, of course, but I can't help feeling that's a bit odd – him being such a great one for the ten commandments…' Rebecca nodded significantly and began to work lard very vigorously into the flour, with the air of one who has a great deal she could say – if only she were not so charitable.

Dido took another apple from the basket, cut into its thick waxy skin – and waited. Now that she was begun, Rebecca would not be able to stop herself.

'…Well it is one of the commandments, ain't it?' Rebecca continued, half to herself, but with one questioning eye upon her companion.

'To which commandment are you referring?'

'Thou shalt not steal.'

'Indeed!' Dido's knife stopped again. She stared at Rebecca. 'Are you suggesting that Mr Portinscale has been stealing?'

Immediately Rebecca looked frightened. 'You won't tell anyone I said it, will you, miss?'

'No, no, of course I shall not. But are you sure of it? What has he stolen?'

Rebecca looked about her, as if she feared that the black-leaded range, or the clothes-horse, or even the coffee grinder, might somehow be concealing spies. When she was quite satisfied that they were alone, she dusted the flour off her hands. 'Cake!' she whispered.

'Cake?' The notion of the dry, severe clergyman purloining – and secretly devouring – cake was delightful, but scarcely believable. 'Cake?'

'And pie.' Rebecca smiled as she poured a little water into her bowl and began to stir. 'No end of it gone from the pantry, so his housekeeper says. Right angry she was about it and ready to beat the skin off the back of the poor boot boy. And then she found crumbs!'

'Crumbs?'

'In the reverend's study.' Rebecca shook a little flour onto the scrubbed wood of the table, lifted her pastry out of its bowl and took up her rolling pin. 'Now, what do you say to that then? Stealing cake out of his own pantry!' (It was clear that, to Rebecca, the fact that it was his *own* pantry only compounded the crime.)

'It is quite...extraordinary.'

'It certainly is. And another extr'ordin'ry thing is he ain't getting no fatter for it – nor is he stinting himself on his meals neither.' She set about her rolling, nodding sagely. 'If you ask me, that looks like he's *feeding someone* – secret like, you know.'

Chapter Twenty

...But, Eliza, I am sure I cannot conceive <u>who</u> the reverend gentleman might be feeding. He is certainly not a man who is noted for random acts of charity. Nor can I believe him to be one who would keep a good deed hidden.

So, whatever can he be about? Does this theft from his own pantry have anything to do with his odd conversation with Francis?

It is quite remarkable the way in which, once one has begun upon solving a mystery, one discovers so many strange and inexplicable things that it is impossible to know which are of importance and which are not. Indeed, I believe that we live surrounded by all manner of strangeness: that our neighbours all have secrets to hide, of which we know nothing until one chance circumstance causes us to begin enquiries.

Well, I am quite sure that you are shaking your head over that idea, for I know that you believe me to be too suspicious in general. I have not your remarkable talent for thinking only the best of my fellow men and women.

But I am growing quite uneasy about the Reverend Mr Portinscale.

At dinner I asked Francis the purpose of Mr Portinscale's visit and he <u>said</u> that he had come to discuss poachers. By Francis's account, the Rev. Mr P. believes that, since

Mr Harman-Foote cannot be persuaded to take strong measures, the other gentlemen of the neighbourhood should unite against this 'wicked assault upon property'.

Francis was, as you may imagine, no more anxious to exert himself in this cause than he is in any other. Though Margaret, I might add, took a rather different line. She was all for a little hanging and transporting – and opined that a man-trap or two would not go amiss either.

By the time we were got onto dessert, she was considering the merits of flogging. But enough of the pleasant dinner-table discourse of this household! It would be cruel if I were to continue; I should only make you discontent that you are not here to join in such elegant diversions!

To return to Mr Portinscale. Is it possible, Eliza, that he knows something of Miss Fenn's death? Could he have killed her in a passion of rage and abhorrence when he discovered that she was not the virtuous woman she appeared to be?

The facts of his having made his offer immediately before her disappearance and his obvious discomposure at her refusal do rather tell against him. And I have been considering again Mrs Philips' account of his 'attentions'. She reports that they had continued all summer; that the pair were quite in the habit of walking out together 'nearly every fine day'. Now, that would seem to suggest that Miss Fenn, if not exactly encouraging his attachment, was, at least, fond of his society.

Does that not seem rather remarkable to you, Eliza? That such a very handsome, passionate woman, firmly attached to another man, should freely choose to be in company with such a dull fellow as Mr P? Although, perhaps I should bear in mind that Mr Portinscale might have been a very different man then – before his hair became thin and his own resentment and self-consequence got the better of him.

And there is the annotation in the bible to consider too: Miss Fenn's feeling response to Mr Portinscale's discourse upon the tenderness of husbands – which might also suggest that she felt some affection for the speaker...

No, I cannot make it out at all!

I try again and again to look into the heart of this remarkable governess and find mysteries and contradictions at every turn.

If only she had had a confidante: a friend with whom she shared at least some portion of her feelings and her hopes. She certainly does not seem to have confided in her pupil. Which is, I suppose, not to be wondered at. To talk with any degree of freedom to a girl of thirteen would be extremely indelicate. But maybe there was some other friend. I think I had better consult with Mrs Philips over this.

For I must at any rate go to the abbey again today. I cannot be at ease in my mind until I have replaced the letter in the bible. I cannot keep it. I had considered making a copy before returning the original; but that did not seem honourable.

She paused in quite a glow of virtue – but then felt compelled to add:

Nor do I find that it is necessary, for every word is fixed in my memory.

Dido rather fancied that her feet were wearing a path between Badleigh Vicarage and Madderstone Abbey. But it was a pleasant walk, she reflected as she hurried once more through the wood.

She paused upon a footbridge that crossed the busy little stream. From here a broad ride led away into Madderstone village. The trunks of the overarching beeches were as grey and sombre as cathedral stone; but the leaves burnt red-brown upon their curving branches – and also on the floor of the ride. The day was mild and the sun was fetching up a slightly spicy scent from fallen beech-mast. Pigeons murmured comfortably and, somewhere close by, a woodpecker was, once again, at work.

As she rested, the scene enlarged. Mr Lomax appeared in the ride, walking towards her with long, hasty strides. He seemed to be in some agitation: his head was bowed in thought, his hands clasped behind his back. He kicked at a pebble with such violence it rustled away through the fallen leaves and splashed down into the brook.

'Miss Kent!' He stopped abruptly as he caught sight of her. There was such a look, such a fierce struggle for composure, as made her fear the meeting was unwelcome. But at last he bowed and came to stand beside her on the bridge – and seemed willing either to rest there with her, or to accompany her back along the ride if she wished it.

He had, he said, been paying a call at the abbey. 'There is a degree of acquaintance. We have met when I have visited a friend in Shropshire…'

He stopped speaking and regarded her so intently that she began to wonder whether there was something amiss in her appearance. However, it soon transpired that it was not her *looks* which were at fault.

'Mr Harman-Foote,' he continued in a tone of quiet control, 'has been telling me of his wife's distress at the horrible discovery in the lake: her unwillingness to believe that the poor woman took her own life.'

'Oh!' Dido turned her eyes resolutely upon the water gliding away beneath them; she watched a bright leaf as it spun around in an eddy, trapped by the pressure of water.

'He informs me that you have undertaken to help her prove there was…some other cause of death.' She stole a glance at his handsome, clever face. The brows were raised in a question, the strong jaw set in obstinate disapproval – but there was anxiety in the grey eyes. 'Is it true?' he asked.

She fixed her gaze once more upon the spinning leaf and reminded herself that his ill moods ought to concern her no longer. Now that her refusal was given she should be no more upset by his displeasure than pleased by his compliments.

'Yes, it is true,' she said firmly. 'And I am very sorry if you do not like it. But if you had seen the poor lady's wretchedness I am sure you would agree that I must help her.'

'I have had the pleasure of knowing you too long to ever doubt your compassion. However…' His fingers beat restlessly upon the wooden rail of the bridge.

'Your judgement is against me?'

'My judgement…' he began hastily. 'Or rather my advice…' He stopped himself. 'But, no, I am sorry. I have no right to advise you, Miss Kent. You have not chosen to bestow that privilege upon me.'

She coloured uncomfortably at the allusion and there was a short pause, filled only by the song of water and the woodpecker's stutter. She knew that, in a moment – when he had regained his composure – he would begin talking upon indifferent subjects like the well-bred man that he was: a remark upon the weather perhaps, or the beauty of the season...

And that would be worse than his disapproval! She did not wish for indifferent subjects. She might talk of those with everyone else in the world. But with him she had learnt the exquisite pleasure of reason, of ideas discussed and argued in a rational manner. And she found that she could not relinquish it.

'Very well,' she said, raising her face with an inviting smile. 'I shall not ask your opinion of my conduct; but what is your opinion of the subject?'

'The subject?'

'Do you believe that the coroner was correct in declaring for suicide?'

'Ah!' He looked wary. 'I have no reason to believe him *incorrect*.' He replied cautiously.

'Have you not? Perhaps Mr Harman-Foote failed to mention to you the very material fact that Miss Fenn's letters have been removed from her room.'

'No. He mentioned it. And perhaps I should add that he also mentioned the loss of the young woman's ring – for I am sure that is the next matter you will bring to my attention.'

Her smile broadened. 'And do these strange thefts not suggest to you that someone has a secret to hide – some motive for wishing the circumstances surrounding

Miss Fenn's death to remain in obscurity?'

'That, I grant you, is one interpretation.'

'You believe that another is possible?'

'I do.' He said gravely. 'Do you wish to hear my interpretation?'

'Most certainly!'

'Well, Mrs Harman-Foote's suffering at the discovery of the corpse is very evident; it is entirely possible that someone with her best interests at heart might remove the remembrances of her friend in order to prevent her dwelling upon the unpleasant subject.'

'But there has been no such effect. The losses have only added to her distress.'

'I did not say the actions were well judged,' he countered, 'only that the motives might be kindly.'

'I see.' She was forced to consider his theory carefully. It was possible. 'And this person who has Mrs Harman-Foote's best interests at heart, would, I suppose, be her husband?'

'Perhaps,' he acknowledged with a slight inclination of his head.

'Yes – and there was a hint of tobacco smoke in the room when we entered it,' she mused, 'which rather leads me to suppose that Mr Harman-Foote had been there just before us.'

There was a fleeting smile from the gentleman at this bit of cleverness, but it was quickly suppressed. 'And you have suspected him of removing the letters in order to hide his own guilt?' he asked.

'You must at least grant that it is a possibility.'

'A rather remote one, I think.'

'No!' she cried, stung by the note of dismissal in his voice. 'Not so very remote! Not when everything is taken into consideration.'

'Everything?' he repeated. His eyes narrowed suspiciously. 'And what is this "everything" which must be considered?'

'Oh!' Dido found herself fairly caught. For now she must either allow him to think her suspicions unfounded and unreasonable, or else put forward her proofs – and reveal the extent of her investigation.

She hesitated a moment over the desire of preserving his good opinion and the pleasure of disputing with him – but the latter won the day. And, fixing her eyes once more upon the turning leaf – which was now beginning to sink beneath the weight of water – she launched herself upon an account of everything which argued against suicide: the coins, the housekeeper's opinion that Miss Fenn had recovered from her melancholy, the position of the corpse in the pool...

He listened in silence, his hand all the while gripping the wooden rail of the bridge – his knuckles gradually whitening as her tale progressed.

She ended with an account of the letter in the bible. She had meant to leave it out, but, when she came to the point, she found that her case was incomplete without it, and her pride would not allow her to suppress it.

She finished her tale. Somewhere, deep among the trees, the woodpecker laughed to itself.

He became aware of his hand which seemed to be attempting to crush the rail of the bridge. Slowly he uncurled his fingers. 'And what was the import of this letter?' he asked stiffly.

She blushed but resolutely drew the letter from her pocket. 'You may read it for yourself.'

He hesitated and she amused herself by imagining that conflict between propriety and curiosity, so familiar to herself, now taking place within his dignified bosom. Finally he took the letter and she watched him in silence as he read both pages, sunlight and the shadows of leaves shifting constantly across his frowning face.

He finished and stood for a moment, his hand, with the papers still in it, resting upon the rail of the bridge, his eyes fixed thoughtfully upon her. A muscle moved restlessly in his cheek. He seemed to be forcing back angry words.

'The lady had a secret…attachment.' he said quietly at last.

'Yes, it would seem that she had.'

'And this is the end of your compassion for Mrs Harman-Foote? You are able to defame the reputation of her dead friend!'

Dido recoiled. 'It is unfortunate – but I could not have guessed…'

'And the best comfort you can offer the poor lady,' he ran on without seeming to hear her, 'is that her own husband is the guilty man; guilty not only of gross immorality, but of murder too!' He stopped. His hand had curled into a fist around the papers.

'I wish with all my heart,' she said, 'that the evidence were different – that it pointed to entirely different conclusions. But I cannot regret undertaking the enquiry. The fear of uncovering inconvenient truths should never make us content to accept lies.'

'You forget,' he said in a voice of quiet restraint, 'that I am not permitted to comment upon your conduct.'

'I beg your pardon,' she cried angrily, 'I rather thought that it was you that had forgotten it.'

'No,' he said, struggling against himself, quite shocked by the violence of his own emotions. 'I am not questioning your behaviour, madam, only your conclusions.'

'And what, pray, is amiss with my conclusions?'

'Nothing at all, except that they are ill-founded and entirely erroneous.'

'Oh?'

'I assure you,' he said, hastily returning the papers, 'Mr Harman-Foote did not write this letter.'

'But how can you know?'

'By the writing. He and I correspond from time to time on matters of business. This is certainly *not* his hand.' He bowed with great formality and hurried away: too angry to remain with her a moment longer.

Chapter Twenty-One

My Dear Eliza,

I congratulate you. I had no idea of your possessing the gift of premonition! It is quite remarkable.

When I returned home from Madderstone this afternoon there was awaiting me your letter, written three days ago and cautioning me against 'provoking poor Mr Lomax unnecessarily when he arrives at Badleigh'. Now, how could you know – without supernatural power – that I would do such a thing? I am quite sure that you have never detected in my extremely docile and accommodating nature anything which might be suspected of deliberately provoking a gentleman.

But I regret to inform you that you are doomed – like Cassandra of old – to have your wise warnings disregarded. You may consider Mr Lomax most thoroughly provoked. He has not spoken one word to me since a little meeting between us which occurred this morning. He has spent all evening at piquet with Margaret: which I consider to be a very bad sign indeed, for I am sure only a very strong desire of avoiding conversation could overcome his abhorrence of cards.

Dido, sitting rather stiffly upon her narrow bed, paused and leant her head against the sloping ceiling. The rain was once more pattering upon her dark window and the house becoming quiet as the family retired. Rebecca's weary feet had already tramped past her door and now there was only the ticking of the clock on the landing and the occasional creak of settling floorboards.

But she could not sleep. Now that she was alone, fragments of her conversation with Mr Lomax would recur, and Eliza's letter was also oddly disquieting. It was not in Eliza's nature to detect faults in anyone, least of all her beloved sister, and yet there had been in this morning's letter a rare hint of criticism. After anticipating Mr Lomax's provocation, she had continued:

...I wonder sometimes, whether your quick wits do not make you just a little outspoken. Please do not misunderstand me, Dearest, I know that you never express an opinion which is not sound, and very clever, but I fear that sometimes gentlemen may misunderstand you.

Dido, do you remember the Reverend Mr Clarke who came to stay with the Fordwicks when we were one and twenty? He was a very pleasant gentleman, with three good livings – and so very much in love with you! I was quite sure he would make you an offer. But you would argue so with him!

Dido could not help but feel it was a little unfair of her sister to mention the Reverend Mr Clarke. For she had not exactly *argued* with him... She had done no more than tell him she disapproved of pluralism in the clergy – and light-coloured morning coats. And those were opinions which were better expressed immediately, for a wife could certainly not have kept them to herself *after* marriage – not if she were married to a man such as Mr

Clarke, who was possessed of three livings – and a rather pale morning coat…

No, she assured herself, she was not argumentative… only honest. She bent her head once more over her page.

However, Eliza, I do not quite agree that Mr Lomax's being provoked was <u>unnecessary</u>. For if the poor misguided man will persist in expecting me to be what I am not, then I must conclude that his disappointment is inevitable. He has no reason to suppose me reformed since our last meeting in Richmond; no cause at all to suppose me less curious or more inclined to rest contented with half truths when a little effort might uncover the whole.

Well, I suppose he is now congratulating himself upon his happy escape; for this morning's little discussion must have proved to him how very unquiet his domestic life would have been had I accepted his offer of marriage.

She stopped. To her very great surprise a tear was splashing down upon the letter. And now a fit of sobbing seized her, shaking her whole frame – and even the frame of the bed. It was quite unaccountable: she had never in her life indulged in such an excess of sensibility – had always supposed herself quite incapable of it. But the pen was slipping from her hand, smearing the counterpane with ink, and the writing desk was clattering to the floor. She was curling up upon the bed.

Astonishing – impossible – though it seemed, Miss Dido Kent, that most composed and determinedly rational of creatures, was giving way to a fit of hysterics.

* * *

This outburst was all the more remarkable for following on a day of the most rational and useful pursuits. The little disagreement with Mr Lomax had not overset her at the time. Indeed, she had been rather pleased with her own composure in the face of his anger and, although she had rested about a quarter of an hour upon the bridge after he left her, at least seven and a half of those fifteen minutes had been spent in considering, not his displeasure, but his information.

It was *that*, she had rapidly decided, which must concern her. His ill temper was his own affair. She would not give it another thought... But his certainty that Mr Harman-Foote had not written the letter was of the first importance. It not only disproved her strongest suspicion, it also pointed a way forward for her investigations.

And, upon this subject, she had even had the grace to admit that Mr Lomax's impatience was well-founded. It had, of course, been very stupid of her not to think before of comparing the handwriting, for such an undertaking might serve not only to discount the innocent, but also to uncover the guilty man.

Tapping her fingers on the rail of the bridge, she counted out the objects of her suspicion – the men whose handwriting she must try to get a sight of.

There was Mr Portinscale – though how she might gain a look at his writing she could not yet determine; and there was old Mr Harman – some correspondence of his might survive in his daughter's possession, or in the library at Madderstone; and there was Captain Laurence... She stopped. But, of course, she knew the captain's writing already! She recalled the looped characters of the message written to Penelope on the *Navy List* – and hurriedly unfolded the letter she was holding...

No. She was quite sure that there was no likeness at all. The writing of Miss Fenn's 'Beloved' had no loops upon it. It was strong and straightforward with a vigorous forward slant.

Dido was on the point of putting up the letter when, quite suddenly, it flashed into her mind that the hand was not entirely unfamiliar to her. Spreading out the page in the dappled sunshine of the wood, she became quite certain that there was something about it which she recognised. She had seen a hand rather like it – and seen it recently. But where? The actual details eluded her – but the suspicion was extremely useful in dispelling any lingering solicitude over Mr Lomax's behaviour.

She folded the papers away and turned resolutely towards Madderstone. She would busy herself about her mystery: she must begin to look about her for examples of handwriting – and she must also discover whether Miss Fenn had had any confidante who could be applied to for information concerning Mr Portinscale's offer of marriage.

She certainly had no time to waste upon idle regrets.

Chapter Twenty-Two

Dido found Mrs Philips busily watering plants in Madderstone Abbey's great hothouse and lost no time in bringing forward a question about Miss Fenn's friends and acquaintances.

'No, miss,' said Mrs Philips, setting down her pail and pressing a hand to her back as she straightened up, 'I don't reckon there was anyone hereabouts that Miss Fenn was what you might call *intimate* with – though she always had a pleasant word for everyone, I'm sure.'

'There was no one she visited?'

The housekeeper frowned thoughtfully and Dido waited with the sun shining through the glass and warming the back of her head.

'No.' Mrs Philips pinched a dead leaf from a myrtle bush. 'At least,' she said, 'she'd not paid many visits since she stopped going to call on that Mrs Pinker.'

'Mrs Pinker?'

'Yes, she used to visit *her*; but she wasn't from round here. Lived over Great Farleigh way I believe.'

'And did Miss Fenn visit her often?'

The shadows of clustering vine leaves shifted across Mrs Philips' face as she struggled to remember. 'She used to go to her once a week…on a Thursday afternoon,' she said. 'That is, she used to go the first few years she was here. Used to drive herself over there in the pony carriage. But she'd left off going lately – I mean a year or two before she disappeared.'

'I see.' Dido was very disappointed to find that the friendship had lapsed before Mr Portinscale's courtship began. But the information might be of use. If Mrs Harman-Foote could be persuaded to make her carriage available, a visit to Great Farleigh ought to be made. Mrs Pinker might not know how the clergyman's advances had been received but she might be able to tell something of Miss Fenn's character and connections. Yes, she thought, she would call upon Mrs Pinker at the earliest opportunity. It was at least something to be doing. Activity, and having something to think about, seemed to be of the first importance with her just now…

Meanwhile, her companion was dusting a little earth from her hands and looking anxious. 'Miss Kent,' she began, 'I wonder whether I might make so bold as to ask how you are going on with finding out about the ghost?' As she spoke she looked out through the vine's crowding foliage to the ruins, just visible beyond the despoiled lawns. 'Have you found out what might be carrying on over there? Pardon me for asking about it, but Mrs Harman-Foote told me you'd been kind enough to say you would…look into it.'

Dido was forced to confess that, as yet, she had no notion of what might be 'carrying on over there'.

'Ah dear,' said Mrs Philips. 'I was in hopes you might be able to talk a little sense into the housemaids. They're all full of it and now Mary-Ann says she's so scared of the ghost she means to leave at Christmas. I declare, miss, I'd be very glad if you could get to the bottom of all this business of lights and haunting.'

'Lights?' repeated Dido rather puzzled – and then she remembered Lucy Crockford mentioning lights being seen in the gallery.

'Yes,' said Mrs Philips, looking very troubled. 'There certainly *are* lights, miss. At first I paid no attention to what was being said – I thought it was all in the girls' heads. But then Mrs Jones came to me and said *she* had seen a light in the old ruins – when she was coming back late from her afternoon off. "Dear me!" I thought. "We are in a sorry state if such a steady old thing as Mrs Jones is taking fancies into her head!" So the next night – close on midnight – out I go myself. And, sure enough, there was a light! Just a faint one – and darting about a bit.'

'Like a ghost?'

The housekeeper looked at her shrewdly, her brows raised. 'Well, miss,' she said, 'I wouldn't know about that on account of never having seen a ghost. But I've seen a lantern being swung about as it's carried – and that's what it looked like to me.'

'Did it, indeed?' Dido stepped past the pots of marjoram and myrtle and pressed her face to the warm, steamy glass so that she could see the jagged walls and broken arches of the abbey more clearly. But the great nave of the abbey church presented only a blank wall. The gallery faced out across the parkland and no light upon it would be visible from the house. 'Now who would be carrying a lantern about up there so late at night?' she mused.

'Someone up to no good,' said the housekeeper with great conviction.

Someone up to no good upon the gallery. For some reason the description brought Captain Laurence immediately to Dido's mind. A memory struck her with such force that she reached out to hold the gnarled trunk of the vine. The damp, peaty heat of the glasshouse seemed to be choking her.

She was remembering how the captain had come to inspect the gallery on the day that the bones were discovered. He had been so very interested in the place. His manner had been so secretive… And he had seemed to be searching for something…

Was it possible that Captain Laurence had returned to the ruins to continue his search – at night, when he might do so unobserved?

'You are quite right to remind me, Mrs Philips,' she said with sudden determination – and very pleased indeed to have a fresh cause of activity. 'I believe I should be paying much more attention to what is "carrying on" over in the ruins.'

The housekeeper's words had not exactly reminded Dido of the ghost in the ruins, for she had certainly not forgotten it; but they had served to recall her to its possible significance.

For she now remembered that the captain had behaved rather strangely when he visited the scene of the accident. She recalled how very thoughtful he had been – and how interested he had been to discover that Penelope could see the pool at the moment when she fell.

At the time, this circumstance had passed almost unnoticed. But now – now that she knew him to have had some foreknowledge of the skeleton's presence in the pool – it took on a great deal more significance…

Was it possible that he been considering a connection between Penelope's fall and the murdered woman?

At the beginning of this business – at the time of the inquest – Dido had herself suspected such a connection. But lately she had been drawn away by other matters and had rather overlooked the haunting… Perhaps that had been a mistake. Perhaps in pursuing the ghost she might discover something about Miss Fenn's death. She should visit the ruins again to see whether this late-night visitor, this carrier of a lantern, had left behind any evidences.

She bade a rather abrupt farewell to the housekeeper, left the house and hurried busily along the gravel path towards the ruins, the air of the autumn morning raw and cold against her face after the clinging heat of the hothouse. Over on the lawns among the felled trees, a wagon was being loaded with great logs and a pair of big, placid workhorses were dragging away tree stumps, the rattling of chains and the shouts of their driver carrying clearly in the stillness. A raven rose from the abbey walls, crying harshly as she approached.

She walked meditatively across the cloisters, where little stunted hawthorns had broken through the stone flags worn smooth by the feet of long-dead nuns, and passed through a fallen wall into the remains of the nave. And, as she did so, she heard a sound from the gallery above – slight though it was, it echoed about the high, damp walls. She held her breath and listened intently.

The sound came again – a slow, heavy footfall.

She crept very carefully across the broken pavement, and peered up into the gallery. There was a man up there: a dark figure against pale grey sky, framed by an arch of stone. For a moment the power of her expectations caused her to see Captain Laurence; but then there was a slight movement and the shape resolved itself into Henry Coulson.

Without hesitating to think what she was about, she gathered up her skirts and quietly climbed the steps.

Mr Coulson had his back turned towards her. He was walking slowly along the gallery, studying the floor as he went. About halfway along he stopped, bent down, picked something up, then looked about and picked up one, two, three more things before tucking them all away inside his coat. Dido was upon the tips of her toes, her fingers clutching tightly at the ivy for support as she endeavoured to see what he was gathering so carefully; but the bulk of his body obscured her view and, try as she might, she could not make it out…

He straightened up – and turned around.

'Miss Kent!' he cried. His face became very red; he laughed nervously. 'You quite surprised me!' He hurried towards her. 'I was…just looking about me, you know.' He insisted upon taking her hand and shaking it, whether she would or not. 'I declare I am monstrous glad to see you, Miss Kent!' he cried. 'For, d'you know, you are the very person I have been thinking I must talk to?'

'Indeed?' said Dido, stepping into the gallery's dank atmosphere and looking up at him with some surprise. He was a thickset young man with a decided air of fashion, untidy fair hair and rather weak, pale eyes which were blinking and peering in the shadows of the gallery. Now that the first shock of being observed was over, he was regaining his usual air of easy familiarity.

'Yes indeed! I'll warrant you are just the woman to help me! As soon as I set eyes upon you, I said to myself, now there's a remarkably clever woman and I'll wager fifty pounds she's the very person to advise me.'

'I am sure I should be very glad to be of service to you, Mr Coulson, but I do not know…' Dido was now attempting to peer beyond him, without seeming to do so. She was particularly anxious to see whether there was anything still lying upon the flagstones.

'And good-natured too,' he cried, 'which is just as I thought. Now then,' he said leaning easily against a pillar, 'what do you think of this surgeon fellow – Paynter? For I expect you've known him for ever.'

'Mr Paynter,' said Dido very much astonished at the question, 'is a very respectable man: very knowledgeable, and exceedingly well regarded in his profession.'

Mr Coulson's small eyes narrowed above his rather snubbed nose. 'Is he now?' he said keenly. But then he laughed. 'Well, I daresay he does well enough. But I'll warrant his patients die a great deal, do they not? Come, they do, don't they?'

Dido stared. 'I am sure,' she began rather warmly, 'that they die a great deal less…' She stopped, realising that she too was now talking nonsense. 'I am sure,' she said with careful precision, 'that Mr Paynter's patients are a great deal less likely to die for consulting with him.'

'Yes, but he is just a country fellow. Why, I'll wager a

thousand pounds he scarcely knows Galen and Harvey and has never heard of Edward Jenner!'

'As to that,' said Dido doubtingly, 'I hardly know.' She could see beyond him now – and was quite sure that there was nothing lying on the floor of the gallery – nothing but one or two green and brown feathers. 'I never heard Mr Paynter speak of those gentlemen,' she said, 'but, really, I know nothing about his acquaintances.'

'Excellent!' he cried, very well pleased. 'That is just as I thought! An ignorant country fellow!'

Dido was uneasy: she did not quite like him being so well satisfied with her information. 'Why do you think so badly of Mr Paynter?' she asked.

'Oh, it is nothing. Merely that I went to the inquest, you know, and there was this bumbling fellow talking – and the whole room listening and saying how much he was to be trusted on account of him being "a very clever medical man", which, you see, I could not help laughing at!'

Dido looked up at him sharply. 'You mistrust Mr Paynter's testimony?'

He smiled knowingly and tapped the side of his nose. 'I think he knows nothing at all and had better be disregarded,' he said.

Dido's last visit of the day was to the front of the house – in search of Mrs Harman-Foote. She wished to solicit the use of the carriage – and also to make a few more enquiries about Miss Fenn's acquaintances. For a little reflection upon the matter had brought her to suspect that Anne Harman-Foote might know more than she was telling about 'the woman who had brought her up'.

She was fortunate enough to arrive in the drawing room just after the children had quitted it for the nursery dinner. The room – and the mother – had a rather fagged, weary appearance. There were toys and books everywhere: a wooden doll lolled against the elegant gilded leg of a chair with a decidedly wine-flown appearance; spillikins sticks, toy soldiers and a ragged Latin grammar covered the sofas. Anne had her hair pulled down about one ear and the imprint of a small hand upon the pale grey silk of her gown in what appeared to be plum jam.

Dido brought forward the name of Mrs Pinker, but Anne immediately shook her head. No, she was quite sure she had never heard of the woman.

Might she have forgotten?

Oh, no. She never forgot a name. And, as for the carriage, of course it would be at Dido's disposal whenever she wished. 'But,' Anne added anxiously, 'I doubt I shall be able to accompany you. My poor Georgie is suffering from the most distressing bilious attack and I cannot leave him alone so long as it would take to travel there. It is a principle of mine *never* to leave my children when they are sick.'

Dido readily assured her that her help would not be necessary in the search for Mrs Pinker – for it would, in point of fact, suit her rather well to go to Great Farleigh alone.

But Anne continued with an account of poor dear Georgie's symptoms, which was a great deal more detailed than it had any cause to be. To distract herself from it Dido formed a representation of the Battle of Blenheim with the soldiers upon the sofa, then picked up the Latin grammar and began idly to look it over – discovering stale cake crumbs adhering to several of its battered pages...

'But, now,' continued Anne in a dangerously businesslike voice, 'we must talk about Mr Lomax. When he called here this morning I was most particular in bringing the conversation around to you.'

'Oh!' Dido put down the grammar. 'I do not think you had better trouble yourself with recommending me to Mr Lomax after all,' she said as firmly as she could. 'He and I have argued – you see he does not approve of my interesting myself in Miss Fenn's death.'

Anne regarded her with alarm. 'You did not talk to Mr Lomax about *that*, did you?'

'Why, yes.'

'My dear Dido, that is not a subject to discuss with a gentleman! When talking to a man a woman must *always* avoid any topic upon which disagreement is possible – it is a principle of mine.'

'But even if such a principle were sustainable before marriage,' Dido protested, 'it could not be maintained *after*.'

Anne looked puzzled. 'Why,' she said, 'I do not believe that Mr Harman-Foote and I have ever found it an inconvenience.'

Dido was silenced. She let Anne talk on about Mr Lomax – and turned her mind to thinking about cake instead...

Chapter Twenty-Three

Great Farleigh was a large, populous village which had almost grown into a town with the aid of a particularly fast-flowing stream and a half-dozen or so mills and weaving sheds which had been established along its banks. The narrow streets were filled with people intent upon business, and with wagons carrying sacks of grain to the miller, logs to the sawmills and bales of cloth from the manufactories. Builders were at work upon the ragged remains of a village green, raising a new row of cottages, and their loud shouts and oaths were added to the rattle of carts, the whine of sawmills and the ceaseless low thunder of the great waterwheels.

Dido held up a hand as if to protect herself from the noise as she descended from Madderstone's carriage in the grimy, confined little yard of the inn – for her head ached dreadfully from the tears of the previous night – and quickly made her way into the inn's chilly parlour where, in keeping with the general busyness of the village, no one was at leisure to attend her. A quarter of an hour's perseverance produced little information – or refreshment: only a pot of cold, bitter coffee, a shrug of the shoulders and, 'No, I can't ever remember hearing of no Pinker... Well, maybe she lives here, maybe she don't... I couldn't say.'

So she determined on making more enquiries in the village, but was met at the inn door by Jed Waters, the Madderstone coachman, who was, very kindly, intent upon accompanying her, 'on account of the folk round here being a bit rough in their manners – and you not used to their ways, miss.'

She thanked him, but insisted upon his remaining at the inn to refresh himself and his horses. 'For we have had a seven-mile drive,' she said. 'I am sure you are in need of rest before returning.'

And she made her way back across the busy, cobbled yard – wondering a little as she did so about those seven miles which lay between Madderstone and Great Farleigh. Now that she came to consider it, she saw that seven miles was a great distance for a lady to travel alone in a pony carriage. And yet, such was the esteem in which Miss Fenn had been held, she could not doubt that a different conveyance would have been put at her disposal, had she desired it.

What had been her motive in driving herself so far? Secrecy perhaps? Had she wished her employer's household to remain ignorant of her exact destination? This idea quickened Dido's interest and made her more determined than ever to discover all that she might about the mysterious Mrs Pinker.

But when she reached the archway that led into the street, she was forced to stop. A large cart was just turning into the yard at a rapid pace with a horseman riding beside it. She stepped back into the shadow of the inn's walls and they clattered past her without seeming to notice that they had almost run her down.

'Hey fellow!' shouted the rider to a passing ostler. 'Has the London coach gone? Damn my luck! I'll wager fifty pounds it has!'

Dido turned immediately at the sound of the familiar voice and saw Henry Coulson, swinging himself out of his saddle – and being reassured by the ostler that, no sir, the coach weren't yet come, but it'd likely be here in ten minutes, for he was almost sure he'd heard the horn very faint…

'Why, I'm monstrous glad of it, for I'd have been in a fine pickle if I'd missed it. Now,' handing a coin to the man, and gesturing at the cart, 'you make sure this box is safely stowed aboard. It's mighty important it gets to town today.' And, with a tap at his nose, he was off through the parlour door.

Dido watched him go with great interest and wondered very much why he should put himself to the trouble of bringing his box here. A London coach passed within two miles of the abbey and stopped every day at the Red Lion in Badleigh…

She could not resist stepping closer to look at the box which the cart driver and the ostler were now, with some difficulty, lifting out of the bottom of the deep cart. It seemed rather heavy, though small to be the only cargo in such a large cart: long, and narrow, it was made of deal and clasped at the corners with iron plates.

'What's he got stowed in this, solid gold?' grunted the ostler.

'I don't know,' replied the carter quickly. 'Ain't none of my business what he's got in it. I just drive it for him.' And he lowered the box onto the cobbles as if he wanted rid of it.

Dido peered over his shoulder as he bent down and read the label pasted on the lid. *To John Kenning, Leadenhall.* How very interesting…

The carter was climbing back onto his seat and gathering up the reins, eager to be gone. The ostler looked up.

'Can I help you, miss?'

'Oh!' She blushed and stepped back hastily. 'Oh, no thank you… That is… I wondered whether you might direct me to the haberdasher's shop.'

He did so, but as he was talking, she kept her eyes upon the box – and noticed that there were one or two damp leaves clinging to it, and that a very thin trickle of liquid was now running from the edge of one of its iron plates, forming a little dark stream through the dirty cobbles. And then, as she thanked the ostler and started off across the yard, she became aware of a smell. It was very faint, but it was something other than the usual inn-yard odour of horses, dust and sour ale: something sweet and very slightly rotten. And she was almost sure that it was coming from the box…

There was no more information to be got about Mrs Pinker in the haberdasher's shop than there was at the inn. It seemed that the good people of Great Farleigh bought their laces and their cottons and their knitting-pins as rapidly as they did everything else, and had no time at all to talk about their neighbours. The woman behind the long counter shook her head at Dido's questions, astonished to be asked about anything other than haberdashery. However, a woman with a pair of whining children hanging upon her skirts did interrupt her hurried selection of shirt buttons long enough to suggest that Dido might make enquiries at the post office.

It was an excellent thought and Dido praised the buyer of shirt buttons so warmly for it, that she was rewarded with a little smile – and a few hasty directions.

The directions took her back to a muddy lane beside the inn, a tiny room adjoining the stables and a very old man upon a very high stool who was so exceedingly short-sighted that he was obliged to hold the letters he was sorting within a half-inch of his spectacles in order to read their covers.

And…yes, he certainly knew Mrs Pinker. He continued with his work.

Might he be so very kind as to direct her to the lady's house?

He slowly lowered the letter he had been reading, pushed his spectacles to the very end of his long nose and studied her. He seemed, after all, to be the one inhabitant of the village who had time to spare. She waited. A couple of fat, sleepy bluebottles buzzed loudly in the window. At last he shook his head with a 'Well, well,' as if he were somehow shocked at her enquiring after Mrs Pinker.

'I beg your pardon?' said Dido.

'Nothing! Nothing at all!' He hurriedly picked up another letter and hid his face behind it. 'Out along the Upper Farleigh road, that's where you'll find her. 'Bout half a mile out. Green gate in a high garden wall. You can't mistake it.'

'Thank you.'

She turned to go, but, just as she reached the door,

he said something else very quietly – something which sounded rather like, 'I doubt she'll be able to oblige you.'

She stopped. 'I beg your pardon?' she said again.

'Nothing! Nothing at all!' he said, very busy with his letters.

The noise of the village faded rapidly as Dido made her way along the road which led to Upper Farleigh. The muddy street became a broad, steep track and the crowding houses gave way upon one side to fields of stubble, yellowing hazel thickets and hedgerows bright with rosehips and hawthorn berries. Upon the other side of the road were now more prosperous-looking cottages with honeysuckle fences and mounded onion beds.

As she walked, she wondered about Mrs Pinker, the kind of house she kept here – and the nature of Miss Fenn's acquaintance with her… And of one thing she was certain: such a very busy village would be an excellent place for the keeping of a secret. Perhaps both Miss Fenn and Mr Coulson had discovered how to use that fact to their advantage.

The old man's grudging information was accurate. She found the wall and the gate – which was unlocked – and let herself into a rather pleasing, but overgrown, little garden. The air was full of the heady scent of crab apples fermenting in long grass, and from a branch of the ancient apple tree hung a low, lopsided swing. A great mass of rose bushes gone wild clambered about the gate, snatching at her hands as she replaced the latch. A pigeon was warbling comfortably to itself somewhere close by, and a little tabby cat was trotting along the cinder path to greet her.

The house, old and low-built and more than half-covered with ivy, was too large for a labourer's cottage, but certainly not a gentleman's dwelling… The home of a shopkeeper perhaps, she calculated…or a family that was prospering in a humble trade… It was altogether a rather surprising establishment for such a woman as Miss Fenn to be visiting…

The cat, as attentive as a footman, conducted her to a porch where a dilapidated hobby horse was propped beside a low old door. A minute or two of knocking produced at last an elderly maid and the information that it was quite impossible to see the mistress.

'Why, she's gorn away to her sister's on a visit, miss! She won't be back these three days yet.' The maid shook her head in amazement at Dido's ignorance of these facts.

'Oh dear. That is a great shame, I was hoping most particularly to speak with her. I have made quite a long journey.'

The maid sucked in a breath through her teeth and shook her head again. She seemed to be a woman who was continually surprised by the folly of her fellow creatures. 'You ain't come here on business are you?' she said pityingly.

'Well, yes, in a manner of speaking.'

The maid shook her head and all but echoed the words of the man in the post office. 'No, no! Mrs Pinker won't be able to oblige you…madam. She ain't taking no more. She ain't taken none this last twelvemonth.'

'Oh.'

The maid curtseyed and, with a final shake of her head in compassion for the simplicity of her visitor, she was upon the point of closing the door. Dido thought rapidly, eagerly trying to guess at the precise nature of Mrs Pinker's 'business'. 'I wonder,' she cried hurriedly, 'I wonder whether you might be able to…advise me…'

The maid waited with an air of great impatience, her hand still upon the door.

Dido looked about her – at the hobby horse – and the swing. And she considered also the insolent interest of the man in the post office – and the alteration in the maid's address – that telling change from 'miss' to 'madam' as soon as she suspected that the visitor was, 'come on business'.

An idea occurred.

'Perhaps,' she said, 'you might be able to suggest another establishment. You see,' she continued slowly, watching the woman's face closely, 'a friend of mine is very anxious to place a child in the care of just such an experienced, respectable woman as your mistress. If Mrs Pinker is no longer taking in children, I would be very grateful if you would be so kind as to suggest another woman to whom my friend might apply?'

Before she had finished speaking, Dido knew, from the maid's manner, that she had guessed aright. Mrs Pinker's business was, without doubt, the care of children.

The maid sighed impatiently. 'Well, I don't know… There's Mrs Hardwick, I suppose. You might try her. How old is the little 'un?'

'About eight…or nine,' Dido hazarded.

'Oh no!' cried the maid. 'No, Mrs Hardwick's like

the mistress, they don't neither of them keep 'em on that old! It's up to seven she keeps girls – and not beyond five for boys. They need schooling after that, that's what the mistress says.'

'Yes…yes, of course.'

'Is it a boy or girl?'

'Oh! It is a…er…girl.'

'Well then your friend might try Mrs Nolan's school in Bath.'

'Mrs Nolan…?' said Dido. A memory stirred at the sound of the name, but she could not quite make it out.

'Yes, yes,' the maid replied and repeated the name with emphasis, as if it were one which all the world ought to know. 'Mrs Nolan. It's her Mrs Pinker sends her girls on to. Holds her in very high regard, she does.'

'Thank you.'

The maid bobbed and began to inch the door closed.

'Oh, please, just a moment,' cried Dido eagerly. 'There was something else which I wished to ask.'

'Yes?' There was a long sigh.

'I wondered whether you might recall an acquaintance of mine – a Miss…' She stopped, remembering the recent careful change in her own status. It was, probably, a courtesy extended to all women who did 'business' with Mrs Pinker. 'Mrs Fenn. Mrs Elinor Fenn?'

'Oh!' The maid pushed back the door a little way and peered at the visitor, showing interest in her for the first time. 'Yes,' she said warily, peering around the door's edge. 'I recall the mistress speaking of her. But that was a long time ago her little 'un was here. Before I came.'

'So you do not know what became of her child?'

'No, I don't,' she said flatly. 'And, pardon me for speaking plain, but if I knew anything I wouldn't tell it. It's the rule – Mistress says I'm never to talk about the little 'uns. Folks have secrets, she says, and it's part of our business to help keep those secrets. And that's what I told the young gentleman when he came here.'

'The young gentleman?'

'Ah – the fellow who came asking about Mrs Fenn two months back. And the mistress told him the same I know – for I don't reckon she liked the look of him any better than I did. But he was set on finding out...' She stopped with a suspicious look. 'What's happened to this Mrs Fenn that everyone is asking about her?'

'Oh nothing has happened to her,' said Dido quickly. Clearly news of the inquest had not yet spread to Great Farleigh – and probably would not until a report was printed in the newspapers next week. 'I just wondered...'

But the maid – mindful perhaps of 'the rule' – was now edging the door closed again.

Dido thanked her and turned back along the cinder path wondering who the 'young gentleman', can have been. And why had he been asking questions?

And where had she heard the name of Nolan before?

She was almost back to Great Farleigh when the answer to this last question occurred – and the memory brought her to a standstill in the lane between the hawthorn hedges and the cottage gardens, her eyes staring, her hands pressed to her mouth.

Mrs Nolan was the keeper of a school in Bath. She was, in fact, Penelope's guardian...

Chapter Twenty-Four

...And so you see, Eliza, my two mysteries, Penelope's accident and the skeleton in the pool, are now joined together!

I knew all along that they must somehow be connected!

But the discovery has thrown all my ideas into a great muddle and, if you are not so indulgent as to allow me to share my perplexities with you, I believe I shall run mad!

You see, I have made the necessary calculations and – unless my arithmetic deceives me – it can certainly be made to fit. I mean <u>it is possible that Penelope is Miss Fenn's child.</u> There was gratification in this discovery for a mind such as mine which delights in patterns and connections and the complete absence of coincidences.

But I soon began to see that there is little cause for rejoicing.

For, supposing Penelope is indeed Miss Fenn's daughter – what kind of sense does this make of recent events? What force has brought her back to the very place at which her mother met her death – and at the very time at which that death is discovered? And what am I – as a determinedly rational woman – to make of the ghost which Penelope saw? Was it somehow conjured into being by the discovery – or rather the proximity – of her mother's remains?

Now, you see, I am got into a morass of coincidence and supernatural happenings which does not suit me at all!

But I intend to confine myself entirely to reason. I shall not allow my fancy to get the better of me. The only sensible course of action is to make some quiet enquiries into Miss Lambe's background with a view to determining whether she is indeed the child that Miss Fenn placed in Mrs Pinker's care.

You would laugh if you could see me just now, Eliza, for I am writing this from the kitchen. My writing desk stands upon the table here between the knife box and a great dish of curds, and I am in perpetual danger of mistaking the salt pot for my sand shaker. Rebecca is abed, suffering from a sudden and rather surprising attack of the asthma, and her assistant is gone out upon errands. So I am deputed to keep the spit wound up and to watch over the rising of the bread. I only hope I may acquit myself well. At least I have a warm and quiet place in which to think.

And my thoughts are rioting!

I have spent a <u>great deal</u> of time wondering about the mysterious 'young gentleman' who lately visited Mrs Pinker. I do wish that I had had an opportunity to ask the maid about his looks. For I am sure his identity is of the utmost importance.

Who is he? Why is he making the same enquiries that I am making? And is he the person who has stolen the letters and the ring? His being described as a <u>young</u> man, makes it almost impossible he can be Miss Fenn's 'Beloved'.

Maybe he is Captain Laurence. The captain might, I suppose, be considered young – at least by a woman as elderly as Mrs Pinker's maid – and I cannot escape the idea that he is deeply involved in this business...

I have just had a little interval in which I wound up the

spit and removed the cat from the curds. And, while I was about it, I began to consider Mr Coulson.

Perhaps Mr Coulson is the mysterious inquirer. I know he is a visitor to Great Farleigh. And I keep remembering his words to me on the gallery: his implied contempt for Mr Paynter. Why should he wish the surgeon's testimony to be distrusted? Is he, also, attempting to prove that Miss Fenn was murdered? Is that why he would discredit the surgeon? For, after all, it is largely upon Mr Paynter's evidence that the inquest verdict rests.

Yesterday, I fell in with Mr Paynter himself – I found him here in the kitchen consulting with Rebecca – and I took the opportunity of enquiring whether he is at all acquainted with Mr Coulson. He considered the question carefully as he always does and replied that he was 'only very <u>slightly</u> acquainted with the young gentleman'. But there was certainly that in his manner which hinted at disapproval: a suggestion that he would not wish the degree of acquaintance to be any greater. So I rather suspect that Mr Coulson's criticisms have been general and sustained enough to reach his ears.

But I cannot think of a reason why Mr Coulson should interest himself in the business of Miss Fenn's death, any more than I can imagine what he might have been conveying in his malodorous box.

No, I cannot make it out at all.

But at least I can now see my way forward. I must make enquiries into Penelope's history. It cannot be impossible to find out just who she is. After all, <u>someone</u> maintains her at Mrs Nolan's school. The great object must be to discover who it is that pays her allowance.

* * *

Dido soon began upon her enquires into Penelope's birth, but it would seem that there was not a great deal to know upon the subject.

Lucy Crockford, though assuring Dido that she knew *everything* about dear Pen, that they were like sisters and would not for the world keep secrets from one another, could only say that Penelope had been at Mrs Nolan's school since she was five years old; that she had been raised to the status of parlour boarder several years ago; and that she was certainly the natural daughter of *somebody*. Although Lucy, being such an extraordinarily sensitive and generous woman, had never found the circumstances of birth a barrier to friendship. She was much too tender-hearted to blame the child for the faults of the parents…

'Yes, yes, of course,' said Dido. 'But how did you become acquainted with Miss Lambe? Have you known her long?'

'Oh! No, I would not say I have known her *long*. But I have often observed that time alone does not determine intimacy. It is rather a matter of disposition, you know. And Pen and I are so remarkably well suited that I believe we were intimate within seven days. And she is so *very* happy to be with us you know, and I am sure…'

'But, in point of fact, when did you meet her?'

'About six weeks ago – when Harriet and I were last in Bath. Captain Laurence introduced us.'

'Did he indeed?' said Dido with great interest. And, as she spoke, she was able to glance across the room at the gentleman in question, for the conversation was taking place in the drawing room of Madderstone Abbey, where a large party was collected for the evening.

Just now, the captain was standing with his back to a roaring fire telling a story which involved a great deal of energy and expression, 'alarms', 'overwhelming odds', and 'French privateers'. Margaret, Silas and Harriet sat before him listening attentively and Lucy was wanting to join them. She began to rise from her seat, but Dido placed a delaying hand upon her arm. She could not allow the opportunity for conversation to pass. Soon the whist table at which Mr and Mrs Harman-Foote, Francis and Mr Lomax were all engaged, would be breaking up – the company dispersing…

'And how did Captain Laurence become acquainted with Miss Lambe?' she asked.

'I do not know,' said Lucy carelessly, 'I have never asked.'

Dido sighed. Sometimes she found the lack of curiosity in others very hard to forgive.

'But,' continued Lucy in a thrilled whisper, 'he was quite determined that we should become friends, you know. For he said that he esteemed us all so much he must have us love one another!'

'Indeed!' Dido looked across again to the captain as he smiled broadly in the ruddy light of the fire, his strong white teeth very prominent in his weather-beaten face. There was a great deal too much self-congratulation in the smile for her taste.

At tea he had devoted himself to Penelope, who had made a brief appearance in company that evening – her first since her accident. Now she had returned to rest in her bedchamber, but while she had remained below the captain had been so very solicitous for her comfort and welfare that Dido had wondered how Lucy could look on with every appearance of goodwill and complaisance…

She realised suddenly that the captain had ceased talking – that he was now returning her gaze. His smile broadened.

She turned back to Lucy quickly. 'And Penelope knows no more about her own history?' she asked.

'Oh no! Though of course she remembers her mother quite distinctly!'

'Does she?' cried Dido in surprise – but then distrusted. 'And what, exactly, does she remember?'

'She remembers the sweetest, most beautiful face in the world bending over her cradle – a voice, angelic in its softness, singing her to sleep… All that kind of thing, you know – for it is quite impossible to ever forget a mother's love.'

'I see.' Dido detected more of romance than memory in all this. 'But she has never asked Mrs Nolan…?'

She stopped, aware that her companion was no longer attending. Captain Laurence himself was now approaching and Lucy was happily making room for him to sit between them on the sofa.

'You are talking of Miss Lambe?' he asked as he sat down and arranged his bristling brows and side-whiskers into a look of compassionate concern. 'I was,' he said turning to Lucy with a very particular look, 'very glad indeed to see her so much recovered. For I know, Miss Lucy, how very, very anxious you have been about her.'

Lucy smirked and exclaimed.

Dido watched and listened with great interest as the

captain talked on in a low insinuating voice. She could not help but admire the way in which every concern for, every attention to, Penelope was now explained away by his overwhelming anxiety for Lucy's peace of mind.

'...And so you see, Miss Lambe has told me that she is experiencing no great pain in her head; so you *must*, I *beg* you, cease to distress yourself by imagining any such thing. Come now, will you *promise* me that you will not lie awake at night any more worrying about it...?'

It was all so very cleverly done! And no doubt Lucy – predisposed as she was to believe whatever suited her – had cause enough to think him 'attached'.

Dido glanced about the room to see whether anyone else was taking note of the very particular attention he was paying. But it would seem that she was their only audience. On one side Silas, overheated by Mr Harman-Foote's enormous fire, was beginning to wheeze and cough, and Harriet was entirely taken up with chiding him and placing a screen to protect him, for all the world as if he were a delicate girl. And on the other side, the whist players were intent upon their cards and a conversation on the perennial subject of poachers.

'It's a mystery to me, Lomax, where the devil the birds are all going,' boomed Mr Harman-Foote. 'They can't be eating them all – they must be getting 'em off to sell in town somehow, but I'm damned if I know how they're doing it, for the keepers have been out looking at every cart that leaves the village. Why, I rather take my hat off to 'em. Clever devils ain't they...?'

'...And I am particularly grateful to you, Miss Kent...'

'I beg your pardon?' Dido turned back hastily to find that the captain was now regarding her with a look of great feeling.

'I know,' he said, 'that you have been doing the poor invalid the greatest of services – I refer of course to your efforts at discovering the cause of her fall. Such an explanation would' – a solicitous glance here at Lucy – 'help to put all our minds at rest. And I am sure there is no one better qualified for the undertaking.'

'I hardly know about that,' Dido replied. 'For I am not at all certain what qualities the task might require. But if overweening curiosity and a frivolous mind which cannot allow the smallest detail to pass unnoticed are called for – then perhaps I may make some claim.'

'You are too modest!' he cried with habitual gallantry. 'But I cannot allow you to escape the compliment so easily, for I hear too much about your intelligence and quickness of understanding to doubt you are capable of solving any manner of perplexity.'

'Thank you,' she said quietly, rather wishing he would not lean so close, nor speak in such a softened tone. It was, she knew, no more than his manner – the duty of charming all women which his vanity imposed upon him. But, beyond his shoulder, she could see Lucy becoming very annoyed at having to share his attention.

'I should be very grateful if you would tell me what you have discovered in your search. And' – he leant closer still, sinking his voice so that only she could hear – 'there is the other matter – the mysterious disappearance of Miss Fenn's letters. My cousin tells me that you are making enquiries into that too…'

Dido drew back, shocked that he should know of the letters, and offended by the familiarity of his manner. She opened her mouth to protest; but her words were drowned in an exclamation from the card table. 'Mr Lomax! Are you forgetting that spades are *trumps*?'

She looked across to see the unfortunate Mr Lomax stammering an apology as he frowned distractedly at the game. And she was wondering whether her imagination was flattering her in suggesting that his eyes had been only just withdrawn from her corner of the room, when all other considerations were driven out by such a scream from above their heads as seemed to shake the very walls of the house.

There was a moment of complete stillness in the drawing room as the echoes died away along the stairs and hallways of the old abbey. Everybody seemed to be staring at somebody else.

And then everybody was moving and talking at once.

Silas Crockford's voice rang out, with unusual clarity, above the rest. 'It was Penelope!'

Lucy was taken with hysterics, and Captain Laurence was forced to attend her. Silas, Francis and Mr Lomax were running into the hall, but Harriet was ahead of them all, crying out, 'It is of no consequence. Do not worry, please. I will go to her.'

And Dido, neatly avoiding Lucy's clutching hands, was running after her friend immediately. She slipped past the gentlemen who were all come to an uncertain standstill at the foot of the stairs – very eager to encounter any danger, and yet unable to pursue it into a lady's bedchamber.

She caught up with Harriet on the turn of the stairs. 'Is Penelope alone?'

Harriet shook her head. 'No... At least I thought not. I thought that Nanny was sitting with her...'

They were on the landing... At the door... Dido pushed it open...

The only light in the room came from the fire, burning low upon glowing embers with a small flame or two flickering unsteadily, sending fingers of light and shadow across the ceiling and the bed-hangings. There was no attendant – only Penelope sitting up on her bed, her face terrified. She turned to the door as Dido and Harriet hurried in.

'Oh! She was here!' she cried. 'I saw her! The Grey Nun was here at the foot of the bed!'

'It was a dream,' said Harriet soothingly. 'Nothing more.' She went to the bed and tried to persuade her charge to lie down.

But Penelope resisted feverishly. 'No, no! I was awake. I was quite awake! And she was just there, you know,' she insisted, pointing a shaking finger. 'I had just fallen asleep and then I woke up. And there was a figure in a very ugly grey gown like nuns wear. And there was a light. And a great big hood so her face was quite covered up.'

'No, no...'

'Yes!' Penelope's poor eyes seemed to be starting out of her head. 'She spoke to me in an odd sort of voice – such as I suppose they call *hollow tones* in a book. And I thought I should die of fright...'

Harriet shook her head, and continued to talk quietly and calmly about dreams and tricks of the firelight and the injury from which Penelope was not yet quite recovered...

Meanwhile Dido had followed the direction of the pointing finger and was looking closely at the spot by the bed's foot where the ghost was supposed to have appeared. She stooped down and touched the bedpost lightly, raised her finger and studied its tip…

Just then the door was opened by poor Nanny, full of tearful apologies for having 'only just gone down to the kitchen with the tray. And she had only been away a minute or two. And she was right sure her old legs *couldn't* have taken her there and back any quicker than they did. And Miss Harriet knew full well that she never had been one for wasting time gossiping in the kitchen…'

Harriet left the bedside to confer with her and send her off with a reassuring message for the company below. Dido went to Penelope. 'The Grey Nun spoke to you?' she whispered eagerly.

'Yes.' Penelope seized her with hot little hands, very anxious to be believed.

'What did she say?'

'She said…'

'Now now,' said Harriet turning back towards them, 'it will not do at all to dwell upon it. It was nothing but a nightmare. Least said soonest mended.'

But Penelope clung on, her eyes wide and pleading. 'She *did* speak. I am quite, quite sure it was not a dream. You believe me, do you not?'

'Yes…' Dido looked down thoughtfully at her own fingers, rubbed them together a little. 'Yes, I think perhaps I do believe you.' There was a protest from Harriet, but she continued. 'Can you tell us what the Grey Nun said to you?'

'Oh! She said that I am in great danger. She said that I must get away from here as soon as ever I can.'

Chapter Twenty-Five

Dido left the bedroom immediately and hurried out onto the landing, eagerly looking to right and left. There was no one in sight. Down in the hall the company was yielding to Nanny's message and Mrs Harman-Foote's entreaties. Everyone was returning to the drawing room. She could hear their voices fading away. She started down the stairs. The drawing room door was just closing; Nanny was hurrying off to the kitchen; there was only one person left in the hall – it was Mr Lomax.

And he was watching her with a very troubled expression – as if he were suspecting her motives for hurrying away so promptly to Penelope's room; and yet he seemed reluctant to leave her and return to the drawing room…

'Did you see anybody?' she asked a little breathlessly as she reached the hall. 'Did you see anybody come down the stairs just now – after Harriet and I went up?'

'The old nurse came down to assure us all was well.'

'Nobody else?'

'No.' He looked at her with concern. 'You seem distressed.'

She had no time to reply to that. She was too occupied with suspicion and calculation to give much thought to anything else. 'Who exactly was in the drawing room just now?' she said distractedly. 'Can you remember? When we heard the cry, was there anyone who was not with us?'

He raised his brows, started another question, but then, upon seeing her look of impatience, stopped. He hesitated a moment – reluctant to encourage whatever investigations now occupied her. But then he gave a sigh. 'Well,' he said, considering carefully. 'Mr and Mrs Harman-Foote, your brother and I were all at the card table. Mr and Miss Crockford and your sister were beside the fire. Miss Lucy Crockford was on the sofa by the pianoforte…and,' he added, suddenly averting his eyes from hers, 'Captain Laurence was there too and, I believe, talking *very* entertainingly to *you*.'

'Yes,' she said, only half-listening as she struggled to remember the position of everybody as exactly as she could. 'Yes, you are quite right.'

He frowned and fell into a thoughtful silence.

'So, who was missing?' she said, busily checking everyone off on her fingers.

'That young fellow who talked so much at tea about felling trees,' he said, rousing from his reverie. 'I do not believe he was in the drawing room.'

'Mr Coulson? No, I think you are right.' She looked thoughtfully about the quiet, empty expanse of marble-floored hall. Fine mahogany doors led to library, drawing room, dining room and billiard room and, all but hidden under the shadow of the great staircase, another smaller door led away to the offices. 'I wonder,' she said, 'where that gentleman is now.'

'Why, he has gone back into the drawing room now with the others. He joined us here in the hall a moment or two after you and Miss Crockford went upstairs.'

'Did he indeed!' she cried eagerly, eyes brightening, her face alive with rapid thought. 'But he did not come down the stairs?'

'No.'

'Mr Lomax, can you remember *from where he came*?'

'I hardly know…' He was becoming more puzzled every moment: more and more at a loss to understand what she was about.

'Please, try to remember. Is it possible that he came from over there.' She pointed towards the door that led to the offices.

'It is possible that he did. I cannot be sure. We were all shocked and there were a number of people in the hall. What does it matter whether he came through that door or another?'

'Because,' she said, 'there must be back stairs in this house like any other.'

'Miss Kent,' he cried, unable to hide his exasperation any longer, 'I am afraid that I do not now have the pleasure of understanding you. I am sure Madderstone Abbey *has* back stairs or its servants would be very seriously inconvenienced. But I am quite at a loss to know why those stairs should concern us now.'

'Because Mr Coulson could have come down them, of course. He could have left Miss Lambe's room, slipped out along the landing before Harriet and I reached it and come down the backstairs into the hall.'

He shook his head in bewilderment. 'But why

should you suspect him of doing so?'

'Because something – or somebody – appeared to Penelope just now, and I do not believe it was either a ghost, or a nightmare.'

He looked extremely grave and she was very sure that he was going to make some remonstrance concerning unnecessary curiosity, but, to her great surprise, he only said, 'Why? Why should you suppose such a thing?'

She held out her hand and he looked into it. 'Candle wax?' he said.

'It was upon the bedpost near where this *ghost* had stood. It was still warm and soft when I found it – just spilt from a candle. And I think you will agree, Mr Lomax, that an apparition does not require artificial light – but a man impersonating one does.'

'It seems a very wild idea,' he protested. 'Are you suggesting that the gentleman disguised himself as a ghost on purpose to frighten Miss Lambe? What possible motive could he have for doing something so very strange – and cruel?'

Dido bit thoughtfully at her lip. 'The motive I cannot explain – yet. But it may be possible to prove my theory.'

'Indeed?' Try as he might, he could not keep the interest from his voice. 'I should be very glad to hear how you might *prove* it.'

She looked from the sweeping staircase to the little door in its shadow. 'If my surmise is correct,' she said, 'then he must have discarded his costume somewhere between the bedchamber and the hall – and he would have had little time in which to conceal it.'

'His costume?'

'Oh, Mr Lomax!' she cried impatiently before she could stop herself. 'Is it not obvious?'

He again considered leaving her and returning to the drawing room, but found that he could not. 'No,' he said as calmly as he could, 'I am afraid it is not obvious to me at all. I am very sorry to be so dull-witted.'

'Well, when – *if* – Mr Coulson appeared to Penelope as the ghost, then he had on a grey nun's habit. But I do not suppose that he was dressed in that fashion when he arrived here in the hall – I think you might have remarked upon it if he had been.'

'Ah!' he said, smiling in spite of himself. 'Yes, I think that even I might have noticed such a detail!'

'And so,' she said, 'I shall see whether I can find it before he has a chance to retrieve it.'

She started up the stairs and, after a moment's struggle, he followed her. 'May I accompany you?' he said. 'I should be very glad to see your proof.'

'I am all amazement! I had expected you to advise me against interfering.'

'And would you heed me if I did?'

'Ah!' There was a moment of confusion, but the urgency of her quest overruled everything. 'I fear that I might not,' she admitted.

'Then I shall not make myself ridiculous by offering counsel which I know will be disregarded.'

They reached the top of the stairs and turned into the passageway which led away to the back of the house; it was wide, well carpeted and panelled in fine oak, embellished with the staring heads of long-dead stags. Dido had expected to find a door to the kitchen stairs leading from it, but they arrived at its end and a large window overlooking an inner court, without encountering any such door.

'How strange!' she cried, turning her back to the window and looking along the length of the passage. 'I was quite certain that there would be a door.'

Lomax picked up a candelabra which stood upon the window sill. 'There most certainly is a door,' he said, 'but it has not been allowed to spoil the beauty of this panelling.'

Holding the light close to the wall, he began to make his way slowly back towards the landing. 'Here it is!' He stopped, pushed at the wood and opened a small door.

'How very clever of you!'

'Thank you!' he said, standing back for her to enter. 'I am glad to be of service.' Looking up at him as she passed through she saw that he was smiling slightly. She rather suspected that the grave, dignified Mr Lomax was beginning to enjoy this little adventure.

They stepped out of the carpeted passage onto cold stone. The light of the candles showed narrow, unrailed stone stairs twisting downwards between lime-washed walls. From below came echoing sounds as of knives and china being cleaned and an occasional voice raised above the din of work. There was a smell of damp and fried meat, leather and boot-black.

'Well,' said Mr Lomax, looking about him. 'I see neither a nun's habit, nor any place in which one might be concealed.'

'No,' admitted Dido. 'Nor do I.'

They started down the stairs, the sound of their feet echoing harshly against the stark walls. About halfway down there was a shuttered window. Dido stopped, pulled open the shutter and looked behind it. There was nothing hidden there.

The stairs ended in a narrow lobby from which doors led away to kitchen, scullery and laundry. On the bare white wall hung the usual row of labelled bells by which servants were summoned to the front of the house, and at one end of the lobby was the door which led into the main hall. At the other end, hard by the stairs, was a kind of wooden screen beside an outer door – through which an icy draught was blowing.

Mr Lomax shivered and shook his head. 'I think, perhaps, you have failed in your proof.' He sounded almost disappointed.

Dido turned restlessly from one door to another. 'It must be here… There was no time in which to take it anywhere else.' She stared about her. Inspiration struck. 'Ah!' she cried and stepped behind the screen. 'Did you never play "Hunt the Thimble" when you were young, Mr Lomax?'

'Not with any great success,' he admitted as he held up the light and followed her into the cold gloomy space by the back door, where there was a great assortment of old muddy boots and pattens – and pegs upon which the servants' outer garments were hung.

'The trick,' she said as she began to take cloaks from the wall, 'is always to put the thimble somewhere where it does not look out of place – among small ornaments, or jewellery, that kind of thing…' As she spoke she had been hurriedly handing articles of clothing to him and by now he was holding two old woollen pelisses, a fustian jacket and a sackcloth apron. 'And of course, if one wished to hide a garment... Ah!'

She turned in triumph, holding, in one hand, a loose grey hooded habit, and, in the other, the belt of rope which had secured it.

For a moment they stood in that wretched, cold little porch smiling delightedly at one another like a pair of high-spirited children. Her cheeks glowed and her eyes shone. He began to laugh. 'You are remarkable, Miss Kent!'

Without seeming to know what he was about he took a step towards her – or maybe she moved towards him. When she considered it afterwards, Dido could not be quite sure which it was...

But she recollected herself, blushed, turned away, replaced the habit on its peg and began to cover it with the other things.

He took a step back, held the candle a little higher so that she could see more clearly. 'So...you do not wish Mr Coulson to know that you have found him out?'

'No,' she mumbled as he handed back the last of the housemaids' pelisses, 'I would rather he did not. I need to think matters over...'

They stepped out into the lobby and paused a little awkwardly. The sounds of the kitchen echoed about the bare walls: the rattle of wooden pails on stone flags, the scrubbing of a table and the raking of coals. She wished he would not look at her so very intently.

'Miss Kent,' he began cautiously, 'do you suspect that this strange occurrence – this "haunting" – is connected with Miss Lambe's fall; or with other late events – I mean the discovery of the body... In short, is this a part of your *investigation?*'

She avoided his eye and stared at the long, unsteady shadows which the candlelight was stretching from their feet, listened to someone whistling a hornpipe somewhere in the kitchens. A score of evasions ran through her mind, but she put them aside. 'Yes, it is,' she said quietly.

'And what conclusions do you draw from this discovery?' He nodded in the direction of the screen and the habit.

'I conclude...' She stopped herself and shook her head. 'Mr Lomax, I think you are forgetting our last conversation upon this subject. I do not believe it is a matter we can discuss without falling into argument.'

The light of the candles flickered across his face showing powerfully conflicting emotions which puzzled her. There was a struggle carrying on; and it ended with: 'I believe I may have spoken a little too...strongly when we discussed the matter before. I am sorry if I offended you.'

The words were said so very stiffly she could not immediately take in their meaning. But when she was quite sure that he had indeed made an apology, she stared. Whatever could have brought about this change of heart? She was quite at a loss to explain it.

'If,' he continued, 'you were to do me the honour of confiding in me again, I should...endeavour to listen more calmly.'

She smiled: vastly pleased, though still very puzzled. 'It is very good of you to offer it,' she said demurely. 'I appreciate your kindness – indeed I appreciate it far too well to put it to the test.'

'You do not choose to share your ideas with me?'

'I think it had better not be attempted. For even if you succeeded in...listening calmly. Even if you said nothing at all, I should *know* that you disapproved.'

He considered this for a moment. 'But it would seem,' he pointed out with his usual impeccable logic, 'that you already *know* all about my disapproval. You have pre-empted me and are already suffering my imagined strictures. So what is to be gained from reserve? Might you not as well confide in me? The exercise might prove useful to you. Speaking thoughts aloud is frequently a means to understanding them better.'

'Yes. Talking – to the right person – can, sometimes be a great help…' She put her hand to her head. There was something about his solid, reassuring presence and kindly grey eyes that made her long to share her thoughts with him. But his eagerness to help, his valiant attempts to avoid censuring her, were inexplicable! She was too puzzled and confused to trust his sudden change of heart. 'Come,' she said abruptly, 'we had better return to the drawing room.'

'I see,' he said, deeply offended. 'I am not "the right person". You would like to talk – but not to me.'

'I think I had better not,' she said turning away.

'I suppose,' he said quietly, 'that you would prefer to confide in Captain Laurence.'

'Captain Laurence!' she cried, spinning back to face him and seeing his cheeks red with emotion. But, before she could say another word, the drawing room bell in the row above their heads clanged into life. They both stared up at it. Footsteps could be heard rapidly approaching from the kitchen.

Mr Lomax seized her arm. They ran together for the door, and only just succeeded in gaining the hall before a footman sauntered out behind them – still whistling a hornpipe under his breath.

Chapter Twenty-Six

It was jealousy! That was the cause of Mr Lomax's change of heart. Jealousy of Captain Laurence!

Dido could not even frame the thought without laughing out loud.

'I do not see what there is to laugh about,' said Margaret sourly as they got into the carriage. 'In my opinion the evening was quite spoilt by that unpleasant little episode. Such a scream! When I was young, girls were not brought up to make such an exhibition I am sure!'

'Poor young lady cannot help having a nightmare,' said Francis mildly. 'Not to be wondered at. Her brain is not yet set to rights.'

'Quite so,' murmured Dido and they all lapsed into silence, shivering a little, for the coach seemed very cold after the heat of the abbey's good fires.

But when she looked across at the dark outline of Mr Lomax, swaying slightly as the carriage began to move, coat collar turned up, hat pulled down: when she thought of him as being consumed by Shakespeare's 'Green-eyed Monster' – and upon no better evidence than the captain's commonplace gallantry in the drawing room – she felt her lips once more forming themselves into a smile.

But now the carriage was creaking and crunching over

the gravel of the sweep; the lights of the house were left behind; her smiles passed unseen, and censured only by herself.

Indeed, she *ought* not to smile. Jealousy was a very severe character flaw – not something to be taken lightly. But Dido now found, to her dismay, that this discovery of weakness – this proof that he was not the model of perfection she had taken him for – did not diminish her affection at all, and she was fallen so deeply into love that a flaw could have all the charm of a virtue. Which was a very great shock to her, and a mighty revelation, for she had lived six and thirty years in the world innocently supposing only merit to be loveable.

Suddenly the carriage lurched to a standstill – and Margaret screamed.

'What the devil?' Francis let down the glass and peered out into the night, letting in a foggy damp which caught at the back of Dido's throat.

There was an answering curse from the coachman, quickly suppressed with an apology. 'Thought I saw someone sir,' he called. 'Looked like a fellow running across the lawn from the old pool.'

Francis leant out further. 'Can't see a thing…except, what's that over there? Looks like a lantern swinging about.'

'Where? In the ruins?' asked Dido. 'Is the light upon the gallery in the ruins?' She tried to look for herself. But the carriage was in motion again now and Margaret was demanding the glass be put up before the carriage lining was spoilt by damp.

'Yes, it may be in the ruins,' Francis conceded as he

secured the glass and settled back into his seat.

'Oh! I would dearly love to know what is carrying on there.'

'Then you had better ask the intrepid captain to investigate,' said Mr Lomax quietly.

Dido made no reply to that – and passed all the rest of the journey silently condemning her own cruelty. She should say something. One slight remark hinting at her low opinion of the captain would suffice. She could say enough, even in the presence of Margaret and Francis, to make him comfortable. It was barbarous to remain silent and allow his suffering to continue! But she found that she could not make up her mind to do away with his jealousy. It was just too delightful – and too convenient.

For while he remained jealous he would listen without condemning her. He would be prepared – perhaps even willing – to discuss her mysteries in order to prevent her confiding in the perceived rival.

Ah, dear! And she had been used to think of love as an ennobling and elevating passion. She had never imagined it could be the cause of such unkindness.

'You look pleased,' said Mr Lomax as he handed her from the carriage. 'The evening's discoveries have been helpful to you?'

'Oh! Yes, thank you.' They walked slowly up the vicarage steps and she stole a glance at his face in the pale light shining out into white mist through the open door. There was a kind of hope and expectancy...

Just one small, slighting remark about Laurence would be enough...

Instead, she paused as they came into the hall and said

quietly. 'I have been reconsidering your kind offer, Mr Lomax.'

'My offer?'

'Your offer to be my confidant. I think I should like very much to talk matters over with you.'

'Ah! I am sure I am very honoured.' He bowed, took the shawl from her shoulders and looked about the hall. Francis was gone away to the library to put the finishing touches to a sermon and Margaret was just climbing the stairs. He suggested they walk into the parlour, and there, beside the sunken embers of the fire, she told him of her visit to Great Farleigh – and her suspicion that Penelope was the daughter of Miss Fenn.

'It seems – if I am permitted to make such an observation – a rather overstrained conclusion.'

'No, it is not a conclusion: it is a *suspicion*.'

'I beg your pardon. It seems a rather overstrained *suspicion*.'

'Perhaps it is; but I mean to test the truth of it by finding out about Miss Lambe's history.'

'I see.' He was standing by the hearth, one hand resting upon the chimney piece and he now turned his face away to stare down at the dying fire. She suspected that he disapproved this course of action but was making a valiant attempt to hide this opinion. After a short pause he said, 'May I ask how Miss Lambe's…parentage might prompt the cruel trick which was played upon her this evening?'

'I think someone wishes to drive her away from Madderstone. It does, I grant, seem a rather strange method of persuasion,' she added hastily. 'But, knowing

Miss Lambe's romantic disposition, I cannot help but think it might be an effective one.'

'Upon that point, I must give way to your superior knowledge of the lady's character,' he said graciously, his eyes still fixed upon the embers. 'But do you suspect Mr Coulson of acting on his own behalf, or do you believe he took on the role of ghost at someone else's prompting?'

Dido smiled at his determination to suppress any hint of censure and there was a short silence as she collected her thoughts. 'I believe,' she said slowly at last, 'that it is perhaps Mr Harman-Foote who wishes Penelope to leave the neighbourhood. I think he may have persuaded Mr Coulson into the charade.' She hesitated: there was an idea gradually forming in her mind which she particularly wished to try out upon him. 'You see,' she said carefully, 'if Penelope is indeed Miss Fenn's daughter, then the man to whom she wrote that very…affectionate letter – the man she addressed as "Beloved" – must be suspected of being the father.'

'Yes,' he agreed, raising his eyes at last from the fire and looking at her rather anxiously.

'And the reputation of that man would be endangered by the girl being here in the neighbourhood. His good-name might be best guarded by frightening her away.'

'But you are forgetting, Miss Kent: Mr Harman-Foote cannot be Miss Fenn's "Beloved". As I have had the pleasure of explaining to you – the handwriting in the letter is certainly not his.'

'No, no,' she cried immediately. 'I am not forgetting it at all.' And then, ashamed of her sharpness, she went on more gently. 'I confess it was very foolish of me not to have considered the handwriting before. I am particularly grateful to you for drawing it to my attention.'

'I am very glad to have been of service to you.'

'But,' she continued, 'although I accept your conclusion that Mr Harman-Foote cannot have been the man to whom Miss Fenn wrote, I think that, after all, he might have prompted Mr Coulson to play the part of a ghost.'

He said nothing – only raised his brows.

'It is possible he was acting not on his own behalf – but for the sake of someone else.'

He still said nothing, but he had turned to face her now; his elbow was resting on the mantleshelf, the tips of his fingers just touching one another.

'You see,' she said, 'I have given some thought to your suggestion that Mr Harman-Foote stole the letters and the ring in order to protect his wife from pain.'

'Yes?'

'And might not Miss Lambe be frightened away for the same reason?'

He rested his chin upon the tips of his fingers. 'This would suppose that Mr Harman-Foote knows the secret of the young lady's parentage.'

'Yes it would,' she said eagerly, 'and that would be entirely possible if...' She stopped for she was in grave danger of stumbling into indelicacy. But in her mind she could not help but see the luxury of that bedchamber – so very ill-suited to a governess. She lowered her eyes. 'It may be that the man guilty of...indiscretion with Miss Fenn was a friend of Mr Harman-Foote's – and someone his wife esteems very highly indeed.'

'Who, precisely, do you have in mind?'

Dido kept her eyes upon the floor. 'The late Mr Harman – her father,' she said quietly. 'If Mr Harman-Foote knew anything to Mr Harman's disadvantage, he might be very eager to protect his memory – for the sake of his wife's peace of mind.'

There was a rather long silence in the room. Dido still did not choose to look at her companion; but his eyes rested upon her very steadily. Their expression however was troubled and considering rather than critical.

'I wish,' he said at last, 'that I could deny the possibility of such a confusion of guilt and deception as you are suggesting.'

'But you cannot?' She raised her eyes at last. He was standing with his chin resting upon his steepled fingers – which was always a sign with him of deep thought.

'No,' he admitted with a heavy sigh. 'I cannot. I must, at least, concede that you are justified in being suspicious. There is certainly something very strange carrying on at Madderstone. There is guilt of some kind.'

'And in return for your admitting so much, I will grant that you were right to caution me when we spoke in the wood. Investigation – even truth itself – can be a dangerous and hurtful thing. You did well to put me upon my guard. But – be assured – I mean to proceed with the utmost care. I have not yet spoken one word to Mrs Harman-Foote which might lower her opinion of her governess. Nor shall I – unless the cause of justice absolutely demands it. And I shall be particularly careful to keep from her these suspicions against her father.'

He smiled. 'I am extremely glad to hear it,' he said. 'And I am sure I should have expected no less of you. It was very bad of me to doubt your humanity – or your delicacy of feeling. In future Miss Kent, I shall endeavour to judge you less hastily, and prove myself worthy of your confidence.'

'And I shall try to listen calmly to any opinions which you offer,' she said.

His smile broadened. He took a step closer, fixing his eyes upon her and holding out his hand. 'Then perhaps we may find that it is possible for us to disagree – to even express our disagreement – without injuring our esteem of one another. I should be very glad to think that open and honest discussion were possible between us.'

Dido coloured as she took in all that this proposal might mean – but there was more pleasure than pain in her confusion. 'Perhaps we shall,' she said. She rose and, with a great show of solemnity, placed her hand in his, wondering very much whether he hoped such an arrangement might end at last in marriage: a marriage in which this pleasurable kind of dispute was allowed to continue…

Meanwhile he was looking as if he did not quite know what to do with her hand. He held it a moment; perhaps he was on the point of carrying it to his lips. But then, all at once, he let it go, stepped away from her and searched around for another branch of the subject with which to distract himself.

'It might,' he began rather abruptly, 'be useful to know something of Miss Fenn's life before she came to Madderstone – have you made any enquiries into that subject?'

'No…at least, I have not been able to discover much.'

Dido looked down at the grate – at the soft grey ash and the last faint red pulse of the embers. 'Mrs Harman-Foote seems to know nothing except that the Fenns were neighbours of her mother-in-law in Shropshire and…' She stopped. An idea had occurred. 'Mr Lomax,' she said slowly raising her eyes to his. 'I believe *you* have an acquaintance in that neighbourhood?'

'Ah! Yes, I have.' He held her gaze and smiled – understanding exactly the request which was in her mind without a word of it being spoken. He hesitated; her eyes brightened eagerly in the faint glow of the fire…'Very well,' he conceded, rather against his own judgement, 'if you wish it, I shall write to my friend and ask what he knows of the family.'

'Thank you! It is very kind of you.'

'Well, well…' He was beginning to think he had better not stay with her any longer; she was too dangerous; she might persuade him into anything. But still he kept his place by the hearth. 'And in the meantime,' he said, 'you will continue your investigations by enquiring into Miss Lambe's history?'

'Yes – though I confess I do not yet know how I shall go to work on it.'

'Might I be permitted to make a suggestion?'

'Of course you may.'

'If it is within your power, I would advise you to accept Miss Crockford's invitation and accompany her and her sister when they convey Miss Lambe to Bath.'

'Oh?' she said, much surprised. 'Why should I go to Bath?'

'I have two reasons for recommending it. Firstly, I

think that it would provide the safest – and most discreet – opportunity for discovering whether your speculations about Miss Lambe's origins are correct.'

'You think that I ought to make enquiries of Mrs Nolan?'

'No,' he said with a shake of his head. 'I do not say, exactly, that you *ought* to do so. I am your confidant, remember, not your advisor. I only suggest that going to Bath may be a little safer than pursuing your enquiries here.'

'You believe then that there is danger here? That there is a murderer among us?'

'I believe that it is *possible*.'

She considered this for several minutes. The last remains of the fire were beginning now to dull and drop away through the grate. The room was becoming cold and dark: his face only just visible, a black, brooding outline against the red glow. 'And what,' she asked at last, 'is your other motive?'

'I beg your pardon?'

'You said that you had two motives for recommending I join the party to Bath. What is the second?'

'Oh,' he said with a smile, 'merely that I must be there myself next week and it would give me particular pleasure to be allowed to accompany you to the theatre.'

He took her hand again, and this time he allowed himself the indulgence of kissing it.

Chapter Twenty-Seven

...Is it possible, Eliza? Could a man and woman exist in a state of well-mannered disputation, listening to and expressing contrary ideas without any loss of respect: the views of neither being subsumed within the judgement of the other? And could this form the foundation of marriage?

I know not! It seems very far removed from any marriage which has fallen within my observation. And yet, I cannot help but think that Mr Lomax has conceived of such a miraculous union — and that he is now intent upon proving to me that it can be achieved!

I am sure it is an experiment quite as interesting as any Mr Paynter has undertaken — and one which, were it published, might add a great deal to the sum of human knowledge. But I am beset by doubts. What would happen if there were a very serious disagreement of principle: if one party was adamant in holding fast to an opinion which the other considered utterly wrong? For our opinions inform our decisions and direct our actions. Might the time not come when difference of opinion led to serious disapproval of conduct? And that <u>must</u> lead to a loss of respect and affection...

Well, I suppose this is something which only time — and experimentation — can discover. And, I should certainly be very glad to go to Bath and carry on the experiment there, for I fear the house will feel very dull indeed after Mr Lomax leaves us tomorrow.

But the signs are not good for my being allowed to go. The subject is now under perpetual discussion here at the vicarage, and Margaret has a great deal to say upon the subject of 'expense' and 'not imposing upon the goodwill of the Crockfords' and even of 'there being nothing to be achieved from such a visit at six and thirty' – by which I suppose she means that I am unlikely to return with a new name on my tickets.

At times I am sorely tempted to disclose my true situation...

And of course I have another reason, besides this enquiry into the science of human nature, for wishing to go to Bath. I am very anxious indeed to find out just who Penelope is. This second haunting <u>must</u> increase the suspicion that she is the daughter of the dead woman.

But, at present, I have no chance of even getting back to the abbey to pursue my enquiries – much less travelling to Bath. For Rebecca is still gasping and sneezing in her bed, young Mary is busy with the marketing, and Margaret has had Francis get horses for the carriage and gone to pay a call upon Mrs Harman-Foote. So I am once more in charge of the bread, the spit, the curds and the cat.

And, by the by, it is to the latter that you must attribute the smudged writing of this letter: it is no fault of mine. Puss has been walking about the table and trying to put herself between me and the page this last quarter of an hour. She is now settled upon my lap and purring a kind of counterpoint to the spit's ticking.

Monday night's 'haunting' has disturbed me greatly. I

want very much to be <u>doing</u> something. But I am neither able to get out of this kitchen, nor am I even certain what it is that I ought to be doing.

Even my scheme to help Silas is not prospering. He declares himself heartbroken at the prospect of Penelope's going, but I have not yet seen a single line of his poem. Harriet informs me that most of his time is now spent in shooting and lounging about with Mr Coulson — and very angry she is about it too! The effects upon his health are, I believe...

She broke off as a loud knocking sounded on the kitchen door. The cat leapt up with such a look as seemed to suggest the noise was Dido's fault and stalked away.

She opened the door to find Harris Paynter on the step, a thin mizzling rain silvering his dark coat. He was come, he said, to visit Rebecca.

'For I hear,' he said, coming in and shaking moisture from his hat, 'that she has been sick some days.'

'She has indeed and I sincerely hope that you can cure her.' Dido stepped to the fireside and began to turn the key of the spit, for it was all but unwound. 'We are in a great muddle without her.'

'Oh dear!' He shook his hat again, sending drops of water hissing against the range. 'I am sorry... I did not know.' He hesitated a moment, looking very disconcerted, then excused himself and hurried away to make the examination.

Dido stood for several minutes upon the hearth rug, staring after him and wondering very much why he should feel it necessary to apologise for the sickness of his patient. It seemed to be yet another conundrum which she could not answer – one of many surrounding her at present.

She had basted the meat and put the bread into the oven when the surgeon reappeared, crossed immediately to the range and threw a handful of something onto the hot coals. 'I am sure Rebecca will be quite well by tomorrow,' he said, turning to the door and putting on his hat.

She tried to delay him with a question, but he seemed determined upon going and, pleading another case which urgently required his attendance, hurried off into the rain.

'How very strange,' she said as the door closed behind him. 'Did it seem to you, Puss, that the good surgeon was anxious and guilty about something?'

The cat expressed no opinion upon this subject; she was entirely taken up with watching the sparks which were now flying from the range, her nose 'twitching delicately at the strong odour accompanying them.

Burning feathers! It was a horribly familiar smell to Dido, for it had been her grandmother's favoured restorative (in Grandmama's opinion, the pleasanter scents of lavender and aromatic vinegar only encouraged silly girls to swoon). She crossed to the fire and saw that a bundle of brown hens' feathers was being rapidly consumed in the heart of the embers.

How very odd. Why was Mr Paynter disposing of feathers? She stared down into the glowing red cave of the fire, her mind moving rapidly as she recalled his plucking of the chicken at Madderstone. And then other ideas began to occur...

Chapter Twenty-Eight

...Feathers, Eliza! Feathers! Have you noticed how very many feathers there have been blowing about in this mystery?

And yet I had not thought to consider them until now.

Well, I have made up the deficiency: the last hour of my time has been devoted entirely to the consideration of feathers. I have visited poor Rebecca (who is now most miraculously recovered) – and learnt a great deal. Her information has answered one or two troubling questions – and started half a dozen more.

There was, at first, a certain reluctance to talk. For 'the mistress' would be very angry if she knew what had been carrying on. Though she (Rebecca) had not known that she would be so 'poorly' and throw the whole house into a muddle...

At last, however, upon an assurance that I would not speak a word to the dreaded 'mistress', the story all came out.

It would seem, Eliza, that Rebecca has been the subject – or rather, the victim – of one of Mr Paynter's 'experiments'. You see, the surgeon has been investigating 'what it is that makes folk like poor Mr Crockford wheeze so much.' And, noticing that 'rich folk wheeze more than ordinary ones', he was taken with the notion that it might be the result of what Rebecca calls 'a bad masma' coming out of the feathers in their beds. And so he decided to subject some 'ordinary folk' – people that had not feather beds – to this poisonous miasma in order to see whether it made them ill.

Surely only Mr Paynter could have embarked upon such an odd undertaking!

He has supplied bundles of feathers to villagers in Madderstone and Badleigh, and paid them sixpence apiece to place them beneath their pillows. And the result? I confess my own curiosity made me quite impatient to know it. But it would seem that Rebecca has been the only one to produce so much as a single wheeze – though I am assured that 'old Jonas Wells reckons the feathers charmed his warts away. And Mary Ann, what's kitchen maid up at the abbey, is <u>sure</u> they made her dream about the man she's going to marry.'

To Rebecca's great astonishment however, Mr Paynter is interested in neither wart charms nor lovers; but she tells me that he has not entirely given up his idea of feathers causing asthma. He now believes that, while most people have the constitution to withstand the noxious vapour arising from them, some – like Rebecca and Silas – have a weakness to it and so become ill.

It seems to me to be a rather wild idea. For, I ask you, Eliza, if feathers are a cause of sickness, why do birds appear so very healthy? But I don't doubt poor Silas will now be denied the comfort of a feather bed as well as port wine and rich food... Ah well, if he is saved from another bad attack of the asthma, I suppose the sacrifice will be well made. For the last one very nearly killed him.

And it was in fact <u>that</u> consideration which started an entirely new train of thought and led me back to my mystery. For, you see, I believe this experiment, besides explaining Mr

*Paynter's plucking of Mrs Philips' chicken, may also throw
some light upon the haunting of Penelope's bedchamber…*

*But as yet this is only surmise; there is nothing decided,
nothing fixed; and I will not expose myself by claiming a
solution which I may later be obliged to retract. I must
give the matter a great deal more thought. There is one very
important question which I must ask – and I must ask it in
such a way as not to betray my interest.*

*I have been walking about the house this last half-hour
endeavouring to find a situation in which I may think all
these things over in peace; for the rain continues steadily
and the moss hut is unattainable. I am now at the table
in the parlour, but I cannot hope to remain undisturbed
for long. Margaret will soon return… Ah, I hear footsteps
approaching already. I had better hide my letter or there will
be impertinent questions. Oh, Eliza, the comfort of being
sometimes alone!*

The parlour door opened and Dido found that she must
hastily put away her look of discontent, for the intruder
was not Margaret, but Mr Lomax.

'Miss Kent,' he exclaimed, coming to a standstill in
the middle of the room with a look of great confusion,
'I have had the most alarming letter…' He stopped as
he saw the anxiety on her face and held out a reassuring
hand. 'Forgive me – I should not have been so violent.
There is nothing to distress yourself about. No bad news
from any of our friends. I only meant that I have received
a letter which has puzzled me very much. I cannot make
out what it means.'

'Indeed?' She invited him to a seat and for a moment

they faced one another in silence across the green baize tablecloth. Rain pattered on the window beside them. He looked as if he did not know how to go on. 'May I ask who this letter is from?' she prompted.

'It is from my friend, George Lockhart,' he replied, then, seeing her blank look, he added, 'George lives in Shropshire – very close to old Mrs Foote.'

'Oh yes!' cried Dido with rising interest. 'I recall – it was to him you were to apply for information about Miss Fenn's family?'

'It was.'

He pressed together the tips of his fingers – causing her to ask: 'And what has he told you that is making you think so very deeply, Mr Lomax?'

'He has told me that there is no family of the name of Fenn living in that neighbourhood.'

'Is he quite sure?'

'Oh yes. He is certain that there is no family called Fenn residing within thirty miles of Mrs Foote's home.'

'How very strange,' she cried. 'I was sure that Miss Fenn had come from that county. I thought that her family were neighbours of Mrs Foote and that is how she came to be recommended to the Harmans. But perhaps,' she said, considering, 'I may have mistaken Anne's information... Perhaps it was an acquaintance Mrs Foote formed in town... But no,' she added, 'no, all the gossiping ladies of Badleigh and Madderstone are quite *sure* that Miss Fenn came from Shropshire...' She stopped.

He was frowning over his linked fingers and she understood his looks well enough to know that he was far from comfortable. There was something else to tell – something which he was reluctant to broach.

'My friend George is a...singular fellow,' he began slowly. 'He is very persistent. Once he is presented with a puzzle he cannot rest until it is solved.' He smiled. 'In fact, I know of only one person who can equal him for finding things out – and that is yourself.'

'Then Mr Lockhart must be a remarkably capable and intelligent man!'

'I shall not, of course, contradict you,' he said with a gracious inclination of his head. 'But I confess that, in the present case, he has been a great deal more...*diligent* than I asked him to be.'

Dido found herself rather warming to the unknown Mr Lockhart. 'And what has he discovered?' she asked eagerly.

'He has discovered Elinor Fenn. He has discovered that, until twenty two years ago, Elinor Fenn was living in Mrs Foote's own house.'

'Oh! But I thought you said that there was no one of that name in the neighbourhood.'

'Ah no,' he said gravely. 'I said that there was no *family* of that name.'

'You are too precise!'

'Not at all. The science of disputation requires precision. Besides...' He could not suppress a smile. 'Are you not always reminding me of the importance of noticing details?'

She opened her mouth to argue, but could find nothing to say, and he continued with insufferable self-complacency.

'Elinor Fenn did indeed reside in Shropshire. She was, in point of fact...' He stopped – his uneasiness was returned now. 'She was a maid in Mrs Foote's household.'

'A maid!' cried Dido – her resentment all forgotten in the shock. 'Elinor Fenn was a maid before coming to Madderstone?'

'It would seem that she was.' He looked down at his linked fingers. 'You must understand,' he said, after a moment's struggle, 'that I did not *ask* George to pursue the topic so far...but he saw fit to make enquiries through...tavern talk, the gossip of stable yards... I know not what.'

'Did he indeed?' cried Dido whose regard for Mr Lockhart was increasing rapidly. 'How very shocking! And what did this gossip reveal?'

He frowned at her severely, but continued. 'It revealed that the young woman disappeared from her employer's home...'

'Twenty-two years ago?'

'Yes. And it is supposed – as it generally is in such cases – that the reason for her sudden removal was—'

'She was with child!'

He inclined his head reluctantly and Dido sat for several minutes eagerly considering his information. 'And do the men of the taverns and stables have anything to say about who the father of her child might be?' she asked.

'No,' he said with a reproving frown. 'They do not. And,' he added hastily, 'before you suggest it, no, I shall *not* ask George to make any further enquiries. In my opinion, the matter has been carried quite far enough.'

There was something about the set of his jaw as he

spoke which determined her against pressing him. Instead she considered the information which Mr Lockhart had supplied.

'I suppose,' she mused, 'that Miss Fenn's simple possessions – the coarse hairbrush, the old bible – *might* suggest poverty.'

'She lived in comfort at Madderstone,' he remarked, the note of distaste and disapproval very strong in his voice. 'It would seem that her sin was rather well rewarded.'

'Yes, but…'

'But?' He regarded her questioningly.

'It is so very strange,' she mused. 'That her history should be so…dishonourable.' She hesitated to go on with the subject; she sensed his discomfort at its indelicacy – and yet, she was too puzzled, too intrigued to stop. 'Miss Fenn appeared to her neighbours to be such a virtuous woman.'

'Then it would seem her neighbours were deceived.'

'That is just what Mr Portinscale says. But I find it very hard to believe.' She frowned out of the streaming window at a dripping strand of climbing rose, which scraped to and fro across the glass. 'You see, Mr Lomax, I have always had a great idea that we cannot hide our true selves from our neighbours. At least,' she added, turning back to him with a smiling shrug of the shoulders, 'those of us who live in the country cannot. In the hurry and busyness of a town it may be different. But here in the country – where we lack other diversions – I believe we will *always* find out the true nature of our neighbours.'

'I grant,' he said, 'that in the country a great deal of time is devoted to knowing our neighbours' business.'

'And yet, here was Miss Fenn, residing in a country village and so surrounded by a hundred voluntary spies, but she contrived to keep her character completely hidden. Do you not think it quite extraordinary?'

'It is, perhaps, unusual,' he admitted. 'But I believe that, in this case, you must give up your "great idea" to proof and reason. The evidences are all against you.'

Yet she could not give it up, and his urging only made her more determined upon defence. She thought of the simple possessions; the notes written upon sermons; the text above the bed. She began, with great determination, to look around for proofs and reasons of her own. 'Perhaps she was not guilty…'

'Her guilt is proved. There is the child – and this sudden removal from her employer's house.'

'And yet,' she pursued, 'perhaps it is possible that she was innocent… It might be,' she said, leaning eagerly across the green baize as a new thought occurred, 'it might be that the sin was not mutual.'

He looked startled as her meaning struck home. 'I do not think you had better go on,' he said with grave disapproval.

But there was no preventing Dido now, for she had seen the salvation of her 'great idea' – it lay in the ancient wrongs of her sex. 'Her being with child might be the result of a man's sin only,' she cried. 'Everyone knows of the…nuisances which young maids sometimes suffer in great houses. The crime might not be mutual. After all, a man is stronger than a woman – perhaps her consent was not given…'

She stopped. There was a look of disgust upon his face. She comprehended at last the very great impropriety of describing such a scene to a gentleman – and looked hastily away from him. But there was no recalling her words; they seemed to echo about Margaret's grim parlour.

Mr Lomax stood up. 'I think our conversation had better end, Miss Kent, if we are got onto such subjects.' But he stopped with his hands clenched on the back of a chair. 'Does this not demonstrate to you,' he said with quiet control, 'the very great danger of conducting these arguments – when they lead you into contemplation of scenes which no lady should allow to intrude upon her thoughts?'

Dido turned to the window, and met the faint reflection of her own red face on the dark streaming glass. The very ticking of the clock on the mantle had a shocked sound to her ears; and her own father's silhouette seemed to be regarding her with a look of displeasure which the original had rarely turned upon her.

But her nature was one in which embarrassment was always more inclined to produce justification than remorse...

'Mr Lomax,' she protested, 'I thought I was to be allowed to disagree with you.'

'It is not your disagreement which troubles me. But...' He put a hand to his brow, 'But I must blame *myself* when I allow the pleasure of conversing with you to draw you into unsuitable subjects.'

'Are we not to attempt an equal and open discourse?'

'Yes, but...'

'Such a discourse is quite impossible if there is to be an embargo upon every subject which touches upon misdemeanour – every subject with which the world decrees a lady must not "concern herself"?' She smiled. 'If there are to be such restrictions, you know, we might as well give up our experiment at once and confine ourselves to conversations upon the weather and the state of the roads.'

'I suspect,' he said grimly, 'that you might have dangerous opinions even upon turnpikes and rain-showers.'

There was rather a long silence in which the rose clawed urgently at the window and the severe black outline of old Mr Kent continued to glower reproachfully at his daughter. But then there was a sound of the outer door opening, footsteps in the hall, and Margaret's querulous voice calling out, 'Rebecca, I see that the front step is still not swept!'

Lomax's knuckles whitened upon the chair's back, his voice shook. 'I wish,' he said low and urgent, 'that I could make you understand how very painful it is to a man to hear a woman he esteems…' he hesitated, looked down upon his hands, 'a woman he loves – talking upon such indelicate subjects.'

Dido coloured, but she must speak. Margaret's steps were already crossing towards the parlour.

'I believe,' she said – scarcely speaking above a whisper, 'that true delicacy, consists not in remaining silent about the evils of the world – nor even in being ignorant of them. I am convinced,' she said, finding at last the courage to raise her eyes to his, 'that *real* feminine delicacy consists rather in having right opinions of those evils. And I hope,' and this last was a positive whisper for Margaret was now in the room, 'I hope, Mr Lomax, that, in the course of our acquaintance, you have never had any cause to think my *opinions* indelicate, corrupted or unfeminine.'

He opened his mouth to reply, but Margaret was upon them and he could only smile, bow and excuse himself, leaving Dido alone with her sister-in-law – and struggling to look as if nothing of consequence had passed between them.

Chapter Twenty-Nine

An early escape to the moss hut had now become absolutely necessary. Never had Dido been more in need of solitude; but the rain continued and Margaret was wanting to be listened to.

Margaret was, in fact, in high good humour just now – for dear Mrs Harman-Foote had sent for her – actually *sent* for her. Dear Mrs Harman-Foote wished particularly to consult with her – as one mother to another, you know – about whether young Georgie should be sent to school. For Mr Paynter had advised that he should and had written her a very considered letter upon the merits of plain living in a school. But, of course, she did not wish her husband to know anything about her consulting the surgeon. And so she had *confided* in Margaret, for she knew that she could rely upon her good sense and it seemed that it was a principle of hers…

The day was beginning to draw to a close before the rain held off and Dido was able to escape, at last, from this account of Margaret's triumphant intimacy at the great house.

She slipped out thankfully into the garden's dripping trees and scent of damp earth, and hurried along the gravel path which skirted the side of the house: her mind endeavouring still to interpret the slight smile, the bow which Mr Lomax had made before leaving her alone with Margaret... What had they signified? Assent to her claim? Or doubt...?

There was a peremptory rapping as she passed the library window; she stopped and turned with a dreadful sinking of the heart. However, it was not Margaret knocking; it was Francis's thin face and grey whiskers pressed against the glass, his finger beckoning her in.

'I would just talk with you a moment, Dido,' he said when she joined him. 'Alone, you know. It would not do to...' He waved a hand in vague indication of... something – Margaret perhaps.

Dido closed the library door and went to warm herself at the excellent fire, while her brother settled behind his desk and looked at her in a troubled way. Francis was the oldest of the Kent brothers – in looks, though not in years. He had dark, almost black eyes, narrow features, a high-domed balding head, and particularly large side-whiskers which his sister suspected him of growing so that he might hide from his wife behind them when he was not able to employ a book or a newspaper for that purpose.

Here, however, in the fire-lit sanctuary of his own small room, there was no shortage of books. He had inherited his father's collection and had added to it until it overflowed the shelves to cover every available chair and table. Books were stacked upon his desk and he was now peering around them.

'Ahem, yes. Well, it's this Bath plan, you see...'

'Yes, what of it?' Dido asked briskly. Years of experience

had taught her there was little to be gained from waiting for Francis to finish his sentences. 'You do not wish me to go?' She removed a dictionary and two volumes of Ovid from a chair and sat down.

'Well, as to that... I daresay it could be... And God knows, you've had few enough treats lately.' He gave a quick smile, reminding her suddenly of the kindly older brother who used to read the *Arabian Nights* to her. He opened a drawer in his desk, took something out and hurriedly pushed it towards her. It was a little pile of five gold sovereigns. 'Buy yourself something pretty while you are away – a cap, or a gown or...' He gave another vague wave – clearly at a loss to know what it was that women spent money on.

Dido considered the coins – and his offer – eagerly. She knew there were but a few shillings left in her purse; and, since her regular allowance had disappeared with Charles's bank, heaven only knew when such riches would be within her grasp again. And the visit to Bath represented an opportunity of being with Mr Lomax – continuing their 'open and honest discussion' without Margaret's agonising intrusions.

But still she hesitated. 'I would not wish to rob you, Francis.' She always felt a kind of awkward pity for him and, besides, the money and the holiday would be dearly won if they were to be the cause of more arguments and economy in the vicarage. 'Are you certain it will not inconvenience you?'

'No,' he said, looking steadily at her, his black eyes bright under bushy grey brows. 'Take it, Dido. Take it and go to Bath. I hope things are not got quite so bad that… I should think I can give my sister a few pounds without being obliged to teach Latin lessons again, or I would not…'

'Oh!' Dido put her hand to her mouth as sudden understanding flooded her brain, blotting out for a while even solicitude over Mr Lomax. 'Of course!' she cried delighted at the memory. 'I had forgotten, Francis, you used to take in pupils before you came to Badleigh!'

'*I* have certainly not forgotten it,' he said feelingly. 'Though I do not see why…'

But she was not listening. '"You have been in my situation. You know how difficult it can be!" That is what Mr Portinscale said when he came to visit you last week!'

'Dido!' cried Francis raising a finger. 'I do believe you are *still* in the habit of listening at keyholes! I thought you had grown out of it years ago. I remember Grandmother Kent saying…'

'I was *not* listening at a keyhole,' said Dido with dignity. 'I was quite across the other side of the hall. Mr Portinscale just happened to be talking very loudly – and you had left the door open.'

Francis smiled.

'But my point is,' she said hurriedly, 'that you and Mr Portinscale have both taught little boys their Latin. *That* is the situation you have shared.' Several ideas were coming together in her head now as she remembered the rest of the conversation. 'Francis,' she demanded, 'why did Mr Portinscale come to see you that day? Why did he wish you to intercede with Mr Harman-Foote?'

'Ahem. Well, I do not think…' Francis avoided her

eyes and began to open the largest tome on his desk. 'It was not a matter he would want… Now, if you will excuse me, please, I am rather busy. There is a reference I wish to find for Sunday's sermon…' He put on his spectacles and turned a page.

But Dido was not about to allow a mere brother to evade her questions. She had had many years practice at teasing brothers. She leant across the desk and laid both hands upon the page of his book. 'I shall not leave your library,' she said, 'I shall not cease talking to you until you tell me.'

'Really, this is too bad! You cannot—'

'Did he confess something to you?' she said, smiling up at him and still holding her hands upon his page. 'He did, did he not? He confessed that he had lost his temper with young Georgie. He had struck him, had he not? I know that he had. I saw the bruise!'

Francis gave a long sigh. 'I wonder that you need to trouble me with questions when you *know* so much without…'

'You mean, of course, that I am right!' she cried, tapping her hands delightedly on the book. 'And when you said he should confess all because "*he* is master at Madderstone", you were not referring to Mr Harman-Foote at all, you were referring to Georgie himself.'

'Yes,' said Francis with a resigned sigh. 'I was. You are quite right. Now will you give me some peace?'

But Dido was thinking – without lifting her hands. 'And so you did not intercede for him?'

'No, I did not,' said Francis, with a defeated sigh. 'It would have done no good. That young imp truly is master at the abbey. If he told his mother what had occurred, poor Portinscale would lose the favour of the great house and *my* interceding would only turn Mrs Harman-Foote against me as well, and then Margaret would...' He tried to inch his book out of the sisterly grasp.

'And now,' said Dido, 'the young imp rules Mr Portinscale as well. The unfortunate man is reduced to buying the child's silence – with cake.'

Well satisfied with herself, she released the book, picked up her money and hurried away at last to the damp, but blissful solitude of the moss hut.

Here was one small mystery solved, she thought happily as she settled upon the bench... No, when she considered carefully, she saw that there were *two* mysteries solved. For a little reflection upon Margaret's dull account of her visit to the great house revealed also a solution to Mr Paynter's secret correspondence with Mrs Harman-Foote!

Why, this was turning into a remarkably successful day!

She checked herself abruptly, shocked at her own hard-heartedness. How could these thoughts occupy her so entirely after the affecting interview with Mr Lomax? Within the last hour a man had told her that he loved her – and here was she thinking only about Latin lessons and cake!

How very shameful. Was it possible that her own ideas were of more importance to her than a man's regard? Perhaps, she thought guiltily, she was constitutionally unsuited to love, and Mr Lomax was destined to become no more than a memory, like Mr Clarke...and the other men she had danced and flirted with as a girl.

No. She shook her head immediately with an affectionate smile and watched the black branches of the damson trees drip yellow leaves and water drops into the long grass. No matter what the outcome of their 'experiment', he would always be dear to her. His virtues – and his faults – would always form her very ideal of what a man ought to be.

Mr Lomax's rights revived, but the high spirits of successful mystery solving brightened the prospect. Now she was inclined to be sanguine. The bow and the smile had certainly been favourable…

Chapter Thirty

The party left for Bath two days later, the travellers gathering at the abbey for breakfast before sunrise. And Dido was very glad to be one of the company. She entered the hall of the great house that morning rich and happy; secure in the prospect of five days' freedom and with spirits to enjoy all the anticipation and bustle of an approaching journey: the shuffling in the gravel of the horses as the carriage was drawn up outside; the shouts of the coachman echoing in the grey dawn; the carrying-down of trunks and those odd, muttered arguments which always break out among footmen who never *can* agree upon the best way of stowing boxes.

The smell of chops and toast and coffee issuing from the dining room was very welcome indeed and she was hurrying towards it when a loud voice called out her name. Mr Harman-Foote was standing at the door of his library, holding a candle against the gloom.

'Miss Kent, may I speak with you a moment?'

She followed him into the library where he set the candle down among the papers on a table and begged her to take a seat. But he remained standing himself, his red face frowning, his large hand tapping restlessly among the papers – uppermost of which was the new plan of his grounds. The library fire was but recently lit and the chimney drawing badly: a smell of wood-smoke filled the air and thin grey wisps could be seen twisting about in the candle's pool of light.

'Wanted to ask you something,' he barked at last, so very abruptly that anyone less familiar with his ways would have been offended. Dido only smiled and waited. 'Those letters…' he began, and stopped.

'Letters?'

'Yes. The letters you saw in Miss Fenn's room – or rather you didn't see 'em. For I understand they were gone when you came there.'

'Yes.' She studied his face carefully but could not guess what he was about. His colour was habitually so high that his emotions were very difficult to judge.

'Well—' His fingers drummed upon the plan. 'Point is, I've been wondering. Have you found 'em? Have you got any idea what became of 'em?'

'No, I am afraid not.'

'Ah!' He sat down beside the table, knees spread wide, his hands planted upon them. 'I'm very sorry to hear it. It's a bad business: a very bad business indeed. A lady's correspondence is a private thing, you know. Should be treated with respect. Don't like to think of it falling into the wrong hands. Don't like it at all.'

His disappointment seemed real. There was, overall, such an air of honesty – and of delicacy too, despite the clumsy manner, that she was tempted to trust him… She hesitated; but the sounds of preparation from the hall were becoming louder and more rapid now – they had not long to talk…

'I agree entirely, sir,' she said quietly, meeting his eyes. 'In point of fact, I had rather wondered whether you might have removed the letters yourself – in order to prevent their falling into the wrong hands.'

He started at her words and she discovered that it was, after all, possible for his face to become a little redder. 'By God!' he bellowed good-humouredly. 'William Lomax is right about you, my dear! You're a damned clever young lady!'

'I thank you for the double compliment, sir. I am almost as pleased to be thought young as clever!'

He laughed heartily and insisted upon the accuracy of both words – with a gallantry of intent if not of manner. 'But, you see,' he continued, 'the point is, you are quite right. I did mean to take the letters away…'

'And you went to the room just before Anne and I?' cried Dido, thinking of that little trace of tobacco smoke.

'You are quite right! I did. I left Portinscale and young Crockford in the billiard room and slipped away upstairs pretty soon after dinner.'

'But…'

'But,' he said leaning forward, his hands still clamped upon his knees, 'I was like Old Mother Hubbard. The cupboard was bare.'

'The letters were already gone from the desk?'

He nodded. 'Not a single one left!'

'I see.' She was forced to consider this for several minutes, her eyes fixed meditatively upon the blue-grey skeins of smoke drifting about the candle-flame. 'And do you know,' she asked at last, 'whether any other member of the company went to Miss Fenn's chamber that night? Did you see anyone else on your way there?'

He shook his head. 'Saw no one, I'm certain of it. Only the surgeon.'

'Mr Paynter?'

'Just coming away from poor Miss Lambe's room. Last visit of the day, he said. And, to do that fellow justice, he's been very good. Three times every day he's been here. More than a bump on the head merits, in my opinion – but then, every man knows his own business best.'

'Yes, of course,' said Dido a little absently – for she was now watching her companion very closely and wondering how much he might know about the woman his mother had recommended as governess…

'Those letters, Miss Kent, they must be found, you know. Found and destroyed.'

'Destroyed?' She raised a questioning brow.

'Well, you know…' he looked down, slapped his plump hands upon his legs. 'The poor lady is dead. No need to rake up old secrets. No need at all.'

'Secrets?' began Dido eagerly. 'You believe…'

But the gentleman had now returned to his old refrain. 'Why, it's a bad business,' he declared, sitting back in his chair. 'A bad business all round! I tell you honestly, Miss Kent, I wish the poor lady could have been left in peace where she was. I wish young Henry'd never taken it into his head to drain that pool. It was a foolish trick!'

'A trick!' She leant forward across the papers on the table. 'Mr Harman-Foote, am I to understand that Mr Coulson did not have your permission to breach the dam?'

'No, he did not! I never gave my permission for it. Would *never* have given my permission. Told him so as soon as ever I saw what was going on!'

Dido stared.

'Why,' said he, 'if you do not believe it, look here upon our plan. There, do you see?' She followed the thick pointing finger and saw, drawn quite clearly in the neat black lines of the draughtsman, the shape of the little lake in exactly the same place it had always been. She looked more closely and saw there, among the grand new vistas and terraces, the outline of the watercourse – completely unchanged.

She had been entirely mistaken! It would seem that the question to ask was not: why had the damn been rebuilt? But: why had it ever been broken down?

'*Mr Coulson* chose to drain the pool?' she asked.

'Yes.' Said Mr Harman-Foote. 'But it seems it was James Laurence that persuaded him into it. It was some foolish notion of *his*.'

Chapter Thirty-One

...Well, here I am, Eliza, in this scene of pleasure and dissipation, Bath: and settled at the White Hart, in a comfortable and spacious dining room with a very fine view of the Pump Room's entrance. As usual, whenever I find myself in this town, I am wishing that I had the superiority of mind to be properly disgusted with it. But shops, society and amusements do have their charms even when one is six and thirty and I am not altogether sorry that I have come, though I am by no means certain that I shall succeed in gathering the information I require.

I have met Mrs Nolan.

She is mistress of a small, but well-respected school in Gay Street, who sometimes keeps on girls as 'parlour boarders' when they have no settled home; but unfortunately Penelope is the only young lady occupying that position in her household at present — so there is no close companion to whom I can apply for information.

I suppose Mrs Nolan is a little over fifty years old and she has more than a hint of the North Country in her voice. She has a pale, soft, placid appearance — except for her eyes which are small and black and particularly shrewd. She wears the most remarkable hats I ever set eyes upon, with a great many ribbons and large silk flowers in surprising places. But, though the hats are silly, I suspect the head beneath them is sensible enough.

Yesterday I contrived a tête-à-tête and attempted to ask about Penelope's connections – in a roundabout way. I was not at all successful! I was given to understand that 'the poor lass has not a soul in the world to care for her but me, for I've had the charge of her since she was but five years old'. And, when I pressed to know who it was that had placed her at the school, I was immediately put off. 'Nay, Miss Kent, that is a kind of information which a woman in my situation never discloses.'

Ah well, I suppose I should not have expected her to confide so easily; and I am sure I respect her the better for her discretion. I have not yet determined how she is to be worked upon, but I think I must make a great effort to secure her trust.

Mr Lomax is not yet arrived in Bath, and will not be here until the day after tomorrow. So I fear there will be little time for our 'honest and open discourse'. I was amused, by the by, that you should consider the experiment we have undertaken 'a little dangerous'. What possible danger can there be in our only talking to one another?

Silas has neuralgia; got, so Harriet says, from sitting in a draught in the carriage. He has taken laudanum and has been in his chamber all day. Harriet has taken Lucy away to the shops – where I suspect she is sedulously guarding her from the captain's dangerous company. And I am at peace beside my window – which is very pleasant indeed after the noise and confinement of our journey. The late afternoon sun is shining down in the street, making the stone of the buildings glow. All the fashionable hats of the hurrying ladies – and the fine figures of the gentlemen loitering in the Pump Yard

– appear to great advantage in its cheerful light. Little knots of people are gathered under the colonnade and…

Ah, now that is very interesting, Eliza!

I have recognised one of the figures lounging under the colonnade. It is Captain Laurence! And he is in conversation with an elderly, rakish-looking man whose appearance I do not like at all! He has a fat, dissipated face, a scarred cheek, a quizzing glass – and a <u>very</u> ill-mannered interest in every young lady who walks past him… And the captain – yes, I am not mistaken – the captain, though he has neither the ugly countenance nor the glass, certainly shares the interest. There now! the two of them are putting their heads together and grinning insolently at a little party of schoolgirls.

How very distasteful! I wish that Lucy could see it; it might work her cure.

I confess I am increasingly puzzled by the captain. He is, I am sure, engaged in some very deep scheme. Though I suppose that his contriving to get the pool drained does rather argue against his having killed Miss Fenn – unless he is a very strange murderer indeed: one who <u>wishes</u> the world to know of his crimes.

Upon reflection, I rather think that he is not the guilty man himself; but that he knows something about the poor woman's death. You will remember that, according to the housekeeper, he was in the habit of following Miss Fenn. Well, is it possible that he followed her upon the evening of her death? That he saw her go to the pool and afterwards suspected that she met her death there?

But why should he wish to bring the remains to light? And why should he do it now – after being content to let them lie hidden for fifteen years?

Ah! Here are Lucy, Penelope and Harriet walking up from Cheap Street towards the colonnade! In a moment they will see the captain. I pray Lucy may see enough of his behaviour to disabuse…

But no, it is not to be. Laurence has seen them first. He is pointing them out to his companion in a very insolent way and…and he is hiding from them! It is true, Eliza, the intrepid captain has fled behind a pillar and his friend is shielding him. There now, the women are passing quite unaware and turning away towards Bath Street.

How very strange. Why did he not wish…?

But now L, H and P are out of sight and the captain and his friend are visible again; they have stepped out into the sunshine – they are looking after the women. Laurence is talking fast and earnestly – explaining something to which the other man is listening very attentively indeed. Oh, I wish I could make out their words! The fat man is exceedingly well amused by what he is hearing. His red face is smiling broadly. He is clapping the captain upon the back as if in congratulation. They are sauntering away. Oh Eliza! I do not like the unkind looks upon their faces at all.

Dido laid down her pen and was on the point of stepping to the window to see where the gentlemen might be going, when the door of the dining room burst open and such an apparition appeared as put her in mind of some fellow in a play of Shakespeare's 'with his doublet all unbraced… Pale as his shirt, his knees knocking each other…'

Not that there was a doublet exactly to be 'unbraced', but the general effect was the same. Silas was certainly pale and exceedingly dishevelled: his black curls were

falling about his face, his shirt was open at the neck –
and his knees were shaking violently as he stepped into
the room, holding out a paper.

'It is done!' he declared in a momentous tone.

Dido could only stare, uncomprehending.

'My poem. It is done.' His face was bright with a
kind of confidence and triumph she had never witnessed
there before. He pushed the tumbling hair out of his eyes
and smiled. 'I have never known such r...remarkable
inspiration, Miss Kent. Never!'

'Indeed! But I thought that you were unwell...'

'And so I was. But the laudanum... It set my b...
brain on fire. It conjured up such visions!' He crossed
to the table and sat down beside her, his poem still
clutched in his hand – the paper trembling slightly with
his emotion. 'I did not believe it possible! But Henry
says it is always so. He says those r...romantic fellows
take opium every day and are none the worse for it.
Henry says there's not a p...poet alive who can write a
line without the stuff...'

'I did not know,' she said coolly, 'that Mr Coulson was
such a great authority upon poetry.'

'Oh yes! He has been telling me all about it. I have
talked a great deal about my poem with Henry and he
has been helping me enormously.'

Dido watched him a moment, considering carefully.
Then she drew a slow breath and fixed her eyes upon the
window. 'You do not think,' she suggested lightly, with
every appearance of indifference, 'that perhaps you allow
Mr Coulson to influence you a little too much? He is,
after all, only a distant relation.'

'N...No,' stammered Silas. 'He is the n...nearest male relation that I have and so, you know, the n...nearest thing to a b...brother that I have.'

'Is he?' she asked quickly, abandoning her scrutiny of the window.

But Silas was too restless and too full of his own genius to hear her. 'The poem all came to me in a vision, you know. It was as if I was p...possessed: possessed by a higher p...power! Will you read it, Miss Kent?' he said, pressing the paper upon her and springing to his feet. 'I beg you will tell me honestly w...w...what...' he began; but by now he was at the door and even his new-found confidence could not stand against her actual unfolding of the page and preparing to read. With a blush and one more nervous smile he was gone.

Dido sat for several minutes considering what had passed, before turning, rather apprehensively, to the paper in her hand.

To her relief, it contained only four verses. Clearly 'It is finished!' had not alluded to the whole ballad, but only to that part of it which she was to show to Penelope. For all the influence of the narcotic, the lines were written in a firm, slanting hand and the title 'The Nun's Farewell to her Lover' was underscored by a thick black stroke which only faltered slightly.

She spread the page on the table and read:

The moonlight floats upon the pool
And gleams on grass and sedge.
The dew lies thick. The woman's skirts
Are darkened at the edge.

Upon the mere's dark, reedy verge
The lovers take their leave.
She bends and presses close her love
And begs he must not grieve.

'From this day forth a stranger I,
Must ever be to thee.
But know, beloved, no other can
Match me for constancy.

Another's lips may speak fair words
While I'm by cold vows bound.
Yet falsehoods oft in speech are hid,
And love in silence found.'

Dido read the poem through several times and sat for some time staring at the page. It disturbed her – though she could not think why…

Nor could she quite determine whether there was anything to be gained from showing the work to Penelope. The veiled declaration of devotion might be very much to the purpose, but she rather doubted the poetry had the power of recommending its author… Though Penelope was not likely to be discriminating… Its brevity might count for more with her than anything else – for the *idea* of a poem would certainly appeal more than the prolonged study of one…

She looked again at the paper with its four neat black verses. And again there was a kind of a jolt: a shock almost of recognition…familiarity…

Why did the poem disturb her so much?

Still pondering she rose from the table with a heavy sigh and stepped closer to the window to gaze out upon the darkening town. The first lamps were already lit; over in Cheap Street carriages continued to rumble by, but the Pump Yard was very much quieter now as people hurried away to dress in preparation for the dinner hour. A few ladies were still gazing into the windows of shops; a chairman rested on the pole of his vehicle, smoking a short stub of a pipe; and, in the gathering shadows of the colonnade, two lovers lingered, too wrapped up in one another to heed the approaching dusk.

It was the sight of the couple which at last brought inspiration to Dido. It led her wandering mind through a very natural series of connections, from the tangled affections of her young friends to a consideration of the very great dangers of a passionate nature – and so to that other passionate and dangerous attachment of Miss Fenn to her mysterious correspondent...

She turned hurriedly from the window and seized Silas's poem. Holding it up eagerly in the fading light of the window, she studied it closely.

Yes, that was what had disturbed her! Not the verse – but the hand in which it was written! The letters were small and black with a marked forward slant. It was not exactly the hand of Miss Fenn's 'Beloved' – but it was very much like it.

Chapter Thirty-Two

'Harriet,' said Dido next day as they were walking together in the Pump Room, 'how was your brother educated? Was he sent away to school or was he placed with a private tutor?'

'Why ever do you ask?' cried Harriet in surprise. 'Upon my word, Dido, I never knew a woman like you for asking odd questions!'

'I am only a little curious.'

'Oh, you are always a little curious, and I tell you honestly, that it will not do. Curiosity, you know, is something that old spinsters are always laughed at about.'

'Yes,' said Dido, taking her arm. 'But I am sure *you* will not laugh at me. For we are two old spinsters together are we not? We may defy the world.'

Harriet gave her most weary smile. 'But I do not see why you should care about Silas's education.'

'Oh, it is just that he writes such a very…interesting hand and I rather wondered from whom he had learnt it. For, you know, we all write a little in the style of the master who taught us.'

Harriet frowned and studied her companion rather suspiciously for a moment before shrugging up her shoulders. 'Unfortunately,' she said, 'Silas's poor state of health prevented his ever going away to school. He was educated chiefly at home; his only tutors were friends of the family.' She considered a moment. 'Mr Portinscale taught him for a little while,' she said.

'I see.'

Dido fell into a reverie at that and they walked on in silence. This information did not lie at all easily with everything else that had come to light. How could Mr Portinscale be the illicit lover of Elinor Fenn? How could *he* have written that cold letter ordering her to forget him? He was the man who had made love to her openly – and offered her marriage, was he not?

'Shall we join the others,' said Harriet, gesturing towards Captain Laurence and Penelope who were standing beside the well-head, very deep in conversation.

'Oh yes,' agreed Dido a little absently, and they began to make their way up the long room – their progress much impeded by the crowd.

In point of fact, the company in the Pump Room this morning was 'thin'. Everybody had said that it was so and it had been generally agreed among them that it was too early in the season for truly fashionable people to be in Bath. Dido believed it all, and, aloud, she lamented it with as much energy as her companions; but privately she hoped that she might never have to form part of the company when it was 'thick'.

There was quite enough crowding for her taste. There was a perpetual movement of people through the doors, and such a noise of restless feet and chattering voices as echoed about the elegant Greek pillars and high ceiling, almost overpowering the efforts of the musicians in the gallery who seemed, sometimes, to be fingering and sawing at their instruments in vain. Outside, the sun was just breaking through after a heavy shower, and, within, the smell of wet umbrellas was mixing with that of greenhouse plants and the warm, sulphurous breath of the spring. The very floor was shaking beneath its weight of fashion and it was not until they were within an arm's length that she was able to distinguish anything that was passing between the captain and Penelope – although, alerted by the earnestness of their manner, she was struggling hard for their words all the way along the room…

'…And so you see, I have my orders. Tomorrow I must go up to town to make my preparations,' the captain was saying as they drew close. 'And within five days after that I must be aboard my ship.' He took both Penelope's hands. 'At such a time,' he continued in a low, urgent voice, 'at such a time, Miss Lambe, a man becomes bold. It is not to be wondered at, you know, for he has need of all the courage he can command – knowing what hardships and dangers lie ahead of him.'

'Oh yes!' cried Penelope fervently, 'You are all so very, very brave. I am sure the navy is such a body of men as… Well, I am *quite* sure there is no one else like them in all the world! Except perhaps,' she added anxiously, 'for soldiers – for I would not wish to be unfair upon them, you know. But then, though they are called upon to fight, they may stay upon the land and do not have to go to sea – which I am sure is a great deal more comfortable. So sailors you see,' she finished with conviction, '*are* the bravest after all.' She smiled serenely and, catching sight of Dido and Harriet, turned eagerly to them for confirmation. 'Sailors are the best and bravest men in the whole world, are they not?'

Laurence saw them now. 'Miss Crockford, Miss Kent.' He bowed, released Penelope's hands and looked so very discomposed that Harriet and Dido's suspicions were immediately raised against him.

Had he been upon the point of a *declaration*?

They stood together a few minutes: all rather ill at ease, but for Penelope who had noticed nothing at all and was now busily enumerating the hardships of naval life, through battle, storm and privateers to what must be 'the greatest inconveniences imaginable caused by the motion of the ship. I mean the sliding about of food upon the table and the falling out of beds and so forth...'

As she chattered, Dido's eye was drawn away to a bench beside the great clock, from which the schoolmistress, Mrs Nolan, was watching. She was sitting very straight, with her hands clasped upon the handle of her umbrella: her face sharp and watchful in the shadow of her vast white cap and the elaborate bonnet which covered it. A cluster of flowers hanging low upon the brim half-obscured her eyes and gave her rather the appearance of a small, wild creature peering through undergrowth. But it would seem that she too had noticed the captain's 'attentions' – and they had made her uneasy.

And it occurred immediately to Dido that her uneasiness might provide a very useful opening for conversation. Perhaps this was the moment to try for her confidence... Declaring, rather abruptly, that she was tired and must rest, she left Harriet to chaperone Penelope, and made her way purposefully back towards the schoolmistress.

'My dear, Mrs Nolan,' she cried with a smile as she approached, 'you are looking very worried. Are you afraid of Miss Lambe's tiring herself with walking about too much?'

'Nay.' Mrs Nolan shook her head and set the flowers flapping about her eyes. 'She's a stout lass, and I doubt a little knock on the head has turned her into an invalid. But...' she raised her umbrella in Laurence's direction and gave it a little shake, 'I'm right *vexed* to see her walking about on yon fellow's arm.'

'Oh?' said Dido in a tone of innocent surprise. 'Do you not consider the captain a suitable acquaintance for the young lady?'

'Suitable? Eeh, no!' Mrs Nolan lowered the umbrella, folded her hands over its handle and gave Dido a doleful stare. 'Pardon me for saying it, Miss Kent, but I'm accustomed to speaking my mind, and I tell you honestly, yon captain is such a fellow as I swear is sent to test and torment poor honest schoolteachers like myself. For I declare there ain't no way of keeping young ladies safe from his sort.'

'Is there not?' said Dido, deeply interested. 'And how...?'

'As if the cost of candles for the schoolroom wasn't trial enough,' Mrs Nolan ran on, with all the appearance of a woman who is launched upon a favourite complaint and will not be easily turned aside from it. 'And folks being so tardy over paying their fees! As if such things weren't sufficient torment, there must be men like that one sent to make us miserable!'

'Dear, dear,' said Dido. She took a seat beside the schoolmistress, her head tilted in sympathetic attention.

'Aye, a woman in my situation lives in terror of such fellows as that. One hears such tales, Miss Kent!'

'Does one?'

'Eeh yes! Ladders set up at bedroom windows in the dead of night and young lasses carried off to Gretna in the twinkling of an eye. Or worse...' Mrs Nolan tapped at Dido's foot with her umbrella to emphasise her point, '*not* carried to Gretna at all – if you gather my meaning.'

'Oh heavens! How shocking! I confess I had heard...' Dido bent a little closer. 'But do such things truly happen?'

'They do, my dear. Though...' her face reddening. '*Never* in my establishment, I assure you.'

'No, no of course not! I would not have thought it.'

'Twenty-six years, come next Lady Day, I've been educating my lasses and not one has ever come to harm. And a schoolmistress's reputation is her livelihood you know, Miss Kent. I've seen a school or two closed down because there's been a breath of scandal – for the parents cannot trust then, you see.'

'Dear, dear! What a very great worry it must be for you!' Dido regarded her companion with great interest. But, unfortunately, the others were approaching now and Mrs Nolan was reaching out with the umbrella to tap Penelope on the arm with a 'Well now, my dear, I think you have walked enough for today.'

And it was quite impossible to re-engage her in conversation, for a moment later Lucy and Silas also appeared and then they were all in a group talking together.

Silas had been very busy securing places at the obligatory entertainments of Bath. He had tickets for a concert in the assembly rooms that evening, and there was a theatre box taken for tomorrow. 'A b…box which holds n…nine. So we are in hopes, Mrs Nolan that you and P…P… Miss Lambe will be kind enough to join us.'

Meanwhile Dido was considering the schoolmistress's words – and concluding that the very best way to work upon her would be to somehow save Penelope from the captain. That would certainly create a high degree of obligation – in fact it might *just* overcome her reserve and bring her to confide who it was that paid the girl's allowance…

Chapter Thirty-Three

The evening's concert included – according to popular report – some of the foremost performers in the country. However, Dido knew that the foremost performers in the country were to be met with everywhere – under a great many variations of taste and talent – and she did not look forward to the evening very eagerly.

Her own taste for music was not great. She would rather have the sweet strains of pianoforte and harp in the background of her mind than the foreground. And, in the event, she found that she had scarcely ever enjoyed music better than she did now as she sat under the brilliant chandeliers of the concert room and peered around the tall feathered headdress of the lady in the next row to catch a glimpse of hautboy and fiddle. For here, she found, she was free to worry away at her mystery, while the duty of listening deterred other people from talking to her.

And, altogether, she had probably more pleasure in the entertainment than Lucy who declared that she 'loved music more than any creature alive', and 'music was an absolute necessary of life to her' – but who passed her evening fidgeting about and watching the gentlemen lounging at the sides of the room; and certainly more than poor Penelope who yawned through the full two hours, observed that 'there was no understanding a word of Italian singing,' and wondered from time to time 'how anyone could make their fingers fly about so fast – and keep it up so long too.'

Dido was very comfortably occupied through the first act with running through the many questions in her mind – and with watching the seats of grandeur round the orchestra. Here she discovered Captain Laurence's fat companion of the colonnade, accompanied by a fashionable woman with a great deal more face paint than bodice; and she fell to studying the lady with particular interest. The gay apparel and the slight, pleasing figure suggested youth – but the thick white painting of the face told of age concealed...

'My dear friend, at last I have you alone!' Lucy's whisper startled Dido from her reverie. She looked about her to find the first act concluded, Penelope and Harriet walking off with Silas and Captain Laurence in quest of tea – and Lucy taking the empty place on the bench beside her.

'Had we not better go to drink tea?' Dido said quickly and attempted an escape. She was, at any time, uneasy to be addressed as Lucy's 'dear friend', and just now she was particularly unwilling to have the train of her thoughts disturbed.

But Lucy took her arm, held her securely in her place and leant close as people hurried along the aisle beside them. 'There is a great secret which I must tell you about,' she said in a low, thrilled voice.

'Oh!' Fond though she was in general of secrets, Dido

doubted that she wished to hear this one. She cast longing eyes towards the inviting little tables under the balcony, where the urns were bubbling and hissing comfortably and 'the cups that cheer but not inebriate' were setting out. A very pleasant scent of hot tea and sweetmeats filled the air.

But Lucy was blushing and fidgeting with her fan. 'Captain Laurence,' she whispered, 'is to go away from Bath for two days tomorrow.'

'Oh, but that is no great secret! He has told us of it himself.'

Dido attempted to stand up; but Lucy held hard to her arm. 'There is a very particular reason for his going,' she whispered. 'He is going to make preparations.'

Dido detected danger in the words and ceased trying to escape. 'What kind of preparations?' she asked, searching Lucy's face closely – and noticing a thick, unbecoming layer of powder and rogue laid over the freckles.

'Preparations for our marriage.'

Oh dear! Dido's heart sank. 'But why,' she asked impatiently, 'must we whisper about the business in this way?'

'Because no one is to know anything about it until after we are married – and then you know, no one will be able to stop it.'

'A *secret* marriage!' cried Dido aghast, staring at her companion who was sitting upon the edge of the bench and swinging her feet like a delighted child. 'And in haste too! I do not believe it!' Indeed she could not, *would* not believe it. Not even of her!

Lucy looked a little disconcerted. Her feet stilled.

'Why?' urged Dido desperately. 'I can see no reason for secrecy. You are of age – no one can prevent your marrying the captain if you have set your heart upon it. Why cannot it all be honest and open?'

'Oh!' Lucy shrugged, spread her fan and pretended to study the peacocks painted upon it. 'But Harriet would want to prevent it, you know. And dear, dear, Laurence is so *very* afraid of losing me!' She blushed and looked towards the tea tables, where the gentleman himself was leaning easily against one of the columns, cup in hand. 'For he knows how excessively it grieves me to cause anyone pain. He says he cannot be easy until the matter is settled beyond any danger of persuasion.'

'Does he indeed!' Dido was almost overcome with apprehension. She was *sure* Captain Laurence was engaged upon strange and devious schemes: he knew something of the death of Miss Fenn; he consorted with unpleasant men with fat leering faces – and, by Harriet's account, the morals of his friends were as objectionable as their countenances. In short, he was not to be trusted. Lucy risked too much by putting herself into his power in this way…

But she did not know how to act. The instinct of nature cried out to her to run immediately to Harriet, who was now tranquilly sipping tea at one of the tables, and tell her all – to prevent at all costs this dangerous concealment. But the power of reason kept her still on the bench at Lucy's side. For what would she achieve by disclosure but an instant rupture between the sisters – and a hasty marriage?

Wit alone could prevent this elopement.

She shifted uncomfortably upon the narrow bench as the cacophony of voices echoed about the high ceiled room. 'Upon my word, Lucy,' she pleaded earnestly, 'you risk too much by going away in secret with such a man. Your good name...'

'Oh! You are too careful! I do not wonder at *your* never having married! True love knows nothing of caution!'

Dido's face burnt with more than the heat of the crowd; but she had time neither to think about the comment, nor be wounded by it. And Lucy hurried on. '*Dear* Laurence's mind is quite made up,' she said, 'I cannot think of myself. I *must* do as he wishes.'

There was a short pause here; they were disturbed by a large party of ladies bustling past to regain their seats, and Dido took the opportunity to reform her thoughts. Perhaps she was only hardening the silly girl's resolve by arguing against her. As they reseated themselves she said cautiously, 'I am very grateful for your confidence...'

'Oh!' cried Lucy, taking her hand. 'It is only natural I should trust such a steady creature as yourself! There is a kind of *solidity* about your reflections which I am sure I know how to value – even though it is very different from my own quick, lively character.'

'Thank you.' It was not the most pleasing compliment she had ever received, but Dido smiled graciously nonetheless.

'And besides,' ran on Lucy, 'I have a particular reason for confiding in you. Dido...' she looked quickly about the crowded concert room, setting her curls bobbing, and clasped together her hands like a little girl at prayer. 'I need your help,' she whispered.

'Ah! Well…'

'No. Please listen to me. We have not much time to talk. You see, there is to be a letter for me – a very *important* letter.'

'And it will be from Captain Laurence, I daresay.'

'Yes. He must send me news of what is arranged, you see. But Harriet is so suspicious! I know she looks at every letter I receive. So, you see, I have no choice…'

'…but to make me complicit in your deception!'

'Upon my word!' cried Lucy in a voice that was suddenly quick and sharp. 'I am only asking you to watch for the letter and, if you should see it, hide it from Harriet and hand it quietly to me. I do not think that so great a test of friendship!'

'No,' said Dido, forcing herself to speak soothingly. 'Of course it is not.'

She was sick at heart, almost overwhelmed by a crowding host of fears which were all the more painful for being so very ill-defined; but she dared not risk losing Lucy's confidence: for retaining it seemed to offer the best – the only – chance of working against the marriage.

Chapter Thirty-Four

...Oh Eliza, what am I to do? I am miserable – and angry too with Lucy for having entrapped me in so invidious a position. It is monstrous to deceive Harriet – and yet I dare not speak a word. And my only comfort is in writing this account to you. I am like the man in the fable who must whisper to the reeds, 'King Midas has asses' ears.'

And I sincerely hope that you will forgive me for likening you to a bed of reeds!

But, if the very worst should happen: if this marriage should take place and Harriet afterwards discover that I have appeared complicit in it, I beg that you will bear witness to my motives – which, from the very beginning, have been fixed upon prevention.

I cannot sleep tonight for thinking about the business and I have fallen into my vicarage habit of writing in bed by candlelight. Though I do not know that, if my mind were completely at ease, I should get much sleep, for the lights in the street and the ringing calls of the watchman telling the hours make the night rather uncomfortable for a country-woman.

The great question – the question to which all my thoughts recur – is this: why should Captain Laurence insist upon a <u>secret</u> marriage? To say that he fears Lucy may be persuaded out of her consent is arrant nonsense. He is certainly not so modest he cannot see how much she is in love with him! And he must know as well as Harriet or I that opposition would only harden her resolution of having him...

But then, when I consider the scene he was enacting with Penelope in the Pump Room, I begin to fear I understand him.

His address was very particular – and his confusion upon being disturbed very evident. I cannot doubt he was upon the point of declaring himself. And yet, Eliza, not even James Laurence can hope to marry <u>two</u> ladies at once.

This, I am sure, is his plan: he will marry Lucy and secure her twelve thousand pounds (or whatever portion of it the estate can be made to pay) and then, while everyone remains in ignorance of the marriage, he will persuade Penelope into an elopement. And, before she discovers that she cannot become his wife, her reputation will be so far compromised that the poor friendless girl will have no choice but to accept the shameful 'protection' which he offers.

He must, of course, be prevented. But how? Neither Penelope nor Lucy will listen to me unless I have solid proof. And there can be no proof – not until Lucy is actually married to the rogue. And then her misery will be assured – together with the misery of her brother and sister.

This is more than enough worry to keep me awake, without the continual passing of link boys and chattering gentlemen. And there is another small point which has begun to trouble me – Silas's poem. I cannot quite be easy about Silas's poem. I have had at the back of my mind all day an uneasy suspicion that there is something else odd about it, besides the hand in which it is written...

I have just been looking the poem over again. Perhaps it is his use of the endearment, 'beloved', that troubles me – and the odd similarity between 'No other can match me for constancy' and the expressions of everlasting love in Miss Fenn's letter. There is, when I come to consider it, a rather close affinity in the ideas expressed… Almost as if Silas might have read her declarations. Eliza, do you think it is possible that Henry Coulson has those other letters – the stolen ones – and he has shown them to Silas? Is that perhaps what Silas meant when he said that Henry had been helping him with his poem?

The letter arrived next day – directed to Lucy in Captain Laurence's unmistakable looped and sprawling hand. It was lying upon the table of the inn parlour when Dido and Harriet returned from the shops where they had spent two hours and a half attempting to complete the very exacting commissions with which Margaret had charged them. And rarely had a little bit of sealed paper looked so very dreadful and ominous.

Dido swept it up and put it away in her pocket while Harriet was still occupied in telling the boy where to set down their parcels; then she dropped into a chair.

'Why!' cried Harriet. 'You look well and truly done-up. And I think you had better not be walking out to Sydney Gardens with me now. For, when all's said and done, there is no need to "make a labour of our leisure", as the saying goes.'

Dido hesitated. It was arranged that they should meet Lucy and Penelope in the gardens and, if she did not go, then she would be able to delay handing the letter to

Lucy... But, she would also delay her own knowledge of what it contained – and she did not think she could bear that.

'No,' she said a little unsteadily. 'I am quite well, thank you. The walk will be refreshing after loitering about so long at shop counters.' She smiled, struggling hard for composure.

And, within a quarter of an hour, they were out again and crossing the sunny Pump Yard. It was a bright day and warm for the season. The sun glowed on the creamy yellow stone saints of the abbey church's west front, and its fine pinnacles stood out sharp against a cloudless blue. The peculiar white dust of Bath was rising in little clouds about everyone's feet and the prospect of a walk among trees and shrubs was pleasant; but Dido's anticipation of it was very much spoilt by the presence of the letter in her pocket.

What did it contain? When was the elopement to take place? How much time had she in which to prevent it? These questions were running so continually through her head that she was not aware of Mrs Nolan's approach until she called out a greeting.

'Upon my word,' cried Harriet as the schoolmistress joined them, 'you look as if you have lost a crown and found a farthing!'

'Eeh now! Don't tease me, I beg, Miss Crockford. For it is a great deal worse than that. I've found *this*.' She held out a letter which was so very like the one in her own pocket that Dido started at the sight. Here were the same large black characters, the same paper, the same post office mark; the only difference was in the name and direction. For this was addressed to *Miss P. Lambe*. 'It arrived not half an hour ago, and I think I know who it is from,' continued Mrs Nolan.

'It is Captain Laurence's hand,' said Dido quietly – and immediately saw that she had confirmed the poor woman's worst fears.

'Eeh! Well, I decided straightaway I'd out after my young lady with it and see if I can't talk sense into her, for if it's come to this then matters are pretty bad.' She shook the letter fiercely.

Dido sighed and echoed the sentiment internally. Indeed, matters were pretty bad: if Laurence was corresponding with Penelope, then there could be no doubt of his having reached an 'understanding' with her too – nothing less could authorise it. She gazed up helplessly at the carving on the sunny church wall above their heads and wished that the stone angels there who laboured perpetually up Jacob's ladder might carry with them a prayer for assistance; for she was beginning to fear that this tangle was beyond mortal ingenuity.

'I doubt Penelope will heed you,' said Harriet to Mrs Nolan as they all walked on together. 'Her notions are all romantic, you know.'

It was a point upon which three such sensible women could not but agree and they continued in rather gloomy silence along the shady north side of the church and past the Lower Rooms. Dido was turning over in her mind the evidences for Captain Laurence's plans of seduction and considering the ingenuity with which it was all carrying on.

'But what I cannot quite understand,' she confessed as they came to the road beside the river and paused to allow the passing of a smart curricle, 'one point which still rather puzzles me is this: how was Captain Laurence's acquaintance with Miss Lambe begun? I can imagine a handsome, plausible man going on very well once he has a fair opportunity. But how does he begin? How does he get an introduction?'

'Lord! My dear Miss Kent, young fellows these days scarcely need an introduction! Not in public places such as this.' And Mrs Nolan scowled about her as they hurried through the dirt of the road – as if the very streets of Bath were her personal enemies. 'They begin by watching, you see – you may be sure I had noticed the captain and his fat friend watching the poor girl a week or more before he acted. And then he played his trick…and it was such an old, worn-out trick as only an innocent like Miss Lambe *could* be taken in by.'

'Oh?' Both Harriet and Dido looked at her with interest.

'Aye,' she said, 'for it was nought but the old game of picking up a lady's dropped handkerchief. In the Pump Room one morning, not six weeks past! That's how he forced himself upon the poor lass's attention.'

'I see.' Dido knew the trick well. In her youth she had dropped a handkerchief or two herself, though she had always found it a rather unsatisfactory stratagem, since they had invariably been retrieved by the *wrong* gentleman.

'But,' protested Harriet with a frown, 'that's a game two must play, is it not? For, when all's said and done, the handkerchief must be dropped before it can be returned.'

'Oh Lord!' exclaimed Mrs Nolan. 'You are nigh as innocent as Miss Lambe herself! In Bath these days fellows such as yon captain carry a ready supply of ladies' handkerchiefs in their pockets – aye, and fans too. And then it is all, "I beg your pardon, but I was sure it fell from *your* hand. In this crowd it is so difficult to determine..." And very clever it is, for, of course, the less the lass believes it, the more flattered she is.'

'How very...unpleasant,' said Dido.

'Aye. But the difficulty,' she confided, 'lies in ensuring that it does not become anything worse than "unpleasant", if you take my meaning.'

'Yes,' murmured Dido and Harriet. And they all stopped, as if by common consent, looking down upon the sluggish river flowing from beneath Pulteney Bridge and at the gulls which wheeled above it, crying out as harshly as the men in the crowding boats. For a moment they were all lost in the awful contemplation of that great chasm of 'worse than unpleasant' which gapes just beneath the intercourse of the respectable world and threatens always to swallow up incautious members of the fair sex.

But, all at once, Dido's considerations took an entirely different turn...

'Pardon me, Mrs Nolan,' she cried, 'but did you say that Captain Laurence has been acquainted with Miss Lambe for *only six weeks?*'

'Yes.'

'Well, that is very odd – very odd indeed.' She frowned thoughtfully and turned to Harriet. 'I understood from Lucy,' she said as they all walked on to the bridge, 'that it was about then that he introduced Penelope to you.'

'It was,' said Harriet.

'Aye, that's right,' confirmed Mrs Nolan, 'I remember it perfectly well. It was no more than two days after he had so kindly "picked up her handkerchief".'

'How very strange.' Dido fell into a reverie.

They turned onto the bridge and made their way as best they could between the carriages passing on the busy road and the people loitering about to look in the windows of the little shops.

'Why...' said Dido slowly at last, '...was he in such a very great hurry to make that introduction?'

'Why,' said Mrs Nolan, glancing a little uneasily at Harriet, 'to get her invited to the country, I suppose, so that he might carry on his attentions there.'

But Dido shook her head. 'No,' she said with emphasis, 'I do not think so. I am sure that cannot have been his motive. It is very stupid of me not to have thought of this before! I am quite sure he could have pursued her more conveniently here, where, as you say, the public places allow a great deal more license than is ever possible in private parties.'

'Aye,' agreed Mrs Nolan slowly, 'I suppose that is true enough.'

'And,' continued Dido eagerly, warming to her theme, 'since the good captain seems also to be in pursuit of Lucy, his schemes *must* have been made more dangerous by the introduction.'

Harriet nodded. 'I confess,' she said, 'I had wondered...'

'I am *sure*,' cried Dido, 'that he had another reason for wishing Penelope to be at Badleigh – or else...' she added, her mind firmly fixed upon that tantalising possibility of Penelope being Miss Fenn's daughter, 'or else he wished her to go to Madderstone Abbey!'

'But why should he wish her to go to Madderstone?' asked Harriet in a puzzled voice. And Dido was struggling for a plausible answer when she became aware that Mrs Nolan had stopped walking.

She turned back and saw that the schoolmistress was staring intently into the window of one of the bridge's little shops – though, since it offered *The Finest Gentlemen's Tailoring*, it did not seem to provide much interest for a widowed lady. The flowers and foliage of her bonnet, the wide expanse of white cap below it, almost obscured her face, but, upon the little bit of pale cheek which could be seen, muscles were working fitfully – as if something in the conversation had struck a chord.

'Mrs Nolan?' said Dido, stepping back to her. 'Do you agree with me that there was something strange in the introduction?'

'Oh dear! I hardly know I'm sure, Miss Kent!' She left the window and hurried on so fast that Dido and Harriet could scarcely keep pace with her.

They found Penelope and Lucy in Sydney Gardens, amid the arching beauty of ornamental trees, standing upon one of the pretty little iron bridges which span the new canal, with all the reflected red and gold of turning leaves shimmering upon the water below. Though their arms were linked, they were not talking but seemed rather to be engaged upon private reveries, for, while Lucy's head was thrown back in soulful contemplation of the autumnal scene, Penelope's attention was smilingly turned upon a little child who was clinging to the hand of his nursemaid and taking unsteady steps across the grass nearby.

Harriet hurried forward immediately with a greeting, but Mrs Nolan held back. Beneath the nodding flowers, her soft white face puckered into a frown. And Dido hesitated at her side, feeling that she understood precisely the apprehension she was experiencing.

For the moment of handing the letter to Lucy was upon her – and she still knew not how to prevent disaster... She looked again towards the two girls standing on the bridge in their fluttering white muslins. Something must be done – and done quickly – to bring them both to disillusion... And yet she dared not offer a word of advice... She dared not even tell Harriet the truth...

Mrs Nolan had drawn out her letter and was reading the direction of it – as if she hoped that somehow it might have changed. Her eyes were narrowed against the sharp sunlight and shadows which were shifting across the paper; she held it closer to her eyes to make out the writing...

And all at once Dido saw, in that one simple movement, the answer to all their difficulties!

She touched her companion gently on the arm. 'I too have something to deliver,' she said quietly and, taking the letter from her own pocket, she held it out for Mrs Nolan's inspection.

'Eeh dear me!'

'I wonder,' said Dido hurriedly, 'whether you might permit me to deliver *both* letters.'

Mrs Nolan looked a little uncertain, but relinquished her letter and Dido stood for a moment looking down at the two pieces of paper with their black sprawling directions: so innocent looking, so very dangerous – and so very, *very* alike...

'It is,' she remarked, 'extremely difficult to make out the writing in this light, is it not?' She swapped the letters about in her hands and smiled.

There was a moment of puzzlement on the schoolmistress's face – and then a dawning of understanding. 'Eeh! Miss Kent! You would not!'

But Dido did not reply. She was already running along the path towards the bridge. Lucy and Penelope were walking towards her, their faces flushed with sun and exercise, their bonnet-strings streaming behind them in the breeze.

She looked down just once more at the letters, frowning with all the appearance of a woman dazzled. She held out a hand to each of the girls.

They each took a letter and their faces showed immediate recognition of the hand-writing. They turned aside preparing to break the seals – their movements mirroring one another so exactly they might have been engaged in a country dance.

They stopped, back to back. Dido held her breath.

They seemed to stand frozen for an eternity of seconds in the sunlight as people sauntered past. The child on the grass stumbled and began to cry.

Slowly the girls turned back to face one another. The wind flung back a bonnet string, cracking it like a whip. Lucy's face burnt red with fury; Penelope's was pale and trembling, a tear creeping slowly from one eye.

'Miss Lambe, I believe this letter is directed to *you*.'

'And this, I think is *yours*.'

Stiffly they made the exchange. A moment later the glorious sound of tearing paper reached Dido's ears, bringing with it the very comfortable conviction that Captain Laurence's schemes were defeated.

Chapter Thirty-Five

Dido was very well pleased with her solution of this problem. Her triumph made her rather confident of succeeding at last in all her other undertakings and she had an appearance of great satisfaction and self-congratulation when she entered the theatre the following evening. Mr Lomax noticed it as they met in the lobby and, as they were all taking their seats, he remarked that the air – and the *company* – of Bath seemed to agree with her.

As he spoke, he cast a meaningful look at Captain Laurence, who had now rejoined their party and was being very attentive to Dido – no doubt as a consequence of the cold looks he was receiving from Lucy and Penelope.

Dido only smiled and acknowledged that the air suited her very well. There was no time for further explanation just then, for everyone must look about them and admire Bath's grand new theatre.

The bright fresh paintings upon the ceiling and the rows of boxes rising up on their bronze pillars, glorious with scarlet linings and gilt lattices, were a fine sight to behold. The audience (though it was, by common consent, as 'thin' as the company in the Pump Room) was aglitter with jewels and feathers and silks. And upon the stage there were all manner of gaily painted scenes and clever tricks with lights and machinery to be admired.

Indeed, amid all this opulence, there was but one dull thing – and that, unfortunately, was the wit of the playwright.

The play itself proved to be a poor old threadbare thing, and throughout the first act Dido's attention was perpetually wandering from it. She soon found a great deal more to interest her in Captain Laurence's wanderings about the building than she did in the worn out maxims and jokes of the actors.

The captain seemed to be no better amused by the play than she was herself. He left their box before the first scene was over and, thereafter, he was forever appearing first in one part of the theatre and then in another. She could not help but wonder what he was about and it became a kind of game with her to guess in which box she would detect him next.

'Do you know,' she whispered eagerly to Mr Lomax as the first act ended, 'who the man is that Captain Laurence is talking to now?'

Lomax followed the direction of her eyes to a box almost opposite their own where the captain had now joined the elderly rake of the colonnade, and his well-painted lady. 'That,' he replied rather stiffly, 'is Lord Congreve: the man who owns half the land in Shropshire, and has a great deal of influence at the Admiralty besides – which is no doubt the reason for Laurence courting his favour.'

'I see!' cried Dido her interest deepening. 'But I think you do not like His Lordship?' she added as she noticed a look of marked distaste spreading across her companion's face.

'*I* have no opinion of him at all,' he said with great dignity. 'It is *you* who are so very occupied with James Laurence and his acquaintances that you cannot keep your eyes upon the stage.'

Dido suppressed a smile – and continued to look at the captain's acquaintances. The fat lord was listening intently, as Laurence – with one hand resting familiarly on the noble shoulder – talked earnestly into his ear. As he listened he stroked the old scar on his cheek very thoughtfully – and looked in their direction.

Whatever was Laurence communicating? His plan for Lucy and Penelope's ruin was at an end; yet he seemed still to be scheming…

'I w…wonder at Laurence being seen in c…company with that fellow,' whispered Silas from his seat behind. 'I'll w…warrant the friendship's not known about at Madderstone!'

The expression upon his face suggested he knew something in particular to the disadvantage of 'that fellow', and Dido was about to ask what exactly he meant; but the play was beginning again and his attention was returning to the stage.

So she fell instead to examining Lord Congreve's companion again. And that little painted face set in motion such a *very* interesting train of thought that soon 'the two hours' traffic of our stage' was passing by quite unregarded. Dido recalled all the things which she knew about His Lordship – and an idea began slowly to form in her head: an idea far stranger than the fiction acting out before her. And yet, she assured herself, it was an idea based entirely upon reason, facts and observation.

It certainly allowed for no shadow of coincidence or superstition – perhaps even the ghost itself might be rationally explained by it...

As they all came out upon the stairs at the end of the play, the very great pressure of the crowd bore Dido and Mr Lomax away from their companions and authorised her to cling rather tightly to his arm. Indeed it was only by pressing herself against him that she could save herself from being carried away by a careless troop of passing gentlemen. She seized upon this moment of jostling intimacy.

'Are you familiar at all with the lady accompanying Lord Congreve?' she asked urgently. 'Is she his wife?'

He looked surprised by the sudden application. 'No,' he said, gravely disapproving, 'she is not. His marriage ended unhappily some years ago. The young lady with him tonight is his mistress.' He turned away as he spoke and held out a hand to guard her as a drunken man staggered by.

'You call her young,' said Dido. 'About what age do you suppose her to be?'

'What a very strange question!'

'But I think it is a rather important one. Please? Do you know her age?'

He sighed and shook his head. 'She is reported to be barely sixteen,' he said reluctantly. 'His Lordship has the reputation of...associating with very young women.'

'Yes,' said Dido remembering the peer's behaviour under the colonnade. 'I rather suspected it.'

She lapsed into a very thoughtful silence and they

were carried forward down the stairs on a hot tide of coloured headdresses, dark evening coats and bare white shoulders. The memory of that white powdered face was still intriguing her. 'It is a puzzle,' she said as they came to rest upon the last landing. 'A very great puzzle. Why should such a young woman paint her face so very thickly?'

Lomax looked down at her laughing: brows raised over questioning eyes. 'Miss Kent!' he cried. 'I would never have expected to find you so much interested in appearance and cosmetic!'

'Oh, but on this occasion, I am, Mr Lomax! I really believe...'

'What is it?' he said, matching her seriousness immediately. 'What is it you believe?'

'I believe that that lady's face paint might be a key to Madderstone's mysteries.'

He looked bewildered – and rather irritated; he particularly disliked her speaking in riddles. Struggling hard for patience he began, 'I am afraid I do not quite...'

But she was not listening. Her attention was fixed upon the hallway just a few steps below, where a discourteous footman was now making way for a disdainful Lord Congreve and his companion.

Then, all at once, she was on the move, weaving rapidly through the crowd on the stairs and slipping off the loop of ribbon which secured her fan to her wrist. She reached the bottom of the steps just as the manservant succeeding in clearing a passage for his master; she turned in apparent confusion and nearly ran against His

Lordship – there was an ill-bred oath. She stepped back in confusion – and somehow contrived to drop her fan. It slid most satisfactorily across the floor and came to rest just in front of the couple. She bent to retrieve it – and so was able to look full into the face of the young woman as she stood up and apologised for inconveniencing her...

And it was just as she had thought: the startled white little face was extremely youthful: almost a child's face – but so thickly coated in grease and powder that tiny cracks were evident about the mouth and eyes.

But, seen as close as this, the face had another secret to reveal...

Chapter Thirty-Six

Dido woke next morning from a light, restless sleep, to the clattering of milk-pails and pattens on the inn doorstep. She lay for a minute or two staring up at the dusty red wool of the bed's canopy as she once more ran over the ideas which had occupied her long into the night: the face of Lord Congreve's companion; His Lordship's ill-bred interest in very young women; the scar upon his cheek; Mrs Nolan's information that Congreve and Laurence had watched Penelope several days before Laurence made his move with the handkerchief; Silas's suggestion of some particular vice which would make the peer's acquaintance unacceptable at Madderstone…

And, once it was all recalled, she found that she could lie still no longer.

She jumped up and stood beside the room's small window, gazing down upon the early-morning street and the milkmaids who were now hurrying away from the inn, the empty pails swinging lightly on their yokes, and at a cart which was drawn up to bring fowls and vegetables from the country.

There was in her head such a picture of guilt and deception! And yet she was still like a little girl in the schoolroom endeavouring to fit together her map of Europe. Some pieces fell into place very neatly indeed

– but there were gaps and missing pieces which left the continent woefully incomplete. She could not finish her lesson – she could not even be sure that the pattern she had formed was correct...

There were still details to discover. She must ascertain from Silas exactly what it was that he had hinted at last night. But the most pressing business was to speak to Mrs Nolan. It was absolutely essential to know for certain who it was that had placed Penelope in her care: who it was that maintained the girl. When that was established, then perhaps she would know how to proceed.

However, they were to leave Bath this very morning and she had only an hour or two in which to persuade the schoolmistress into confiding. Within five and twenty minutes she was dressed and making her way out of the inn's door.

The light was strengthening now as the sun rose. Two men were throwing down water on the steps and sweeping dirt away into the gutters. The farmer's cart was just finishing unloading its goods and, as Dido passed it, she detected a sweet, slightly rotten smell which reminded her sharply of the inn-yard at Great Farleigh...

She turned quickly and saw a boy swinging the last basket from the cart onto his shoulder. Through the wickerwork there protruded several brown and green feathers of game birds.

A smile of satisfaction spread across her face and, as she began to walk slowly across the Pump Yard towards the upper town, she was fitting another small piece of her map into place.

* * *

Dido could not help but feel hopeful about her errand. There had, she reasoned, been marked signs of gratitude in Mrs Nolan's address since the scene in Sydney Gardens – a disposition to regard Dido as a special friend for the service she had rendered in separating Penelope from Captain Laurence. There had even been moments when she had detected an inclination to confide – but caution had always intervened.

Somehow the confidence must be won this morning. A great deal depended upon it – for she was sure that, once she had it, she could find the countries which were still missing from Europe…

She brightened at this thought – and hurried on with such determination that she almost ran against a gentleman just then descending the steps of his house. He drew back immediately with a bow, a well-mannered apology – and a look of earnest admiration…

A look to which Dido was not insensible, despite the preoccupation of her mind. He walked off – but paused twice to look again before turning away into George Street – and she continued on her way amused and delighted to find that the animation of mystery-solving could add such charm to her person. But, as she approached Mrs Nolan's house, her mood became more sombre – her manner businesslike.

She was admitted by a housemaid and shown into a parlour which could never be mistaken for belonging to anyone but the keeper of a school, it was crammed so full with fancy work. Everything, from the six or seven worked footstools, to the pictures in coloured silks hanging upon the walls and the imitations of china crowding the mantelpiece, attested to the accomplishments of Mrs Nolan's 'lasses'.

'Well, I am right glad to see you Miss Kent,' cried the schoolmistress, standing up to receive her, and seeming not to mind the earliness of the hour at all. 'I'd have been sorry not to have wished you goodbye before you start out on your journey and I particularly wished to see you alone so that I might thank you for dealing so neatly with that little business over the letters. It was very cleverly done indeed. For neither Miss Lambe nor Miss Lucy Crockford had to admit that they had been mistaken – and you know that counts for a great deal with young people.'

'I believe it counts for a great deal with people of any age,' said Dido smiling. 'But I hope Miss Lambe has not been too much hurt.'

'Eeh well, there were a few tears when she was on her own in her bed, I daresay. But it'll be got over. She's not the sort to mind it long. And,' she leant forward and tapped Dido's arm, 'I reckon what's needed is another fellow for her to fall in love with – someone a bit more suitable, eh?'

Dido agreed to it wholeheartedly, and congratulated herself upon her work of the previous afternoon – when Silas's poem had been shown to Penelope – and had been *very* favourably received. 'The Nun's Farewell to her Lover' had in fact been declared 'so sweet, and so very clever and just exactly like the poems one read in books. Or rather better; for one understood just exactly what was meant by it. Which was not always the way with poems in books…'

'And, in the meantime,' pursued Dido, intent upon making the most of the present opening, 'there is another little matter concerning Miss Lambe about which I hoped to talk to you.'

'Eeh well,' said Mrs Nolan, turning away and smoothing the threads of an indifferently worked cushion. 'I think I know what that is. It concerns her going to Badleigh does it not?'

Dido studied the schoolteacher's averted face, very sensible under the extravagant coquelicot ribbons of her cap. 'Yes,' she said, 'it does concern her visit there…'

'Aye, I guessed from the way you looked at me so sharp upon Pulteney Bridge yesterday that you suspected I knew more about that than I was telling.'

'And do you know more than you were telling?'

'Eeh yes, to be perfectly candid with you, Miss Kent, I do. And I'm still right uneasy about it…' She hesitated again. Dido waited in silence. 'I've been awake half this night wondering whether I ought to speak to you about it. For, if there's trouble brewing, maybe you can put things right.'

'I shall certainly do everything within my power to… put things right. And, of course, you may rely upon my discretion.'

'Well,' said Mrs Nolan raising her eyes. 'The fact of the matter is, I never was happy about her going off to be with the Crockfords.'

'Because you knew Captain Laurence would be close at hand?'

'Aye, there was that. But there was something else too…' She stopped and turned her eyes once more upon the cushion as if appraising its pattern. She did not seem to know how to go on.

'Did you,' Dido prompted, 'know that Miss Lambe had…connections in that neighbourhood?'

'Yes, I did.' Mrs Nolan seemed to make up her mind to disclosure. She looked up, her gaze straight, honest and sensible. 'The lass herself knows nothing about it of course. She knows nought of her own history. I was told to tell her nothing. But her mother…or rather I should say, the lady who sent her here, she lived very near the Crockfords – at Madderstone Abbey.'

'Oh!' cried Dido. She could scarcely draw breath for fear of saying something which might prevent the schoolteacher from continuing. 'And…this lady was…?'

'Miss Fenn. Miss Elinor Fenn.'

'Oh!' It was quite impossible for Dido to sit still a moment longer. She absolutely must walk about. She could not think while remaining stationary. Excusing herself, she went to the window and found some relief in gazing out at the steep sunny cobbles and a couple of chairmen labouring up the hill. 'Are you quite sure?' she asked, turning back into the room. 'Are you quite sure that it was Elinor Fenn who sent Penelope here?'

'Oh, aye. Though I never met her.'

'Did you not?' asked Dido sharply.

'No, but I am quite sure of the name. There were letters and money sent; and for the first two years I wrote to her from time to time to tell her how the lass went on – so I am very sure of the direction too. I always fancied she was companion to a lady at the abbey, or something of that sort.'

'A governess,' said Dido rather absently, 'she was a governess. But,' she paced back across the room, 'I do not quite understand. Miss Fenn has been dead for fifteen years…'

'Dead? Poor soul! But I always suspected it.'

'And has no one paid Miss Lambe's allowance in all that time?'

'Eeh! Miss Kent, I wish I was such a rich woman I could keep on lasses for nought. But no… No, the fact is, about fifteen years ago – just two years after Miss Lambe came here – the money for her maintenance stopped coming. Naturally I wrote to Miss Fenn to enquire about the matter.'

'Yes, of course.'

'And, after a short delay, I received a reply. Not from the lady herself – but from…a friend of hers. This letter said…now what was it…? It said Miss Fenn was "no longer able to meet her obligations with regard to the child" and he – the writer of this letter – would in future pay what was necessary. And – all credit to him, Miss Kent – he's never missed. Never been so much as a day late sending the money. Which leads me to suppose…' she stopped and primmed up her lips.

'To suppose that he is the girl's father?'

'Aye – though of course, it is none of my business to have an opinion. And I only mention the matter to you because you might be able to make sure the secret don't get out. You see, Miss Kent, I know how gentlemen can turn when their secrets are exposed. They're inclined to get angry – and stop paying the money. I wouldn't want ought to happen that'd hurt the poor lass – for she's a dear soul. Not so very clever – but as good-hearted as you could wish.'

'Yes, she is. I agree that she must be protected.' Dido turned back to the window to hide her eagerness and asked, as calmly as she could, 'Can you tell me the name of this gentleman who maintains Miss Lambe?'

'Aye. His name is Mr Foote – Mr *Harman*-Foote I believe he calls himself now.'

Chapter Thirty-Seven

Dido hurried down Gay Street, her mind busy with the notion of Mr Harman-Foote being Penelope's father. Very carefully, tentatively, she tried to fit this new piece into her map...

It explained a great deal: that reluctance to have Penelope stay at Madderstone which she had detected in her first conversation with Mr Harman-Foote after the accident; his determination to prevent his wife discovering the truth about the death in the lake; his persuading his mother to recommend Miss Fenn as governess.

She was very reluctant to think the genial master of Madderstone a murderer – but this latest information pointed to a powerful motive. Had he drowned his former mistress in order to silence her passionate demands which, had they become public, would certainly have prevented his very advantageous marriage? Maybe Captain Laurence had come to suspect the liaison and his investigations into the matter were a preliminary to exacting money in exchange for silence – that was a stratagem she believed the captain to be quite capable of...

But no. She shook her head, deeply dissatisfied. There were yet pieces which did not fit into the map at all: the handwriting which argued against Mr Harman-

Foote being Miss Fenn's lover; and Laurence's distasteful conferences with Lord Congreve; and there was still the strange appearance of the ghost to be accounted for.

And then there was one point which troubled her more than any other: one small, but very disturbing fact. It would seem that Mrs Nolan had never met Elinor Fenn...

The town was becoming busier now: the chairmen were much occupied with getting people to the hot baths and the sweet smell of fresh bread and pastry was drifting from half a dozen little bakeries – turning Dido's thoughts inevitably towards breakfast. And, despite the urgent demands of her mysteries, she was becoming rather occupied with chocolate and hot buns as she once more crossed the quiet Pump Yard and came to the front of the White Hart.

But there she encountered a sight which rapidly returned her thoughts to business. A post-chaise was drawn up outside the inn door and a groom was just stowing aboard a box and greatcoat which she recognised immediately as belonging to Captain Laurence.

'Is Captain Laurence going to Portsmouth to join his ship?' she enquired of the groom.

'Oh no, miss, he's going back to his family in the country first.'

'To Madderstone Abbey?'

'Aye.'

Now that, she thought, coming to a standstill beside the inn door, was odd: very odd indeed. She had been quite sure that, after the failure of his scheme against Lucy and Penelope, Laurence would simply take himself off to sea. Why was he returning to Madderstone? She did not like it at all. If he was still scheming – if he had still an interest at Madderstone, then matters might be more complicated – and dangerous – than she had supposed…

She stepped hurriedly into the inn's public parlour in the hope of snatching a word with him alone, but was instantly disappointed.

Just inside the door there was a high oak screen which formed a kind of dark, ale-scented passageway with a dirty, stone-flagged floor, from which stairs led to the upper chambers. And, as she stepped into the passageway, Dido heard Laurence's voice talking in the parlour on the other side of the screen. He had company.

'…I promise I will do it…' he was saying hurriedly.

She turned away. She was upon the point of continuing up the stairs (or so she assured herself afterwards).

'…If those letters are there to be found,' said Laurence, 'I promise I will find them.'

Such an invitation to eavesdropping! Resistance would have required the ethic of a saint – and Dido had never pretended to sainthood. She stopped.

'Why, you're a good fellow, Laurence,' drawled a lazy voice. 'A damned good fellow and you won't find me ungrateful.'

She puzzled over the voice a moment – knowing she had heard it before, but uncertain where, until the scene in the theatre lobby recurred. Her dropped fan, the insolent oath. The second man was certainly Lord Congreve.

'Yes, get the letters and burn them,' he was saying now. 'All I want is to have the whole business covered up. I had hoped I'd get what I need out of this…' He stopped; there was a sound as of a hand striking a table. 'But the infernal woman didn't… Well, no matter, it seems she did not rob me after all. All I want now is for it to be covered up. I've no interest in the little miss. Just get the letters and destroy them.'

Chairs scraped across the stone floor as he spoke, footsteps approached the screen. Dido turned to hurry away; but as she went she caught the captain's repeated assurance that there was nothing for His Lordship to worry about – that everything would be settled safely.

Dido fled up the dark stairs. Suspicions were turning into certainties, new fears presenting themselves, and plans forming so very rapidly that her map was almost made up by the time she arrived at the door of the private dining parlour.

Lord Congreve was at the root of it all! It explained so much.

She pushed open the door – and saw Mr Lomax just rising from the window seat to make his bow.

'Miss Kent, I am sorry to call upon you so early,' he began quickly, taking a step towards her, his face anxious. 'But I have been uneasy since our conversation in the theatre last night – your interest in Lord Congreve. I have been blaming myself ever since for not warning you sufficiently…' He hesitated, aware perhaps that she was as agitated as he was himself. 'I was concerned about your…investigations,' he said, eyeing her more closely. 'I wished to warn you to take no interest in that wretched fellow's affairs. They are not…'

'They are not the kind of thing a lady ought to concern herself with,' she finished for him, closing the door and stepping into the room. 'Yes, I am aware of that – though I am very grateful to you for taking the trouble to warn me of the danger.'

He watched her uneasily as she crossed to the window and looked down into the street where the chaise was just drawing away. 'However,' she said, 'I am also aware that Captain Laurence is, at this moment, setting off for Madderstone – upon business for "that wretched fellow". And,' she added distractedly, 'he *must* be prevented from completing that business. The safety of a friend of mine depends upon his being prevented.'

She put a hand to her brow, almost overwhelmed by the thoughts rushing in upon her. Mr Lomax stepped back to the window seat. 'You had better sit down and tell me all about it,' he said quietly.

She hesitated. He would not like many of the things which she had to say: he would be shocked – disgusted, perhaps, to hear them from her lips. But the words were on the point of spilling out of her. It would be agony to hold them back. She *had* to speak.

And, perhaps this was the moment at which all their theories must be tested. For, if he could bear to hear her now without objection, then that miraculous union might yet stand within the compass of belief.

She sank down gratefully on the window seat and drew in a long breath. Behind her she could still hear the agonising sound of chaise wheels speeding towards Madderstone Abbey, and around her the inn was coming to life: footsteps echoed on the stairs as the maids carried up hot water, voices were calling out below in the public rooms and the smells of coal smoke, hot bread and coffee filled the air. The day was advancing; soon she must return to Madderstone and face the difficulties and dangers which awaited her there.

But, for now, she could indulge herself in the exquisite relief of talking – of sharing her ideas with a mind she knew could meet hers in understanding.

She folded her hands in her lap, as demure as a child preparing to recite a lesson, turned her face into the sun's warmth and began to 'tell all about it' – starting with the information she had gained upon her recent visit to Mrs Nolan, and the conversation between Captain Laurence and his friend which she 'happened to have heard as she passed through the parlour just now.'

By the time she reached this point he was watching her with interest: the tips of his fingers were coming together… 'And so, you believe that Mr Harman-Foote is Miss Lambe's father?' he said as she paused.

'No.' She continued resolutely, without apologising for the indelicacy of the subject – for it had to be said; but she turned away her face to the window so that she was watching the smoke of the town's breakfast fires roll across the sunny roofs as she said, 'No, I do not believe that he is Penelope's father at all.'

'You think the schoolmistress is lying?'

'No, no, I am sure her information is correct – so far as it goes. I believe Mr Harman-Foote has indeed supported Penelope these last fifteen years. But, it does not necessarily follow that he has been prompted by either duty or guilt. I think his only motive has been benevolence.'

'That,' he acknowledged, consideringly, 'would accord well with his character. I have a great regard for the man and I would be very happy to believe him innocent. But what is your proof?' He stopped, smiled. 'You see, Miss Kent, I have such confidence in your reasoning that I am sure you *have* proof.'

'And your confidence is not misplaced. My proof lies in the behaviour of Captain Laurence. You see,' she said, 'I believe the captain knew that Miss Fenn had gone to the pool on the day of her death – and suspected that she had died there. But, for fifteen years he said nothing of his suspicions – and then, about two months ago, he began making enquiries. He followed the same trail as I did, through the information of servants, to Great Farleigh – and Penelope. And he also persuaded Mr Coulson to drain the lower pool.'

'But this is no proof of your case!' he cried. 'Laurence's most probable motive was to expose Harman-Foote's guilt and subject him to blackmail.'

'No, no,' she said eagerly. 'I do not think so. If his intention was to get money from Mr Harman-Foote, why did he not approach him with his discoveries? Why did he come here to Bath – and tell Lord Congreve?'

'Congreve?' The gathering interest in Lomax's face was all swallowed up in alarm. The very name seemed to make him uneasy.

'What would you say,' continued Dido eagerly, 'if I told you that His Lordship is Penelope's father?'

'Ah!' he frowned and hastened to supply an explanation himself; in order, no doubt, to save her 'concerning herself' with unsuitable information. 'You believe that Congreve...

forced his attentions upon this woman Elinor Fenn – when she was maid to old Mrs Foote. That he got her with child. And that, out of compassion, Mr Harman-Foote persuaded his mother to recommend her as a governess.'

'Do you not think it possible?' she asked.

'No!' he protested warmly. 'No I certainly do not!'

She tilted her head and looked up at him questioningly. 'And what, pray, is the weakness in my reasoning?'

'I regret to say there are so many weaknesses I scarcely know where to begin.' His face was frowning severely in the sunshine, criss-crossed by the shadows of the window-leads. 'A disgraced maid become a governess! It was most unsuitable. And yet you believe that two such respectable people as Mrs Foote and Mr Harman were complicit in the deception?'

'I believe that they must have both known the truth of the young governess's history. Otherwise the plan could not have been carried out.'

'No!' he cried. 'This is very poor reasoning. I knew Mrs Foote. She was a very proper lady. She would not have taken part in such a business.'

'So, I cannot convince you that this story is true?'

'I am afraid you cannot. It is nonsense... That is,' he added, recollecting himself, and bowing slightly awkwardly in the confined space of the window seat. 'I would not contradict a lady...'

'No, no Mr Lomax,' she cried immediately, 'you are forgetting that there is to be open and honest discussion between you and I. Please contradict me as much as you wish. You must be as free to mention my errors as I am to mention other people's crimes.'

'Must I?' He looked at her in surprise – then laughed, set his elbow on the edge of the window and leant towards her, shaking his head. 'Then I *shall* contradict you. My dear Miss Kent,' he said in gentle challenge, 'I would suggest that you are talking nonsense.'

'Yes,' she said, smiling serenely up into his eyes. 'I know that I am.'

'You know?'

'Yes, of course this tale is arrant nonsense! And yet,' she added, 'you failed to mention the one most startling piece of evidence against it – the very comfortable bedchamber which was allotted to Miss Fenn at Madderstone.'

'The bedchamber?' he repeated, rather confused by this sudden turn of events. 'Why should that be significant?'

She hesitated over answering the question. A part of her would have liked to jump up at this point and walk about the room – for there were a great many ideas and suspicions crowding in upon her now and her mind was always clearer when her body was in motion. But she did not wish to move away from him. Honest and open discussion was, she found, rather pleasantly conducted at rest together upon the sun-warmed window seat, where his long fingers played restlessly within inches of her face and she could see the tiny dark flecks which the sunlight revealed in the grey of his eyes.

'In the theatre,' she said, striking out into another branch of reasoning, 'I suggested to you that the key to all our mysteries might lie in the face of Lord Congreve's present mistress.'

'Yes, I remember.'

'Well, afterwards – in the lobby – I contrived to

look more closely at that young lady's face.'

'And what did her face reveal?'

'It revealed a great deal of grease and powder; but not quite enough – not enough to hide a blackened eye, a bruised cheek and a split lip.'

'Congreve!' he cried in a voice of controlled fury. The restless fingers formed an involuntary fist. He smote the ancient frame of the window and set the panes rattling.

'Yes,' she agreed. 'I believe him to have been the source of the injuries – for I remember Harriet telling me once that it was his unkind treatment of his wife which ended his marriage.'

'In God's name, I wish – for the honour of my own sex – that I could repudiate it. But I cannot.'

'Very well then,' she said solemnly, 'the young lady's face reveals Lord Congreve's nature – the behaviour he is capable of towards women.' For a moment there was no sound within the room except the soft flap and stutter of flames on the hearth. But from below came the shouts of coachmen and the ringing of plates and tankards upon tables – reminding Dido that they must soon be disturbed. Hastily she picked up the third – and final – thread of her reasoning. 'Yesterday,' she said, 'when we were all discussing His Lordship, Mr Crockford remarked that the captain's connection with him would be disapproved at Madderstone. He seemed to hint at a particular reason for that disapproval.'

Mr Lomax was watching her intently, his fingers just tapping slightly against one another.

'I meant,' she said, 'to ask Mr Crockford to explain his remark. For you know, masculine disputes are generally better known to gentlemen. But perhaps *you* can supply the information, Mr Lomax. Why is Mr Harman-Foote Lord Congreve's enemy?'

'Ah!' he cried, 'I am not sure that is a question...'

'...that a lady should concern herself with. But,' she ran on hastily, 'I find that I *must* concern myself with this question of the gentlemen's enmity. For I believe it is all to do with the scar upon His Lordship's cheek – and Mr Harman-Foote's reputation for having fought and marked his man.' She paused, brows raised. 'I am right, am I not?' she said. 'The man he fought many years ago *was* Lord Congreve?'

He nodded.

'And the cause of their fight was?'

'My dear Miss Kent, gentlemen do not discuss the cause of a duel!'

'Then gentlemen are very foolish indeed,' she cried impatiently. 'I am sure no woman would put an embargo upon a subject which might uncover the guilt of a murderer! Upon my word, I begin to suspect that between considerations of what women must not think about and men may not talk of, a great many crimes go undetected!'

'But, it is a matter of honour not to disclose the name of a lady...'

'Ah!' she cried, well satisfied. 'So, there *was* a lady involved in the dispute between Mr Harman-Foote and Lord Congreve!'

He groaned and passed his hand across his face. She seemed to defeat him at every turn.

'Very well, then,' she continued. 'And, to spare you the

dishonour of speaking her name, I shall supply it myself. It was Lady Congreve, was it not? It was His Lordship's ill-treatment of his own wife which Mr Harman-Foote sought to punish in that meeting?'

'It was. However,' he said, finding suddenly a new angle of attack, 'I am sure that your hitting upon the name is no more than a lucky guess. For I defy even you to produce any proof of your surmise.'

'No,' she said with dignity. 'It is not a guess; it is an hypothesis.'

'An hypothesis?'

'Yes, for once we assume that she was the cause of the fight, the events at Madderstone become a great deal more comprehensible. Consider the matter carefully: more than twenty years ago, Lady Congreve suffered such ill-usage at the hands of her husband that she removed herself from his house. And Mr Harman-Foote fought His Lordship over the matter. And…' Her face was glowing with something of the fervour that can be seen in those high-spirited women who follow the fox-hunt. 'And, at about the same time as Lady Congreve disappeared, a governess appeared at Madderstone Abbey – upon the recommendation of the Foote family: a friendless woman who, apparently, had no relations, no connections.'

'But,' objected Lomax, 'the governess was Elinor Fenn.'

'No,' insisted Dido quietly. 'The governess was *Lady Congreve*. A homeless fugitive, after her flight from a wretched marriage had left her utterly destitute.'

She had certainly won her companion's attention. He was leaning towards her, his brow gathered into a frown of concentration, his fingers tapping together as he considered.

'I believe,' she continued, very eager to strengthen and elaborate her case, before he could begin to doubt, 'I believe that the key to the name – Elinor Fenn – might lie in the matter-of-fact character of old Mrs Foote. Called upon to introduce Her Ladyship under a new identity, the poor woman found that invention was beyond her, and she fell back upon a name fresh in her mind from her maid's recent departure. But the one point which convinces me that I am right is the bedchamber.'

'You think a great deal about this bedchamber.'

'I do indeed. You see, I can conceive of a country gentleman like Mr Harman taking in – out of compassion – a viscountess, and hiding her under the guise of a governess. But I am sure he would be quite incapable of consigning her to an attic!'

Lomax shook his head. 'It is a fantastic – an impossible tale! That a lady of such standing should take on the post of country governess…'

'It may be fantastic to a man,' said Dido with quiet feeling, 'but I believe it would fall within the comprehension of many women: we have so little power over our own destiny, Mr Lomax, we slip so easily from comfort – even luxury – into poverty. We have so little that we can truly call our own…' She sat for a moment looking down at her own hands folded in her lap.

And he watched her in silence, the telltale muscle in his cheek moving slightly in the way it always did when he was forcing himself to hold back words.

'Consider the situation of a woman such as Lady

Congreve,' said Dido at last. 'A woman who finds herself living in fear of her husband's violent temper. She has no power, no right even to remove herself, much less take any wealth with her. Even a viscountess might be compelled to seek employment in such an extremity.'

'Well,' he conceded with a heavy sigh, 'Congreve's vicious nature would certainly have made concealment necessary for his poor wife.'

'You believe then that I am right?'

'Ah! I did not quite say that,' he cried hastily. 'I admit that there are evidences in support of your theory; however there are also arguments against it.'

'Indeed? And what are they?'

'Principally the character of Lady Congreve. She was, by all accounts, a very religious woman…'

'And so was Elinor Fenn,' countered Dido quickly. 'I am by no means suggesting that the lady changed her character with her name. Indeed, I rather consider Her Ladyship's piety to be a point in my favour. For I believe there is evidence of scruples. Consider the verse in the Bible which had been underlined. It was the second part of the commandment which was so very important to her. St Paul begins by demanding obedience from women; but he then insists upon a man's kindly treatment of his wife. And I believe Lady Congreve found comfort in considering that, by his abominable behaviour, His Lordship had been the first to break the sacred pact of matrimony.'

But still he insisted upon disbelief. 'It would all have involved such a degree of calculation,' he objected, 'not only upon the part of Lady Congreve, but of others too. Compassion, I believe, is rarely carried to such extremes.'

'But,' she said, 'there is one circumstance which might have made Lady Congreve's friends particularly willing to assist her. You see, she was with child when she left her husband; and I believe this provides whatever explanation is still wanting for her desperate scheme – and her friends' compliance in it. If it was feared that her husband's vicious conduct not only threatened her own safety, but also put at risk the life of the child she carried, might not very religious, moral people feel that the highest duty was to protect that young life?'

He considered her words in silence. Meanwhile the noises about them were becoming louder. The old staircase of the inn was in such constant and heavy use now that the panelled walls of their parlour were shaking a little. Harriet, Lucy and Silas must soon make their appearance.

'Have I convinced you, Mr Lomax?' she ventured to ask.

But he avoided admitting the force of her arguments. 'And do you believe that Congreve discovered his wife – and exacted a terrible revenge for her desertion?' he asked.

She would have dearly loved to make him acknowledge defeat. It would have been delightful to have him admit the superiority of her reasoning – but, unfortunately, it was an indulgence for which she had no time.

'No,' she said in a great hurry, 'I do not think that His Lordship was the murderer. For I am quite sure that Laurence carried out his investigations in order to please his influential friend. I believe the two men met about two months ago and, when Laurence heard the tale of his new acquaintance's divorce, he remembered the coming of the governess to Madderstone. *That* is what prompted him to begin his enquiries.'

'I see.'

Harriet and Silas could now be heard talking on the landing.

'And all this,' Dido ran on hurriedly, 'argues for Lord Congreve wishing for information about the fate of his wife – and that of course rather rules out his having murdered her.'

'That is soundly reasoned,' he acknowledged. 'But if Congreve is not the murderer, then who is it that you suspect? And why should you believe Congreve's latest commission to Laurence to be so dangerous, if he only wishes for the business to be covered up?'

A hand turned the lock of the parlour door. 'Because,' Dido said urgently, 'Lady Congreve was a remarkably clever woman. I have been thinking it all over for half the night, and I believe that Captain Laurence has not yet discovered her most dangerous secret. And it is,' she added, 'of the greatest importance that he never does discover it. That is why he *must not* be allowed to find the missing letters.'

Harriet and Silas were actually in the room now; but, fortunately, they were too busy arguing over whether Silas should wear a flannel waistcoat for the journey to take any notice of the couple in the window seat. Lomax leant close and, in his anxiety, laid his hand upon Dido's arm. 'Why?' he whispered. 'What do you fear the letters might reveal?'

'I fear they will reveal that His Lordship is mistaken in thinking his wife stole nothing from him. You see, Mr Lomax, I believe that when Lady Congreve left her husband's house she defied those laws which said she could take nothing. She took with her something of very great value indeed – something which was the cause of her death. And, if her husband ever discovers that she robbed him, he will stop at nothing to retrieve his property.'

'Good God! Explain yourself, please! I do not like to see you involving yourself with the affairs of such a man as Congreve. I would advise against it if I dared, but I fear my very opposition would make you more determined…' Without his knowing it, the pressure of his fingers on her arm increased and their urgent warmth moved her more than any words of persuasion.

'But I cannot explain it yet,' she answered regretfully, 'for I do not yet understand it all myself. I must send a message to Great Farleigh immediately; and I need to find out who stole the letters and the ring; and I *must* look again at the pieces of gold and silver which were taken from the lake…'

Chapter Thirty-Eight

The last hour in Bath passed in a muddle of rapidly packed boxes and conflicting anxieties. Dido knew not whether to worry most about Captain Laurence speeding towards Madderstone ahead of them, or the ideas which were swarming through her head – or the effect which the communication of those ideas had had upon Mr Lomax.

And, at the end, the drawing up of the chaise at the door took her entirely by surprise and she ran down the stairs into the dark passageway with a band-box in her hand and the ribbons of her bonnet still untied – to find Lomax himself waiting for her in the gloom.

With an urgency which was surprising – but not entirely unpleasant – he seized her free hand and drew her around the end of the screen. The public parlour – a black-beamed room with high settles and smoke-yellowed plaster – was empty now, but for an old grey deerhound stretched out upon the dirty flags in a patch of sunlight. Mr Lomax took the band-box from her and set it down on a table scarred with the notches made to reckon card games and the sticky rings of tankards.

'Miss Kent,' he said quickly, 'you must take great care that Congreve does not know what you are about. He is a vile man. You cannot conceive what he is capable of.'

'I have seen that young woman's face.' she said quietly, 'I can believe him capable of any evil. But do not fear. If all goes well, he will suspect nothing – he will continue to have no interest in Madderstone. And if all does not go well…' She hesitated. 'If Captain Laurence succeeds in finding the letters, then there may be danger – but not for me. It is someone else who will be at risk.'

'Who?'

She shrugged up her shoulders. 'I do not yet know. But someone else at Madderstone has a great secret to hide. From the beginning, someone has been working against me: stealing the letters and the ring, attempting to stop me from discovering the truth.'

'The murderer?'

'No, I am almost certain that the person who killed Lady Congreve has already answered for that crime in the highest court of all. The murderer, I am sure, is dead – but someone yet living wishes the identity of the killer to remain hidden.'

The horses were stamping outside now and Harriet was calling out that time and tide waited for no one. Lomax studied Dido's face closely, his expression very grave. She was still unable to tell how her revelations had affected him. Was he angry, or only concerned for her safety?

'There is one question which I must ask you,' he said, with quiet urgency. 'There is one very important subject we have not yet talked of – and that is, what do you mean to *do* when all is discovered? Will you approach the coroner? Do you wish me to act for you? I will be in Madderstone again in just a few days…'

'Oh no!' she cried in alarm.

His look told her that she had confirmed his worst fears. 'You do not intend to take any action?' he said quietly. 'You mean to keep the identity of the dead woman a secret?'

'No possible good could come of revealing it,' she said quickly, 'and there might be a great deal of harm. No, believe me, her identity – everything – must remain in the obscurity that she desired.'

His look darkened. 'And you are to decide this?' he said raising an eyebrow. 'May I ask upon what authority you, and you alone, are to decide what is to be revealed and what is to be kept hidden?'

Dido drew herself away from him stiffly. 'Upon the indisputable authority of my knowing what no one else has taken the trouble to discover,' she said.

'That is arrant nonsense!' He passed his hand across his face. 'You *must* inform the authorities of what you know. It is entirely contrary to the law to keep information to yourself when a murder has taken place.'

She stared up at him in defiant disbelief. 'Why?' she demanded. 'Why do you insist that I must supply the coroner's court with information you did not even wish me to seek out?'

The muscle moved in his cheek as he forced back angry words. 'Because,' he said, his face all stony composure and insufferable self-righteousness, 'you are privileged to live in a civilised land and it is your duty to abide by its laws.'

'But the laws of this civilised land did nothing to save the poor lady who died,' protested Dido. 'She lost everything she owned in order to protect her child from her husband's cruelty and in the end gave up her life to guard her secrets. No, Mr Lomax, you must excuse me, I will *not* expose those secrets now, to satisfy laws which are wrong.'

'Why, I am sure that every thief in the commonwealth thinks that our laws against burglary are wrong – and every killer would see murder go unpunished if he could!'

'You would call me a criminal, because I will not agree with you?' she cried with energy.

'I would call you a criminal because you are intent upon breaking the law! We cannot, any of us, disobey laws simply because we do not like them.'

'Can we not? Well, I certainly cannot do what I know is wrong simply because there happens to be a law about it.'

'Oh!' he cried bringing his hand down upon the table and making the band-box leap an inch into the air. 'This is argued like a woman!'

'I beg your pardon,' she said coldly. 'But I am a woman and it is hardly to be expected that I should argue against my nature.' She picked up the band-box and turned away.

'I am sorry,' he said quickly, 'I should not have spoken so violently. I only meant that these considerations fall far outside a woman's usual sphere.' The muscle moved restlessly in his cheek as he struggled for composure. 'Nothing in your experience has prepared you for making a decision of such a very serious nature. It is natural – it is amiable – that you should put private feelings before public duty. But…'

'No, you are wrong, Mr Lomax,' she said, with chilling composure. 'I am very well prepared to make this decision. I am prepared by six and thirty years of being a woman with no independent fortune. I understand Miss Fenn's wretched plight as no man ever could – and I will never betray her.'

She curtsied and walked off around the screen, just as Harriet bustled into the passage to remind her that only early birds catch worms and they must put the better foot first.

Chapter Thirty-Nine

If Dido could have chosen the luxury of solitude she would probably have deemed herself incapable of bearing with company. But having no such choice and being shut into a carriage for several hours with three other people, she found that she could endure well enough by only turning her thoughts inward and being rather silent.

She certainly had more than sufficient thoughts to fill the tedious miles between Bath and Madderstone. And the first and most melancholy of her thoughts was that their experiment had failed. It would seem that, after all, it was *not* possible for a man and woman to exist in a state of well-mannered disagreement. She had been right to anticipate a moment when difference of opinion must lead to disapproval of conduct.

Perhaps it could all be explained by Mr Lomax's theory of 'a woman's usual sphere'. For, if such a thing existed – and there was also a corresponding 'sphere' usual to men – then nothing of importance could be communicated between the sexes; their experiences and their natures differed so widely they never could agree upon important matters.

Perhaps the only happy marriages were rather silent ones…

She sighed and leant her face against the cold, lurching window-glass. If this were the case, there seemed to be no escaping the thought that she was herself constitutionally unsuited to marriage. For she doubted it was in her nature to be restrained and uncommunicative in the most intimate connection of a woman's life.

When she was got to such a pitch as this, there was an uncomfortable suspicion that tears might not be very far away and some kind of diversion of her thoughts was absolutely necessary.

And so she sought refuge in the mysteries of Madderstone. For they at least offered the possibility of solution – unlike the horrible dilemma of the spheres…

She set herself to consider the stolen letters. If she was to prevent their falling into Captain Laurence's hands, then she must discover who had taken them – and discover it quickly. As the carriage rattled on, she fell to a careful consideration of the nine people who had been at the dinner table on the day the letters were stolen, running over everything she knew of their whereabouts during that all important interval between dinner and tea.

Harriet had been with Penelope, Anne had been with Dido herself in the drawing room and, by Lucy's account, Captain Laurence had been making love to her in the conservatory. Mr Harman-Foote testified to Silas and Mr Portinscale having been with him in the billiard room. And that left only Henry Coulson unaccounted for! But…

'Oh!' she cried involuntarily.

'Dido, whatever is the matter?' demanded Harriet.

Dido looked about her and saw, to her surprise, that

the scene of barren common-land and furze bushes beyond the carriage window proved them to be many miles from Bath. The carriage was cold and gloomy with late afternoon – and becoming colder every minute. Opposite her Silas and Lucy were drowsing, their two heads drooping closer and closer together and nodding in time to the jolt and creak of the wheels.

'Harriet,' said Dido eagerly, but speaking low so as not to wake the others, 'do you remember the night we all dined at Madderstone two weeks ago – the night on which the letters were taken from Miss Fenn's chamber?'

Harriet looked surprised and put the book which she had been attempting to read into her lap. 'Yes,' she said with a frown, 'I remember it. But, Dido, I hope that this is not a beginning of odd questions…'

'No, no. The questions are not odd at all. They are very sensible ones which I should have thought to ask before. After dinner you went upstairs to sit with Penelope, did you not?'

'Yes ' – with great resignation – 'I did.'

'And the chamber which Penelope was given at Madderstone was in the same wing as Miss Fenn's room, was it not? They were within a few doors of one another.'

'Yes – though I do not see why you should be so very interested…'

'Harriet, I want you to think very carefully – this is, I believe, very important. I *must* discover what happened to those letters. Do you understand?'

'I understand that you are intent upon meddling. Why must you always be wanting to discover things?

"Let sleeping dogs lie," that is what Papa always said.'

Dido sighed. Now they were got to Dear Papa and proverbs all at once! It was going to be a great struggle to get any information at all out of Harriet.

'That evening,' she persisted, 'did you hear anyone come up the stairs and go to Miss Fenn's bedchamber?'

Harriet hesitated a moment, then: 'Well, since you ask, Mr Harman-Foote came by.'

'You are sure it was him?'

'Yes.'

'How can you be sure?'

'Why, Dido, I do believe the old inquisitors of Spain could not match you for tormenting a person with questions!'

'Harriet, why are you so sure that it was Mr Harman-Foote?'

'I know because he came past Penelope's room just as Mr Paynter was leaving it. He – Mr Paynter – had come to visit Penelope, you see – that is why I had been called away from the drawing room immediately after dinner. We went up to Penelope's chamber together, he made his examination and then, as he left, I went to the door of the chamber with him. As he went out, he met Mr Harman-Foote in the passageway.'

'I see,' said Dido. 'That certainly accords well with Mr Harman-Foote's own account of events. But it was not he who took the letters. Are you sure you heard no one else?'

The pale outline of Harriet's face looked mutinous in the gloom, as if she would protest against Dido's torturing her again. But then she seemed to change her mind. She frowned as if considering the question rather carefully, and turned to look through the window, at the yellow grass, the hunched shadows of furze bushes and the gaunt, long-legged sheep which grazed among them. 'Yes,' she said slowly, 'I remember now: there *was* someone else. It was Henry Coulson.'

'Indeed? Harriet are you sure?'

'Oh yes.' Harriet turned back, but the faint light of the window was behind her now and the encroaching evening together with the deep shadow of her hat made it impossible to read her exact expression. 'It was certainly Mr Coulson,' she said firmly. 'There can be no doubt about it. I was sitting on my own beside Penelope, you see, and I heard steps coming up the stairs so...so I went to the door and looked out – and there was Mr Coulson!'

'And what was he doing?'

'Why, he was walking along the passage – he went into Miss Fenn's chamber.'

'You are sure of it?'

'Oh yes! I remember it very clearly. Now are you satisfied?'

'Yes,' said Dido, drawing her fingers thoughtfully through the moisture on window-glass. 'Yes, I am satisfied. But how odd, how very odd...'

And she fell into a sad reverie – for Harriet's account had confirmed her very worst apprehensions. Matters were as dangerous as she had supposed, and rather more difficult of solution than she had feared. She sat for some time in silent contemplation of the scene beyond the window where a few sharp, cold stars were beginning to wink out in the darkening arch of the sky. Sheep turned stern yellow eyes to follow the carriage, their chins rotating as they chewed meditatively. An icy little draught crept around the glass of the window, making her shiver and pull her cloak tighter about her shoulders.

Henry Coulson posed a great many problems – his role in the mysteries of Madderstone was complicated and, although she suspected a great deal, there was much of which she was still uncertain…

She turned back to Harriet who was once more attempting to read. Her book – held up high to catch the light – was obscuring her face.

'Harriet, I have been meaning for some days past to talk to you about Mr Coulson.'

'Oh?' Harriet lowered the book an inch or two and looked rather apprehensively over the top of it.

Dido looked at Silas, but he was sleeping soundly, his cheek now resting upon the side of Lucy's bonnet, his own hat sliding forward over his face. 'Who,' she asked bluntly, '*is* Henry Coulson – exactly.'

Harriet sighed and lowered the book an inch further. 'Exactly? Let me see… By his account of himself to Silas, it would seem that he was third cousin twice removed to old Mr Harman. But, as you know, he was orphaned when he was a boy and Mr Harman paid for his education.'

Harriet delivered this account briskly and raised the book once more to her eyes – though there would scarcely seem to be enough light for reading in the rocking carriage.

'And what relation is the young man to *you*?' insisted Dido.

Harriet sighed loudly. 'Dido, this really is becoming

very tiresome! Am I to have no peace in which to read?'

'It is a great deal too dark to read and conversation is our only resource. Please indulge me by answering my questions. We aging spinsters have so few pleasures!'

'You are impossible!'

'What relation is Henry Coulson to your family?'

'Oh well! If his account of himself is correct, I calculate that he must be the great nephew of our second cousin – but on the father's side only.'

'That must have taken a great deal of time to work out,' remarked Dido. 'I wonder that you put yourself to the trouble of establishing it.'

Harriet's only answer was to raise the book and pretend to read.

'The other day,' said Dido conversationally, 'Silas revealed something very interesting about Mr Coulson.'

'Did he?' The book did not move.

'I understand – from what Silas told me – that, although in absolute terms Mr Coulson is only a distant connection, he is, in fact, your nearest living *male* relation.'

'Perhaps,' said Harriet with a great show of indifference. 'There does seem rather to be a shortage of men in Dear Papa's family.'

'In fact…' Dido leant impatiently across the swaying carriage and pushed down the book so that she could look into Harriet's eyes. 'Mr Coulson is next in line to the entail on your father's estate, is he not? He will inherit Ashfield if…'

Instinctively both women turned to look at Silas's face, pale and delicate under the wide dark brim of his hat.

'…if,' Dido finished in a whisper, 'anything should happen to your brother.'

'Yes.' Harriet sighed and closed her book with a snap. 'Now, Dido, why are you inquiring so minutely into my family's concerns? It is very impertinent.'

'On the contrary it is very pertinent – in the proper sense.'

'Now you are being satirical! And you know…'

'Yes, my dear Harriet, I know you do not like it. But I think you may forgive me when you know the direction of my enquiries.'

'Very well then, you had better explain yourself.'

'Well, Mr Coulson's relationship to you accounts for all his attempts to discredit Harris Paynter. You see, I realise now that Henry Coulson does not mean to throw doubt upon the testimony Mr Paynter gave at the inquest, at all – which is what I thought at first. All these slighting remarks about the poor surgeon have been aimed at Silas.' She cast another concerned look at the sleeping boy who had been bundled by his careful sisters, not only into a flannel waistcoat, but also two overcoats. 'He hopes to make your brother careless of Mr Paynter's sound medical advice, does he not?'

Harriet hesitated and then put her hand to her brow as if in relief. It was perhaps a comfort to talk of something that had been weighing upon her mind for weeks. 'Yes,' she admitted, 'I believe he does. Mr Coulson has next to no fortune of his own, you know. I daresay it would suit him very well indeed if Silas succumbed to the asthma. But there are none so blind as those that will not see. I *cannot* make Silas distrust the tiresome man. He thinks

Henry Coulson is the greatest friend he has ever had!'

Dido sank a little deeper into the damp-smelling leather of her corner and shifted about her cold feet in an attempt to revive a little feeling in them. 'You are right,' she said. 'Mr Coulson is a very tiresome man indeed. I have known from the beginning that he was up to no good. But it was not until I first understood the great lengths to which Mr Paynter is going to help your brother, that I began to divine the cause of Mr Coulson's defaming the surgeon. And then, of course, a great many other matters were brought within my understanding – matters such as the haunting of Penelope's bedchamber.'

'Do you believe Mr Coulson was the cause of that?' cried Harriet, interested in spite of herself.

'Oh yes, I have been sure of it from the beginning. But at first I believed he had acted on behalf of somebody else. Now I can see the cruel masquerade for what it was: a bid to take advantage of Penelope's credulous nature in order to frighten her away from our neighbourhood.'

'But to what end?'

'That is what puzzled me – until I began to suspect the exact nature of Mr Coulson's relationship to your family, and then, of course his motive was clear.'

'Was it?'

'My dear Harriet, besides your brother being cured of his asthma, what could be more inconvenient to Mr Coulson than the poor boy's marrying and fathering a son? And I happen to know that Silas had confided his feelings for Penelope to "the best friend he has ever had".'

'Ah! Of course!' Harriet sighed discontentedly. 'Oh, I wish with all my heart we could be rid of the troublesome man, but I see no hope of his leaving Madderstone. He will stay, I am sure, until his dangerous *friendship* has destroyed Silas.'

'Well now,' said Dido with great satisfaction, 'we come to my point: the reason why I believe you may become reconciled to curiosity and impertinent enquiry. You see I believe that these besetting sins of spinsterhood have led me to a solution of your problems.'

'Have they?'

'I would reveal it, but I fear you would think me satirical.'

'Dido, just tell me.'

'Very well then,' said Dido, 'I think that you should speak to Mr Coulson yourself, and represent to him the very great desirability of his leaving.'

'That would not do at all. He would not listen.'

'Oh, but I think he would. For, if he should seem reluctant, you might just mention to him the blood and the feathers which litter the ruined gallery at the abbey: suggest that they – and the lanterns which are seen in the ruins at night – should be brought to the attention of Mr Harman-Foote. I think that once you have done *that* you may find him much more willing to oblige you by taking himself out of the neighbourhood.' The lights of cottages were now beginning to appear beyond the carriage windows and, as she looked out at them, Dido's smile broadened. 'And if you find the gentleman is still inclined to be awkward, you might mention that I saw him in the inn yard at Great Farleigh, delivering to the London mail-coach a box which smelt *very* strongly of game.'

There were stronger lights now shining into the

carriage and showing Harriet's face staring in half-smiling disbelief, as the wheels began to rattle loudly into the yard of the inn at which they were to stop for the night, shaking their companions awake.

They all climbed out into the welcoming lamp- and firelight that poured out of the open door onto the cobbles, stamping their numb feet and attempting to rub a little warmth into their hands. The others hurried indoors, but Harriet hung back and caught at Dido's arm. 'Are you sure of this?' she asked.

They paused a moment in the encroaching dusk of the yard, where the edge of the year's first frost cut through the smells of horses and wood-smoke.

'Oh yes,' said Dido with great conviction, 'Mr Coulson has certainly been assisting the poachers – and, I don't doubt, making "a mint of money" from the business. The carts carrying the felled trees to the sawmills at Great Farleigh have also been carrying away Mr Harman-Foote's woodcock and partridges. And the ruins have made a very convenient place in which to hide the birds till they can be removed. Mr Harman-Foote is known to be lenient towards poachers, but I do not believe even he would countenance his kinsman abusing his hospitality in such a way.'

'Oh this is wonderful news!' cried Harriet joyfully, 'I shall take the first opportunity of speaking to Mr Coulson!'

She hurried away indoors, but Dido stood a moment longer in the aching cold. 'Now,' she said quietly to herself, 'the question is whether I have finished with Mr Henry Coulson, or whether he has yet another, more dangerous, role to play in these mysteries.'

Chapter Forty

My Dear Eliza,

'Strange things I have in head that will to hand!'

Someone says that in one of Shakespeare's plays I believe, and tonight I find myself in accord with the poor fellow. And so I shall begin upon a letter which it may be I shall never send. For my head is full of strange things which must be expressed before they can be understood and, since I have no one to whom I may speak them, I needs must write them down. Yet I do not know that even your patient affection can bear with the outlandish ideas which torment me tonight.

I have the parlour fire to myself now — which is a very great luxury. Although it is only nine o'clock, Margaret is gone away to bed with a headache. Francis is engaged upon a sermon; at least, he is in his study, deep in the perusal of a large book — though since it seems to be the writings of some old Greek philosopher that he is reading, I doubt the parishioners of Badleigh will gain much from it. So, I have been left to myself, with a precious handful of coals still in the box on the hearth — and a whole three inches of candle! It is a cold night — and very foggy. The fog was gathering with the dusk as I walked home from Madderstone four hours ago.

My business there was to look again at those pieces of gold and silver which were discovered with Miss Fenn's body. And I regret to say that I found among them something which I had been sincerely hoping <u>not</u> to find…

Dido hesitated. She was approaching now those outlandish ideas of which she had warned her sister. She bit the end of her pen and gazed down into the red cave of hot coals as she wondered how best to express her darkest suspicions; suspicions which were all built out of such very tiny details as seemed of no importance on their own – details which anyone else might have passed over entirely, but which clung to her brain like burrs and briars on a gun-dog's coat after a day's rough shooting.

If you have been attending as you should to all my accounts, Eliza, you will by now be aware of some very great problems and discrepancies in the account of Miss Fenn which I have so far pieced together. To borrow a phrase from dear Harriet: it will not do at all. And the most incongruous fact is still the letters in the bible. I have, as yet, said nothing to Anne about them – nor about the true identity of 'Miss Fenn'; but the time draws near when I <u>must</u> decide what she is to know and not to know – as well as determining how Mr Portinscale is to be persuaded that there was no suicide…

The letters seem to prove that there was a lover: a man who lived close at hand (the evidence for his proximity is, you will recall, the absence of a post office mark on the letter's cover and Miss Fenn's reference to seeing him '*again and again*'). *But this accords so <u>very</u> ill with the neighbourhood's opinion of the woman that I find myself going over the words of the letters, in the hope that I might yet discover some other meaning concealed within them.*

And then there is that very jarring fact which has preyed upon my mind since my visit to Mrs Nolan: her assertion that <u>she had never seen Miss Elinor Fenn.</u>

This is inexplicable, Eliza. How could it be that Miss Fenn had never called upon her daughter in Bath? When the child was with Mrs Pinker, she had visited her every week without fail, going to the considerable inconvenience of driving herself fourteen miles in a pony carriage in order to do so. This argues a very natural and amiable maternal attachment, does it not? And yet this attachment was done away entirely when Penelope came into Mrs Nolan's care! Why?

Dido set her pen aside with a restless motion, chafed together her hands, then dropped a coal or two more onto the dying fire. She crept closer to the hearth until her feet were resting upon the fender and her face warm, even though the cold night air continued to chill her back. Her tired eyes watched the coals gently pulsing from black to red and her thoughts were so very strange she could not help but wonder whether she was like dear Mr Cowper when he looked into his fire – 'myself creating what I saw'. But there was a kind of sense and pattern to her ideas – a way of fitting together all the pieces to make a complete map – even though it was one with a very surprising geography indeed.

She picked up her pen, determined upon writing down her incredible tale, even if, when it was finished, she had not the courage to publish it.

You see, Eliza, when I began to look for the cause of this change, I was reminded of one other very slight discrepancy in the accounts I have heard of Penelope's going to Mrs Nolan's school. Lucy told me that Penelope had been in Bath since she was five years old — and Mrs Nolan herself confirmed that account in my first interview with her. But, Mrs Pinker's maid told me that girls were not sent from the house in Great Farleigh until they were <u>seven</u>.

Is not this rather strange? It alerted me to a possibility which can make comprehensible a great many of the mysteries which surround me. The possibility which has been tormenting me these past two days. Eliza, I do not believe that the child Mrs Pinker cared for was Penelope at all. I believe there was a switch made at the time of the removal to Bath, and, while her own child was hidden somewhere close to Madderstone, Miss Fenn <u>pretended</u> that Penelope was her daughter…

Small flames began to lick at the coals, brightening the room, lighting up the noble black profile of old Mr Kent in his frame, and sending shadows dancing across the ceiling. Out in the foggy night a fox barked sharply. Dido brushed her pen against her lips as she thought. Were her suspicions too fantastic? She had tried to ground each new idea in fact — that was a principle which her brother Edward had taught her. And Edward had once won a medal for debating at Cambridge. But he had never told her what one was to do when facts led to monstrous suspicions against the most innocent-seeming people. The great logicians of the university seemed to be entirely silent upon that point.

She sighed. What else could one do but follow the trail of reason relentlessly to its end?

Of course the next question must be: why was the exchange made? And I think that the reason lies in Miss Fenn's remarkable determination to keep a particular secret from her husband.

As I told Mr Lomax at Bath, I believe Miss Fenn was an exceptionally clever and resourceful woman. (And I apologise, by the by, for my continued use of that name. I know that I ought to write instead of Lady Congreve, but I have known her too long as Miss Fenn to be comfortable with any other name.) Now, although the abominable laws of our land decree that a woman fleeing her husband's ill-usage may take nothing with her, I believe that this remarkable lady contrived to steal one thing which he valued very highly indeed – and, having taken it, she was forced to do all that she could to keep it concealed. Even the friends who had helped her knew nothing of it. Because if Lord Congreve had known, he would never have rested until he had got back his property.

You see, Eliza, the key to it all lies in another little detail: a piece of information I got from Mrs Pinker's maid, but the significance of which I have only just begun to suspect. As I have said, girls did not leave Great Farleigh until they were seven years old. It was <u>boys</u> *who left that establishment at five.*

Dido bent eagerly over her writing desk, her pen scratching rapidly in the red firelight, her eyes bright, one small foot tapping rapidly upon the brass fender: impatient now to get it all told.

Miss Fenn had contrived, in fact, to steal from Lord Congreve his son: the heir to his title and estates. That is what he had always been uncertain of: the sex of the child she had borne. He feared she had robbed him of the next Lord Congreve and he could not rest until he had discovered the truth. That, you see, is why Captain Laurence began his investigations. But, of course, he found only what Miss Fenn had intended her husband should find if he searched: a daughter. The 'little miss' about whom His Lordship cared so little he did not even trouble to protect her from the captain's own selfish schemes!

Well, I think I begin at last to understand Miss Fenn (and upon further reflection I am quite determined to continue with that name – she deserves to have a title quite different from that of her brutish husband!). She was, in fact, the religious, upright woman that her neighbours believed her to be. And when I next see Mr Lomax I shall be sure to tell him that my 'great idea' has been vindicated entirely...

She paused, a smile softening her anxious face; but a moment later she had recollected herself and her pen was driving fast across the page.

The poor woman was quite determined to protect her son from the influence and example of such a vicious father. Titles and fortune were of no importance to her beside virtue and she set about hiding her son so effectively he would be *protected even after her death. The web of deceit which she wove cost her her life in the end, Eliza – and I cannot bear to think that she might have died in vain. Lord Congreve shall <u>not</u> find his son if I can prevent it.*

And so, of course, you will now understand the urgency – the absolute necessity – of my finding those lost letters. For, if Captain Laurence gets to them first, I fear he will discover his mistake – and Lord Congreve himself will descend upon Madderstone to retrieve his stolen heir.

I cannot yet be sure exactly what the missing letters are about, nor who wrote them. But I think they may reveal the whereabouts of the boy – and <u>that</u> I believe is the reason for their removal. Somewhere here in the neighbourhood of Madderstone or Badleigh is the true son of Elinor Fenn, and I cannot help but wonder whether it is not he who has, from the very beginning, been working against me and trying to prevent my discovering the truth about his mother's death.

Well, tomorrow is All Hallows and, at the ball, I intend to lay a trap for the culprit. I hope I shall learn the final truth behind Miss Fenn's death – and the haunting of Madderstone Abbey.

But first I must speak to Mr Portinscale and persuade him that the grave must be moved…

Chapter Forty-One

The next morning was still, and thick with fog; hundreds of spider's webs festooned the bright hawthorn hedges. The air was cold and damp on Dido's face as she made her way along the lane to Madderstone church, and the sheep that bleated and coughed about her were all but invisible in blank white fields.

She was come in search of Mr Portinscale, but, near the vicarage, she caught up with young Georgie who was dawdling homeward along the narrow muddy lane with his ragged Latin grammar under one arm and pausing from time to time to stuff his pockets with the glistening brown fruits that had fallen from the horse chestnut trees. The sight of him reminded Dido of another little matter which she wished to resolve.

'Well, Georgie,' she said politely as she fell into step beside him. 'Did you have a pleasant lesson with Mr Portinscale?'

'No.' He turned up his fat pale face – the nose slightly pink with cold, the tassel of his cap falling into one eye. She noticed that the bruise was healed now. 'I don't like Latin,' he said sulkily.

'But you like cake, do you not?'

'What?' He stopped under the dripping yellow leaves

of one of the chestnuts and looked up at her in great surprise. 'What do you mean?'

'I mean, of course, that you like the cake which Mr Portinscale gives you. Though I think, Georgie, you had better eat a little less of it, if it makes you bilious.'

'How do you know about that?' he demanded, his face reddening, his small eyes shifting about suspiciously above his plump cheeks.

'Oh! I just know,' said Dido brightly and walked on along the lane so that he was forced to trot to catch up with her. 'It is, you see, something which happens to ladies if they remain unmarried. When they reach a certain age they begin to know everything about everyone else's business.'

'Do they?' His eyes widened. He bit his lip, considered the unmarried ladies of his acquaintance – and seemed to find proof of her assertion. 'What else do you know, Miss Kent?' he asked with cautious respect.

'Well, let me see. I know that Mr Portinscale gives you cake to prevent your telling your mother that he once… lost his temper with you.' She gave a little wink and touched her finger to her cheek.

'Oh!'

'And there is one other thing that I know, Georgie.' She stopped walking for they had come now to the lychgate and she could see the thin black figure of the parson disappearing among the mist-shrouded gravestones.

'What else is it you know, miss?' asked Georgie anxiously.

'I know that you are being very unwise.' She looked down at the fat, indulged little face: the pale eyes blinking rapidly with worry. 'You had better make your peace with Mr Portinscale,' she said gently. 'I do not think he will strike you again.'

'He won't!' the boy cried indignantly. 'For if he does…'

'No, Georgie,' she said with a shake of the head, 'you must not tell your mother of what happened. For, you see, if she thinks your present teacher is unsuitable then she will certainly send you away to school.'

The soft little mouth fell open in horror.

'You would not like school at all, Georgie. My brothers have told me all about it. You see, in schools, teachers strike their pupils whenever they wish.'

Mr Portinscale was standing on the north side of the foggy churchyard. One hand rested upon a low bough of the ancient yew tree, his hat was pulled low over his eyes, his angular figure bent over in contemplation of the suicide's grave.

Dido stopped as she first caught sight of him – though she had come there to find him. She had spent several hours of the past night devising and rehearsing the case she must put to him – and was rather well pleased with the argument she had prepared. But there was something private in his attitude: something of the attitude of prayer in his earnest gazing upon the raw little mound of earth among the dead yellow grass and broken dock stems. She was on the point of turning away when he looked up and saw her.

He turned to her and swept off his hat with a bow and a courteous greeting. But when she stepped forward and mentioned a particular reason for seeking him out – a subject upon which she wished to talk – he frowned sternly.

'I would by no means wish you to think me unwilling to converse with you Miss Kent,' he said solemnly, turning his hat about in his hands, 'but I hope that you are not intending to revive the very unpleasant discussion of…'

'Miss Fenn's death,' she finished briskly, with a glance at the grave. 'Yes, Mr Portinscale, I am afraid that I must. You see, I have learnt something – during my visit to Bath – something which I think you ought to know about that lady.'

'Indeed! Have you?' His voice attempted indifference, but his face was all interest.

And Dido, sure that this was all the invitation he would allow himself to give, made only a hasty plea for his complete secrecy before entering upon an account of the governess's true identity and the cause of her sojourn in Madderstone – suppressing only the existence of the child. She did not look at him as she spoke, fixing her eyes upon anything rather than his face – the brown decaying petals of Mr Paynter's roses on the grave, the mossy stones of the wall, an old gravestone half-sunk down into the ground and lying aslant in the fog, the round arch of the church window with a candle glowing within.

Before she had been speaking for two minutes, his hand was once more upon the bough of the tree, his hat beating gently against his knee. His long sombre face, framed in clerical white, was fixed upon her, his eyes scarcely blinking. When she finished and finally looked up at him, he swallowed hard. 'I cannot believe…' He began in a voice of great emotion. But he was unable to continue.

'It is all true, I assure you, Mr Portinscale.'

He looked hastily away. He beat the hat harder upon his knees. 'It is extraordinary,' he said in a struggling, uneven voice. 'But of course,' he said with a great effort to give his voice the certainty of the pulpit, 'I cannot allow this information to change my decision. The Lord God judges us not by our titles and birth. The sin of self-murder is as heinous in the highest in the land as it is in the lowliest of mortals.'

'I do not doubt it,' said Dido earnestly. Her voice was low and, in the fog and the stillness of the graveyard, it had a close sound – as if they were within doors. 'But, Mr Portinscale, I believe you must reconsider your decision. For I do not argue about rank – but only *character*.'

'Character?'

'Yes. Do you not see, that you have grounded your understanding of the lady's character upon a false belief?'

'I beg your pardon.'

'Forgive me,' she said very quietly, 'for alluding to those very *personal* matters which you were so kind as to confide in me. But you have believed for fifteen years that an illicit attachment was the cause of her refusing your offer of marriage, have you not?'

'Yes, but...' He stopped. The hat stilled in his hand; his face became very thoughtful indeed.

'But,' said Dido, 'I beg you to recollect her words now in the light of your new understanding of her situation. She spoke of an attachment, she said that you would never witness her marriage to another man.'

She stopped and waited for him to consider. A crow settled on the slanting gravestone and set up a hoarse cry. She stole a look at the clergyman's face and saw there amazement and dawning understanding – the beginnings of a revolution in his ideas, which was slowly doing away the resentment of fifteen years' standing.

'Her words were true, Mr Portinscale. She was attached, very unhappily attached, to a cruel, unworthy husband…'

He did not speak; but he did not need to. She could gather everything she wished to know from his face. There was dawning upon it a gentler look than any she had ever seen there before. All those lines which seemed to drag down upon his face were easing; his thin lips moving in the uncertain beginnings of a smile. There, beside that wretched grave, the woman he had loved, the woman who had been dead for fifteen years, was restored to him, her virtue unspotted – her character as perfect as he had once believed it to be.

There was, Dido was sure, only one thing wanting to secure Miss Fenn's place here upon the holy side of the churchyard wall.

'It was of course impossible for her to marry you,' she said quietly. 'But I am very sure that she wished it. That is why, when she was forced to refuse your offer, she tried to convey to you something of her reasons.' She watched the tentative smile gain power on his thin, severe face. 'Having discovered a good, religious man, so very different from her vicious husband, I make no doubt she wished very much that she might give him her affection and spend her life with him.'

Mr Portinscale was silent for a long while and then said only, 'Thank you. Thank you, Miss Kent, for telling me this.' Dido doubted it were possible for him to say more. But he took her hand and shook it warmly.

Then he excused himself and turned purposefully towards his church. As he walked away he put on his hat. And he put it on the very back of his head – with a sort of a tilt to it...

Chapter Forty-Two

Dido returned to the vicarage well pleased with the morning's work and found a letter awaiting her in the hall: a letter which Margaret assured her she did not have time to read now, for if she did not begin preparing for the ball immediately she would look a fright and be a disgrace to her family...

Margaret was herself standing upon the stairs in curl papers, with a candle in her hand, and very eager for the moment of setting out. It always pained her to lose a single minute which might be passed at the great house.

But, since the letter was written in an unfamiliar hand, there was no restraining Dido's curiosity and she began immediately upon opening it in spite of the torrent of chiding pouring over her head. Margaret retaliated by walking away with her candle – leaving not enough light to read by. Dido hurried into the parlour and knelt upon the hearth to catch the dull red glow of the fire.

The letter was from Mrs Pinker. Written in carefully rounded characters, it was an answer to that enquiry which she had sent before leaving Bath.

Dear Miss Kent,

I am much obliged to you for your letter I am sure, and regret I was not here to receive you when you was so good as to call upon me.

Well you ask me about Mrs Fenn's child and I don't know what I should say and I was very much minded not to answer your letter at all — for all that would have been so very ill-mannered. For a woman in my position should know how to keep other folks' secrets. But she was a very pleasant lady and I was vastly sorry to hear she was dead and drowned in that pool. Which everyone is talking of now on account of it being written about in the newspapers, which I always say is the great evil of newspapers, for once a thing is written in them it does seem everyone knows about it.

And I am like you in thinking she didn't murder herself, for all it says so in the newspaper. For she was not a mad woman — nor a bad one neither. And it would be a fine thing if you could find out the truth so they could put her in the churchyard. And so I have thought about it a great deal and I think I had better answer your question. Though I hope you will not tell it to anyone else — in particular that nasty fellow that came to my house two months back.

Well, you was right to think the poor lady's child was a boy — for it was. Poor little Harry Fenn. I remember him very well indeed.

And I hope my telling you will, as you say, help you find out just what happened to the poor lady for she was a good woman and <u>mighty</u> fond of that little boy. And sometimes when she must leave at the end of her visit she would cry so I thought she would break her heart. And

*she would hold him and call him 'my beloved'. Always
'beloved'. That's what he always was with her.*
  Yours Sincerely,
  Deborah Pinker

Dido sat before the fire staring at this letter until Rebecca
appeared. 'Mistress says dinner's to be on table in half
an hour and the carriage is to be at the door the minute
you're finished eating.' She hesitated and gave one of her
rapid looks about the room as if ensuring 'the mistress'
was not concealed anywhere within hearing. 'You want
me to help you with your hair, miss?'

'No... No thank you...'

Dido fled to her attic, but, instead of arranging her
hair, she sat upon the bed and continued to stare at her
letter – her mind rearranging everything which she had
thought she knew.

She remembered the passionate affection of Miss
Fenn's letter to the 'Beloved'. *I love you. I will always love
you. No other woman will ever love you as I do.* And at
last she understood those words! They were not an illicit
declaration to a lover; they were the age-old cry of the
devoted mother to her son!

Now, at last, everything which had seemed
contradictory in the character of this extraordinary
woman was explained. How strange it was that everything
she had uncovered had led her finally back to the general
opinion of the neighbourhood. Madderstone's governess
had been as upright and pious as she had seemed.

Then she recalled the exact words of the reply to Miss
Fenn's letter... And here was a subject which must keep

her sitting on the bed even after Margaret had begun to call out impatiently from the landing below.

Of course her mistake had been to assume that the reply was written by the person to whom the letter was sent. And that assumption had been ill-founded: the writer had not used the personal pronoun, but had written instead of '*one whom you profess to love*'. The reply had, in fact, been sent by the person into whose care Miss Fenn had given her son.

And this realisation opened a new vista, the existence of which Dido had suspected before – but had hoped would prove illusory.

The guardian of the boy had been unwilling to relinquish him – had, in fact, been absolutely determined against giving up the child – even though the poor woman had resolved upon reclaiming him.

For some reason, this person had wanted to keep the boy as desperately as the mother wished to take him back. *That* had been the cause of her death. It was the boy's guardian she had gone to meet beside the pool. And he had killed her in order to prevent her reclaiming the child…

But who had that guardian been…? And who was Harry Fenn?

Chapter Forty-Three

The ballroom at Madderstone Abbey was the finest apartment in the neighbourhood. It was furnished with two great chandeliers and mirrors in which 'Goliath might have seen his giant bulk'; there was a wide marble chimney piece at either end of the room; fat cherubs done in plaster clung to the ceiling, and there was such a delicious expanse of floor as must make the feet positively itch to dance.

Into this wonderful room, on every All Hallows Eve, all the gentry and half-gentry of Madderstone and Badleigh were invited, and many a young miss looked forward to the evening as the pinnacle of her winter engagements. But Dido had deeper causes of anticipation as she entered the room that evening and made her curtsey to her hostess. Tonight she was determined that all her questions must be settled: the last mysteries of Madderstone solved – and its unquiet spirits finally laid to rest.

A very fitting undertaking for All Hallows Eve!

Her first business upon joining the gathering circle of guests beside one of the hearths was to look about for Mr Lomax. He was there, standing on the opposite side of the hearth with his hands behind his back and his head courteously inclined towards Lucy Crockford, who was talking to him very earnestly. He was unable to do more than bow a greeting – which was entirely unsatisfactory, for it was beyond even Dido's hopeful penetration to detect complete forgiveness in a bow...

She sighed a little and allowed her eye to wander on about the little crowd of her friends and neighbours, all dressed in their finest clothes, and she fell to wondering... who among them was Harry Fenn?

One of these young men in their best breeches and dancing pumps and frothing cravats was the son that Elinor Fenn had taken such pains to hide. But which one...? She thought of a young man, apparently orphaned...adopted and raised upon someone's charity.

And her gaze came to rest upon Henry Coulson.

He was lounging against one end of the mantelpiece with such a sour countenance as made her quite sure that Harriet had already spoken to him about the mysterious boxes which were finding their way to Great Farleigh. His was the largest, most elaborate cravat in the room, got up with so many twists and so much starch that he seemed scarcely able to turn his head. And he had got himself from somewhere a very foolish-looking single eyeglass which depended on a chain from his waistcoat.

Harriet – looking remarkably well in a blue-trimmed gown and braided headdress – was standing a little way from him and occasionally throwing him a cold look as she talked to Harris Paynter. Next to her was Lucy, talking to Mr Lomax, but breaking off from time to time to swing her fan irritably and cast a resentful glance in the direction of Captain Laurence.

Laurence had taken up a position at some distance

from the hearth – almost in the centre of the room. With his right arm swinging about as if it held a sword, he was talking with great animation to a little bevy of enthralled young ladies. He was too far away for Dido to catch his words, but she detected in the shaping of his lips 'navy', 'French privateers' and – more than once – 'very grave danger'.

Close beside her stood Silas, who seemed to be attempting to explain 'Mr C...Coleridge's beautiful, moving b...ballad about an old sailor and a d...d... dead albatross,' to Mr Harman-Foote – who was looking frankly perplexed.

And Mr Portinscale, she now saw, was just approaching their circle, making an exaggerated obeisance to his hostess and congratulating her upon 'that exceptional elegance and propriety of all the arrangements which never fails to make the All Hallows ball the most delightful of occasions...'

He then lowered his voice and continued to talk very quietly to the lady. Dido was almost sure she caught the words 'churchyard' and 'reconsidered'; but unfortunately Laurence's narrative was becoming louder as it reached its crisis: he had progressed from 'grave danger', through 'overwhelming odds', to 'mortal peril'. He and his men were now 'fighting for our lives'. His voice was positively echoing about the room – and two of the enthralled young ladies were giving refined little screams and looking as if they might faint away at any moment.

The end of Mr Portinscale's speech was sunk in the naval skirmish. But a moment later Anne came to Dido with such expressions of delight and gratitude as confirmed its import – and caused more than one head to turn in their direction.

'I *knew* that you could persuade Mr Portinscale into removing the grave,' she declared joyfully. 'I was sure from the very beginning that you were the right person to do it. And I am never wrong about these things you know.'

Dido smiled graciously, but there was no time to talk further, for the dancing was soon to begin and Anne was very busy about finding partners for everyone. She hurried off, instructing Dido over her shoulder to 'come to me tomorrow so that we may talk it all over.'

No sooner had she gone than Mr Lomax appeared, released at last from Lucy's conversation, and congratulated Dido rather stiffly upon her success. 'I am sure Mrs Harman-Foote will be much more at ease once her friend rests within the churchyard,' he said. 'This at least was well done.' He stood for several minutes, hands clasped behind him, frowning as if he knew not what to say. The memory of their last interview in Bath was enough to silence them both.

'It is gratifying to know that you approve some portion of my conduct,' she said – and stopped, distracted from his looks of displeasure by an awareness that news of the grave's removal had now spread through the circle by the fire – and turned everyone's attention towards her. Over in the room's centre Laurence talked on unabated, but here beside the fire, conversation had stopped for a moment...

It was not an opportunity to miss. 'I am sure,' she said, addressing herself to Mr Lomax, but making no attempt to lower her voice, 'I am very glad to have been of service to Mrs Harman-Foote. And I have in fact discovered another comfort for her.'

'Indeed?'

'Yes. When the thief took Miss Fenn's letters – there was one overlooked. Not all her correspondence was lost. There is still one letter in the back of her bible.' Dido stopped. Captain Laurence continued to declaim, but she was sure that she could detect a kind of attentive quietness behind her. She was sure that one person at least in the circle round the fire was listening with particular interest… But who was that person?

She was on the point of turning to look when she became aware that Mr Lomax was addressing her hastily – upon an entirely different matter: that he was, in fact, soliciting her hand for the first two dances.

She was distracted: her attention powerfully torn. The company behind her resumed its conversations. The moment for discovery was lost.

'You do not wish to dance with me?' he asked, misinterpreting her confusion and looking grave and offended.

'Yes,' she cried in distress. 'I should like to dance with you very much indeed. But I am afraid I cannot.'

'I promise I shall not revert to the subjects which distressed you in our last interview. We shall go down the entire set in silence if you wish. Indeed,' he added, raising his brows and beginning to smile, 'I think I would rather enjoy a little companionable silence between us.'

But still she shook her head. 'I am afraid I cannot dance with you, Mr Lomax' she said regretfully. 'Not now. You see, I have other business on hand. I have set a trap.'

'A trap?' he cried in alarm. 'Whatever are you about now?'

'Well,' she explained in a hasty undertone, 'everyone, here beside the hearth, heard me speaking to you just now. Whoever stole Miss Fenn's letters now knows there is another yet remaining in her chamber. And I am *sure* that just as soon as the dancing begins that person will go to find that one last letter.'

'Oh! And you mean to go to the bedchamber, to see who comes?'

'Yes. So you see, I *cannot* dance.'

It hurt her deeply, for, she would have dearly loved to dance with him just once, and, as things stood between them, she might never have another opportunity. But she was sure that Harry Fenn – or his envoy – would go now to retrieve the letter and if she was not there in the room waiting, she would never know the truth about Miss Fenn's death…

There was moonlight falling through the tall windows of Miss Fenn's chamber as Dido quietly opened the door. Behind her, the faint strains of the first dance were echoing up the stairs; and before her the shape of the window was drawn in white light across the floorboards and a broad square of Turkey carpet. The light fell diagonally across the high bed, catching the corner of the bedside table and the old black bible lying upon it.

She tiptoed into the room – going first to the bible to reassure herself that the letter was still there within the back cover, then to the window seat, where she found that only a little rearranging of a curtain would conceal her. And there, with her cheek resting against the cold glass, she waited, her ears straining to catch the sound of approaching feet, and her eyes becoming gradually more accustomed to the faint light, until even the curving tails of the Chinese birds were distinguishable on the bed-hangings.

Who would come?

Henry Coulson. It would be Henry Coulson for sure, she told herself. For there was the name to consider. Did not 'little Harrys' always grow into men called Henry? And the account Harriet had given of Mr Coulson was so vague – nothing was known here in Madderstone of his parentage, save what he had told himself...

Yes, it would be Henry Coulson – she would not even countenance the other darker thoughts which kept trying to insinuate themselves into her brain. And yet, those darker thoughts had prompted her to lay the trap wide – including in its scope everyone who might possibly be the thief. She had let them all know of the letter's existence...

There was a slight sound out in the passageway. She lifted her feet onto the window seat and drew the curtain about her. Steps approached rapidly – as if the walker knew exactly where he was going – then stopped outside the door of the chamber. There was a pause, filled by the faint sound of a waltz.

The lock turned. The door opened slowly. Dido's hands tightened about her knees. The light of a candle flickered round the room and footsteps – firm, but light – crept across the floor, tap-tapping on the boards, softer on the carpet. Now the intruder was come to the bed. And – straining for it – she caught the sound of a candle being set down, the sound of pages turning. And then, as she held her breath and listened with every fibre of her being, Dido detected the one noise she had most dreaded hearing – the slight rustle of a silk gown.

It struck her like a blow in the face: confirming all her worst fears – and making her angry. She jumped to her feet, pushing aside the curtain and flooding the chamber with moonlight.

The figure by the bed gave a cry, dropping letter and bible together, and the candlelight showed the white staring face – of Harriet Crockford.

Chapter Forty-Four

For a moment the two friends could only stand and stare rather foolishly at one another.

'I hoped so much,' stammered Dido at last, 'that it would not be you, Harriet. I would rather it had been anyone else…'

'It was a trick!' cried Harriet and the hurt of betrayal was as strong in her voice as it was in Dido's. 'You meant me to come here. That is why you told me about the letter.'

'I told everyone about it,' Dido reminded her. 'But I knew the only person who would come to retrieve it was the person who stole the rest of Miss Fenn's correspondence.'

'But you suspected me of being that person?'

'I could not help but suspect you after you lied so very badly to me in the carriage. When you tried to convince me that Mr Coulson had taken the letters, I knew that you must have something to hide.'

'How did you know…?'

'Oh Harriet! it was so very obvious. You said that you were *on your own* in Penelope's room when you heard Mr Coulson pass the door. But, by your own account, Mr Paynter had come up with you immediately after dinner to see his patient. You were not alone until after the surgeon left you. And it was as he left that Mr Harman-Foote came to the room – and found the desk already empty. Mr Coulson could not have taken the letters.'

'Oh.' Harriet suddenly became aware that the letter itself was lying still upon the floor, she picked it up hastily and stowed it away in her pocket. 'You shall not have it,' she said, setting her chin determinedly.

'I do not need it. I know what it says – and I know who sent it.'

Harriet sat down upon the bed. 'And what do you mean to do about it?' she asked with a great attempt at calm.

'That,' said Dido, turning away to the window, 'rather depends upon you, Harriet. It depends upon whether you are prepared to right those crimes and injustices which you have been trying so hard to conceal.' She fixed her eyes upon the lopped trunks of the trees below the window which appeared like fallen giants in the moonlight. 'And you must start by telling me the whole truth of what you know and why you took the other letters.'

'Dido, please, it will do no good. There is no need to rake up what is past. Least said…'

'Least said soonest mended!' cried Dido, turning upon her angrily. 'Harriet, I cannot believe that even now you will quote maxims instead of really *speaking* to me! Let sleeping dogs lie – that was Dear Papa's favourite saying, was it not?'

'I shall not stay to hear you speak disrespectfully of my father!'

'Yes you shall!' cried Dido, more angry than ever.

'Upon my word you shall. For if you do not, I will speak to Mr Wishart instead.'

'You would not!' said Harriet and, although she made no appeal to their friendship, the thought of it filled the grand bedchamber as real as the moonlight and the faint scraping of the fiddles.

Dido hesitated.

'How long have you suspected me?' asked Harriet.

'Almost from the beginning. Though I have tried hard to put the thought away from me. I believe it was when the ring was stolen that the first doubts intruded. Mrs Harman-Foote said something interesting then. She said that a visitor could not wander away to her bedchamber without her knowing about it. And I could not help but think that there was one visitor who had an unusual degree of freedom in this house. Your role as Penelope's nurse would enable you to move about the upper floors undetected.'

'I see.'

'And of course, you were quite determined to nurse Penelope – and to nurse her alone. Even Lucy noticed your determination – though she entirely misunderstood its cause. Why Harriet? What was the real cause? Were you perhaps afraid of what Penelope might say in delirium?' Dido left the window and began to pace restlessly about the room, finding some relief in movement and words. 'And when I insisted upon your having a companion in the labour, your choice was very telling indeed. You chose the oldest servant in your household – the oldest, the most loyal and, I suspect, the one who already knew the secrets of your family. Indeed, I am convinced that, besides yourself, old Nanny is the only person alive who knows those secrets.'

Harriet only clutched at the post of the bed, following Dido's restless motion with her eyes. 'Tell me what you know,' she said.

'Enough. More than enough, I assure you. I know who sent that letter.'

'But how? How can you know it?'

'From the writing. Oh you tried very hard to deceive me when we talked about it in Bath. Silas's hand is so like that of the letter I could not doubt that he had been taught by the man who wrote it. But Silas was educated at home…'

'Not entirely.'

'No – you tried to mislead me by mentioning Mr Portinscale. But that would not do. Silas might have learnt Latin from the local clergyman, but he would not have gone to him to learn his letters.' Dido stopped walking and fixed her friend with an earnest gaze. 'It was your father who taught Silas to write, was it not?'

Harriet looked stubborn.

'Oh why will you not admit it? I believe you are reluctant to confess it all even to yourself!' She began again to pace about the room. 'Your father taught Silas to write – and there is a likeness in their writing. The hand in the letter seemed familiar to me because your father wrote it. Admit it, Harriet. Please admit it. Your father sent letters to Miss Fenn – letters which you were determined to destroy, because they revealed the…arrangement which he had entered into with her…'

'Oh hush, hush,' cried Harriet, flapping her hands. '"Prating tongues never…"'

'No Harriet!' cried Dido in exasperation. 'If we must have proverbs, let us try this: "Tell the truth and put the devil to flight"!'

Harriet moaned gently. 'You cannot know so much, it is impossible…' She stopped herself; afraid of what she was admitting.

'I do,' said Dido, putting her hand to her brow. 'When looked at in one way all the evidence began to make sense. Little details which had only made me uneasy before, took on entirely new meanings: things like Silas's poem…'

'Silas's poem? Indeed, I certainly do not understand you now!'

'No?' Dido paced to the side of the bed, picked up the bible and set it gently on its table again – rather as if she would propitiate the ghost which haunted the room. 'At first,' she said, 'I thought it was only the hand those verses were written in that disturbed me. But then I found I couldn't get them out of my mind and – despite my affection for your brother – I could not quite believe it was his excellence as a poet which had fixed his words in my brain.'

Dido looked down at Harriet sitting upon the bed in her pale evening gown. The candle standing beside her showed a long strand of hair which had escaped the silk bands of her headdress, hanging down across one ear. A pink rose pinned at her breast had shed petals into her lap. Her eyes were fixed – she was merely waiting. It would perhaps be kindest to continue – to tell all she knew and hope to convince Harriet that further pretence was impossible.

'There are, in fact, three interesting points about

the poem,' she said. 'There is, first of all, the use of the endearment 'beloved' and the expressions of unswerving affection which Silas uses – ideas which put me very much in mind of Miss Fenn when I read them. To begin with, I thought that perhaps Silas had somehow read a similar letter to the one I had seen – that perhaps Mr Coulson was our thief and he had shown the letters to him. But now I know that Mr Coulson has had no hand in this – and I think instead that Silas had actually *heard* her declarations.'

'Oh!' Again Harriet's hands moved rapidly in a suppressing motion – as if she could not bear to have such things said aloud.

But Dido hardened her heart and standing at the foot of the bed, she continued. 'Silas is no genius,' she said. 'A little opium might inspire a great romantic to compose exquisite poetry. But for a dear, prosaic boy like Silas, the only visions that came were drawn from...*memory*. Memories which are lost to his waking mind.'

'No, no,' said Harriet, shaking her head violently.

Dido could not but take the denial for confirmation. 'You see, the second point of interest is that verse of description with which the poem opens.' She turned her eyes upon the window and quoted:

The moonlight floats upon the pool
And gleams on grass and sedge.
The dew lies thick. The woman's skirts
Are darkened at the edge.

'It is, when considered carefully, a rather, unusual description, is it not?' she asked.

'It is certainly not very great poetry,' said Harriet in a

choking voice which struggled for indifference.

'No – but why should he choose to describe the hem of her skirts?'

'I hardly know.' Harriet now sounded genuinely puzzled.

'Do you not? I do. The answer is given in the next verse – *She bends and presses close her love*. Harriet, why must the nun bend down to embrace her love? And why is the writer of the poem looking at her skirts?'

There was no reply. Now Harriet was beginning to catch her meaning and was thrown back into silence.

'She must bend,' continued Dido quietly, 'because it is a *child* to whom she is bidding farewell. The whole scene is described from a child's point of view!'

She turned away from the bed and moved restlessly to the window. Gazing out into the strange, distorting white light of the moon, she looked beyond the fallen giants to the broken outline of the ruins – all black and indistinct in the moonlight, but for the great east window standing out gaunt against sky – and the dark line of trees which marked the old pool. Their crowding shadows seemed capable of hiding all manner of meetings and partings and secrets…

'It was down there, beside the pool that he bade farewell to his mother, was it not? When he was five years old.'

She looked back and was just in time to see Harriet raising her hands to cover her ears. 'You know full well,' she cried, 'that our mother died when Silas was born.'

'No.' Dido went back to her and gently removed the hands, holding them firmly in her own. 'No,' she said. 'Silas's mother died here in the pool – two years after that parting. She died because she wished the man to whom she had given her son to relinquish him. And he could not bear to do that. The boy was too important to him.'

Harriet merely held her eyes in a tortured stare. Dido found herself wishing for tears – they would at least seem natural. But Harriet was not by nature a weeper. 'You see, I was sure that someone had killed in order to avoid giving up the child. So I looked about Badleigh and Madderstone to determine who might have stood in such desperate need of a son that he might kill in order to retain him. And who, I thought, could need a son more keenly than a man with a dead wife, two dearly loved daughters – and an entailed estate?' Dido's lips were stiff, reluctant to pronounce the words which seemed like a death blow to her friend. 'Mr Edward Crockford,' she said, 'the man who was so very determined to provide for his daughters – he would have had a powerful motive for murder.'

Suddenly Harriet gave a cry that had more of tortured animal in it than human being; seizing her candle she jumped up and ran to the hearth, took the letter from her pocket and held its corner to the flame.

'You will never prove anything!' she cried as the yellow light of burning paper flared across her pale, terrified face. 'The other letters were all destroyed weeks ago.'

Dido watched the paper burn: watched grey ash fall from it onto the fender. It was a satisfying sight, for she saw in it the final defeat of Captain Laurence. Now, all the letters were gone. Congreve would never know the truth!

Harriet dropped the burning letter into the hearth

and fell onto her knees, her hands covering her head as if the accusation was a blow from which she must protect herself.

In spite of everything, Dido's heart rebuked her for unkindness as she looked down upon the bowed head, the clutching hands. Never had she been more inclined to condemn her own love of mysteries. That her curiosity had led her at last to this – to the torture of a friend! And yet…it could not be right to rest content with half-truths when they concealed past crimes – and present injustice…

'Harriet, please listen to me.' She knelt down by the hearth and gently pulled Harriet's hands away from her ears. 'You cannot hide the truth in this way. I do not need the letter for evidence – there is another proof.'

'What?' cried Harriet, her eyes wide, the muscles in her face working in anxiety. 'What is this other proof?'

Dido looked down at their joined hands. Harriet had ceased to struggle against her now and her hands lay passive, as if she awaited her own sentence of death. 'Yesterday,' she said, 'I looked at the pieces of gold and silver taken from the lake with Miss Fenn's body. Harriet, they are not all coins.'

'Not coins?' repeated Harriet. 'I do not understand you. What are they?'

'Two of the pieces which I had at first taken for misshapen shillings, are buttons – silver buttons – just such as your father wore.'

'No! No! I will not listen to you.'

'You must. Those buttons were torn from his coat as that poor woman struggled against him.'

Harriet began to tremble. Her hands twisted until they were gripping her friend's. Her eyes pleaded. Her lips moved again – but no sound came from them.

'You have known it all the time, have you not?' said Dido. 'That is why you have been working against me to obscure the truth – taking the letters and the ring. But now,' she continued with all the force of conviction, 'you must listen to me. You must help me put right some of the wrong that your father did. If you do not, I swear I will take those buttons to Mr Wishart and tell him that his inquest must be reopened.'

'I do not know what to do,' said Harriet, her eyes darting desperately to and fro. 'I do not know what Papa would have wanted…'

'No! No! You must not think of what he would want. The time has come, Harriet, to think for yourself.'

Harriet only stared wildly. In the silence, the ghostly strains of a violin just beginning upon Montgomery's Reel crept into the chamber. The two women faced each other over the candle's flame, the light flickering across their cheeks and throwing long shadows up the pale chimney piece and seeming to make the birds and foliage move upon the bed-hangings. Dido looked defiantly into her friend's eyes. Pity was tearing at her – but she must not give in to it. There was a greater duty to be performed here than the everyday obligation of friendship. Justice must be done. She gripped tighter at the cold hands which lay unmoving in her grasp.

And then, at last, Harriet bowed her head. 'He had no choice,' she said, her voice scarcely above a whisper. 'It all started in kindness to my mother, you see. She was dying – the only thing she wished to hear was that she had borne a son. She asked… He could not hurt her. He told her that the baby was a boy… And after that…' She broke down, shaking her head helplessly.

'And after that,' Dido continued for her, 'it occurred to him that the deception might be carried on. He told the whole world that his third child was a son. And, for the first few years nothing more was needed to perpetuate the lie than a nursemaid utterly devoted to the family – and that he had ready to hand.'

Harriet nodded, her eyes still staring down upon the candle. 'No one else knew the child was a girl.'

'Except for you?'

'Yes. I found out when Silas…when the child was but a few months old. I was twelve, you know and very anxious to help care for the new baby…'

'But you told no one the truth?'

Harriet's head jerked upward. 'No,' she said simply. 'Papa told me not to.'

'Yes, of course.' Dido listened a moment to the slight drumming of feet which now accompanied the reel. 'But I suppose he always knew that after a few years he would need to take some other action.'

'He had business interests in Great Farleigh – we have a mill there,' explained Harriet matter-of-factly. 'I believe that is how he discovered Mrs Pinker's establishment.'

'And so he was lucky enough to encounter Miss Fenn – a woman who needed a daughter as badly as he needed a son.'

'Yes. The exchange was made when the children were five. And all would have been well. All was well for two years. No one suspected anything. And then,' said Harriet plaintively, 'she attempted to go back upon her word.'

'She could not bear to see the boy growing up without knowing her.'

Harriet nodded.

There was one question which Dido knew she must ask, though she dreaded hearing the answer. 'Did you know?' she said quietly. 'I mean, did you know fifteen years ago that your father had killed Miss Fenn?'

'No...' Harriet stared down at the candle flame, her face working in shifting expressions of misery. In the silence voices and laughter echoed up from the hall below – the company was going in to supper. 'Yes...' whispered Harriet. 'That is, I do not know whether I knew or not. I never knew for sure. I knew that he was gone to meet her that evening. I knew that she was never seen again...' She drew a long shuddering breath. 'But...' she spread her hands and looked up at her friend. 'Is it possible to know something and not to know it at the same time?' she asked.

'Yes, I believe it is.'

'And what,' whispered Harriet, 'do you mean to do now?'

'I mean,' said Dido firmly, 'to lay the ghosts of Madderstone to rest for once and for all.' She stooped down and blew out the candle on the hearth. Then she took Harriet's hand. 'Come,' she said, drawing her to her feet and leading her across to the window.

With the candle extinguished the moonlight was gaining power in the room. Showing up rich embroidery and well-polished mahogany – and the shabby bible and the severe text above the bed, *Thou God seest me.*

Dido had a strong sense of being in the presence, not only of her God, but also a ghost. In this room of outward luxury, a woman had lived out a simple life: a life of renunciation. For Lady Congreve had withdrawn from the world as surely as any old-time nun – even taking a new name, as nuns did.

'"I was wrong to ever agree to this pretence,"' said Dido quietly as they came to the window and looked out together into the moonlit grounds. 'That is what she wrote, you know. And I think it was not only her longing for her son which made her say it. Harriet, I believe she had determined upon ending the deception – and that is why she had become happier in the last few weeks of her life. She was no longer struggling against her conscience. She had acknowledged to herself the deep injustice of the arrangement she had made with your father.'

'Injustice? Dido, what exactly are you talking of?'

'I am talking of the one person you and I have not yet mentioned. I am talking of Penelope; the little girl who was sent away from her family, because she was not the son that everyone wished her to be.'

'Oh!' Harriet tried to snatch away her hand but Dido held it firmly.

'This is the price you must pay for my silence, Harriet. If you wish me to hold my tongue – if your father's name is to go untarnished – then you must let your sister come home.'

Chapter Forty-Five

By next morning the fog was entirely cleared away. The sun shone as Dido and Mr Lomax walked beside the lower pool, and the trees blazed forth gloriously against a cloudless blue sky. The pool was almost returned now to its old level; an enterprising pair of ducks had already taken possession of it and scores of curled, bronze oak leaves drifted across its ruffled surface, driven by a brisk, cold wind.

They stood upon the bank in silence for a while: her hand just resting on his arm.

'Will you tell me the end of the story?' he asked quietly at last. 'Your countenance this morning seems to say that the "business" which took you from the ballroom yesterday was successfully completed.'

'Yes, it was.' She looked up into his brooding face. His eyes were fixed upon the peacefully sculling ducks, his jaw set in obstinate disapproval. 'But if I tell you about it, it will be the cause of another quarrel between us. I fear,' she said quietly, 'that we must give up free and open discussion, for it will always end in my arguing like a woman – and your being displeased.'

He sighed heavily. 'To quarrel when there is no possibility of changing one another's mind is a fruitless indulgence. If you are so kind as to honour me with an account of last night's events, I will undertake – I will *endeavour* – not to express opinions of which you are already aware.'

She searched his cheek for that restless little muscle, which always betrayed him when he reigned in his anger; but she could discern no sign of it. However she did notice that the sunlight was once more bringing forward the dark flecks in his eyes. She hastily turned her own gaze upon the pool and the ducks, and began her account.

Soon, she knew, she must tell him of the conclusion she had come to in the journey from Bath. But, for now she would indulge herself with talking freely to him – perhaps it would be the last time that such intercourse was possible.

As she talked they walked on about the edge of the pool and climbed the steps at its end. From time to time she stole a look at his impassive face. There was an occasional shake of the head; but, in view of his undertaking, she interpreted these as expressing wonder rather than disapproval.

She finished her tale as they arrived at the spoilt lawn and came to a standstill upon the once-smooth turf which was now deeply gouged by horses' hooves and cartwheels. They stood for a moment, looking towards the irregular outline of the ruins, the blue sky showing brightly through ivy-clad arches and the great stone rose of the east window.

'And so,' he said meditatively as they walked on, 'you knew that it would be Miss Crockford who came to retrieve the letter?'

'Oh! No.' She hesitated a moment. Like Harriet, she had known – and yet not known. 'Perhaps...' she confessed – for she was quite determined that, come what may, there must still be complete honesty between them. 'Perhaps I should have been more certain if I had not wished with all my heart for it to be untrue. Until the very last moment I was hoping it would be Mr Coulson who came.'

'I see.' He looked very thoughtful, and Dido began to understand him. There was certainly disapproval – powerful disapproval. But there was interest too. He would not admit to it, but he was almost as fascinated by the subject as she was herself.

'Well,' he continued, 'I can understand your *suspecting* Mr Coulson of being Harry Fenn. But why should you settle so very decisively upon him alone? That I cannot understand. He is, after all, not the only young man in the neighbourhood of a suitable age and unknown parentage.'

'You are thinking perhaps of Mr Paynter.'

'I am. The surgeon has been at Madderstone Abbey a great deal of late. Harman-Foote himself has wondered at his constant attendance. Paynter would certainly have had opportunity to take the letters – and the ring. And yet, I think you have been prejudiced so strongly against Mr Coulson you have quite overlooked the possibility of *his* guilt. Your reasoning was not sound.'

'Upon my word!' cried Dido. 'You do not approve of my making enquiries, and yet you would instruct me how to carry them out.'

'I disapprove of the use to which you put your powers

of reason,' he countered, 'I do not disapprove of reason itself and I am always very sorry to see it overpowered by prejudice.'

'But, as it happens, you need have no fear in this case; I was not prejudiced. For a while I was very much inclined to suspect Mr Paynter. There were other circumstances which rather suggested him, you see – such as the roses which he laid upon Miss Fenn's grave. But I soon came to see that there was an entirely different explanation for those – and for his frequent visits to the abbey.'

'There was?'

'Oh yes. It is all in the sitting of a gentleman's hat, you know, Mr Lomax!'

'His hat?'

'Yes, have you not noticed that Mr Paynter wears his hat upon the very back of his head?' She laughed at his confusion and he took a firmer hold of her arm to assist her past a great patch of mud where a noble chestnut had fallen. Its wood was all carried away now, leaving only a mass of yellow leaves and spiked green fruit trodden into the dirt. 'Mr Paynter is in love,' she explained, picking her way with care. 'He is in love with Harriet. It is she that has brought him so often to the abbey. He was, in fact, on his way to see Harriet when I met him in the churchyard, and the roses were a gift for her; but he was confused when he met me – he feared, you see, that I might guess his secret.'

Mr Lomax nodded understanding.

'Of course, a country surgeon ought not to be paying attentions to Miss Crockford of Ashfield!' said Dido, 'and so he pretended the flowers were for the grave.' She smiled. 'The poor man was then obliged to return home to gather more before coming on to the house.'

'You are sure of this?'

'Oh yes, I saw pink roses in the sick-chamber on my next visit.'

'No, no, I meant, are you sure of his being in love?'

'Yes, very sure – and I am sure too that she returns his affection. The only point of doubt is whether she will allow herself to be happy with a man she knows her father would not approve.'

Lomax shook his head gravely. 'I fear there would be disapproval on all sides. The whole neighbourhood would cry out against such a match.'

'Oh, I think Harriet might defy the neighbourhood! But Dear Papa is a much stronger influence. He always has been,' she added sadly.

'His plan to evade the entail was – extraordinary,' said Lomax.

'An entail itself is a very extraordinary – a very cruel – thing,' said Dido feelingly. 'It takes away a woman's home and gives it into the hands of strangers! Mr Crockford's crime was monstrous – but some portion of blame must fall upon those inhuman circumstances which prompted him to it.'

He stopped walking and when she looked up she saw that his face was grave, the muscle in full play. She closed her eyes a moment, knowing very well what must follow. Their shared interest in the mystery had brought them thus far in comparative harmony, but the chasm dividing masculine and feminine worlds, that great inescapable divide, was upon the point of opening between them.

'And is Mr Crockford's crime to succeed?' he asked in a restrained voice. 'Is the entail to be evaded? I must ask you, Miss Kent, because it would seem that you have become the arbiter of right and wrong, the sole judge in this case.'

Dido withdrew her hand from his arm. 'If you mean will I publish the facts which I have discovered, then the answer is no, I most certainly will not. If the men of authority wish to posses such information, then let them find it out for themselves! I will not rob my friends and give their home into the hands of such a man as Henry Coulson!'

'Mr Coulson's being weak and foolish does not alter the fact that he is the rightful possessor of Ashfield.'

Dido only clasped her arms about her and looked stubborn.

'Do you mean to do nothing to bring justice about?' he demanded.

But she would not answer him. Still she sought to put off that moment when they must confront the differences which yawned between them. 'Come,' she said hurrying towards the ruins. 'I wish to show you the ghost!'

'The ghost?'

'Yes, for I think I have found out just what it was that Penelope saw upon the gallery.' She began to run away from him through the stunted bushes and fallen masonry. Three crows clattered up from the fallen pillars of the chancel.

He shook his head helplessly and followed her more slowly, looking still very disapproving – but intrigued nonetheless.

'I thought,' he called after her, his voice echoing against the high walls, 'that you had failed to find any clues at all when you came here to search.'

'I thought I had failed,' she said, stopping and turning back as she reached the foot of the night stair. 'But, in point of fact, I had found one very important clue.'

She started to climb and he hurried forward, urging her to take care.

The wind grew stronger as he followed her upward and, by the time they reached the gallery, she was once more holding hard to her bonnet, which was blown onto the very back of her head. She turned back to him, her cheeks glowing, her hair all swept away from her face, her eyes bright with exercise and discovery. 'What do you feel, here just at the top of the stairs?'

'Cold!' he said as he joined her in the gallery. 'Nothing but cold.'

'Exactly so!' she cried with great satisfaction and stepped a little further on – out of the wind.

'But why should you think that significant?' he said. He also moved away from the draught, further into the gallery, where the sun was shining greenish through the curtains of creeper which hung about the arches.

'Does not a feeling of cold always accompany the appearance of a ghost?' she asked, leaning against the old stones and the thick, twisting stems of ivy.

'Why, you do not mean to say that you believe in such things?' he objected. 'What of reason, Miss Kent? What of that rational view of the world which I know you hold as dear as I do myself?'

'But I am being perfectly rational.' She looked up at

him, her head on one side, intent upon teasing away some of his gravity. 'There is reason enough for that coldness at the head of the stairs! It is the draught of air which blows just there. And you know,' she added, 'now that I consider the matter, I rather wonder whether a great deal of what Lucy would call an "unearthly feeling" and "an atmosphere of evil" might not be explained away by an unpleasant draught of air.'

'I will not,' he said firmly, 'believe that Miss Lambe was frightened into falling by a cold draught!'

'Oh but she was! For it is extremely strong. And you must remember that the day of Penelope's accident was even windier than today. I remember, when I looked back from the bottom of the stairs, the wind was so strong just there at the end of the gallery that Harriet's bonnet was almost blowing away, and her cap too.'

'And the draught called a ghost into being?' he said, raising his brows.

'It did indeed! I did not realise it at first, because, you see, *I* knew of no reason why Penelope *should* see a ghost at Madderstone. But Captain Laurence rather expected that she would – and that is why he also came here to the gallery after the accident. He was particularly anxious to figure out just what she had seen.'

'And why was James Laurence so very interested in a ghost?'

'Well, you must remember that Captain Laurence suspected Penelope was the daughter of Miss Fenn. But he could find no confirmation of it. And so he had introduced her to the Crockfords – and caused her to come to Madderstone – in the hope that she would encounter ghosts. In short, he hoped that her being here would cause her to remember something of her earliest years.'

'Because such a memory would confirm his theories?' Despite himself, he was beginning to look less severe – and more interested.

'Yes,' she said. 'And, of course, within a few days of being here, Penelope fell from the gallery – in very mysterious circumstances: causing the good captain to wonder whether her fall had anything to do with her history.'

'And was there any such connection?'

'Oh yes, there was. But he and I were both rather stupid about finding it out. You see, we both noticed that the lake – the place in which the bones rested – is visible from this gallery.'

'No, no,' he objected quickly, 'she could not have seen the bones from such a distance.'

'Of course she could not. That is precisely my point! Look!' she gestured to the view beyond the arches of the gallery: the looming walls and broken outline of the great window; a glimpse of the pool; red-, yellow- and copper-coloured trees; an expanse of blue sky with an arrow-shaped formation of wild geese rippling across it. 'We are too high up here to see any details,' she said. 'Penelope certainly could not have seen anything of significance in the grounds. But both Captain Laurence and I wasted a great deal of time in wondering whether she had. And that prevented us from examining the simple facts of the matter.'

'Very well,' he said, 'and what are these simple facts?'

'There are – I see now – only two facts to consider. First of all, there are Penelope's words "I saw her". And, secondly, there is the absolute certainty that there was no one in the gallery – except *Harriet*. Put those two facts together – with no superstitious nonsense about grey nuns, or theories about skeletons – and you are brought to one conclusion. It was simply Harriet that Penelope saw. And the sight shocked her so much, she stepped backward – and fell.'

He stared, pressed the tips of his fingers together. 'You believe that Miss Lambe recognised her sister at that moment?'

'I am quite sure that she did.'

'But why? For it would seem she had never recognised Miss Crockford – or any other member of her family before.'

'It was because of that draught of air. As I explained, it was blowing away Harriet's cap and bonnet. And, as I have often observed myself, without them she looks positively *young*.'

He rested his chin upon the tips of his fingers – thinking deeply, but saying nothing.

'Lucy told me once,' continued Dido, becoming more serious, 'that Penelope remembered her mother bending over her cradle when she was a baby. Of course, that was impossible. Penelope's mother died when she was born. It was, in fact, Harriet's face she remembered. The face of the young Harriet. It was the first face she learnt to love. And it was that face which was suddenly revealed to the poor girl here on the gallery that day – a ghost indeed!'

She looked up at him eagerly. But his profile was dark

against the bright sky, framed by an arch of grey stone. She wished very much that she might know just what he was thinking, for the moment was come… She could no longer delay telling him of her decision.

'Mr Lomax,' she said quietly, 'you asked me just now whether I meant to do anything to bring justice about. Well, I would not wish you to think that I am motivated only by an insatiable curiosity. I do care deeply for what is right and I do certainly mean to bring about justice.' She hesitated. 'I mean to bring about a woman's justice.'

He looked at her uncertainly. 'And how does that differ from a man's?'

'It is humane,' she said, 'and concerns itself not with agreements drawn up to impoverish women for the enrichment of their male relations; it concerns itself instead with the plight of a girl sent away from her home to grow up among strangers simply because she was not the boy that everyone wished her to be.'

'You are referring I suppose to Miss Lambe.'

'Yes. Penelope must be allowed to come home,' she said with great decision.

'Must she? And how is that to be achieved?'

'In the simplest, most natural way possible. All that is needed is for Harriet to cease opposing Silas's wishes and Penelope will come home to Ashfield as his bride. I have conditioned for it, you see. I have told Harriet I will only surrender the silver buttons to her on their wedding day.'

He gazed steadily at her for several minutes. Sunlight and the shadows of leaves shifted across his face as the wind blew about the hanging curtain of ivy. 'And this,' he said, 'is your notion of justice?'

'Yes it is.' She drew a long breath. 'And, I believe that when you consider how different – how very different – it is from yours... I think you will agree that...' She looked away quickly. 'I think you will agree that our opinions upon some very important subjects will always differ – that they never can be reconciled.'

'Because you will always argue like a woman?'

'And you will always argue like a man.' She smiled sadly. 'Your notion of a woman's sphere distinct and separate from a man's was all too correct, Mr Lomax. I believe our experiment was, from the first, doomed to failure because there is an established barrier – a kind of chasm – between men and women which our words can never cross.'

'And there must of course be words?' he said raising one eyebrow.

'Oh yes,' she insisted – and the quiet propriety of the previous Mrs Lomax was very much in her mind as she spoke. 'I am afraid that for me there must always be words. I never could exist in silence – and that I fear makes me essentially unsuited to the state of matrimony.'

He stood brooding for a very long time. And she waited, her gloved hands resting upon the ancient stones of the gallery's balustrade, her eyes fixed upon a bright beech tree in the park from which showers of leaves were being blown against the sky. She half-regretted their doomed experiment – it had perhaps made her understand herself too well.

'I believe,' said Lomax slowly at last, 'that there is a fault in your reasoning.' She looked up and saw that the tips of his fingers were just pressing against one another. 'I will not dispute the existence of such a divide,' he said. 'Its presence has recently been too painfully obtruded upon my notice for me to doubt its reality. Yet I continue to believe that – were you to do me the honour of becoming my wife – we could be happy together. For, though our words may not cross that divide, I believe our affection might.'

'No,' she shook her head wretchedly. 'It would not, Mr Lomax. It could not. For affection would all be lost in irritation and anger.'

'And what is your evidence for that position?'

'The evidence of a dozen wretched marriages within my knowledge in which argument and disapproval has soured regard and destroyed all vestige of confidence.'

He shook his head. 'No, I will not allow you to put forward other marriages as proof. They can reveal nothing to the purpose, for I believe that the present case is entirely different. In this particular instance the evidence is against you.'

'Oh! Are we so very different from other men and women?'

'Perhaps we are. Witness our recent dispute,' he said, resting his chin on his fingers. 'We certainly cannot agree upon what is just – and I think that we never will. The courses of action which we think proper differ widely.'

'Exactly so!'

'And you have been aware of this dissimilarity in outlook since our last interview in Bath, have you not?'

'Yes.'

'And yet, just now, when I asked you to share with me the story of last night's discoveries, you did not hesitate

– once I had assured you that I would endeavour not to express my anger.'

'No, why should I hesitate?'

'Why, because my contrary ideas of justice might have prompted me to approach the coroner myself with the information you gave me.'

'But I knew you would not!'

'How did you know?' he said, studying her face very earnestly. 'You did not condition for my silence before you began to speak.'

'I did not need to,' she cried. 'I knew that you would never betray me, no matter what you thought.'

He smiled. She began to catch his meaning and quickly turned her face away.

'And upon that confidence,' he said quietly, 'upon that trust, I rest my argument – and all my hopes of future happiness.' He reached out and laid his hand over hers. 'You see, Miss Kent, there is another force at work here besides our words. You and I know – we will always know – that we can trust one another implicitly; and I firmly believe that that trust *can* bridge the divide which lies between us.'

Dido kept her eyes fixed upon the great arch of the ruined window, and upon a black chattering flock of starlings as it was blown about the sky. She could not look at him, nor could she very readily find a reply among the crowding sensations which his words had produced. But very slowly she turned the hand which lay under his. And at last their hands rested palm to palm on the ivy-covered wall. Then, one by one, their fingers interlinked. Their grasp tightened, warm and steady in the icy wind.